The
Bluestocking
and the
Rake

ALSO BY NORMA DARCY

THE REGENCY GENTLEMEN

A Gentleman and a Scoundrel
The Honourable Gentleman

The Bluestocking and the Rake

NORMA DARCY

Montlake
Romance

Text copyright © 2013 Norma Darcy
All rights reserved.

Published by Montlake Romance, Seattle

www.apub.com

Amazon, the Amazon logo, and Montlake Romance are trademarks of Amazon.com, Inc., or its affiliates.

ISBN-13: 9781477820896
ISBN-10: 1477820892

Cover design by Laura Klynstra

Library of Congress Control Number: 2014912881

Printed in the United States of America

For Mum,

My inspiration and my best friend.

CHAPTER 1

Longfield Park, Hertfordshire. September 1817.

"AND ARE YOU AWARE," demanded the Countess of Marcham in her most imperious tone, "that the whole county has been expecting you to make Lady Emily Holt an offer at any time these last two months?"

Her son, Robert Holkham, fourth Earl of Marcham, to whom this remark was addressed, did not immediately reply. As he was not completely decided if he *was* about to make Lady Emily Holt an offer, he was a little annoyed by his mother's taxing him on the subject. He did not raise his eyes from a three-day-old copy of the *Morning Post* but pretended extreme interest in the announcements, his dark brows knitted together across the bridge of his nose.

"Horesham is getting married," he said, yawning behind one well-manicured hand, and turned the page as if his mother hadn't spoken.

The third occupant of the room was Mrs. Caroline Weir, Lord Marcham's younger sister, known to all her friends and family as Caro. She gasped and widened her eyes. "Never say so! Michael Horesham? He is forty-five if he's a day. Who is he to marry, pray? Never tell me he caught the beautiful widgeon at last?"

Lord Marcham glanced at her, amused. "I would be very much surprised if Michael gave two hoots if she is a widgeon or not. It is not her intelligence that has drawn his attention. She is what one might call 'a prime article,' an Incomparable, plump in all the right places and, most importantly, plump in the pocket."

"And of course *you* have never been known to make a cake of yourself over a beauty with no brains," remarked his sister.

"Oh, no, not *I*," agreed the earl amiably, completely unperturbed by this comment.

"You *always* take into account a lady's intelligence. You are well known as a man who likes to spend an evening poring over books and enthusing about the latest scientific discovery or the newest production of an opera that has been performed to great acclaim."

He looked up from his paper and smiled sweetly at her. "I spend a lot of time at the opera."

She choked on a laugh. "Not opera *dancers*, Robbie. That is something altogether different."

His lips twitched but he asked, perfectly gravely, "Is it?"

She ignored this provocative remark and said in a wistful voice, "If I could but see you in love, Robbie, with a woman with a little common sense, a well-informed mind, and a modicum of beauty, I would be satisfied."

"No more than a *modicum* of beauty?" he repeated in mock horror. "Dear Sister, *you* might be satisfied but I should not be!"

Lord Marcham was a man used to consorting with the most beautiful women in society. He was used to doing precisely as he wished. At the age of six and thirty, he had long since abandoned listening to the advice of his family, or anyone else for that matter. He was aware that his sister had only his best interests at heart, but he was reluctant to entertain such a discussion before their mother, who, once such a subject was broached, was wearyingly persistent in pursuing it. He'd been expected to marry at any time during the last fifteen years but had, instead, spent the time indulging in the same activities that attracted other well-off young gentleman of his circle. He was something of a rake. His reputation was such that his mother despaired of him ever choosing a wife. But his mother was not a woman to stand idly by while he chose to ignore what he owed to his father's name. His duty was to marry and provide an heir, and she never let him forget it. He knew what was expected of him and had almost come to the conclusion that any well-bred young woman would do. If he could not have love, then why not marry the first eligible female he met and be done with it? And yet . . .

The thought of marrying for duty filled him with dread. Caroline's own marriage had been a happy one. It had shown him the possibilities. He was an incurable romantic at heart and he wanted, if at all possible, to marry for love.

Caroline dimpled. "If she can then add to these qualities a gentleness of character and sweetness of disposition—"

"She sounds to me like a dead bore. Spare me, I beg of you."

"Well, no one ever thought that Michael Horesham would marry—not at his age—not that he is so *very* old, but he has never before shown any interest in matrimony. There is hope for you yet, dearest."

"I am relieved to hear it. To hear you, anyone would think that a person over forty has one foot in the grave."

"Yes, and so you have," she declared.

He smiled. "I'm not there yet; you must wait another few years for that."

"But not so very many, Robbie."

"Little cat," he murmured.

Lord Marcham was a rather good-looking man, well built, with a fine pair of shoulders and a very attractive smile, which he had learned over the years could be used with devastating effect upon women when trying to escape their black books. If he was not precisely what one would call a Tulip of fashion, he was, nonetheless, elegantly dressed for the morning in pantaloons and a snugly fitting blue coat, highly polished Hessian boots, and a cravat of exquisitely tied linen. He was seated by the window in his mother's dressing room as far away as he could get from the fierce heat of the fire, which was blazing even on this summer day in August.

Caroline smiled sweetly and picked up her fan. "But is Lord Horesham's engagement a love match?"

"I think that extremely unlikely," he said with bruising frankness.

"Then why should a man like him enter into wedlock at his age?"

He leaned back in his chair and folded his arms across his chest. "Because he is so *very* ancient, and everyone knows that only young persons are capable of falling in love—isn't that right?"

She playfully poked her tongue out at him. "I didn't mean *that*—you know I didn't. You are deliberately putting words in my mouth to be provoking."

"Depend upon it, a man of his age may expire halfway through the ceremony, after all," he said and then added as he reached for his teacup, "not to mention the consummation."

A glimmer of amusement stole into her eyes. "I meant only that a man who reaches five and forty without marrying is almost certainly happy with his own company. It would be an extraordinary woman indeed who could inspire such a man to love after all those years. You must own the truth of *that*."

"Certainly it is unlikely. But not impossible," he replied, wondering why after years of waiting in vain for just such an extraordinary woman to come into his own life, he was still entertaining any hope at all for Michael Horesham.

"And why would a young woman, half his age, choose him over any other agreeable young man of her acquaintance?"

"A fifty-thousand-pound fortune will inspire a great deal of love—or at least all the appearance of it."

She raised an eyebrow at him. "So cynical, Robbie? Speaking from experience?"

He grunted but said nothing in reply to this. Cynical was something of an understatement. Since the year he'd achieved his majority, he'd been prey to some of the most cunning and ambitious schemes to lure him into matrimony with women after little more than his money. Love, or the appearance of it, was very easy to fake when there was a fortune to be had. He had always hoped for a love match, but as the years went by, the chances of such a union seemed increasingly unlikely. He was well-off and personable, and he had little difficulty attracting women. What bothered him was that he might have been five and sixty with a bald head and a liking for raw onions and corsets, and still they would have pursued him. He was rich, and he was painfully aware that most women of his acquaintance—well, the respectable ones anyway—were as much in love with his purse as they were his person.

"I cannot imagine *you* falling prey to such a woman," remarked his sister.

"Certainly not," he agreed. "But then I am not Michael Horesham."

"No indeed."

The countess, who had been following this exchange with growing impatience, stamped her foot. "Oh, hang Michael Horesham! Didn't anyone hear what I said?"

"Certainly, Mama," her son replied coolly.

"Your latest flirtation has become the talk of the town and has given rise to the sort of conjecture that I deplore. I say again, the whole county is expecting an announcement at any moment."

Lord Marcham set down his teacup, irritated at his mother's continued interference in his affairs. He would marry when he chose to do so, not at the convenience of society—or of his mother, for that matter. "I don't give a damn what the whole county expects," he replied mildly.

"But I do," retorted his mother, shifting herself on the sofa, where she lay amongst an impressive array of cushions and shawls. "You may have no care to the reputation of this family, but I can assure you that I do. And I will not stand by and watch you toy with the affections of a respectable girl. You have gone too far this time, Robert. Your addresses have been too marked—you have aroused expectation in the breast of that young woman and the neighborhood in general. And you may depend upon the girl's dreadful mother having already ordered satin for the wedding. Your father put up with much from you, but this kind of behavior is not seemly in a Holkham."

The earl cast aside the newspaper, stood up abruptly, and moved to the window to look out at the park beyond. It was a fine day, with the first hint of autumn in the air, and the rolling lawns were silvery with dew. He braced one hand high against the paint-work and watched a rider, his youngest sister, Harriet, who was just turned eighteen, trotting away from the house with a groom. He smiled faintly, knowing that as soon as she was out of sight of the house—and their mother—she would in all probability break into an unladylike gallop that would have the groom struggling to keep up with her.

"Who says I am toying?" he asked at last.

His mother shrieked and raised her smelling salts to her nose. "You don't mean that you are serious about this girl?"

The earl shrugged again. "I must marry someone, you know."

"Yes but . . . Lady Emily Holt? Her father's estate is mortgaged to the hilt—surely you know that? He will bleed your coffers dry. Robert, pray be serious."

"I *was* being serious."

The countess gaped and was at a loss for words.

Lady Caroline took up where her mother left off. "Robbie, you are funning," she declared, fanning herself vigorously, an unladylike sheen of sweat upon her brow from the excessive heat of the room. "What does Lady Emily Holt have that any other society beauty does not?"

"A meek temper," he replied with the ghost of a laugh, still with his back to them, watching the riders until they disappeared into the trees. *A quiet, mild-mannered woman who would obey his wishes and see to his every whim . . .*

"A meek temper?" his sister repeated blankly.

Had his lordship turned around at that moment, Caroline would have seen the glint of amusement in his eyes and known that he was funning. As it were, she only heard his words and was concerned that he was about to make the biggest mistake of his life.

"Yes . . . a most desirable accomplishment for a woman."

"And is that what you want from marriage?" she asked. "A mild and meek little mouse who won't say boo to a goose?"

"Certainly it is. I do not wish to be harangued at every turn."

Daughter and mother exchanged worried glances.

"And are you in love with her?" demanded the countess from behind her handkerchief.

The earl burst out laughing and turned around at last. "Not in the least, ma'am."

The countess began to breathe more easily. If his heart were not engaged, then perhaps she could sway him from his choice. She had always hoped her eldest son would make a match of it with the daughter of one of her particular friends, a girl with a huge fortune, even if her figure was a little robust for modern tastes. She was something of a goose and not what one would precisely call clever, but her ladyship thought her son wouldn't care overmuch about that. Lord Halchester's daughter, Phoebe, was a splendid girl—a fine match for her son. "Then why choose this slip of a girl when Halchester's daughter is worth eighty thousand pounds?" she asked. "When I think of all the heiresses you could have had in these last twenty years, beauties, too, some of them . . . and you choose Lady Emily Holt."

"Because they would hate to live at Holme," he replied, examining his fingernails.

"Hate to live at Holme Park?" repeated his mother. "Hate to live in one of the finest houses in the country?"

"Company there is rather thin, Mama, as you know full well. Lady Emily comes from that part of the world and knows what to expect. I would not take a society beauty to Holme and have her wasting away and constantly berating me to move back to London. The parties and pleasures of town no longer hold any appeal for me, and I require a wife who will be happy to live with me in the country. Lady Emily Holt is a respectable young woman and she will do well enough."

His sister stood up and went to him, laying a hand on his arm. "Are you sure, Robbie?"

"Certainly. How could I not be? She is an excellent female."

"And will turn a blind eye to your infamous parties, all-night drinking, and mistresses?" asked his sister, lowering her voice so their mother wouldn't be privy to their conversation.

He smiled sweetly. "My dear Caroline, I cannot imagine what you may mean."

"Hmm," she replied.

"I do *not* have a mistress, and I will wager that these days, I am very often in bed earlier than you are."

"I'm sure you are," she murmured, "but I'll wager not alone."

He smiled affably. "Perfectly alone, I assure you, and I prefer it that way. A man of my advanced years cannot contend with too much excitement, you know."

"What utter nonsense," she declared.

"It is not nonsense. I thought you were always up with the latest on-dit, Caro, but it seems that you have not heard. I am retired."

He watched in dismay as his sister choked on a laugh, clearly unwilling to believe him. Everyone he had told had reacted in the same way. Why was it so hard to believe? Year after year of empty, meaningless liaisons with lightskirts or bored widows had taken their toll. Oh yes, he'd amused himself greatly, and no doubt some men were envious of him, but there surely was more to life? He wanted someone he could laugh with, someone who understood him, someone who was entirely his. He knew that his friends and even Caroline didn't understand it—he hardly understood it himself. All he knew was that he had grown tired of the role he played in public. Some mornings it was a trial to look at himself in the mirror: he didn't like what he saw.

"Since when did a man of your kidney retire?" Caroline asked, amused.

He shrugged. "Since I realized that there are a great many days in my life spent far too foxed to achieve anything meaningful. Whole weeks have passed by that I can honestly say I do not remember a damned thing about. A life of idle dissipation, even for such a wastrel as me, ceases to hold any fascination after twenty years of it."

"Gentlemen in your line do not retire," she said firmly. "And you may think it is amusing to pull the wool over my eyes, Robbie, but I am not Sarah and not as green as you may think."

He laughed and spread his hands. "It's true."

She gave him a knowing look. "And who was that blonde piece I saw you with last week if you are retired?"

He grinned ruefully. "I was merely making myself agreeable."

"Hmm," said his sister again, clearly believing it all a hum.

"I do *not* have a mistress," he repeated, "and I have no immediate desire to change the situation. And really, Sister, it is most improper in you to speak to me of such things."

"And is your heart still untouched after all these years?" she asked softly.

He smiled, his gray eyes twinkling. "Dear Caro, always the great romantic."

She took his arm and led him over to the other window, out of earshot of their mother. "Don't throw yourself away on Lady Emily. Be patient."

"I would say twenty years is patient enough, wouldn't you?"

She stared at him. "What's happened to you? Have you finally given up hope? What happened to the man who wanted to wait for love?"

"He's gone. I cannot wait forever, Caro. This family needs an heir," he replied.

She stole a glance at their mother and lowered her voice. "But you're so . . . so jaded. I think you'd rather read a book these days than . . . well . . . rather than make *love*!"

He looked at her with amusement from under his hooded lids. "Sister, you shock me."

"I am a married woman of the world—well, widowed at any rate—and you, Robbie, were never shocked by a little plain speaking, so don't come the outraged prude with me. When was the last time you looked at a woman and wanted her? I mean really wanted her?"

An awkward silence followed. Lord Marcham felt the truth of her words hit home and resonate with the part inside him that yearned to love. He saw a desolate future stretching out before him, a future in which he was trapped inside a loveless marriage. He wondered if he had left it all too late. Had he run out of time? He was already six and thirty. How much longer could he afford to wait? No, let him take Lady Emily, in sickness and in health, until an heir was conceived. Then, once the future of the earldom was secure, he could rest easy, knowing his duty had been done.

"Then where is she?" he asked quietly. "Where is this paragon? I have waited for her long enough. No, it is time I married. I need an heir. Emily is my choice, and I would ask you and Mama and Sarah to respect my wishes . . . *especially* Sarah, as she is, of all of my sisters, the busiest in my affairs." He kissed her on the cheek. "Have you heard her news, by the way?"

"Yes. Wonderful news," Caroline said absently, thinking that when their eldest sister found out that their brother was planning matrimony with Lady Emily Holt, there would be the devil to pay. Sarah was two years younger than Robert, but she acted as if she were the eldest and the head of the family. Harriet, the youngest of the three sisters, would be over the moon at Robbie's news. Anything her big brother did was perfect in her eyes.

"If she has a son, do you think she will name him after me?" he asked.

"What sort of a name is Lucifer for a baby?" Caroline replied with an innocent look.

The Earl of Marcham snorted in amusement, made his good-byes, and sauntered down the steps of his mother's home in a restless mood. He had by no means been certain that he *was* about to make an offer for Lady Emily, but his mother's outrage at his choice had provoked the devil in him, and he had found himself declaring an interest in the girl when he had not entirely made up his own mind on the subject.

Yes, he found Lady Emily attractive. Yes, she was a kind and generous woman, and he had no doubt she would make a splendid countess.

So let it be Lady Emily Holt. Or any of the other respectable women of Worcestershire. He cared not.

❧

The woman's mother irritated him, the earl decided as he sipped his tea.

The overattentive, almost fawning, desire to please set up his bristles. She was like a spider, spreading her web out wide to catch him.

He was given the best chair, or so she told him, and the best tea served in the best china. He watched Lady Holt, a plump, vacuous woman, titter on the edge of her chair, praising the accomplishments of her eldest daughter, and he felt an overwhelming desire to run in the opposite direction.

Lady Emily sat opposite him, looking demure and shy, and hardly raised her eyes to his face. If she were beyond the age of twenty, his lordship would be very much surprised. He found himself wondering if she would be the image of her mother in thirty years' time.

The earl had traveled from his mother's estate to the Holts' residence expressly to decide once and for all whether he was to make an offer. Emily was pretty, petite, and voluptuous, with blonde artificially curled hair and a small mouth that simpered rather than smiled. He wondered if she had put on her best dress for him. He wondered if her mother made her life a misery in private. He wondered if Lady Emily would rather marry the devil himself than him.

He looked at her closely, trying to detect any warmth in her expression as her eyes rested upon him. Was she being forced into this match by her mother? And if he married her, would he find her a dutiful but unenthusiastic contributor to the more intimate moments of wedlock?

He set down his teacup and suggested that Emily show him the rose garden that he had spied from his curricle.

The mother beamed. The daughter blushed and looked sick.

A shawl and a bonnet were fetched, and soon the Earl of Marcham, the most notorious of men, was alone with the eminently respectable Lady Emily Holt.

"You—you have been away, my lord?" she stammered as they pushed open the gate into the rose garden.

He nodded. "To see my mother."

"And is she well?"

"Yes, I thank you."

A silence fell, and Emily looked away.

"Do you know why I am here?" he asked.

She turned fuchsia pink. He found himself irritated by her blushes, her lack of worldliness, her die-away airs. He had been about for a good many years and had seen more than his fair share of blushing virgins. Many had set their snares for him, and many had failed to entrap him.

He smothered a yawn as she turned toward him.

"You are here to visit my poor Mama, and indeed we are grateful for your kindness," she said.

"My kindness?" he echoed. "Pray what have I done to deserve your gratitude?"

"You have taken an interest in us, even though you circulate in considerably more fashionable circles than ours. We are simple people, my lord."

He doubted that. Her father was an earl, albeit an impoverished one, but they were still an old, noble family and not so poor that they could not afford to put on a show for a prospective son-in-law.

"And yet that is a very fashionable gown you are wearing, Lady Emily."

She shrugged a pretty shoulder, pleased with the compliment. "Oh, this old thing? I have worn it for an age."

"I'm sure I would have remembered if you had . . . Emily. May I call you Emily?" he asked, touching her arm. "I wish to know . . . are your feelings engaged? Forgive my candor, but I must know. You and Thomas . . . is everything entirely at an end between you?"

He knew something of what had passed between Lady Emily and his old friend Thomas Edridge and knew that it had not ended well. What he was less sure of was how greatly the lady's affections had been engaged. He had to be certain that she was not in love with Thomas. He was prepared to give up his own hopes for a love match if he must, but he had no desire to marry a woman whose heart was given elsewhere.

Lady Emily Holt paled and looked at her hands. "Mr. Edridge has . . . has decided that I am not . . . I mean he has . . . other interests."

"I see."

There was a silence.

Lord Marcham watched her face, trying to read her feelings. But she was so calm and pale that he could not detect any signs of her heart having been touched. He tried another approach. "Thomas tells me that you are merely friends. He said that you have told him it was all a mistake, and you had no feelings for him beyond that of a brother. Forgive me, I do not wish to give you pain, but I have to be certain."

Lady Emily Holt raised her chin. "I won't pretend that you do not perfectly understand the circumstances, my lord. Mr. Edridge has . . . has toyed with my affections. He is nothing more than an acquaintance to me now."

He nodded, satisfied. "Then . . . I mean . . . would you do me the honor . . . ?"

"Yes?" she replied breathlessly, staring wide-eyed up at him.

He froze. The words stuck in his throat. Somehow he could not do it. The thought of taking her in his arms sent a spike of dread through him. The thought of waking up next to her every morning for the rest of his life filled him with such a sense of loss that he felt bereft. His heart cried out at the injustice of being quashed by his will. It would not remain quiet. It called to him. It whispered to him to have hope, still, when he thought all hope had gone. Caroline had been right; however attractive Lady Emily was, he simply couldn't do it. He cleared his throat.

"Would you do me the honor of escorting me to the lake? I have a fancy to see it."

"Of course," she replied demurely as she led the way along the path.

❧

"Well, child, well?" asked Lady Holt as soon as his lordship had driven away.

Emily blushed and stared at the floor. Her mother came toward her and took her face between her hands. Emily lifted her eyes.

"Well, child? Has he asked you?" Lady Holt demanded.

The young woman knew what it meant to her mother. She knew that the new gowns and bonnets had all been for his benefit. Her mother regarded her with such a sense of expectation that Emily felt trapped. To let down her family after such expense, to be a disappointment to the people she loved so well—she could not do it.

"Oh, Mama," she began.

Lady Holt beamed. "You are engaged then? Tell me, Emily, is it true?"

She stared at the floor, her mouth refusing to work. Lord Marcham was everything a young woman could wish for: handsome, titled, and rich. Her parents yearned for a match between them. How could she let them down? Perhaps, given time, Lord Marcham would indeed propose; she had felt certain he was about to do so when they had walked in the garden together, but something had made him change his mind. Perhaps if she pretended a real engagement did exist between them, it would eventually come to fruition, and her mother would not be so dreadfully angry with her. So she stayed silent and let assumptions be made.

Her mother shrieked with joy.

CHAPTER 2

"Have you seen this rag?" drawled Sir Julius Fawcett, crossing his booted ankles and resting them on the table.

Lord Marcham cast a disapproving glance at his friend and reflected that pristine white tablecloths should be absent from the table whenever Sir Julius Fawcett joined him for breakfast. He looked at the paper being waved at him without interest. "No, what is it?" he asked, carving himself another slice of ham.

"A sermon. At least it might as well be."

His lordship reapplied himself to his breakfast. He had come down to London on business to stay at his town house, and Sir Julius, on finding that his old friend was back in town, immediately accosted him at a very unfashionable hour. "Are you taking up religion at last, Ju?" his lordship asked.

Sir Julius shuddered and set the paper down. "Perish the thought."

"Then would you like a slice of ham or sirloin instead?"

His friend waved it away impatiently with a look of distaste. He was an extremely thin man who never seemed to eat, a fact that contrasted strongly with Lord Marcham's legendary appetite. Sir Julius was a good ten years older than his friend and had spent much of his youth abroad, his family having made their money in sugar in the West Indies some years before. Somewhere along the line, the Fawcetts had earned respectability by marrying into the aristocracy, and Sir Julius, the grandson of the union, was now as much a part of the English nobility as Lord Marcham himself.

Sir Julius rubbed his spectacularly long nose. "It's another one of those pamphlets, March. You surely must have heard about them? Every drawing room has one."

"Really? Not mine," said his lordship over the rim of his tankard.

"You will be pleased to learn that you feature in this one—well, she doesn't actually mention you by name, but anyone may guess who she means."

"She?" repeated the earl. "And who is she?"

"The author . . . a Miss Blakelow."

"Never heard of her."

"Well, she has definitely heard of you," said Sir Julius.

"*Everyone* has heard of me, Ju," replied his lordship without a hint of conceit. "My youthful . . . er . . . adventures have made me infamous, you know."

"It's called 'The inexorable pursuit of earthly pleasures by the moneyed classes and the consequences upon the poorest and most vulnerable in our society.'"

Lord Marcham raised his eyes from his plate. "Memorable."

"Isn't it, though?" agreed his friend.

"Are you dining out this evening?" asked his lordship in a valiant attempt to change the subject. "I thought that I might go to Whites."

"Miss Blakelow condemns your morals," said Sir Julius. "She says that a man in your position should know better."

"Indeed?" The earl yawned and cut a sliver of ham from the slice on his plate. "And who is Miss Blakelow to question me or anyone else?"

"'A woman with the highest moral principles,' or so it says here."

"A veritable saint then," replied his lordship when he had swallowed his mouthful. "But I don't answer to Miss Blakelow or her following."

"And she has a following," said Sir Julius gloomily, turning over the publication in his hands so that he might examine the back of it. "She must be making a pretty penny from all this too."

"Good for her."

"March, I do not think that you are taking this at all seriously," complained Sir Julius. "Damn me if you aren't a little too relaxed about the whole affair."

"She is making money from peddling gossip. In my view that makes her no arbiter of moral excellence. I'll wager she has achieved notoriety by sensationalizing the same old stories that have been regurgitated continually since I was eighteen."

"Oh, no, she has done her research. She seems to know an awful lot about you."

Lord Marcham fixed his rather hard gray eyes upon his friend. "Research? What research?"

"She knows about the duel."

His lordship rolled his eyes. "Everyone knows about that."

"No, the *other* duel," said Sir Julius with a meaningful look.

There was a short silence. Lord Marcham thought back the best part of twenty years to the young fool he'd been at the age of seventeen and grimaced. A friend of his father's had accused him of cheating at cards, and Marcham, as hotheaded as he was hotblooded, had told the fellow he'd meet him whenever, wherever, he chose. The attendants at the duel had been sworn to secrecy, and he was as sure as he could be that the doctor hadn't blabbed. Where on earth had she got her information?

"The other . . . How the devil—?"

"Exactly. See? I told you. She knows things. And now all of society knows about it too."

The earl snatched the pamphlet from his friend's hand.

"Third page, second paragraph," said Sir Julius, a hint of triumph in his voice.

There was a silence while his lordship read the offending piece, a frown between his brows. "Devil take her," he muttered under his breath. "Who is the woman anyway?"

"I told you," said Sir Julius with some irritation. "Miss Blakelow. Don't you ever listen?"

"Yes, I heard you the first time, but that does not tell me who she is."

"She knows things," repeated his friend ominously.

"But I've never even heard of the woman . . . wait . . . Blakelow, why is that name familiar to me?"

His friend stared at him. "Her father was your neighbor."

"Was he? Damned if I can remember."

"Sir William Blakelow. Gamester and profligate, and that description could be applied equally to the son. Seems to me that the daughter knows your business, and if I were you, I would look to my household."

The earl threw down the pamphlet. "What do you mean?"

"Ten to one your servants have been blabbing what they shouldn't."

His lordship shook his head. "My servants don't blab—not if they wish to retain their positions in my house. Besides, they don't know anything."

"You'd be surprised," said Sir Julius. "They have a way of knowing everything."

"Well, mine don't . . . not *everything*."

"You may say that, but somehow Miss Blakelow knows about the Diana Ingham affair, and I certainly didn't tell her."

A gleam of annoyance stole into his lordship's eyes. "Does she indeed?"

"She knows you covered it up and that you went to great lengths to do it."

The earl pushed back his chair and flung his napkin onto the table. He remembered how smitten his younger brother, Henry, had been by Diana Ingham. The boy had made a fool of himself. Diana, as clever as she was beautiful, had Hal wrapped around her little finger from the moment she'd met him. It took all his lordship's persuasive powers and a sizable purse to induce the woman to leave the lad alone. Now here was Miss Blakelow, raking up the past when he thought he had buried it so deep that no one would ever find it again. Confound this Blakelow creature—she was going to undo all his hard work!

But drawing attention to her wretched pamphlet would only prove that the words written within it were correct and provide more ammunition for the woman to write another edition. No, the best way to deal with this was to pay it no attention. Pretty soon the ton would find another story for their gossips. He sighed. "Can I not eat my breakfast in peace?"

"I'm telling you, March, you will have to take her to task. Pay her off or something."

"Pay her off?" repeated Lord Marcham. "I will not."

"I will lay odds that she's writing another one."

"Let her. Who is she that she dare question me?"

"She says that she is hell-bent on, and I quote, 'exposing the corrupt attitude of the nobility and their belief that any woman is fair game.' There. Did I not warn you? This chit is a troublemaker."

"You don't say."

"Have you and she . . . you know? Had relations?" asked Sir Julius.

The earl pulled a face. "Hardly, when I can barely remember her name."

"That never stopped you before," his friend pointed out helpfully and received a glare for his trouble. "She's a jilted lover of yours looking for recompense."

"She is not a jilted lover of mine," insisted the earl.

"Did you get her with child? You needn't glare at me like that, March. It's not exactly impossible, is it? It wouldn't surprise me in the least if you had a brat or two come out of the woodwork," said Sir Julius, pulling forth his snuffbox. "You've ploughed a field or two in your time."

"Thank you for reminding me," said his lordship dryly.

"Well, you have," reasoned his friend. "There have been women you'd dropped, throwing themselves into the Serpentine just because you'd found yourself a new lover."

Lord Marcham picked up his tankard and drank from it. "There was only one lady who did that, and she was as mad as a box of frogs," he said, setting down his ale again. He turned to Sir Julius with a look of distaste on his face. "And do we have to talk about this?"

"You ran wild for years. I think your mother was never more glad than when you were sent to war in the Peninsular. She said it saved you from yourself."

"Getting shot at is hardly the method I would choose," said the earl caustically, glancing down at his once-injured leg.

"Well, ten to one she's a harpy," said Sir Julius.

"Who? My mother or Miss Blakelow?"

Sir Julius rolled his eyes. "Miss Blakelow, of course."

The earl looked doubtfully at him, picked up a freshly baked bread roll, and pulled it apart. "A harpy who's the epitome of moral perfection? Hardly. She sounds terribly straitlaced to me."

Sir Julius rubbed his nose thoughtfully. "Then it's not likely you were intimate . . . so why does she have it in for you?"

"Heaven only knows."

"Well, you cannot let her get away with bad-mouthing you. No, no, March, it simply will not do."

"She hasn't bad-mouthed me. You said yourself that she has not mentioned me by name. How do I know that she is referring to me?"

"Because there are too many circumstances that are familiar. And people who know you and who are intimate with your past cannot fail to make the comparison. And those who don't will speculate that it's you anyway. You can't allow that."

"Certainly I can," replied his lordship coolly. "I will not give the woman the satisfaction."

He'd been criticized and hectored by the moral busybodies of the world since he was seventeen. Everything he'd done, from his first affair to the scandalous duel that had almost caused his father to disinherit him, had been food for the gossips. He'd long since learned that many of them were hypocrites who had their own secrets that they would prefer to keep hidden. But this woman had found out about the Diana Ingham affair, which meant she must have spoken to someone whose information was worryingly accurate. What he'd told Sir Julius was the truth; at present he had no plans to address Miss Blakelow on the subject of her pamphlet. But in a few months, when all the fuss had died down, he would deal with her in his own way and in his own time.

"No," he continued, "what I *need* is to finish my breakfast in peace."

Sir Julius ignored him. He tapped one long finger against his nose, appearing to set his rather limited intellect to the task. "What would be the ultimate mortification to a spinster woman of high moral principle?" demanded Sir Julius.

His lordship snorted in amusement and reached for his coffee. "To be ruined by a rake."

Sir Julius Fawcett's face split into a wide smile. "That's it! Damn me if it isn't. Seduce the girl."

Lord Marcham did a double take. "Ju, I was funning. I am not in the habit of seducing moralizing spinster bores. Besides, she may not be a girl at all. She could be ninety for all we know."

His friend's smile grew. "Her father was Sir William Blakelow, and he was five and sixty when he died, so she has to be younger than forty."

"You relieve me," murmured the earl.

"There's no telling what she looks like, though. Those sorts of women are usually spinsters for a reason . . . but that won't matter to you, will it?"

His lordship frowned. "I have standards, Ju."

"You don't have to actually like the girl, just pretend that you do. Miss Blakelow is going to fall in love with you."

"Oh, Lord."

A grim smile settled upon Sir Julius Fawcett's thin lips. "Well, she will soon find that to be the object of desire of such a man is not at all pleasant, that any woman whose name is linked with yours is inevitably tarnished by the acquaintance even if you have exchanged nothing more than words. To be talked about in that fashion is not very nice. She will discover what it is like to be on the receiving end of some of the vitriol she has poured onto others."

"Do you know, Ju, if I didn't know any better, I'd think that she has made you angry."

Sir Julius smiled. "I am angry, I admit, but so are you."

"*Me?* Am I?" replied the earl with a laugh. "How on earth do you arrive at that conclusion? I have already told you that I care nothing for what this nobody has to say."

"You hide it well, but I *know* you. I have known you for years. I know what it means when you get that look in your eyes."

"What look?" said his lordship, laughing and spreading his hands.

"The one you get when someone makes you angry," said Sir Julius, fixing him with a knowing look. "You, dear boy, are preparing for battle."

Lord Marcham smiled, but the expression did not reach his eyes. "Indeed? How well you think you know me. But I assure you that I am utterly uninterested in anything that woman has to say or do."

"Hmm," said Sir Julius. "And I'm Genghis Khan."

CHAPTER 3

THE BIG BLACK DOOR was about to slam in her face.

But the young woman, who had waited a month for the appointment with the earl and who had ridden two miles in the rain to his estate at Holme Park, was not about to be undone at the last hurdle by Mr. Davenham, his lordship's pompous butler, who had been in the earl's employ for years. She thrust her foot into the rapidly closing space between the door and the frame, resisting the urge to yelp as the impact seemed to crush every bone in her foot.

"I must see Lord Marcham," she said, pushing the door back in the startled servant's face.

"I have already informed you that his lordship is not at home to visitors," said Mr. Davenham, his voice becoming high-pitched with panic in the face of this determined young lady.

She brushed past him and into the hall and stood looking about her. It was a large affair with a polished marble floor and paintings of lords and ladies frowning down at her from all sides.

Yes, you may well stare your disapproval, but when your descendant will not keep his appointments, then what else is one to do? she thought.

She suddenly felt the force of her actions, barging her way into a gentleman's home, unaccompanied, when the owner of the house was probably at breakfast, or worse, still abed. She thought again of her home and her family and remembered that her case was desperate. She was sorry for the intrusion, but she needed to see the earl before it was too late.

She was a trim woman, tall, and by no means in the first flush of youth. Mr. Davenham thought her around the age of thirty and someone's governess to boot. She was dressed entirely in black, suggesting a recent bereavement, and the overlarge clothes hung off her slender frame, suggesting that they were someone else's castoffs. The garments were well made but outmoded and shabby, as if they had been made some time ago. Her face was pink and flushed from the exercise of riding, and she possessed a short, slim nose and generous lips that were curved in a smile guaranteed to break down the butler's defenses. Under her bonnet could be seen the frill of a mob cap and a pair of green eyes hidden behind ugly spectacles.

If Mr. Davenham had been fortunate enough to see her without the spectacles and the cap and the prim clothing, he might have thought her an attractive woman, but as it were, he thought her a country dowd and someone's poor relation at that. The suspicion that she was about to claim some link to Lord Marcham and wheedle her way into his purse was not lost upon the butler, nor was the thought that she might be some lightskirt from the earl's colorful youth about to foist a love child upon him. Equally alarming was the thought of what his lordship would do to Mr. Davenham if he let her anywhere near him. He ran a forefinger between his collar and his neck, already imagining his master's hands around his throat. He watched the young lady tuck away a long tendril of chestnut hair. It had escaped from the prim arrangement of her headdress and curled gently against her cheek.

"Well, he will be at home to me when he hears what I have to say to him," she replied, stripping off her gloves. "I have an appointment of some weeks' standing. My father's man of business arranged it, and I am not about to be turned away at the last fence by you or anyone else. I know that his lordship has a policy of not receiving visitors, but this is not a social visit, I can assure you. I am here on business, and I must ask you again to please inform Lord Marcham of my arrival."

"His lordship is *indisposed*," said Mr. Davenham, his slightly protruding eyes almost popping out of their sockets.

"If he is truly indisposed, then I am sorry for it, but if he is, as I suspect, avoiding me—"

"Wait! Ma'am, you cannot go in there!"

The woman had moved swiftly across the hallway toward a closed door from behind which she could hear masculine laughter and excited shouts of encouragement. She placed her hand upon the doorknob.

The butler looked at her so fearfully that she felt sorry for him.

"Madam, please, his lordship will turn me out of the house if I let you in there! Come into the parlor, and I will fetch my master to you."

She smiled at him kindly. "What a silly creature you are to be so afraid of the earl. He must be a tyrant indeed to instill such fear in you," she marveled. "But never fear. He will not seek retribution from you, I promise. Forgive me, Mr. Davenham, but I really will not be put off my purpose this time."

She turned and flung the door wide open and for a moment stood in stunned disbelief, as the scene before her was one that she had not ever encountered before.

The room was dim, the curtains still drawn even though it wanted only fifteen minutes until midday, and the candles burned low in their sockets. Around the table were perhaps ten or twelve gentlemen of differing ages, some with their wigs askew, others with their coats cast aside and cravats undone, chins unshaven, eyes bleary with drink and lack of sleep. The room reeked of alcohol, and the table was littered with empty bottles, wineglasses, and the remains of supper. Several young ladies in varying states of undress sat on the laps of the gentlemen; one couple was engaged in a very indecent embrace on a sofa against the wall. Rose petals were strewn across the tablecloth, and standing in the middle of the table as the centerpiece was a woman, clearly in the process of stripping off her clothes for the entertainment of the gathered male company. The shouts she'd heard had been encouragement to remove the last item of clothing, a rather expensive-looking but decidedly improper undergarment. The half-dressed woman had halted her disrobement as the door was opened and now stared agog at the prim woman looking so coolly back at her.

To the woman standing in the doorway, it seemed that twenty pairs of eyes had swiveled in her direction. Every instinct told her to flee. She most definitely should not be in such a place. She knew that Lord Marcham had a certain reputation; indeed, everyone knew it. But *this*? Who could have expected his debauchery to sink him so low?

"Who's this, Marcham?" asked an elderly gentleman, slurring his words. He turned in his chair and raised his eyeglass, staring at her impertinently through it for some moments. "Have you brought your housekeeper to entertain us? Or is she the village schoolteacher?"

She swallowed hard, lifted her chin, and stared back.

"Nothing to do with me, Henry," said a deep voice from the far end of the room.

"I have come to see Lord Marcham, and I wish to see him in private," she announced in a firm and clear voice.

"I'll wager you do," someone muttered, and there was a rumble of suggestive laughter.

"Mind your manners, Anthony," chided that same deep voice, but there was a hint of amusement nonetheless.

"What do you want with him?" demanded the elderly gentleman named Henry.

"It is a private matter of business," she replied.

"Never 'eard it called that before," said one young woman clad in an indecently low-cut gown.

"Get her up on the table!" suggested a skinny man with a droopy nose, waving his arm aloft. "Let's see what's under that mourning garb."

Several men slapped the table in appreciation of this idea.

"Yes!"

"Capital idea!"

Her hand gripped tightly upon the small pistol buried in the pocket of her cloak. "I have a long-standing appointment to see Lord Marcham at eleven thirty this morning," she said firmly, trying to control the rising sense of panic that was threatening to send her flying from the room but taking strength from the feel of the pistol in her hand.

"Oh, March never keeps his appointments," said another man with bright-blue eyes and a kindly face. "Anyone can tell you that. Famous for it."

"Which one of you is Lord Marcham?" she demanded, her eyes traveling from the handsome man with the blue eyes to another man's puce cheeks to another who had thick gray eyebrows like caterpillars.

"I am Lord Marcham," said a man seated at the far end of the table. He stood up and came toward her, smiling at her in a way that made her feel as if she wanted to take a bath. He was clearly still drunk, and his dress was in considerable disarray. He had long ago discarded his coat and cravat, and his very hairy chest could be seen at the low neck of his shirt.

She balked a little but stood her ground, gripping the pistol ever more tightly in her fingers as he came nearer. Was this Lord Marcham? She had not set eyes on the earl in years, but even so, he looked very different from the man she remembered. He offered her his hand and she chose not to take it. There was another rumble of laughter. He pulled out a chair from the table and invited her to be seated in it with a gesture of his hand. She remained where she was.

"Oh, Prudence, will you not come near the fire at least?" he asked. "You are soaked through."

The rain had percolated through her thick cloak to her gown underneath, and steam was slowly rising from her back. She would have dearly loved to warm herself before the fire, but she did not trust him an inch and stayed where she was.

"Won't you take off your cloak, my dear?"

Given that every man in the room appeared to be speculating about how she looked under her cloak, she declined.

"And what is your name, fair Cyprian?" he asked, smiling, and his friends laughed at the very idea. He was of the same height as her, but she was almost certain that when she had met Lord Marcham before, he had been very much taller than she was. Whoever this man was, he was not the earl, and he had a lecherous look in his eye that turned her stomach.

"You are insulting, sir."

"Am I indeed? And why, may I ask, are you dressed in widow's garb? I don't remember requesting such an outfit. Does your madam imagine any man wants to see a woman dressed in such a fashion?"

He reached out a hand to untie the ribbons on her cloak, and she slapped him away. "I am in mourning, sir," she said, glaring at the man's friends, who seemed to fairly lick their lips in anticipation.

"Are you?" the imposter replied, walking around her as if examining a prize heifer. "You are playing the part of the prude rather too well, my dear. Teasing is all well and good, and I like it as much as the next man, but if you want to get paid, you'll take off your cloak and be quick about it . . ."

"I beg your pardon?" she said blankly.

The man waved a hand at the lady in the thin chemise. "Molly here has kept us more than well entertained without you, but you are a little late for the party, wouldn't you say? You were supposed to have been here yesterday. But I'm sure we can make up for lost time."

Before she knew what he was about, he had seized her by the waist, brought her against his bony body, and kissed her hard on the mouth. She clamped down her teeth upon his lower lip and he yelped in pain. She followed this by raising her knee in a swift but unladylike assault on his unmentionables and the man doubled over, grunting in pain. Guffaws of laughter followed from his friends.

"Enough," said the man with the deep voice, wearily rising from a chair at the far end of the room.

"She kicked me!" the man said, doubled over. "The little shrew!"

"Larwood, calm down."

"Look! I'm bleeding! I'll take her upstairs and show her what—"

"You'll do nothing of the kind. I rather think that there is some mistake. This young woman is not one of your . . . er . . . entertainers."

She pulled the gun from her pocket and aimed it with a remarkably steady hand at the figure that had come forward into the firelight.

The man quirked a brow. "It appears my surmise was accurate," he said.

The room seemed to suck in its breath with anticipation.

"I wish to speak to Lord Marcham," she said, leveling the pistol at his chest, inwardly shaking so much she was amazed she could keep the gun straight. She thought again of her family and her home. She thought of the dire straits they were in and how much she needed the earl's help. Every fiber of her being told her to flee the room before her reputation was in tatters, but she knew she had no choice but to stay.

"And you will have the opportunity of speech with me, once you put the gun away," said the man gently, his hands upturned as if in surrender as he slowly came toward her.

By anyone's standards, he was a handsome man, but she was unable to see him clearly through her wretched glasses. In contrast to the one who had accosted her, he was unexpectedly well kempt. Considering he had spent all night carousing with his friends, his coat and cravat were remarkably well preserved. The only sign that he had been drinking was a gleam in his eyes, which held a slightly wild look, and they rested upon her with an intensity that she found disquieting. He was taller than most of the men of her acquaintance and a good deal broader across the shoulders too. She knew that he would be impossible to fight off should he choose to force his attentions upon her. He smiled disarmingly at her, as if he knew the power this singular expression had upon women. "No one will harm you, I promise."

"Too late for that," she said angrily, wiping her mouth on the back of her hand as if she could wipe away the memory of the kiss.

"You have not been hurt, I hope?" he asked soothingly. "No, I venture to think not. Merely your pride has been wounded."

"I have been insulted in the worst possible manner!"

"I hate to contradict you, my dear, but not the *worst* possible manner. I think there has been some mistake. Mr. Larwood was evidently expecting someone else. Mr. Larwood apologizes, don't you, Harry?"

33

"No, I damn well—"

"Mr. Larwood apologizes most profusely. He is in his cups, ma'am, and not very good at holding his drink. I hope that you might find it in your heart to forgive him. I might also remind you that you came here of your own free will. And uninvited. Let us go to the library where we may talk—"

"I have an appointment with you, sir! And if you had been obliging enough as to keep the previous two appointments with Mr. Healey, my father's man of business, rather than go out hunting, or lying abed, or whatever a rake does when he is not carousing, I would not have needed to come here today."

The man's lips twitched. "Uninvited," he reiterated firmly. "You forced your way in here, when my butler undoubtedly told you that I was not at home to visitors. Whom I choose to entertain in my own house is my business and my business alone. If you feel you have been insulted, then I apologize, but do not ask me for anything more, for I am a selfish creature and will not give it. Now, you may come and sit in my library, where we may be private and discuss this business that you speak of."

"So that you might accost me too?" she demanded.

The earl raised one eyebrow in mild surprise. Then with deliberate slowness, he examined every inch of her, from her old scuffed riding boots to the rain-sodden feather on her bonnet. She felt her cheeks sting with color at his less than complimentary perusal.

"I think that is a little unlikely, don't you?" he said, very, very softly.

She wanted the rich carpet at her feet to swallow her whole.

"Now give me the gun, if you please."

"I don't trust you," she said, setting her chin stubbornly.

"No one points a gun at me in my own house," he replied. He held out his hand imperatively. "The gun, if you please. You will have no need of it while you are here, and it will be returned to you when you leave. You have my word on it."

"Is that the word of a scoundrel and a . . . a . . . *debaucher*?" she demanded.

"It is," he said smoothly, ignoring her insult as he took the gun from her hand. "But it is my word nonetheless."

She looked up at him. "Are you Lord Marcham?"

He bowed slightly. "Robert Holkham, Earl of Marcham. Your servant, ma'am."

"Why did you let your friend insult me? Is this how you treat every gentlewoman who comes into your house?" she demanded.

"Gentlewomen don't make a habit of coming to my house," he replied. "Something to do with their reputations and . . . er . . . mine."

"You are living up to yours, I see," she said.

He gave her a brief smile as he held open the door for her to pass through. "I'm so glad that I don't disappoint you. Shall we?"

❧

Nothing would persuade her to remove her wet cloak, even though she was quite certain that she would catch a chill by keeping it on. She sat perched on the edge of her chair, ready to fly at any moment, and regarded her host with a wary eye.

They were in the library, a large room, clad from floor to ceiling with dark wooden shelves filled with the spines of countless books. There was a large desk, also made of the same dark wood, and the chairs and tables were equally as somber. She thought it a most oppressive room and yearned to pull back the curtains farther to let in the daylight.

His lordship saw the direction of her gaze. "I keep the curtains drawn to protect the books. Can I offer you a glass of wine?" he asked, closing the door behind them.

"No, thank you."

He shrugged. "Suit yourself. I will have one, however . . . I fear I may need it."

"Why, haven't you had enough already?" she asked before she could stop herself.

He paused in the act of pouring himself a glass of wine and glanced at her speculatively, a hint of a smile on his lips. "Do you disapprove, ma'am?"

"I think *anyone* must disapprove. The young gentlemen in our neighborhood look to men like you as role models—"

He frowned at her. "Excuse me, madam, but why exactly are you here? To discuss business or to lecture me?"

She simmered at his interruption. "Business."

"Then let us get to it. I do not need you moralizing at me. Now, tell me what it is that you want of me."

She unfolded the leather case she had under her arm. "I have here papers—"

"I'm not remotely interested in your papers. Tell me what you want."

She bristled and struggled to hold her temper. She took a deep breath and began again. "You recently won a vast sum of money from the owner of the Thorncote estate at the gaming table," she said.

"Yes, what of it?"

"It belonged to my father, Sir William Blakelow—Thorncote, that is—and now belongs to his son, who is every bit as profligate as Papa, but never mind that. It is a large estate, not as large as yours, of course, but it could be made to be very profitable if some money could be spent on it and the right management put in place."

The earl looked perplexed and rubbed his hand against his forehead. "Do you mean to tell me that you haven't come here to tell me that I am the father of your child?"

She stared at him with her mouth agape. *"What?"*

"You don't have a brat that I am expected to recognize?"

"No! I don't have a brat—I mean child. I have hardly spoken two words to you in the entire course of my life!"

"Thank God for that," he breathed.

"You cannot thank God more than I do," she retorted.

"Then you and I have not . . . er . . ."

"No!"

He brightened visibly. "Oh . . . well, that's good. In my youth, you know . . ."

"No," she replied indignantly. "I do *not* know!"

He looked amused and then directed a sudden penetrating glance across at her. "Forgive me, but who are you?" he asked.

She stared at him, waiting for him to recognize her, dreading that he would. "Miss Blakelow. Daughter of Sir William Blakelow."

"Blakelow . . ." he mused, frowning, and then suddenly his brow cleared as it came to him. "Could it be that I am in the company of Miss *Georgiana* Blakelow?"

She flushed and lifted her chin. "Yes, sir."

"The spinster par excellence who has besmirched my reputation?" he said, a gleam of unholy glee in his eye. "Dear me, what am I to do with you?"

"Your reputation was already besmirched, my lord," she retorted with spirit.

"Indeed it was. But I was hoping, Miss Blakelow, to leave my past far behind me. You are the bluestocking recluse who saw fit to drag it all up again, are you not?"

"Just because I do not approve of your ways, my lord, does not make me a bluestocking."

"You wrote a pamphlet condemning my morals, didn't you? Caused a hell of a stir. It was in all the papers."

"I did not mention you, I believe," said Miss Blakelow stiffly. "I did not mention anyone. You assume too much, my lord."

"You didn't have to name me. Everyone knew whom you meant."

"My aunt was hurt very badly as a young woman by just such a man as you. I was sending a warning to all young women to be on their guard."

Lord Marcham half sat, half leaned on the edge of his desk, arms folded. "I see. And do you imagine that many young women will heed your warning?" he asked doubtfully.

"They should, if they wish to preserve their delicacy."

"Their delicacy," he repeated with a harsh laugh. "And how many young women would give up their delicacy and a good deal more to live in a house like this?" he asked, waving a hand to indicate the grandeur around them. "How many women would gladly warm a man's bed for wealth, position, and title and then put a ring on their finger to legitimize their actions?"

"And do you include your fiancée in that flattering description, my lord?" she asked, visibly annoyed.

"My fiancée?" he repeated.

"Lady Emily Holt."

He smiled but no warmth reached his eyes. "You have been listening to idle gossip, ma'am. Lady Emily Holt is not my fiancée."

"No? Then why is news of your engagement spread halfway across the country?"

He stared at her for a long moment of weighted silence. "It isn't."

"I can assure you, my lord, that it is. The talk in Loughton is of nothing else."

He swore under his breath. The Holts had been busy, had they? Well, they would find that Lord Marcham was not a man to be forced.

"There must be some mistake," he replied. "I have not made that young woman an offer."

"She seems to think differently. And you cannot deny that you have been very marked in your attentions," she said coldly, "or that your behavior has given rise to the speculation of the whole neighborhood as to when the wedding will be. If you did not make her an offer, then you will earn the lady nothing but public derision by so singling her out."

He gave a rather scornful laugh. "Dear ma'am, a walk in the rose garden and two drives in the park hardly constitute a love affair, even to your pure and delicate sensibilities."

She lifted her chin. "For a woman associating with a man of your reputation, sir, one glance in a room filled with a hundred people is enough to be remarked upon."

He looked amused at that. "Is that so?" he asked, his eyes twinkling. "Are you not then afraid to be alone with me? Am I so debauched that one glance from me is enough to get you with child?"

She met his look unflinchingly. "It would take more than that."

"So it would," he agreed, watching her. "Lady Emily Holt is no different from any other woman who marries for social advancement, security, and money. She is prepared to wed me despite my shocking reputation because I am rich. She wants fine jewels and clothes and a house such as this. She is just as pretty and mercenary as any other eligible female I know, and if I have to marry someone, I suppose it may as well be her as anyone else. It is a bargain, Miss Blakelow: her virtue in payment for my money. And in my book, that makes her no better than Molly there in the dining room, shivering in her chemise. At least Molly is honest about it."

"And does the future Lady Marcham know you hold her in such high esteem?"

He smiled. "She bears no more love for me than I for her. I need an heir; she likes the size of my . . . ahem . . . purse."

Miss Blakelow felt her temper rising like steam in a boiling kettle. "Are you comparing the poor wretches, the fallen women with whom you associate, to any respectable woman who marries a respectable man for her financial security and that of her children?"

"If she does not do it for love, then yes."

"And yet Lady Emily Holt will agree to be your wife. Wonders will never cease."

He surprised her then by suddenly laughing, and she saw what a devastatingly attractive man he was. When he spoke to her in that way, as if certain of breaking down her defenses with his glib responses and disarming smile, she felt something inside her awaken and respond. It had been a long time since any man had looked at her the way the earl was looking at her now. She felt vulnerable. She steeled herself against him and formed a protective shell around her heart. She did not want to fall for this rake, no matter how engaging he was.

"We are not getting very far with business, are we, Miss Blakelow?"

"You are insufferable," she bit out.

He laughed again. "How true. And so, prim Miss Blakelow with the very kissable lips, what can a dissolute man like me do for you? You do realize that a paragon of womanhood like you should not enter a house like this alone? Do you not fear to be tainted by the very walls?"

"Don't mock me." She stood up and started to pull on her gloves. "I am clearly wasting my time. You are drunk and determined to make me lose my temper."

"Do you know that your eyes flash when you're angry?" he said, watching her. "Or at least I think they do. I cannot see them properly through those hideous spectacles of yours."

"Good day, my lord," she said, scooping up her papers and shoving them back into the leather case.

"Oh, dear, I have upset you. Do remember to say good-bye to Harry Larwood on your way out; he seemed quite taken with you."

Miss Blakelow thought that she might explode with rage. She strode across the room, seized the door handle, and wrenched it open but was halted by his soft voice saying, "That is the door to the servants' quarters, Miss Blakelow. If you wish to make a dramatic exit from the room, might I suggest that the door onto the hallway would serve you better?"

She almost groaned aloud in frustration. Cursing her stupid spectacles, she retreated back the way she had come, narrowly missing tripping over the low table where his lordship's wineglass was perched.

She swept from the room and was halfway across the hallway to the front door when she realized that by deliberately goading her to lose her temper, he had avoided completely the subject that she had gone there to discuss. Determined not to let him off the hook so easily, she spun on her heel and walked back to the library.

Lord Marcham was still where she had left him when she returned to the room. He looked up as she entered and a ghost of a smile flickered on his lips. "Miss Blakestocking . . . not one easily put off your purpose, I see. What a pleasure it is to see you again . . . and so soon."

She tapped her foot impatiently against the floor. "You will allow me to tell you that I find you—" She broke off, suddenly realizing that giving full rein to her temper was hardly likely to get her what she wanted.

"Yes?" he goaded softly. "Do go on."

41

"No."

"You were about to say despicable, shallow, and dissolute."

"No I was not," she said through gritted teeth.

His eyes twinkled. "My manners are deplorable, are they not?"

"My lord Marcham, will you *stop*?"

He gave a low laugh. "As it seems that you are determined to say what you have come here to say, despite my best efforts to put you off, won't you please be seated Miss Blakestock—Miss Blakelow? I will call a truce, and then we may try and be friends."

Miss Blakelow chose to stand. "You have made a lifetime career from fleecing men of their property, have you not?" she demanded.

"I thought we had agreed to call a truce?"

"Do you have any notion what impact your actions have on the families of those men?" she asked.

He shrugged. "I might, I suppose, if I were to put myself to the trouble. But I know that those gentlemen were just as keen to fleece *me* of *my* property," he replied calmly. "I doubt they would have given me a moment's thought as they took up residence at my table. The difference, my dear Miss Blakelow, is that I have rarely been foolish enough to gamble away anything that I wanted to keep."

"So you feel no guilt?"

"Why should I? If they are stupid enough to gamble away the future of their wives and children, then that is their affair."

"My father lost a great deal of money to you eighteen months ago."

"I believe he did."

"And my brother lost yet more money to you trying to win back Father's losses."

"He was foolish enough to attempt it, yes."

"I am here to tell you that we have no more money left to pay you. Thorncote is all we have left, and if you take that, we have nowhere to go."

There was a silence.

"I am truly sorry to hear it, Miss Blakelow. Allow me to offer you my sympathies."

"Thank you but what do you imagine I am to do with those?" she asked. "Do you think your sympathies will provide a home for my brothers and sisters? Do you imagine your sympathies will console my brother at the loss of his inheritance?"

"I *am* truly sorry for your loss," he repeated. "But I say again, your father gambled away what he had no right to. You should be venting your anger at him, not me."

"Oh, I do, I can assure you," she retorted. "Not a day goes by when I don't wish he were alive so that I could tell him exactly what I think of him."

"My dear Miss Blakelow—"

"But there is something you can do as reparation."

He gave her a tight smile. "Forgive me, ma'am, but I do not feel the need to make reparation."

There was a pause. Miss Blakelow moved toward the nearest chair and sank down into it, arranging her hands primly in her lap. She took a deep breath and stared at the floor. "I didn't know that my brother had lost so much money to you until after I had written that stupid pamphlet. I would not blame you if you did not believe me, but I am very sorry now that I wrote it. I know that you are exceedingly generous with your tenants, and none of your servants have a bad word to say about you. I had hoped you might see fit to help a neighbor who has fallen on hard times, a family who will presently be made homeless. I had hoped that even you, my lord, with all your faults, would be willing to help the family of a man who was an acquaintance of your own father's."

"I am sorry, ma'am, but I cannot be responsible for the actions of a few weak men. I am truly sorry for your predicament, but your brother, and indeed your father, knew what they were about when they sat down to play with me. I have no regrets and I feel no remorse."

"Then I am sorry for you," she said.

He looked somewhat taken aback. "Sorry for me? Why should you be indeed?"

She shrugged. "Because it is clear to me that you must be an extremely unhappy man. Lonely too."

The earl stood abruptly and walked to the window, turning his back on her so that she could not read his face. "Don't presume to know me, Miss Blakelow," he said in a completely altered tone that made her flinch.

"I don't want to know you," she answered. "All I want is your assistance."

He turned back toward her in amazement. "My God, you speak your mind true enough, don't you? Well, go on then. Let's have it."

She took a deep breath. "I have never been close to my father. In fact, for many years now I have considered him one of the most foolish men I have ever known. Shocking, is it not, to speak of one's father in such a way? But he drove his wife to an early grave, and he gambled away practically everything we owned. The money, the silverware, paintings, sculptures . . . everything. The house is an empty shell." She looked down at her hands. "Much of my mother's jewelry was sold years ago to pay for his debts, and it is only thanks to her, who hid a little of her own property, that we have anything of hers left. But, that is not getting me to the point, is it? I know that you have issued us instructions to leave within three months, and you will not find us difficult to remove when the time comes; we honor our father's debt to you even if he did not."

"I am glad to hear it."

She looked down at her hands. "W-what do you plan to do with Thorncote once we have gone, sir? Will you sell it?"

"I certainly plan to. I have asked my man of business to set things in motion," he answered.

"Your man of business, yes . . . I suppose you have . . . *other* . . . things to think about," she mused aloud, staring off into the distance.

His lips twitched, coaxed at last out of his ill humor by this blithe comment. "Indeed? And what might those *other things* be, Miss Blakelow?"

She stared back at him, refusing to rise to his bait. "I—nothing. The Thorncote estate has been mismanaged and deprived of money for years. It is good farming land and used to make a tidy profit when my grandfather was alive. But it has been allowed to go to seed, and I do not think you would get a very good price if you sold it in its present condition."

He shrugged. "Perhaps, but any money I get from it would still be an addition to my coffers."

"Yes, but it could be so much more," she said eagerly. She opened her leather case once more and took from it a sheaf of papers. "See here. This was the income in the last year of my grandfather's life. It can be made profitable again."

"This is all very laudable, but I don't want to bring it back to profitability. I lack the will, you see. Let the man who buys it from me do that. I just want shot of it."

"Then let me do it."

He frowned. "What exactly are you asking of me?"

"Don't take Thorncote from us. Let my brother stay in possession of the estate, and let us repay the debt to you from the profits. We can work out a schedule. Every month we will make a payment to you, with interest, until the debt my father and brother owe you is paid off."

There was a long pause while he considered her offer. He looked over at her and folded his arms. "My dear Miss Naivety, have you any idea how much money that is?" he asked.

She stared at her hands. "I imagine it would be a sizable amount," she said in a low voice.

He laughed harshly. "Yes, ma'am, it is a sizable amount," he said with sarcasm. "You would be paying me back into the next century."

She swallowed hard. "We could do it. I know we could."

"I admire your industry, Miss Blakelow, truly I do, and your courage too for coming here to explain your idea to me. But it won't fly."

"Why won't it?" she demanded, a pleading note in her voice. "My father's man of business, Mr. Healey, is a superb fellow and has a great deal of experience in these matters—if only he had not been hamstrung by my father's bleeding the estate dry."

"And there you have hit the nail on the head," said his lordship. "How do you imagine that these improvements are to be made when you have said yourself that you have no money?"

"Well, I have thought of that. If you could loan us the money . . ."

Lord Marcham smiled. "How did I know you were going to say that? You are already in debt to me up to your eyeballs, and you want me to lend you more money?"

"Yes."

"*And* after you have dragged my name through the dirt. Go on then, tell me it all. How much?"

Miss Blakelow pulled another piece of paper from her case and rose to hand it to him.

He looked from the document to her face. "Why so conservative? Why not ask for double that amount?" he asked.

She flushed. "I did think of it," she confessed. "But I did not think you would give it to me."

"No," he replied. "And you were right."

"But, sir, if you would but look at the figures. I can guarantee you a very good rate of return. It represents a very good investment for your money. And with the added bonus of turning a bad situation to good account."

"My dear Miss Blakelow, no."

"But, sir, if you had allowed Mr. Healey to come and explain it all to you—"

He held up a hand. "Spare me from the rigors of farm technology, I beg of you. I cannot think of anything more tedious. Now, is that all?" He moved toward her as he said this.

"Do you wish to keep the paperwork in case you change your mind?" she asked.

"No, ma'am, I do not," he replied, slowly shepherding her toward the door.

"Why do you not come to Thorncote and see for yourself?" she asked, clutching at his arm. "If you were to see the land, smell the earth, you would know that it is a special place."

His lordship relinquished the sleeve of his coat from her clutches. "I am very busy, Miss Blakelow. *Carousing*, you know, takes up all my time."

"And you have not the slightest interest in helping a family whom you are soon to turn out onto the streets?"

"Don't lay the blame for your father's mistakes at my door, young woman—it won't wash."

She bit her lip. "My lord, I beg of you . . . We have nothing else."

He sighed heavily. "I can help find you another place, somewhere that is more within your means . . . if that would help? And I would take that offer if I were you, for I never do anything for anybody if I can help it."

"I don't want to live anywhere else. I love Thorncote."

"You will have to leave there one day when your brother marries . . . or if you marry for that matter," he pointed out.

She shook her head. "I won't marry. And Will has told me that I may stay there for as long as I choose."

"Yes," he replied dryly. "And I imagine that the future Lady William Blakelow will adore having her husband's sister running the place. Don't be such a goose. You will have to leave and that is right and proper."

She allowed him to guide her into the hallway. "You will not even consider it then?"

"No, I will not."

Miss Blakelow turned at the door. "And do you think Lady Emily Holt would be pleased to learn that her future husband has all-night orgies?"

He looked amused. "Blackmail, ma'am?"

"No, I just think that your fiancée should be made aware of what goes on in her future home."

"Be my guest, Miss Blakelow. I know whose reputation would come off worse from such an encounter, and I can assure you, it would not be mine. Yes, my girl, how would you explain your presence in my house while such a party was in progress? Neither your widow's weeds nor your unblemished reputation would be enough to save you."

"She knows then?"

"I have no idea and, furthermore, neither do I care. But I'm willing to wager that she, along with any other female, is more than prepared to put up with it for the pin money I will give her."

"It sounds a rather dismal contract, this marriage of yours. I hope you may find happiness in it."

"Will it do me any good to reiterate once again that I am not engaged to Lady Emily Holt?"

"None at all," she replied, curtsying. "Good-bye then, my lord."

He bowed. "Good-bye, Miss Blakelow, and I shall look forward to featuring heavily as the villain of your next pamphlet."

CHAPTER 4

MISS BLAKELOW PICKED ANOTHER plump blackberry from the briars and tossed it into the basket hanging over her arm. It was late August and they had been enjoying a bout of warm, sunny weather, a welcome epilogue to the summer that softened the impending approach of autumn.

Now that her father's estate all but belonged to Lord Marcham, this was in all probability the last summer that she would spend here and these the last of the fruit that she would pick at Thorncote. She picked another berry and put it between her teeth, biting into the sweet black flesh as she tossed the hull away.

She looked out across the rolling hills and back toward the house that she had considered her home since she was a young woman. It had been her belief that she would spend the rest of her days there, and that she eventually would be carried out in her coffin. But on the turn of a card, her future had been remade, as if her life had been thrown into the air and had landed in a jumble. How long could they stay at Thorncote? When would Robert Holkham come to claim his property? Where would they go then?

She cursed Sir William Blakelow for putting them in this situation. The Thorncote estate had been in the Blakelow family for generations, but through one weak man and his penchant for gambling, they had lost all to their lordly neighbor, who already had more than enough for his needs. Gone by his own hand, in a final act of cowardly betrayal, Sir William had left them saddled with debts that only a miracle could pay off. He had left his name and his gambling habit to his eldest son, William, who was turning out to be every bit as reckless as his father was. He'd tried to win back all that their father had lost with one desperate gamble at the faro table, only to push them even further into debt. It was intolerable. And it did nothing to dissuade Miss Blakelow from the opinion that men were fools.

Sir William, baronet, was her stepfather, her real father having died many years ago. Perhaps if Sir William had been her blood relative, she might have been able to forgive him more easily. Miss Blakelow's mother had married the baronet to provide them with a home, but within three years, she had died, leaving Georgiana in her stepfather's care. Miss Blakelow was only stepsister to the late Sir William's children, but she felt as much a part of the family as if Sir William had been her natural father. He had been a jovial, good-natured sort of man and had shown Georgiana great kindness when she had first come to live at Thorncote, welcoming her into his family as if she were his own daughter. But he was weak, especially when in his cups. He was liable to gamble that which he could not afford to lose and tell people things that Georgiana would much rather have kept private.

Miss Blakelow winced as she pricked her finger on a thorn and took the cut into her mouth to stem the flow of blood. Ten years in total she had lived here and roamed amongst these hills and trees and briars.

What a long time ago it now seemed since she had decided to make her home at Thorncote! She remembered her first glimpse of the house and how enchanted she had been by its high gargoyles and gables. After her mother had died, she had left Thorncote for a London season and all that it could offer a young woman of limited means. Her season had started so well, but when disaster struck and she was disgraced, she returned to Thorncote once again, seeking refuge. She remembered how safe it had felt compared to the world she had just left behind. She had been a young girl of nineteen, thrust into the glare of London society, without a mother to guide and protect her. And she was soon cast out of that very same society when she had fallen foul of her own temperament and her willingness to love and be loved. She had eventually returned to Thorncote, where she had hidden from the world for the past seven years, and where she had expected to live out her days as aunt to her brother's children and to find some sort of contentment in being useful.

No longer was she the green girl who had set the ton on its heels. No longer was she the young beauty who'd had men casting themselves at her feet. She was older, a good deal wiser, and well educated to the hypocrisy of men.

Thorncote had been her solace; the big blue skies above had been a balm to her soul, and the trickle of the stream washed her girlish dreams away. She considered herself lucky. She'd had a second chance at life, and she had grasped it with both hands. She was moderately happy with her lot. To be sure, it was a safe, undemanding existence, and if she did crave a little excitement from time to time, it was only confessed in bed at night when entirely alone.

Now, at the ripe old age of nine and twenty, when she had been considered an old maid for the best part of ten years, her future was about to change again. Who knew where she might go next? Who knew what the future held in store? She had little money. She had no connections of note—none that would recognize her anyway.

She would have to live on her own wits and make her own future as she had once before.

She wiped her juice-stained fingers on the apron around her waist and sighed. Yes, she loved Thorncote, and yes, she had her aunt to accompany her, but if she was honest with herself, she was lonely. William was younger and spent much of his time in London with his friends, her aunt much older and given over to the demands of her ailments. Her younger brothers and sisters were too young to truly understand why she had never married and too old now to require constant attention. She was beginning to feel superfluous; they no longer needed her. It would not be long before they were married with homes and families of their own. And what then for Miss Blakelow? If Thorncote were lost to Lord Marcham, she would have no home and would have to depend upon the charity of her brothers and sisters for her living. The aging spinster, shunted from one sibling's home to the next, as unwanted at one as she was at the other. For however much she was assured that she was welcome to live with one family member or another, the likelihood was that their spouses would not be quite so keen at the thought of living with a poor spinsterly relative. She would have no right to arrange things as she saw fit; she would have to bow to the wishes of whom-soever William married. And if that woman weren't kind, it could be purgatory. She wasn't sure her pride could take it.

How had it come to this? How had all her youthful charm and beauty led her to this impasse? She was not unintelligent; she was not unattractive. Surely there might have been some man prepared to take her on?

She was not ashamed to admit that she had yearned for what every other young woman yearned for—a home of her own, a man to care for, children to love and nurture. But it had been many years now, and she considered that dream to be beyond her reach. Society had put it there. She was too old now to attract any attention, and indeed, she had gone out of her way to acquire a reputation as a bluestocking, a prude, and the very pinnacle of female respectability, because it had suited her needs. She had made her public face with her own hands, carefully erecting each brick in the wall that she hid behind. But now that she had achieved it and was considered by the neighborhood to be a paragon of Christian virtue, she found herself wanting nothing more than to tear it all down. She found the role oppressive; it stifled her passionate and willful nature. She yearned to be herself, to stop playing the part she had created for herself and live as she wanted to live, the world and their opinions be damned.

She was tired of her mourning clothes. She was tired of her position as governess and chaperone to her young siblings. She was tired of pretending to be something she wasn't. She had ritually donned the spectacles and the cap of an old maid whenever she was in company because she wished to be invisible. But now her vanity reared its ugly head and demanded to wear a pretty gown and have men look admiringly at her as they once had.

Why now? she asked herself. Why, when she had been living contentedly enough with her disguise for all those years, did it suddenly irk her so? Was it the smile of a handsome neighbor who made her doubt her own existence? Or was she just a woman, with the same weaknesses, the same need to be desired and loved, as any other? Out here, amongst the briars and the long grass and the oak trees that dipped their branches low to the ground, she could shed her mask and just be herself; the cap and the glasses and the guise of the prim Miss Blakelow stayed in her pocket.

From her position on the rise, she saw a rider approach the house. At first she did not recognize the man, thinking him a visitor to her aunt. But when he swung easily from the saddle and looked about him as if calculating the worth of what he saw, Miss Blakelow recognized the tall, powerful frame of Lord Marcham. He turned and walked languidly into the house as if he already owned every blade of grass on the front lawn.

Miss Blakelow, torn between hope that he had changed his mind and anger at his arrogance, hurried back down the path toward the house. In the hall she handed her basket to the butler, one of the few remaining servants they could afford to keep at Thorncote since her father's death.

"Lord Marcham is visiting with your aunt in the parlor, miss."

"Thank you, John."

The servant discreetly coughed and directed a pointed stare at her blackberry-stained apron. He was a burly man, well into his forties, who had a permanently weather-beaten face and wrists as thick as an anchor chain. He had served in the navy with Miss Blakelow's natural father all those years ago and had been with her ever since.

She smiled and untied the bow at her waist. "Not fit to be seen, am I, John?"

"You are without your glasses, Miss."

"Oh yes, thank you." She fished in the pocket of her gown for the hated spectacles and put them on. The cap followed, smothering her mass of red-brown curls under its frills until not a wisp of hair could be seen. Tying the white cotton strings under her chin, she was almost instantly transformed, and she wondered not for the first time how society was so easily duped by her simple disguise. It had served her well over the years, and she was not about to undo all her hard work by giving in to vanity in a weak moment. She sighed, satisfied that she had once more assumed the role of prim Miss Blakelow of Thorncote, and moved toward the door.

His lordship was standing by the fireplace when she entered the room, a cup and saucer in his hands, looking as if he were having a tooth pulled. His gaze shot to her face as she opened the door, and for a moment he looked so intensely relieved by her arrival that she was amused. Nothing could exceed Miss Blakelow's disapproval of their lordly neighbor, but to see him so uncomfortable appealed to her ready sense of humor. She had been angry with him at their last meeting for refusing to keep their appointment and goading her into losing her temper, but a period of calm reflection had done much to restore her usually buoyant spirits, and as she met him now, slightly chastened by her behavior the last time she had seen him, she was determined to show him that she could be reasonable. Aunt Blakelow was keeping him up to date on the health discoveries she had made when she was last in Bath. These had been many, and by the expression on his lordship's face, he was desperately seeking a means of escape. He set down his cup and saucer and bowed, then opened his mouth to greet her, but his words were drowned out by her aunt's unstoppable tide.

". . . mustard plasters are the thing for that . . . and of course I do recommend the waters at Bath for the gout, you know," remarked the elder Miss Blakelow. "They taste quite awful, but I believe them to be very beneficial to a man suffering from that affliction. Do you suffer from gout, my lord?"

His lordship looked so much taken aback by this very direct question that Miss Blakelow, gently closing the door, was hard-pressed not to laugh.

"Er, no, ma'am. I am fortunate enough to be in the possession of excellent health," he replied.

"Hmm. Well, I am surprised," continued Aunt Blakelow. "From all I hear, it is a wonder to me that you are not riddled with it. Drink and idleness are the enemies of a gentleman, you know. A man should be busy. And if he cannot keep himself busy, then he should find other things to occupy his mind and his time."

His lordship, wrestling with the urge to give this impertinent woman a much-deserved set-down, happened to glance at Miss Blakelow and saw that she was close to laughter. She appeared to be so in danger of losing control that she resolutely refused to meet his gaze, and a devil lurked within him at the thought that he would overset her gravity if it took him the rest of his visit to do it.

"Oh, I have no difficulty occupying my time," said the earl and darted a swift look at Miss Blakelow to see how she bore it.

She did not mistake his meaning: women, drinking, and all-night orgies. A gleam stole into her eyes. "I think my aunt meant *philanthropy*," said Miss Blakelow.

"I am sure she did," he murmured. "But I am *very* philanthropic. I provide a good living and plenty of work for those under my roof."

"Plenty of work, sir?" she asked, meeting his eyes through the thick glass of her spectacles.

"I have needs, ma'am."

"Indeed?" she choked.

"I have a large estate and there is much to be done. My dear Miss Blakelow, what else did you suppose me to be speaking of?" he asked innocently.

"An idle man may very easily give in to corpulence," said Aunt Blakelow at that moment, unconsciously rescuing her niece as she adjusted the arrangement of her considerable bulk upon the sofa.

"So may an idle woman," murmured his lordship, and had the satisfaction of hearing quickly stifled laughter emanate from the other side of the room.

"Remember that," said Aunt Blakelow, waving a finger at him. "But I hear that these days they can do much with corsets, although they are prone to creak just when one wishes that they would not. Mr. Grantham wears one, and you can hear him enter a house even before he has been announced. You might consider corsets when you have a need of them, Marcham."

"I'll bear them in mind," said his lordship.

Miss Blakelow, much amused by the thought of his lordship in a corset, was moved to take a firm hold on her bottom lip with her teeth and went to sit by the fireplace, narrowly missing upsetting the tea tray on the small table.

"How does your mother do?" her aunt asked, and continued without waiting to hear his answer. "Dear Lady Marcham, such a fine woman and such excellent taste. I have often remarked upon it that one rarely finds a person with a better eye for color than the countess. I haven't seen her in an age. Pray, does she not live up at the Dower House?"

"No, ma'am," he replied. "She likes to divide her time between Longfield Park and town."

"London is very well for entertainment, but I dare swear one grows tired of it after a while. Come and sit by me, young man," invited Aunt Blakelow, patting the sofa beside her.

Lord Marcham, who had not been called young man since he was in short coats, resisted the urge to let fly the retort that sprang to his lips. This imperious, forthright woman was fast making him lose his temper, and Miss Blakelow was laughing at him for it. The words of his friend Sir Julius Fawcett came back to him, that the biggest punishment to an uptight bluestocking who had little experience of men was to be the object of the attentions of a notorious rake. He smiled inwardly, took the offered seat by the spinster aunt, and sipped his tea.

"You are a well-looking man . . . although no longer in your youth," remarked the elderly Miss Blakelow. "How old are you?"

"Six and thirty, ma'am."

"Well, you don't look it. Oh, yes, I might be in my dotage, but I can still appreciate a pretty face."

"Thank you," replied his lordship meekly.

"Although you are rather too tall to be considered handsome. Your fiancée is a tall woman, I take it?"

Lord Marcham took the remark with a tight smile. "I have no fiancée."

"Lady Emily Holt."

"Lady Emily Holt is no more than an inch or two above five feet, and she is *not* my fiancée."

"Oh, dear . . . well, it cannot be helped, I suppose. And is she pretty? No, you need not answer that. I cannot believe a man like you would marry a woman who was not. Her father was a handsome man in his day, you know. Blonde, isn't she? Voluptuous too. But she won't age well, Marcham, you can be sure of that. She'll be fat by the time she is thirty, but I suppose you won't mind that once she has given you a house full of little Holkhams, and then you can take a mistress."

His lordship choked on his tea. He opened his mouth to reply and then thought better of it and closed it again.

"My dear Aunt," interjected Miss Blakelow, torn between mortification for her aunt's manners and amusement at the resulting effect on their esteemed visitor. "Lord Marcham is here to discuss business."

"No he isn't," replied his lordship bluntly.

Miss Blakelow colored faintly and looked at him through the thick lenses of her glasses. "No?"

"No."

"Then perhaps you are here to see the estate?"

"I have no interest in your estate, pretty though it may be."

"Oh. Then why are you here? My father's man of business, Mr. Healey, is away on family business."

"I am not here to see Mr. Healey. I am here to see you."

"*Me?*" she replied, astonished. She was unable to think of what he might wish to speak to her about if it was not her business proposal to save Thorncote, for what else could they possibly have in common?

"Yes," he replied smoothly, setting down his cup. "I so enjoyed your visit the other day that I became determined to repay the compliment."

Aunt Blakelow's jaw fell open. "My dear girl, am I to understand you went to visit his lordship unaccompanied?"

Her niece blushed. "I was not unaccompanied. John came with me."

"John?" the earl repeated blankly.

"My father's manservant. I am sure you must remember."

The earl met her gaze, realized he was supposed to be going along with this version of events to save her from a scolding, and tried to recover the situation. "Er, yes, I remember John. Capital fellow. Knew farming inside out, did he not? A very capable fellow, I should imagine."

"He's our butler," Miss Blakelow said as her aunt's face took on an expression of extreme confusion at the notion of John knowing the first thing about farming.

The earl appeared to be struggling to maintain a straight face. "Ah, how convenient it must be to have a man skilled in a great many things. I'm sure Davenham, my butler, wouldn't know one end of a scythe from the other."

Miss Blakelow, remembering the manner of her last meeting with Mr. Davenham and how she had forced her way past him, lowered her gaze. "I think it a little unlikely, my lord, that my visit inspired anything more in you than the desire to box my ears."

He laughed at that. "Do you? Why should you indeed?"

"Because I behaved abominably."

"On the contrary, ma'am, you were touchingly concerned for your family and your home. Your passion did you credit. Now, shall we forget all about our previous meeting? When might I expect you in to receive a social call?"

"You never make social calls," she said.

"I make social calls when I *wish* to make social calls," he retorted.

"Would you like some more tea, my lord?" asked Aunt Blakelow.

"If your niece will consent to pour it for me," the earl replied, smiling.

Miss Blakelow kept her eyes lowered as she shifted forward on the edge of her chair and took the cup from his hand. Her fingers trembled slightly as she sensed his eyes upon her, and she picked up the teapot and began to pour.

"Thank you. I think at least some of the tea has made it into the cup."

Her eyes flew to his and she struggled to keep her countenance. "I beg your pardon?"

His eyes twinkled. "You will allow me to tell you, ma'am, that your spectacles do you no favors."

She raised a brow. "Indeed?"

"You must own that they neither improve your looks nor your eyesight."

"I will own nothing of the kind. My spectacles suit me well enough, my lord, and I will ask you to keep your observations to yourself—"

"I rather suspect that you would see a good deal better without them," he added, leaning back into his chair. "And your appearance would be vastly improved."

Miss Blakelow stared calmly back at him. "I was not aware that I had asked for your opinion on the matter."

"You would look less bookish and, I venture to think, much prettier."

"And I should take the advice of such a worldly connoisseur, is that so?"

He shrugged. "You might listen to worse."

"For your information, my lord, I have no interest in looking pretty—"

He gave her a skeptical look.

"You disagree, my lord?"

"In my experience," he replied, "every woman wants to look pretty, be they five and twenty or five and ninety."

"Did you come here for a reason, Lord Marcham?" she asked. "Or merely to make me lose my temper?"

He smiled, unperturbed. "Tempting though that is, I did in fact come to find out what the morally improving Miss Blakelow is doing tomorrow morning and whether she would consent to drive out with me."

Aunt Blakelow beamed. "Well, I should be honored, my lord. Such an honor to be taken up by you."

The earl, who had in fact meant the younger Miss Blakelow, was momentarily lost for words. From somewhere he found his manners. "I would be honored, ma'am."

"And so you mean to look over the estate, I suppose?" asked Aunt Blakelow. "Well, I'll be happy to show it to you, of course. Might we prevail upon my niece to join us?"

"If you wish it," said his lordship dryly.

Miss Blakelow colored faintly. "Me?"

"Yes, why not, my love? His lordship would like to see the estate, and who better to show him than you?" She offered him a plate of very rustic-looking cakes, and his lordship, used to the fine skills of his French chef, examined them with a fascinated eye but refused them.

"I don't think you would find that at all enjoyable, my lord," Miss Blakelow said.

"My niece and I would be delighted to drive out with you, my lord. She will show you the orchard and the home wood and the water mill. It was once so very fine and so very prosperous, and with your help I hope it will be so again. You will find the estate enchanting, I believe. It has the reputation as one of the finest houses in the county. So well proportioned and handsome. I don't doubt that you will agree that there is none as fine as Thorncote. Not that I mean to say that it is finer than Holme Park, you understand, for everyone knows that your father added much to the house, and it has a deer park and an orangery and—"

"Aunt," interrupted Miss Blakelow hastily. "I think his lordship is well acquainted with the virtues of his own home."

"Yes, my dear, of course he is. I was merely pointing out that Thorncote need not be the poor relation. It can be the equal of Holme Park given the will of those wishing to make amends."

A silence greeted this speech, and Miss Blakelow hardly dared look at their visitor. She did not know the Earl of Marcham but felt sure that nothing was less likely to succeed with him than forcing his hand. She sneaked a peek at his face and saw the hard shuttered look and knew that her aunt had done their cause no favors.

In fact, his lordship was distinctly annoyed. He decided at that moment that nothing would prevail upon him to further the cause of this impertinent woman and her staid niece. He did not know what had possessed him to visit in the first place. He had been on the way back from Loughton and found himself on the road to Thorncote before he had even formed the thought in his head. The estate was exactly as he had remembered it, a modest house set in the middle of good but unremarkable farmland. He had no interest in seeing it returned to its former glory or in assisting two women who had done nothing but lecture him since he had been unfortunate enough to make their acquaintance. But to have this woman try to force him to part with his money had set his back up and had decided him to take his leave as swiftly as possible.

He put his cup down. "Well, I regret to say that I must take my leave of you."

"So soon?" cooed Aunt Blakelow.

"Yes, forgive me, but I have business to attend to," he said curtly.

Miss Blakelow also rose to her feet. "Of course," she replied, thinking that his business probably involved half-naked women. "I will see you out."

"There is no need. I know my way."

She clasped her hands before her. "Very well, my lord."

They walked toward the door together, and Miss Blakelow took the opportunity that was afforded her now that she was out of her aunt's earshot.

"I must apologize for my aunt, Lord Marcham," she said in a low voice.

He raised a brow at her but said nothing.

"She means well but she can be a little forthright."

"Why should you apologize? She is old enough to make her own apologies, after all. Besides, I wouldn't have thought you'd worry overmuch for my feelings."

"I think that she angered you," she said. "And I think that I angered you too."

"What could possibly bring you to that conclusion, ma'am?" he asked, his tone caustically sarcastic.

She bit her lip. "She is old, my lord, and has been a spinster all her life. She has been used to her own way. And I have a frightful temper. That is the truth of it."

"She has been used to no one telling her that her manners are appalling."

"Even by your standards, my lord?" she asked sweetly.

He felt his anger dissipate at the teasing tone in her voice. He glanced at her and laughed somewhat reluctantly. "You will allow me to tell you that I find you impertinent, ma'am."

She dimpled. "And you are a great deal too ready to fly up into the boughs. You have an appalling temper, sir—almost as deplorable as mine."

"I know it," he replied ruefully.

"Are we still adhering to our truce?"

"Just. Although it has been stitched and mended on three occasions already."

She flicked a quick glance at her aunt, who had fallen asleep. "Are we forgiven then?"

"Yes, Miss Blakelow with the very kissable lips, you are forgiven," he said softly.

"I wish that you would not keep saying that."

"What, that you are kissable?" he said.

She blushed painfully. "You know very well—it is a good deal too bad of you to mock me."

"Mock you? Am I mocking you?"

"You no more wish to kiss me than I wish to be the centerpiece at your next dinner party," she hissed under her breath. "I wish that you may stop trying to pretend that you have any interest in me."

"Have I shown any interest in you?" he asked, much surprised. "I thought I had only asked to drive you out to see your father's estate. Forgive me if you misconstrued my meaning. It seems that all I have to do is smile at a woman and she is already planning our wedding."

Just as he said this, she walked into a small table and knocked an ormolu clock flying. She caught it again before any damage was done and set it back upon its base, reddening with embarrassment.

He took out his pocketbook, withdrew several notes from it, and held them out to her. "I will not assist you in restoring Thorncote to its former glory but I will do this: please, go and have yourself fitted for a new pair of spectacles without delay before you do serious harm to your person."

She gaped at him as he took her hand and slapped the money into her open palm. And with that he was gone.

CHAPTER 5

The following Sunday, Lord Marcham attended church.

To say that his presence was unusual was an understatement. Miss Blakelow looked over the heads of the congregation to the Holkham family pew at the front of the church where their esteemed neighbor was sitting, seemingly ignorant of the stir he was creating by his presence. She could only see the rear view of him from where she was seated and was trying to detect from staring at the back of his dark head whether he had in fact fallen asleep.

Lord Marcham was not a religious man. He was seen in church at Christmas and Easter Sunday and very infrequently beyond that. His lifestyle was such that merely setting his big toe over the threshold of Loughton Church was enough to have the neighborhood in an uproar, so why he was sitting cool as you please in the front row, surely aware of the interest he was generating and yet apparently uninterested in anything but those words of wisdom that passed the clergyman's lips, was anyone's guess. The rector seemed particularly flustered by the presence of his lordship and frequently darted a worried glance at his patron lest he find fault in any of the utterances that were put forth for the moral improvement of his parishioners.

"His lordship has never shown any interest in coming to church before," whispered her aunt. "Indeed it is rumored that he does not leave his bedchamber before midday."

"Perhaps our rake has sinned to an alarming degree this week and must seek forgiveness," murmured Miss Blakelow. "Or perhaps the ceiling fell in on his bedchamber and he was obliged to get up."

Her aunt laughed quietly. "You are too cruel."

Miss Blakelow stole another look at the earl from under her lashes. He had raised his eyes to the ceiling and appeared to be examining the dark beams that supported the roof. He wore a bottle-green coat of impeccable cut, and she knew that he also wore pale-biscuit pantaloons and Hessian boots, for she had caught a glimpse of him as he was coming up the path before the service began, at which point she had ducked behind a yew tree to avoid having to speak with him.

She saw the heads of other parishioners bob and roll, and she knew that Lord Marcham's presence was being discussed by others too. She wondered if poor Mr. Norman's sermon had been heard by anyone. The service ended and the congregation stood and waited for his lordship to leave the church before filing in behind him like water down a pipe. Miss Blakelow kept her eyes downcast, sensing his eyes on her but refusing to meet his gaze. She saw him chatting to the rector outside the church as people milled around, and she saw him glance at her and take in her appearance, from her scuffed half boots to the large black bonnet upon her head.

Miss Blakelow pointedly turned away, the circumstances of their last meeting still fresh in her mind. She had not used his money to purchase herself new spectacles; in fact, the crisp notes still sat upon the mantelpiece in her bedchamber as she was undecided as to what to do with them. She was looking around for Mrs. Mount, who had promised to give her Aunt Blakelow a ride home in her carriage, when she was startled to find that she was being addressed.

"Good morning, Miss Blakelow . . . Miss Georgiana Blakelow," Lord Marcham said amiably, with a bow. "How do you do? What a fine morning it is for a drive to church. I really must make the effort to do it more often."

"Indeed you should, my lord," returned Aunt Blakelow. "And a pleasure to see you at church, if I may say so? It has been far too long since we have had your company, my lord, too long indeed. But I am sure you are much too busy to attend our church and probably prefer to attend the dear little church at Holme Park instead."

"If he can get out of bed," Miss Blakelow muttered to herself, glancing away over her shoulder at a late-flowering rosebush festooned with red blooms.

"I beg your pardon, ma'am?" asked his lordship, his eyes twinkling.

She was obliged to turn back to face him and their eyes met. "Nothing, my lord," she replied, although she suspected that he had heard her perfectly well.

"I am glad that I found time to come to church this morning. I am usually . . . *otherwise* occupied on a Sunday," he said, regarding Miss Blakelow as a wicked smile hovered about his mouth.

She took his meaning: women, drinking, carousing, or nursing the aftereffects of all of the above. "Indeed?" she replied, meeting his gaze unflinchingly. "*Philanthropy*, my lord?"

His lips twitched. "Just so, ma'am."

"They have returned to town then? Your . . . er . . . *friends*?"

"Friends?" he asked, looking the very picture of innocence but for the laughter in his eyes. "Plural?"

She blushed faintly. "Oh. But I see now that it was not plural. One lady in particular . . . a favorite of yours, perhaps? And is she known to Lady Emily Holt, my lord?"

His lordship regarded her with weary amusement. "Lady Emily Holt, as I know you are perfectly well aware, is not my fiancée. She is a respectable lady and is not in the slightest bit interested in my . . . er . . . *philanthropic* tendencies."

"Oh, she is. I guarantee it. If she is betrothed to you, I should rather think that she would be interested in them. She would be unlike any other female I have ever known if she were not."

"Including you?" he asked softly.

"Undoubtedly. I would not wish to be made a fool of."

"And if I told you that rumors of my . . . philanthropy . . . had been greatly exaggerated, what would you say then?"

"Merely that you are at church, and it is not seemly to lie before God."

He smiled briefly. "Very true. But perhaps I am not lying."

Aunt Blakelow, who had been following this exchange with some degree of confusion, looked at her niece with such an expression of bewilderment that it was all the latter could do not to laugh. "And do you stay long at Holme Park, my lord?" Aunt Blakelow asked in a valiant attempt to bring the conversation back to normality.

"I am undecided," he replied, flicking a glance at Miss Georgiana Blakelow, who had suddenly become fascinated with the contents of her reticule. "I may return to town within the month."

"Well, that would be a great shame," Aunt Blakelow said. "It would be of all things the most agreeable to have the family back at Holme. I remember when you were young, my lord, and your father was alive and all the family was at Holme Park. There were balls and lavish parties and picnics and skating on the lake at Christmas. It seems such a long time ago now. And Holme seems so empty and forlorn these days, but for the servants, of course. Such a shame to see such a beautiful house unloved. Do you plan to return soon, my lord? Oh, but you said that you were undecided, did you not? Silly me! Well, perhaps my niece and I can add our voices to those who wish to see you happily established here?"

"Thank you, ma'am. We will see," he replied noncommittally.

"Ah . . . there is Mrs. Mount and my carriage ride home. Such a delightful creature but talks ten to the dozen. I can never get one word in from the moment I set foot in her barouche to the moment I step out again. Well, I will take my leave of you. Would you be good enough to escort my niece back to Thorncote, my lord?"

"Oh, there is no need," said Miss Blakelow hastily, coloring up as she spoke.

Lord Marcham bowed as Aunt Blakelow gave him her hand. "Of course, ma'am, I would be honored."

"Of course there is a need, my dear," said her aunt, thinking how the earl seemed to like Georgiana and how convenient it would be if she could persuade him to help them. Yes, he was a rake, but a gentleman nonetheless, a gentleman who had the power to save Thorncote. His lordship's groom would be in attendance so that no impropriety could take place. She trusted her niece. She was no young fool to go throwing her heart after a rake. Let this man escort her niece home and see what could be done. "You cannot walk home alone as I have told you on any number of occasions. It is not at all seemly for a young woman to be abroad entirely by herself. You must be escorted by a gentleman or, at the very least, your maid. Now you go with Lord Marcham and he will see you safely home."

A gentleman rake, thought Miss Blakelow, rolling her eyes. She would surely be safer on her own. "Dear ma'am, I have been walking these lanes alone since I was eighteen!" she cried, a hint of irritation creeping into her voice. "And I have never been accosted once yet."

"There is a first time for everything, my love. Now, do as you are told. These young girls, my lord, always gadding about with nary a thought for their reputations . . . Well, I do hope we will see you at Thorncote again very soon. You know you will always be welcome at our home. And perhaps we shall have a dinner party or something of that nature . . . and perhaps I may venture to hint that Lady Emily Holt might exert her influence and persuade you to stay, in the expectation that she may join you one day in this very church as your wife?"

There was a frigid moment of silence.

"There seems to be a general misunderstanding, ma'am," replied the earl rather coldly. "I am not, nor ever have been, engaged to Lady Emily Holt."

"Oh, you are playing your cards close to your chest, are you not, my lord?" chided Aunt Blakelow coyly, smiling and placing a hand familiarly on his arm. "You young lovers are forever trying to pull the wool over our eyes."

"Young lover?" he repeated, somewhat taken aback. "Me?"

"Oh, yes! We have observed the way that you look at each other, have we not, my dear?" answered Aunt Blakelow, turning to her niece.

Miss Blakelow, mortified to be dragged into the conversation, gave a wan smile and wished that the ground might swallow her whole.

"It is obvious to anyone that you must be in love with her," continued her aunt.

His lordship raised a brow with a look of distaste. "Indeed, ma'am? Then you must be exceptionally clever for you have divined something that no one, not even I, has any knowledge of."

"Oh, my lord," Aunt Blakelow cooed. "You are a cagey one, as dear William would say, a cagey one indeed. Well, I will tease you no longer on a subject that I can see is putting you to the blush, but you may count on my discretion; I will not breathe a word of it to anyone."

"Thank you," muttered his lordship dryly.

Miss Blakelow didn't know whether to laugh or cry. She saw the look of exasperation in his lordship's eyes and found herself applauding her aunt for putting him so out of countenance. But the mortification of her aunt's forthright language, the vulgar manner in which she expressed herself to one so far above their station as if he were the merest greenhorn, put her to the blush, and she braced herself for the crushing set-down that was sure to follow. As much as she enjoyed their neighbor's discomfiture, as much as she was ashamed of allowing her temper to get the better of her when she had burst into his house, nothing was as mortifying to her as listening to her aunt's teasing overtures now as if they were intimate friends rather than the virtual strangers that they were.

She managed to shepherd her aunt toward the waiting carriage, promised faithfully that she would let his lordship drive her home, and was only able to let out her breath once the steps had been put up and her relative was resolutely borne away.

"What a very singular county this is," observed the earl, watching the plume on Mrs. Mount's bonnet wave in the breeze as the carriage rapidly disappeared.

"Singular, my lord?"

"The people of Worcestershire have me in love and betrothed to a woman I hardly know, merely because I have spoken to her publicly on a couple of occasions."

"I rather think it was more than that. It is your behavior that has set tongues wagging, sir. Your attentions have been quite marked, you know."

"Hardly," he replied. "By the same token, they might say that I am in love with you, for I have known you a comparable length of time."

"Ah." Miss Blakelow smiled. "But that will not fly, my lord, for I am not nearly beautiful enough to attract a man like you."

He looked down at her, a smile lurking in his own eyes. "And how, pray, am I to answer that? If I tell you that you are beautiful, you will accuse me of toadying, and if I agree with you, I shall be in your black books."

She laughed. "Exactly right. You cannot win, you know. You had best give it up."

"Bested by a woman?" he cried in mock horror. "No, no, that will never do."

"Then let me assist you out of your dilemma," she said kindly. "I will admit to being less beautiful than Lady Emily Holt, and therefore we can dispense with your theory that the good people of Worcestershire would suspect any attachment between us."

"My dear ma'am, are you suggesting that I am a man who is uninterested in any but the most beautiful of women?" he asked.

"Your past rather proves the point, my lord," she replied. "I doubt you would make yourself agreeable to a woman with an opinion . . . After all, it is not a woman's conversation that interests you."

He was momentarily lost for words. "I see," he managed at length.

"You must own, my lord, that a woman as beautiful as Lady Emily Holt is more likely to hold sway with you than anyone else. If she had a wart and a crooked nose, she would not be half so appealing, no matter how eligible she might be."

"You are wrong, Miss Blakelow. You are wrong indeed."

"Then I might look to the ladies of your past as evidence—"

"No let us not," he interrupted.

"Miss Charlotte Hall was a case in point."

He groaned.

She raised an amused brow at him. "Was she not beautiful, my lord?"

"She was indeed," he replied uncomfortably.

"Well then. Lady Norwood something or other."

"*Mrs.* Norwood-Welch," he corrected. "You seem to know a good deal about my former lovers, Miss Blakelow."

"I listen to the gossip, just the same as anyone else. Then there was Mrs. Maria Stockbridge, and you cannot deny that *she* was beautiful. They called her the diamond of—"

"Miss Blakelow, can we *please* desist from raking up my past?"

"But I am proving my point, my lord. You love the company of beautiful women. And why should you not? You are personable and rich. I am sure any number of women would find you an attractive prospect."

One black eyebrow shot up. "Personable, now, am I? I thought you loathed me?"

"I do," she conceded, without heat. "But I was just stating the facts as I see them. I may not approve of your lifestyle, my lord, but that does not mean that I cannot see your appeal to others of my sex."

"But not you?"

"Oh, no, not I," she said before she could stop herself. "I mean I . . . er . . . you are not the sort of man who would attract me."

"Thank you," he murmured with heavy sarcasm.

She bit her lip, aware that she might have insulted him. "Oh, that sounded even worse, didn't it? Dear sir, I did not mean to insult you, I meant only that—"

"Yes, it's alright. I know very well what you meant."

She threw him a grateful look. "But you will have to own that it is much easier to acquire precisely what one wishes from the men in this world if one is blessed with the looks of an angel. I have often observed it. Men are predictably gullible, are they not, when it comes to women? And Lady Emily Holt is destined for great things, I feel sure of it."

His lordship turned his gray eyes upon her, and once more she found herself being scrutinized. Her breath caught in her throat as she saw the look of cool regard as if he were mentally weighing her up and deciding whether to let fly the stinging retort that she felt sure was on the tip of his tongue. She stiffened under his scrutiny and raised her eyes defiantly to his face.

"You have a very poor opinion of men, Miss Blakelow," his lordship replied at last.

She regarded him warily, not altogether sure of his mood. There was a glint in his eye that told her he had been angered by her words and her insinuation that he was as great a fool for a pretty face as any other man.

"Some men, indeed," she agreed.

"You mean me."

She felt herself color faintly. "I merely point out that you seem only able to fall in love with the most stunningly beautiful women."

"Love?" he repeated incredulously. "Who said anything about love?"

There was a moment's silence while she digested this.

"You did not love them?" asked Miss Blakelow, eyes wide with surprise.

He laughed, but it was a harsh mocking sound. "No, ma'am, I did not love them."

"Oh."

"You will allow me to tell you, Miss Innocence, that women who give up their virtue at the drop of a hat are not the sort of women that men fall in love with."

"Oh," she said again, dropping her reticule, a rather sizable, homemade receptacle that made a solid thud as it hit the ground.

"And I will also add," he said, stooping to pick up her bag, "that it is not at all seemly for a young woman to know of a gentleman's . . . peccadilloes."

"No, my lord," she replied meekly.

"Good God, what have you got in there? A dead body?" he asked, feeling the weight of her reticule.

"It is a book, sir."

"Well, yes, I had realized that," he said, handing it back to her. "Very worthy."

Miss Blakelow winced at his tone.

"What sort of book?" he inquired.

"A . . . er . . . um . . . Fordyce's *Sermons*, my lord."

"I see," he said.

She found her temper rising at the glazed look of boredom that swept his countenance at that moment. She had borrowed the book from a friend in the village. If he were to open the reticule, he would have found *Glenarvon*, the anonymously written novel that was widely known to have been penned by Lady Caroline Lamb. It was a revenge on that lady's former lover, Lord Byron, and although it was entertaining to spot caricatures of the rich and famous within its pages, it hardly fit her bookish image. She would have given anything at that moment to declare that she had read the poetry of Byron and loved nothing better than to curl up in bed with a gothic novel, so that he would not think her the dull creature that he evidently did. But she would not do it. "If you will excuse me, my lord?" she said, bobbing the briefest of curtsies.

He relented. "May I offer to escort you home, ma'am? As a peace offering?"

"No thank you. I had rather walk," she replied, pulling on her gloves.

"Oh Lord, you are giving me that martyr look that all females employ when they are put out. I apologize then, if you must look at me that way."

She struggled with the urge to smile and conquered it. "You are mistaken. I am not at all put out, I assure you."

"Indeed? And is that why you are looking at me as if you wish to push me into that open grave over there and fill in the soil around me?" he demanded.

This time she did smile. "You have not angered me."

"Good. And now you must apologize to me for insinuating that I am shallow, Miss Blakelow."

Her lip quivered. "I did not say that you were shallow, my lord."

"You did. You said that I was incapable of seeing the worth of any woman who was not blessed with superior beauty."

"You are no different than any other man, my lord," she offered.

"And is that supposed to make me feel better?"

"I say only that you cannot help it. It is nature after all."

"It gets better and better," he cried, flinging up his hands in mock horror. "She now says that I have no control over my lustful feelings and that my brain is disengaged when in the company of a beautiful woman."

Miss Blakelow met his gaze and smiled sweetly but made no answer.

He laughed shortly. "Very well, ma'am, that's how it's to be, is it? You will allow me to tell you that you are extremely impertinent."

She dimpled. "And you will allow me to tell *you* that you goad me into incivility and then look outraged when you make me do it."

He stared at her for a moment and then surprised her by laughing. "And you goad me into losing my temper, Miss Blakelow, and I promise you that I did not wish to do it on such a fine day. Come," he said, extending his arm, "let us be friends. I will drive you home, and you may tell me all about the sermon, which I must confess I heard hardly ten words of."

He smiled that smile of his, and Miss Blakelow felt her heart skip a beat. When he looked at her like that, with the impish smile dancing in his eyes, she felt a connection between them, a connection that was as disturbing as it was dangerous, and she wished him at Jericho, or a million miles away from her at any rate. She had once again to remind herself of who he was, of *what* he was. She had to remind herself of all that had befallen her, of everything she had done to achieve her current state of contentment. She would not give it all up for the smile of a handsome man, a smile that she knew very well had been practiced upon the weaker sex and perfected for ultimate effect.

"Now tell me honestly, Miss Blakelow," said his lordship, "how long into Mr. Norman's sermon was it before you fell asleep?"

"I did not fall asleep, my lord," she answered with a faint smile. "I heard every word."

"I turned around at one point, and I thought I detected a distinct nodding of your head during one key passage concerning the fate of the Israelites."

"And why were you watching me when you should have been paying attention to Mr. Norman?"

"Because you are far prettier and not nearly so dull."

She gave him a sideways look. "Flirting with me, my lord?"

He smiled. "A little."

"And have you practiced that speech all morning?"

He shook his head in mock censure. "For shame, Miss Blakelow. Has no one ever taught you how to accept a compliment?"

"A compliment from your lips does not sit well, my lord. It has rather a too studied air to be convincing."

"My word, you speak your mind to me as you wish, do you not, ma'am?" he marveled. "You might wish to know a man before you condemn him merely on the say-so of others."

"I rather think that you forged your reputation with your own hands, my lord. No one forced you into the life that you have led, and you cannot blame anyone but yourself if people judge you by your actions."

"And whatever happened to 'Let him who is without sin cast the first stone'? I would have thought that a fine Christian woman like you would have a little compassion for a man who has lost his way?"

"You have not lost your way, my lord. You chose the route that you have taken. You came into your inheritance far too early, and you had no one to check you. That behavior is allowable in a boy of eighteen but not in a man of six and thirty."

"Please, Miss Blakelow, do not, I beg of you, hold back," he replied, a distinct hint of annoyance in his voice. "Why not say what is really on your mind?"

"Because if I did, you would not help us with Thorncote," she said bluntly.

He stared at her for a long moment, and just when she thought he was about to lose his temper, he burst out laughing. "Frank and to the point, Miss Blakelow. I swear that I have never before met your like."

"I will take that as a compliment, for I believe you meant it," she replied.

He shook his head, regarding her with wonder. "I did mean it! You are a truly remarkable woman, ma'am."

"Thank you."

"You have a way of making me feel five years old again," he said with amusement. "I am sure my father was the most fearsome man on this planet, but I think that even he could have learned much from you."

She winced. *That* touched a nerve. She knew that she deserved it for goading him but it hurt nonetheless. "I have offended you, my lord."

"Not at all, ma'am," he said touching his gloved fingers to his hat, "but I will take my leave of you. I have spied a beautiful woman, and my uncontrollable baser urges force me to her side. Good day."

He strode away without another word toward a petite woman with a riot of golden curls framing her face. Jane Bridlington, daughter of a retired admiral, who lived in Loughton with her parents. She was seventeen, beautiful, and dressed in a fashionable pelisse of blue, complete with military-style trimmings.

Miss Blakelow watched him tip his hat and smile at the girl. *So proves my point,* she thought with an inward smile, as she watched them converse and the young lady blushed prettily.

Miss Blakelow's own heart was still pounding at her audacity for goading him as she had done. She would not have dared speak to anyone as she had to Lord Marcham. But hopefully he had learned his lesson. Rake though he was, he would learn that he needed more than a handsome face and an engaging smile to capture her heart. Miss Blakelow of Thorncote was no fool.

With a satisfied smile she turned to the path that took her back through the fields and home.

CHAPTER 6

LORD MARCHAM WAS ON the verge of walking out.

If he had to endure one more felicitation from the father of a simpering Miss On-the-catch-for-a-rich-husband, he would scream.

What in God's name was he doing here? He never went to these affairs. And he hadn't been to Mrs. Silverwood's ball in years. It was hot. It was a crush. It was every bit as tedious as he'd remembered. And on entering the room, he was very soon furnished with the knowledge that Miss Blakelow had been correct, and news of his supposed engagement to Lady Emily Holt was spread far and wide. He had been congratulated by two persons whom he had no recollection of ever having met before in his life and clapped on the back by several of his friends demanding to know if they might have his mistress now that he was about to be leg-shackled.

When the woman in question, Lady Emily Holt, arrived half an hour later, she started visibly at the sight of him, stared miserably at the floor, and would hardly meet his eye. He made it his mission to inform as many people as he could during the course of the evening that no such engagement existed and told himself that he did not care if her reputation was ruined in the process. He moved purposefully toward his supposed fiancée, determined once and for all that he would make her publicly deny all knowledge of an engagement between them, but she saw him approach and made good her escape before he could work his way through the crowd to her side.

The suspicion that news of the engagement had been spread abroad by Lady Holt was confirmed when he overheard that lady discussing bridal clothes with a group of her friends, declaring that the Countess of Marcham would have no cause to fear that any daughter of hers would turn up to her wedding dressed like a pauper. Marcham, goaded into incivility, muttered that she might dress up like a queen if she chose, but he would not be there to see it.

He reached for a glass of champagne.

Damn and blast Thomas Edridge. His information was sadly mistaken. Thomas had told him that the Blakelows would be in attendance that evening. And for something to do, he'd come along, telling himself that an evening out was what he needed to dispel his gloomy thoughts, and that dancing with pretty girls was much preferable to an evening spent alone in his library with nothing for company other than a book.

He saw Lady Emily stand up with a young man in a wasp-waisted coat, and she moved across the floor as gracefully as a butterfly. The smile she gave the gentleman was truly something to behold. The lucky man glowed.

The earl frowned. *She never looked at me that way,* thought his lordship, watching her with sudden blinding insight. Was the chit in love with Richard Barford?

Damn. How had he missed that? Was he losing his touch?

"March!" cried a voice at his elbow as a hand slapped him on the back.

"Don't you dare," his lordship said through gritted teeth.

Mr. Thomas Edridge, one of Marcham's oldest friends, spread his hands innocently and laughed. "Don't what?"

"Offer me your congratulations."

"Well, I *was* going to ask you if it were true," he confessed. "Is it?"

"No," snapped the earl.

Mr. Edridge grinned. "I thought as much. Couldn't ever see you willingly going up the aisle . . . thought it was all a hum. Told my friend Jim as much when he tackled me on the subject last week. So how have you managed to get yourself engaged when you don't wish to be?"

"Mothers. Two of them. Hers and mine."

"Oh, Lord."

"Quite," agreed Marcham gloomily.

"So dance. Dance the night away with as many pretty girls as you can find."

"No."

"Why not?"

The earl turned. "Because I'd rather hack my arm off with a razor than endure another peal of false congratulations over my impending nuptials."

"March, don't be a fool. Flirt outrageously with every other girl here. Make her cry off."

"I need to go home."

"Home? How can you talk so? Do you know, Rob, I swear you have become middle-aged. Shocking as I know that must sound, I feel it my duty to drop the hint to you."

"I *am* middle-aged," said his lordship, somewhat dismally contemplating this admission.

"Well, I never thought to hear you say that! What has happened to the man I grew up with? What happened to London's most infamous rake?"

"He grew up."

"Oh, tosh! You, my friend, are bored. You need a new flirt."

His lordship groaned.

"A pretty face, a kiss or two, the promise of a little dalliance would put the ink back in your quill . . . There! The blonde chit in the white gown by the door. Isn't she the most heavenly creature? Even you cannot be unmoved by such beauty."

Lord Marcham turned to inspect the vision his friend had described to him. "She is, I will own, a pretty girl."

"A *pretty* girl?" repeated Mr. Edridge. "What is wrong with you, man? She's ravishing."

"But," drawled his lordship, bored with the whole subject, "distinctly un-ravishable. One requires a ring for the fourth finger of her left hand to indulge in any of the activities currently occupying your mind, Tom."

His friend grinned. "No harm in trying, is there?"

"If you have a mind to be leg-shackled before the week is out, by all means try. I won't stand in your way." His lordship smiled. "I retired from my rakish ways quite some time ago. Didn't you know?"

"That's what they *say* to be sure. But no one believes it."

"It's true," the earl protested.

"Have you tired of women? The thrill of the chase? The chance of a kiss behind a husband's back? Don't you miss the excitement?"

"Not in the least," replied his lordship, "and I don't miss being thrown naked out of a lady's bedchamber when her philandering husband returns unexpectedly to town either. *That* I can quite happily live without."

Mr. Edridge grinned. "I heard about that."

Lord Marcham sighed as if in pain. "Everyone heard about it. I climbed out of a bedroom window in nothing but my breeches. I don't think there was a soul in London who did not hear about it."

"Were you foxed?"

"Extremely."

Thomas laughed. "Poor March. And was she worth it?"

His lordship shrugged. "It was enjoyable enough while it lasted."

"Then why have you announced your retirement?"

"Because it's no longer enough . . . not anymore. Not for me anyway." Marcham looked away. Why had he given it up? Because he was bored. Because a pretty face, despite what Miss Blakelow might think, was agreeable enough, but when a woman could not hold a conversation with him, or give as good as she got, or make him laugh, his ardor rapidly cooled. He had begun to question his life: his days filled with the business of running his estates and his evenings with no more taxing a subject on his mind than which coat to wear to dinner. Something was missing. He was lonely. The party at which Miss Blakelow had burst in upon them, the one that Harry Larwood had forced upon him, turning up uninvited with his friends in tow, had served to reinforce his decision to change his way of life. In the midst of all those gentlemen, all he'd wanted to do was send his friends home and go to bed.

"But you cannot expect me to believe that you have vowed to a life of celibacy?" said Mr. Edridge.

The earl looked at his friend as if he had developed a second head. "Now, Tom, you are stretching the realms of possibility too far."

His friend grinned. "Then how?"

"Marriage, dear boy. I am of a mind to get myself a biddable wife who will see to my every whim."

Mr. Edridge looked taken aback. "Marriage? But I thought you just said you didn't want to be engaged?"

"Tom, you numbskull, I said I don't wish to be engaged to Lady Emily. It is not the fact that I am engaged, but the woman to whom I am affianced and the manner in which it came about, that irks me." Lord Marcham sipped his champagne. "One must provide an heir, Tom, and I only know one way of doing that."

"You'll be bored—I'll lay you odds that you tire of matrimony within a month."

"Possibly, but I plan to take exceptional care in my choice."

"Lord," breathed Mr. Edridge.

The earl looked amused. "I was thinking of Jane Bridlington. What say you to her?"

Mr. Edridge blinked at him, and his eyes sought the trim form of Miss Bridlington. "Well, she's pretty enough, I suppose, and if you like her, March . . . but don't you find her a trifle . . . dull? How you could prefer her to Lady Emily, I don't know."

Lord Marcham's amusement grew at his friend's studied air of indifference. "I thought you were fond of her."

Mr. Edridge shrugged nonchalantly as his eyes settled on the young lady in question. "I *am* fond of her. We enjoyed a little flirtation . . . of a sort. She grew clingy, though. Stuck to me like a leech. Be careful there, March—the parents will have you up the aisle if you even look in her direction. The Lord and Lady Holt are nothing to it, mark my words."

"I don't doubt it. And on the subject of the Holts, you did some damage there, Tom, with Lady Emily, I mean, if you but knew it. I think you raised expectation in that lady's breast, if not her parents'."

"I consider myself fortunate to have escaped from such an alliance. Look at her with Barford, staring up at him with those doe eyes of hers. It makes me sick to watch them."

"Did you never think it was an act?" asked the earl.

"An act? To what end?"

"To make you jealous as hell, Tom."

"Me? Jealous?"

"She's punishing you."

"No, no . . . you're way off there, March. Only look at the way she stares up at him. She's quite obviously in love with him."

His lordship shrugged and set down his champagne glass. "Well then. If you're not interested, perhaps I should make Lady Emily an offer?"

"If you wish it," replied his friend stiffly, downing the rest of his own champagne in two gulps.

Lord Marcham turned away to hide a smile. Thomas was looking a trifle bosky; his eyes were glazing over and his countenance was flushed. His lordship had no doubt that Lady Emily's determined flirtation with Mr. Barford was the cause.

"Marianne Blakelow is what one might call 'in your style,'" offered Mr. Edridge.

Lord Marcham's eyes strayed from the demure features of a voluptuous dark-haired beauty he had been admiring on the other side of the room and focused on his friend. "Blakelow? Related to Miss Georgiana Blakelow?"

"The sister, I believe."

"Indeed? And is Marianne here this evening?"

"Mumps."

"Mumps?" repeated his lordship blankly.

"The younger brother has it."

"Oh."

"They were worried that Marianne might have it too so they stayed away this evening."

"I see. And Miss Georgiana Blakelow? Is she here?"

"Thoroughly Moralizing Miss? Lord, no. She doesn't ever come to occasions like this. Far too beneath her."

"You don't like Miss Blakelow?" asked his lordship.

"She makes me want to drop to the floor and say a thousand Hail Marys, and I am not even Catholic. She terrifies me."

His lordship smiled. Truth be told, she terrified him too. That is, the disapproving glint in her eye when she looked at him, as if she had just trodden in something unsavory, the feeling that he would never be good enough to meet her exacting standards, and the suspicion that she had very deliberately set him apart as if she were handling an extremely explosive substance and needed to establish a safe distance.

He admitted to himself that he'd only come to the wretched ball in the vague hope that she would be there too. His eyes skittered around the room, over milk-and-water misses and mother-hen chaperones, and he wished that she were there. Someone to share a joke with, that delicious moment when their eyes would meet after he'd said something outrageous merely to shock her or to force her eyes to his. Something about her intrigued him, and he wasn't entirely sure that the feeling wasn't mutual. He looked amongst the dowagers and the chaperones and saw again what he already knew: that she was not present.

Acknowledging within himself a mild disappointment, he decided that he needed to drown his sorrows in drink to get through the evening.

He was distracted from his thoughts by the sight of Lady Emily Holt standing momentarily on her own with her back to him. In a trice he had left his friend and reappeared at her side, grasped her arm none too gently, and frog-marched her out onto the terrace.

❧

"I did not *mean* to do it," whispered Lady Emily, staring at the floor, her great blue eyes swimming with tears. "Indeed, I am very sorry, my lord, but when Mama asked me if you had made me an offer . . . I couldn't tell her that you had not, after all the expense . . . bonnets and gowns and slippers. Father would have been so disappointed in me . . ."

The rest of this speech was lost as her tears choked off her ability to make coherent speech. Lord Marcham took out his handkerchief and impatiently thrust it at his supposed fiancée.

"You don't wish to marry me, do you?" he demanded.

She shook her head, dabbing her eyes.

"No . . . nor I you. I don't wish to offend you, my lady, but I don't think we'd suit."

"No," she whispered, forlornly staring out at Mr. and Mrs. Silverwood's garden, which was shrouded in darkness but for the lanterns that were strung prettily across the paths.

"Was it your parents who spread this abroad?"

She nodded.

"But why me?" he asked. "There are any number of eligible men in this county who would make you a much more suitable husband than me. I wouldn't let any daughter of mine marry a man like me, earldom or no."

"You are of noble birth and good family. You are also rich. Father's estate is mortgaged to the hilt. We are not as well-off as we appear."

"I see," replied Lord Marcham. "A woman who wants my money to save the family estate. Now where have I heard that before?"

She blinked at him. "My lord?"

"Never mind. You will begin this evening. You will tell everyone that our engagement is at an end," replied Lord Marcham, pacing back and forth across the terrace. "You may tell them that I played fast and loose with your affections if you wish it. Make me the cause—I care not. All I want is that this engagement between us is at an end."

"I cannot, my lord. Please don't ask it of me," she cried, grasping his arm.

"You can and you will."

"But you don't know Mama. She has set her heart on seeing us wed," said Lady Emily. "She will be terribly displeased."

"Bullies you, does she? I thought as much," said his lordship grimly.

The lady sniffed into the handkerchief. "She will be so very angry with me."

Lord Marcham bit back the retort that sprang to his lips that went something along the lines of recommending that she develop a backbone. But he didn't say it and controlled his temper with an effort. In another man, her tears might have provoked sympathy or the desire to comfort the fragile young woman in his arms. But his lordship was unmoved, irritated even, and he wondered how he had ever believed that this woman would make him a suitable wife.

"What are we to do?" she asked mournfully.

He ran a hand through his hair. "I am not going to marry you, my lady."

"Oh . . . I know that, my lord. And I don't want to marry you either."

"Do you have any other relatives?" he asked. "An aunt perhaps? Someone who will stand up to your mother?"

"My aunt is just as frightened of Mama as I am. But my grand-mother is every bit as forthright as Mama. She's her mother, you know, and lives in Harrogate."

"Capital," replied his lordship. "Write to your grandmother and ask her if you may stay with her."

Lady Emily swallowed hard. "I haven't seen her since I was fifteen."

"Even better. Write and tell her how you miss her or some such thing, and wangle an invitation to visit."

"But Mama will never agree to it."

"Your Mama will never know about it," said the earl. "I will escort you there myself."

"Oh, would you?" she breathed. "Dear Lord Marcham, you have been so excessively kind to me."

"No, I haven't," he replied bluntly. "I am being kind to myself, as always."

"Sir?" she asked, a blank expression in her face.

"Never mind. What you need, my girl, is a husband."

"But I thought you just said—?"

"Not *me*," he said impatiently, rolling his eyes. "You need to escape from the controlling influence of your mother."

"Oh, yes," cried Lady Emily, clapping her hands together.

"You need to be mistress of your own establishment, and to do that you need a husband."

A silence greeted this remark. "But, sir . . . who?"

"I don't know . . . Is there no one for whom you have a preference?"

Lady Emily blushed tellingly but she shook her head.

"Are you sure? I thought perhaps you still cherished an affection for Mr. Edridge?"

She shook her head again.

"Well, write to your grandmother. Leave the rest to me."

"Thank you. Dear, *dear* Lord Marcham." She grabbed his gloved hand and kissed it, just as the curtains moved and Lord Holt appeared on the terrace, his face red with drink.

CHAPTER 7

Miss Blakelow did not see Lord Marcham again for a month. She had been absent when he had called to take her and her aunt out driving to see the estate—in fact she had taken great pains that he would not find her at home. Aunt Blakelow was well equipped to show him Thorncote anyway. She knew the place better than anyone else, having been born and raised there. She returned from the drive with a sparkle in her eye, and Georgiana could not help but wonder if the earl had deployed his famous charm in cartloads when dealing with the old lady.

Miss Blakelow had been in the village visiting some of her brother's sick tenants, and when she returned, her aunt was seated by the fire, positively glowing. She removed her bonnet, watching Aunt Blakelow in faint amusement.

"I venture to think that he was very well pleased with Thorncote, my love," said her aunt. "Very well pleased. And who would not be? It is a fine estate—I won't say that it's as fine as Holme Park or as large, but the land is good and the potential is huge. I won't say either that his lordship is ready to make amends, but I fancy we have put a kernel of an idea inside that dissipated head. He may come around."

"Indeed, ma'am?" inquired Miss Blakelow, gratefully taking off her spectacles.

"Oh, yes. He may be a sinful man entirely given over to pleasures of the flesh, but he is not unintelligent and we had a fair conversation. He knows a little about architecture."

"Architecture?" repeated Miss Blakelow in amazement. The only architecture she could imagine his lordship taking an interest in was the structure of ladies' undergarments.

"He was interested in the central tower and whether it was indeed twelfth century. I could not remember—I do not have a head for such things—and I recommended that he ask you. He seemed disappointed that you did not come with us."

To tease me and flirt with me and then pull the rug from under my feet and make me feel ridiculous, Miss Blakelow thought gloomily. *Mock the bluestocking and punish her for writing her pamphlet.* She gave a wan smile. "Did he? That seems unlikely. I hardly know the man."

"Well . . . he asked me all sorts of questions."

"To be sure he did," returned Miss Blakelow, folding up her shawl. "If he wishes to invest in the estate, I imagine he will want to have every detail."

"Not about the estate," said Aunt Blakelow. "About you."

"*Me?*"

"Yes. He asked me why you had never married."

Miss Blakelow froze, her hands resting upon the table for support. "And what did you tell him?"

"Never fear, my dear. I told him that you had suffered a disappointment as a young woman."

Miss Blakelow's face fell. "Dear ma'am, what did you tell him that for?"

Aunt Blakelow blinked at her. "Did I do wrong? I did not give him any details. I spoke only in the most general of terms, I assure you."

"But we had agreed not to divulge anything to anyone. Surely you must realize that to reveal any information, to him of all people, is disastrous? If he were to remember . . ."

"Calm yourself, my dear. He does not remember a thing. How should he indeed? You were a mere slip of a girl then."

Miss Blakelow began to feel sick. She put a hand to her head. "Oh, Aunt, I wish that you had not said as much to him. I had already told him that it was you who had suffered the disappointment, so now he knows that one of us is lying. I would not have had you say such a thing for all the world."

Her aunt stiffened visibly. "Well, I do not see why you should fly up into the boughs about it. How you expect a man to remember some chit of a girl from ten years ago when he has had countless women since is a mystery to me."

Miss Blakelow relented. "I am sorry, Aunt. I am sure there has been no harm done. But we will need to tread carefully from now on. He might be a dissipated rake, but he is no fool."

The door opened, and Miss Blakelow's five younger stepbrothers and sisters burst into the room. The three girls lined up primly on the sofa while the two boys sprawled in their chairs, trying to emulate their eldest brother, a very fashionable young man who lived in London.

"Well, Aunt?" asked Jack, examining the scuffed cricket ball in his hand. Fifteen years old and sports mad, he was darker in looks than his golden-haired, blue-eyed, almost angelic-looking brothers and sisters, more closely resembling Miss Blakelow's coloring. "Is his nibs going to cough up the blunt?"

"Jack!" admonished Aunt Blakelow. "I wish you would not talk in that horridly vulgar way."

"Is he?" demanded the lad, unrepentant.

"It is too early to say."

"He doesn't *look* like an earl," said Lizzy, the tomboy of the family, wrinkling her freckled brow. Slender as a beanpole, she was something of a late bloomer at seventeen, her hair as wild and untamable as a briar. "The only earl I ever saw before was so old and fat that his buttons popped on his waistcoat."

A collective giggle greeted this utterance, and Miss Blakelow turned away to hide a smile.

"Elizabeth, mind your manners," chided their aunt. "To be sure he is a most gentlemanlike man—in public at least—and a handsome one."

"Do *you* think him handsome?" Catherine asked, and Miss Blakelow was surprised to find that the question had been directed at her. Catherine had a knack for asking the very question that everyone in the room wished to know the answer to but was too afraid or too polite to ask—or for putting her foot in her mouth, depending how one chose to regard it.

Miss Blakelow blushed faintly under the eyes of every other person in the room. "Yes, Kitty, I believe one would call him handsome."

"Are you in love with him?" asked Jack, without preamble. He was slouched across one of the chairs with one foot dangling, as he had seen his eldest brother William do on many an occasion. He fancied it gave him an air of cool nonchalance.

"Ridiculous boy," replied Miss Blakelow, laughing. "Of course I'm not in love with him. I hardly know him."

"Well, you women fall in love at the drop of a hat," he continued, as if he had great knowledge about such things.

"Not this one," muttered Miss Blakelow, picking up a periodical and leafing through the pages.

"Probably just as well . . . He's marrying that Holt female."

Miss Blakelow's hand stilled. She looked up and fixed her eyes upon her youngest brother's face. "Lady Emily?"

"Didn't you know?" he asked, turning his green eyes on her.

"No, well, I heard the rumors of course . . . but he said there was no truth in them," she answered.

"The man's got himself into a great deal of hot water."

Miss Blakelow put a hand to her head. She was confused, dazed. And why did she care? "Who . . . what—I mean, why is he marrying her?"

"It's all over Loughton," put in Catherine with eyes gleaming.

"We had it from Hetty Bradshaw who had it from Lady Emily Holt herself," added Lizzy.

"What is?" asked Miss Blakelow, fidgeting with impatience.

"He got caught with his tongue down her throat."

"Jack!" cried Marianne, throwing a cushion at him, looking beautiful even when outraged. She did everything beautifully. She even cried beautifully. The eldest of the children at three and twenty, she was expected by her sisters to make a brilliant match to save Thorncote. The only fly in that particular ointment was her penchant for falling in love with penniless men. "Don't be repulsive."

"Well, he did," said her brother. "It was at the Silverwood ball. They were out on the terrace alone, and he tried on more than he should, and her father caught him and there we are. He's about to be leg-shackled."

Miss Blakelow sensed her aunt's eyes upon her and studiously kept her own gaze lowered. Her face seemed strangely tingly as if all the blood had drained from under her skin. "I'm surprised is all I will say," she said meditatively. "A man of his experience is not one to be trapped like that unless he wished to be."

"You think he was tricked into marrying her?" asked Aunt Blakelow.

"I have no idea. He has to marry someone, I suppose."

"But why her?" said Marianne.

"Because she's beautiful and rich," replied Miss Blakelow quietly.

"Well, if he were to see you without those hideous spectacles, he would know that you are not so weaselly faced as he supposes," said Jack.

"Thank you," replied Miss Blakelow meekly at this backhanded compliment.

"She is not weaselly faced!" cried Marianne, firing up in defense of their eldest sister. "How can you say such a thing?"

"If you would but listen, you would know that I said she wasn't weaselly faced," retorted Jack, vigorously swinging his leg.

"I know those glasses make her look a hundred years old, but never weaselly faced!" continued Marianne, her blue eyes sparkling with tears.

"Oh, Lord, you've set her off again. Jack, how can you be such a clod?" demanded Ned, in a voice that showed he was growing into a fiercely intense young man. Ned, almost eighteen, was very soon to go to Oxford, paid for by his uncle Charles, a gentleman who saw it as his duty to educate his young nephews. Blond-haired and blue-eyed, he was the living image of his father.

"What?" asked Jack, spreading his hands. "All I said was—" He broke off, colored deeply, and stole a swift glance at the averted profile of his eldest sister. "I'm sorry."

Miss Blakelow summoned a smile from somewhere. "No matter. But please, can we drop the weasel reference? I'm not sure my pride can take it," she said with an unsteady laugh.

"Of course," he replied stiffly. "All I meant to say is that you scrub up well when you don't wear those glasses. I think any man would be proud to take you on."

Jack was saved from his embarrassment by the arrival of John, their unlikely butler, who would look more at home aboard a ship than answering the door and greeting visitors. He announced that two gentlemen had arrived to see Miss Blakelow.

John moved forward and presented Aunt Blakelow with a flamboyantly printed calling card. She stared at it blankly and handed it to Georgiana, who regarded the swirling type, set with the name Sir Jeremiah Allen, Baronet, with distaste. Clearly Sir Jeremiah thought himself something rather special.

"Are we expecting them, Aunt?" Georgiana asked.

"Not that I know of. I have never seen this gentleman's name before. Where are they, John?" asked Aunt Blakelow.

"They are in the hallway, ma'am. They didn't seem interested in being shown into the parlor."

Both ladies stood up and followed the butler into the hallway. Two men stood with their backs to them, staring at one of the few remaining sculptures in the house, the thinner man examining it through a magnifying glass. He was dressed all in black, and his hands were long and bony, with veins standing out like bluish rivers under his skin. He dropped the glass where it hung on a ribbon around his neck.

"Fake," he said. "A cheap copy, nothing more."

"Are you sure?" asked his companion in a hushed voice. He was a middle-aged man with artfully shaped silver whiskers. He was trim and neatly dressed and carried a pencil and some sort of journal.

"Certain, Mr. Croft, certain. Many a young gentleman on the Grand Tour bought such fake antiquities. See how we have fragments of different gods all jumbled up together? Rome was flooded with them."

"I need to inform his lordship of the exact value," said Mr. Croft, jotting something down in his journal.

"I would not dignify it with a mark in your book, Mr. Croft," said Sir Jeremiah, and bowed slightly.

Miss Blakelow coughed discreetly, and the two visitors whirled around like startled rabbits. "Can I help you, gentlemen?"

Mr. Croft bowed. "Frederick Croft. Your servant, ma'am. I am Lord Marcham's man of business. And this gentleman is Sir Jeremiah Allen."

The tall, bony man bowed, sneering down his long nose at Georgiana. "Sir Jeremiah Allen, Baronet, of Charmouth House, Miss Blakelow, perhaps you've heard of me? I am something of a collector of fine things." And as he said this, he very deliberately let his eyes travel up and down her figure.

Miss Blakelow raised one brow in polite inquiry.

"Of art, you understand," Mr. Croft put in hastily. "Sir Jeremiah has a reputation for collecting fine and rare antiquities, paintings . . . things of that nature." He paused and cleared his throat. "Perhaps I should explain. His lordship, the earl, has tasked me with selling Thorncote house, and it has been recommended by a friend of the earl's that he ask Sir Jeremiah to accompany me to undertake a valuation of the contents."

Mr. Croft registered the look on Miss Blakelow's face and fell silent. Clearly, he had not wanted to do this; indeed, it appeared that he had rather be anywhere than looking through Miss Blakelow's home when she obviously had issue with their presence.

"And was it Lord Marcham who desired that this valuation be made?" Miss Blakelow asked.

"Yes—well, that is to say, he wished for a valuation of the property—given the sad state of decline of the estate. It was his lordship's sister, Sarah, Lady St. Michael, who desired an inventory be made."

"And what has it to do with Lady St. Michael how much our home is worth?" demanded Miss Blakelow.

Sir Jeremiah balanced his weight on one thin leg and pulled an intricately carved snuffbox from his waistcoat pocket. He flicked open the lid with one thin finger, took a pinch, and put it to his nose, inhaling violently. He snapped the snuffbox closed and put it away again. "Lady St. Michael is a particular friend of mine. She is interested in purchasing the house, but she wants to know whether the contents are of value or—" He paused as his eye alighted on a clock on the mantelpiece. "Or not," he finished, his voice trailing off disdainfully.

Sir Jeremiah moved toward the mantelpiece, ignored the clock, but picked up a small china jug that sat next to it. He turned it upside down and examined the mark on the base. "Ah, I thought so. A Dresden piece. Quite pretty but sadly missing the rest of the set to which it belongs. Mark it in your journal, Mr. Croft."

The other gentleman opened his book and set his hand with pencil poised. "What shall I write down for its value, Sir Jer—"

"Please have the goodness to leave this house immediately," Miss Blakelow said in a tightly controlled voice.

"Lady St. Michael informed me that there used to be a collection of paintings by the Dutch masters," Sir Jeremiah replied, looking down at her as if she were a worm. "She tasked me to look at them and give my opinion as to their value."

"You may tell Lady St. Michael that they were sold years ago," flashed Miss Blakelow. "The gallery, which she no doubt remembers from her visits here in her youth, is now completely empty. My stepfather sold every last one to pay off his debts. There is nothing in this house of value. Now please, respect our wishes and leave."

Mr. Croft closed his journal. "I apologize, Miss Blakelow. I realize that this must be upsetting for you—"

"You heard my sister," said a voice behind Georgiana, and she turned to see Ned entering the hallway, followed by his brother and sisters.

"I can assure you, it won't take us long," Mr. Croft said.

Ned took another step forward. "When we have vacated this house, you may pick over the details at your leisure; until then, you are not welcome."

"We cannot do that, I am afraid," drawled Sir Jeremiah. "You could conceivably sell any remaining items of value, which technically now belong to his lordship. The terms of your brother William's agreement with his lordship stated that the house and its contents were part of the wager. Lord Marcham owns *everything* in this house. I need to see jewelry, paintings, china—"

Ned took a hasty step forward, bristling with anger, but Miss Blakelow halted him with a gentle hand on his arm. She gave his arm a squeeze and a look to let him know that she would deal with it.

Addressing herself to Mr. Croft, who seemed genuinely embarrassed by the whole affair and looked as if he wished the tiles at his feet might slide apart and let him sink through them, Miss Blakelow said, "Then technically, your master owns the clothes on my back too, Mr. Croft?"

The gentleman's discomfiture seemed to increase. "I, er—"

"Perhaps you'd like to look through my stays and stockings?" she asked softly.

Georgiana heard the gasp of her aunt beside her and a collective giggle from her younger sisters. She stared at Mr. Croft but he would not meet her eyes.

"Have the goodness to adhere to my wishes, gentlemen. I can assure you, as the good Christian woman that I am, there is no longer anything of value in this house other than the people who reside in it. There is nothing left. You have my word. I swear upon my mother's grave."

Sir Jeremiah Allen took out his quizzing glass and spied Miss Blakelow at great length through it in so insolent a manner as to bring the heat into her cheeks. "And aren't you a fine piece?" he murmured.

Ned's temper snapped; he broke free of Georgiana's grasp and seized the man by the lapels. Sir Jeremiah cried out and raised a hand to protect his face, thinking he was about to be landed a facer. Ned was not quite eighteen, but boxing was quickly turning him into a very fine figure of a man. "Out," he hissed, manhandling the baronet to the door. "Get out and don't come back."

Miss Blakelow threw a pleading look at John, who took the hint, coughed discreetly, and said, "Your carriage is waiting, gentlemen," as he gently prized Ned's fists from Sir Jeremiah's coat.

"Lady St. Michael will hear of this," the baronet fumed, brushing his assailant's fingerprints from the wide lapels on his coat. "She will hear of this, I say. And Lord Marcham."

John took two steps forward until he was nose to nose with the gentleman, his bulk almost pinning the man to the wall. "I believe you heard what Master Ned told you," he said.

The baronet whimpered.

Mr. Croft attempted a smile. "I apologize, Miss Blakelow. I can see emotions are running high and that is to be entirely expected. If I have your word that nothing of value will leave this house, then that is good enough for me."

Miss Blakelow inclined her head. "Thank you, Mr. Croft. Good day."

The gentlemen departed, and John had just closed the front door upon them when Jack burst out with, "Georgie! Did you see his face when you asked him if he wanted to look through your underclothes? Lord, I nearly died laughing!"

"He deserved to be embarrassed," Ned said crossly. "Barging in here to look over the house. I can barely believe Marcham's gall."

Miss Blakelow sighed and herded her family back into the drawing room. "It is not Mr. Croft's fault, or his lordship's either. Mr. Croft has been asked to sell Thorncote, and to do that he needs to set a value. Lord Marcham is only doing what any man would do in his situation."

"How can you say that, Georgie?" cried Ned. "He sent that—that odious *clod* to examine the few things we have left that Father didn't think valuable enough to sell."

"I don't think that was Lord Marcham's doing," put in Aunt Blakelow, seating herself back in her favorite chair. "His lordship's sister, Lady Sarah, as she was then, was always poking her nose into his affairs. She must have heard about William losing Thorncote to her brother and decided she wanted it for herself. She always liked it here. And it's close enough to his lordship's estate for her to keep an eye on him."

"She's dreadful," Catherine said, pulling her sewing from her workbasket. "Do you remember she came here last summer while she was staying with the earl and told us that the arrangement of the furniture in the drawing room should be changed?"

"Was she the woman who told you that pink did not become you?" asked Lizzy, wrinkling her brow.

Catherine's eyes flashed at the memory. "And she told Marianne that her performance on the pianoforte was nearly as accomplished as her own."

"Odious woman," Marianne chimed in, tucking her feet up under her. "I cannot believe she is to have Thorncote. I'd rather Lord Marcham sell it to a complete stranger than let her live here. I wish something could be done."

Jack rolled his eyes. "Georgie tried, didn't she? And his lordship wouldn't listen. We have no money to pay him back for Will's debts."

Ned paced over to the window, scowling out onto the park and the grass that gently shelved toward the lake. "We have to do something."

"What *can* we do?" Catherine asked. "His lordship has given us three months to leave. The boys will go to live with Uncle Charles, of course, but he doesn't have room for all of us, so we girls will be sent to Mama's sister. But what of you, Aunt, and Georgie? Where will you go? I'm afraid, we will be split up."

A silence answered this prophecy, and the sun went behind a cloud, plunging the room into gloom. "Not if I have anything to say to it," remarked Ned, folding his arms.

"What are you going to do?" demanded Jack.

"I have an idea," said his brother and strode from the room.

❧

John Maynard was outside the front of the house, cutting back the rosebushes that had overgrown the window of the summer parlor. Since the Blakelows had let their head gardener go, John had turned his hand to odd jobs in the grounds. He was no plantsman, but he knew how to chop back a hedge. From here, by the stone balustrade, he could see anyone approaching the house and would have time to dash back inside the house to greet them as the nearest thing to a butler they'd had for years.

John's head snapped up when he heard Ned's footstep on the gravel behind him. John nodded a greeting and returned to his task. Ned seated himself on the stone balustrade and swung his legs back and forth, watching John.

John looked at his young master again. "Mind you don't fall," he said as he snipped the stem of a huge green sucker at the base of the rose.

"I won't," Ned replied, dismissing the drop behind him with nonchalance.

"Are you in trouble, Master?" John asked, throwing the thorny stem into the wheelbarrow.

"Why do you automatically assume I'm in a scrape?" Ned demanded indignantly. "I wanted to ask your advice."

"Oh?" John replied without interest. "Found a girl you like, have you?"

The young man flushed. "No. At least no, it isn't that."

"Good, because I don't understand women at all, so it's no good you asking me."

Ned grinned and sat on his hands. "John?"

"Yes, sir."

"You were in the army, weren't you?"

"The navy. Served under Miss Blakelow's father, Captain Clayton. And a fine captain, he was." His eyes grew wistful but then he caught himself, as if he had revealed too much.

"But you've seen some action?"

"Fought against the French in the West Indies, Master Ned, as the ache in my leg can testify. Why are you asking me all these questions? That's what I wish to know."

Ned closed his eyes, took a deep breath, and said, "Hypothetically, if you were to kidnap a man, how would you go about it?"

There was a long silence.

"I beg your pardon, Master Ned?"

"I think you heard me well enough."

There was an even longer silence.

"Are you funning?"

"No, sir."

John eyed him speculatively and scratched his head. "Hypothetically? You'd need a weapon of some kind. Some rope and something to gag him with. A cart or carriage of some kind to transport the man to wherever you plan to hold him. Some fool willing to drive the cart for you. Some courage, a little luck, and God on your side, because if you get caught, you'll probably hang, and I'll hang along with you because Miss Georgie will want to see me dead for letting you do it."

Ned flushed a little. "How would you do it? Where?"

"Didn't hear what I just said, did you?" John remarked, shoving the pruning shears inside the waistband of his breeches. He sighed and folded his arms. "I'd do it on his own turf, halfway between the lodge gates and his front door so he's not expecting it and none of his household can come running to his aid. I'd do it at a spot where trees overhang the road so you cannot be seen from the house. I'd do it when the gentleman, whoever he is, will likely be fast asleep in his carriage. At night, after he's been out to dine with friends. And if he's in his cups, even better."

Ned nodded, staring off into space, filing away the information for later use. "He's fought duels before, so they say, illegal ones," he remarked, frowning. Clearly this worried him.

"Aye, he's a crack shot. If it's the gentleman I think it is, you'll need a weapon or two and cronies with you to keep the coach driver or the groom busy while you deal with your man. He keeps a pistol under the seat in his carriage, so I'm told. A sack thrown over his head from behind, so he can't see, would do much to aid you, but expect him to put up a fight—even if you stop him from reaching his pistol, from all I hear, he can handle himself in the ring."

Ned ran one finger between his neckcloth and his throat, as if the simple arrangement were choking him. "Would you help me, John?" he asked quietly.

John sighed. "I knew that was coming. Aye, I'll help you. But don't breathe a word to anyone. Not your sisters and especially not your aunt. It'll be all over the neighborhood by breakfast."

"As if I would do such a thing!" Then he realized John was teasing him and grinned again, feeling happier now that he had his promise to help.

John lifted the handles of the wheelbarrow and began to push it across the gravel to the pathway that led around the side of the house. "And if this hypothetical kidnap was to happen the night before his lordship's wedding, Master Ned, I can see as how that would be very persuasive. Very persuasive, indeed."

CHAPTER 8

His lordship awoke to find that quarrymen were trying to batter their way through his skull—or at least that's what it felt like. The pounding in his head made him wish he could take that part of his anatomy off and set it apart from the rest of his body.

Slowly he opened his eyes and was momentarily confused when he could not see anything. It took him a moment to realize that a blindfold had been tied over his eyes and he had been gagged quite roughly. He was sitting in a hard, uncomfortable chair with his ankles bound together and his wrists lashed so tightly to the back of the chair that he was losing the feeling in his fingers. A fine film of sweat was on his brow, and the back of his head felt tight with congealed blood.

"Is he awake?" asked a young male voice.

"I don't know," said another, slightly deeper voice.

"Prod him," said the young lad again. "See if he moves."

"Leave him alone. Haven't you had enough violence for one night?" replied the older boy. "Make yourself useful and get him some water. However much I loathe him, I don't want him dying up here."

"What are you planning to do with him if he won't agree to our demands?"

"Let him fetch you up before the local magistrate for asking *stupid questions*," hissed his accomplice.

Brothers perhaps? his lordship wondered.

"But we can't keep him up here forever. George is bound to find out."

"Then we'll just have to keep him quiet."

Lord Marcham thought back to the events that had brought him to make the acquaintance of his kidnappers. He had been late coming home from his best friend's wedding. The service had been accomplished without mishap, the rings exchanged, and the happy couple waved off, but on the journey home, barely ten miles out of Harrogate, one of his lordship's leaders had thrown a shoe, and the groom had to walk to the nearest inn before a blacksmith could be found, so that it was nearly dark before they set off again.

Mr. Thomas Edridge had married Lady Emily Holt by special license in Harrogate, the lady's grandmother in attendance. The happiness on the face of his best friend was something to behold. He had never seen Tom look so satisfied with his lot.

The world and Lord and Lady Holt were in blissful ignorance of the momentous events of the day. Lady Holt no doubt still believed that her eldest daughter would turn up at the church at Holme Park to wed the Earl of Marcham. She believed that her daughter was at that moment returning from a day out shopping with her friend.

But no invitations had been sent, no flowers decorated the church at Holme, there was to be no wedding breakfast. Lord Marcham was shortly to inform Lady Holt of the news that the wedding of her daughter had already taken place and give her a piece of his mind along with it.

But on the drive home a shot had rung out. The horses bolted and were checked, and the carriage came to a shuddering halt. He could hardly believe his ears. Someone had the temerity, the utter gall, to hold him up on the road that led to his house.

Having drunk a few glasses of champagne to the happy couple, he felt decidedly worse for wear. He frowned, focusing his bleary eyes on the slim youth who appeared at the window. The door was wrenched open, and the wide snout of a blunderbuss nuzzled through and was leveled ominously at his head. His lordship possessed a particularly fine pair of dueling pistols, which unfortunately were under the opposite seat, and he'd been debating how he was going to get to them without having his head blown off when the youth gestured that he leave the carriage and get down onto the road. He reflected grimly that if he had not spent the past half hour fantasizing about telling Lady Holt *exactly* what he thought of her, he might have been more alert at the first shout of the brigands to halt, and he might have stood a chance of escaping this situation without loss of his purse.

All these reflections had passed through his head in a matter of moments, and he grimaced as the highwayman cried, "Stand and deliver!" from behind a red neckerchief—it seemed to his lordship that he shouted merely to set the bells ringing in his ears. As soon as he set foot on the road, he was pushed from behind into the door of his carriage, and a hessian sack was jerked down roughly over his head. He lashed out with his fists, but a blow to the back of his head silenced his protests. Now he found himself lashed to a chair and wondered what on earth they were planning to do with him and what their demands were.

Footsteps approached, and the earl gathered that he was in a room with bare floorboards and the faint musty smell of disuse. It was hot and airless and dark. An attic, perhaps?

"How is he?" said a third voice that was considerably older than the other two. Lord Marcham was surprised. He'd begun to think it was nothing more than a boyish prank, but the presence of an older man suggested something more sinister.

"Coming around, we think," said the older lad.

"His head has stopped bleeding at last," said the man, and Lord Marcham felt a hand on the back of his head and tried not to wince as it touched his wound.

"Do you think we should give him some food?" asked the boy.

"And have those fists loose again? No, I thank you," replied the older youth. "Marcham, can you hear me?"

His lordship was determined that if he ever got his hands on this young whelp, he would beat him so hard that he wouldn't be able to sit down for a week. He raised his head, indicating that he was awake.

"I'm going to take the gag off you to give you some water. If you make a sound, it will be very much the worse for you, do you understand?"

As this was said into his ear as if the boy were talking into an ear trumpet, his lordship was hard-pressed to keep his temper, but he nodded his acceptance.

"Here we go then. And remember, no noise."

Fingers fumbled at the back of his head and then the gag fell loose. His lordship felt the blood rush into his numbed lips and worked his mouth to ease the pain. A cup was pushed against his mouth before the circulation had returned to his lips, and he spilled most of the water down his chin. Slowly he found the right angle and drank deeply.

"Where am I?" he rasped when the cup was cruelly taken away.

"Somewhere safe."

"What do you want from me?" snapped his lordship. "Money?"

The lad pulled up a nearby chair, and the earl heard it scrape against the floorboards. "Amongst other things."

"What other things? What am I to you?"

"You are the man who killed our father."

There was a silence.

His lordship frowned. "Who was your father?" he asked.

"Sir William Blakelow."

The earl paused. "I think there must be some mistake."

"I think not, Marcham. You killed him."

"Master Ned, don't say so," said the man's voice gently.

"It's true! He did, I tell you! Father would never have killed himself but for him. But if you don't want to hear what I have to say to him, then you had better leave now and go back to your work," snapped the lad.

"Very well," replied the man, and then his lordship heard the sound of his footsteps as he walked away.

There was a pause before the lad continued, "But that wasn't enough for you, was it, Marcham? You were not happy with that. You won't be happy until our entire family is out on the streets. My brother Will is in debt to you so deep that we're about to lose everything because of it. You've destroyed this family."

"What are you going to do with me?" asked his lordship.

"We want your signature on some papers," replied the youth.

"Is that so? And do you imagine that any signature of mine without a witness is legal?"

There was a pause.

"Didn't think of that, did you?" taunted the earl softly.

"You will sign those papers."

"Or what?"

The boy stood up and untied the blindfold around Marcham's eyes. The earl winced at the sudden glare of candlelight in his face.

"Or," continued the lad, "you will be kept here until you do."

"And do you imagine such a fearsome prospect will have me breaking into a sweat?"

The youth called Ned stepped forward until his face was inches away, and Marcham felt his breath on his face. "You are due to be married tomorrow," he said, appearing to enjoy himself. "Breach of promise if you don't turn up, isn't it? Now who's the one who didn't think things through?"

"You had better hope and pray that I don't ever get my hands on you, boy."

Ned's smile became a snarl. "Sign my sister's papers or you will not be attending your own wedding."

He shrugged, unconcerned. "Then I will miss my own wedding. I will not give in to blackmail."

"Lady Emily will never believe you. She will think you jilted her."

"Perhaps I was about to jilt her anyway?" said his lordship with a hard smile.

The lad looked surprised. "You're bluffing. You wouldn't do that. You are not so blasé about your word as a gentleman."

"Do you honestly think a man like me gives a damn about that?" demanded the earl, laughing incredulously.

"You are a man of your word, if nothing else. What do you think society will think of you when you jilt Lady Emily Holt at the altar? From what I hear, she was practically the only woman who would agree to marry you. You will never find a wife after that."

"Oh, the innocence of youth," mocked Lord Marcham. "That just shows how little you know about women."

"Sign those papers."

"Go to the devil," recommended his lordship.

❧

Two days later Miss Blakelow was drinking hot chocolate in bed, contemplating the morning ahead, when she heard the strangest noise. There was a loud thud, scuffling, and the distinct sound of a man's voice yelling "George!" There was another bang, more scuffling, and the sound was quashed and the house was silent once more.

Frowning, she climbed out from under the bedclothes, walked to the door, and opened it. Standing still for a moment, she paused to listen. Suddenly Jack burst into the corridor from the stairs that led up to the attic. He held a bowl in his hands and nearly dropped it at the sight of his eldest sister.

"What are you doing, Jack? What was that noise?" asked Miss Blakelow.

"What noise?"

There was another bang from the attic and Jack coughed noisily.

Miss Blakelow's eyes narrowed. "What is going on in this house? Food disappearing from the kitchen, bloodstained rags in the laundry, noises in the attic. Do we have a hermit living up there?"

"George! George, can you hear me?" shouted a man's voice from upstairs, followed by another loud bang and the sound of scuffling.

Miss Blakelow barged past her brother and ran lightly up the curved stairs to the attic. She burst in upon a scene of disarray.

A man was bound tightly to a chair that had toppled over onto the floor, and he was struggling to move the chair against the floorboards, presumably trying to break free of his bonds, making as much noise as possible in the process. He was being ruthlessly gagged by Ned, who was sitting astride him, using his weight to try to quell his struggles, as if he were breaking in a horse. A jug of water was set on an old trunk, and food was scattered all over the floor, the plate smashed into pieces.

"What on earth is going on here?" demanded Miss Blakelow, who picked up a candelabra from where it sat on an old chest and held it aloft so that she might survey the room.

Everyone froze. Ned turned to his sister with a face of resignation. Then his gaze slid to the face of his younger brother, and he glared at him with disgust.

"Well done, Jack. Now look what you've done. I knew I should never have told you about this."

"Who is that man?" asked their eldest sister in a frigid voice.

She moved the candelabra and gasped as she recognized the face of the Earl of Marcham. He lay on the floor and turned his head to look at her as she stared back at him.

"What is he doing here?" Miss Blakelow demanded.

"We've kidnapped him," said Jack.

Ned Blakelow glared at his brother for that admission. "We're keeping him here, until he agrees to our demands."

Miss Blakelow moved farther into the room. "What demands?"

"That he hand over Thorncote to us," said Ned belligerently.

"Give me strength! You foolish boy, this is not the way—surely you must see that. Untie him at once."

"Oh, but George, you will ruin everything!" cried Jack.

"To be sure I will," replied Miss Blakelow, setting the candelabra back down. "And you, Ned, will not be going to stay with Uncle Charles in London unless you release him this minute!"

Lord Marcham observed this scene with mild amusement. The bluestocking had turned into a tigress. He could hardly believe his eyes. Who was this woman? Surely not the prim and prudish Miss Blakelow? The voice was the same. The lips were the same. But where were the cap and glasses? Where the garb of the widow? Before him was a young woman with chestnut hair about her shoulders, her threadbare nightgown momentarily backlit by the light from a branch of candles, showing him in one heart-stopping moment what he had already suspected: Miss Blakelow had a *very* pretty figure.

"Release him at once," demanded Miss Blakelow.

"But George! You don't understand!" cried Jack.

"Untie him this instant," she said. She moved toward his lordship and crouched on the floor. "He's been bleeding. What have you done? What can you have been thinking of? Do you wish to land us all in Newgate?"

"He was hit over the head," said Ned.

"I can see that, thank you," replied Miss Blakelow dryly, reaching forward to untie the gag at his lordship's mouth.

"George?" asked Lord Marcham once the gag was freed.

She smiled apologetically down at him. "It's a family pet name."

"I thought . . ." He coughed. "I assumed that the George they spoke of was a man. An older brother, perhaps."

"And if you are disappointed, my lord, and think that because I am a woman they will escape a sound chastisement, you much mistake the matter!"

Jack and Ned stared sheepishly at the floor at this remark.

"I don't doubt it," said Lord Marcham, laying his head back against the floorboards.

"Jack, bring me that water," commanded Miss Blakelow.

Her brother hurried to obey.

"George," repeated his lordship with eyes closed. "I like it. It suits you."

Ned and Jack untied the bindings at the earl's hands and feet, and they helped him into a chair. His lordship gingerly stretched out his legs and arms to ease his cramped muscles.

Miss Blakelow looked him over carefully. He looked pale, and his clothes were much creased, and there was blood on his shirt.

"Jack, find John and have him take the bath up to Will's room. Then find a clean shirt—one of Will's will have to do, I hope that it might be big enough—and have Betsy bring up hot water for his lordship to wash. And some food too. Oh, and Jack, before you go, check that Aunt Blakelow is still in bed. We don't want her stumbling across Lord Marcham in her nightgown."

"Are you intending to bathe me as well, Miss Blakelow?" asked Lord Marcham, an imp dancing in his eyes, his question spoken so softly that his words reached her ears alone.

"Be quiet," she replied, avoiding his eyes.

"I would welcome your assistance."

She dipped a cloth into the water. "You wouldn't, for I would scrub you from head to toe."

He smiled at some secret thought, and the look he gave her brought the heat into her cheeks.

"Just what I was thinking, ma'am . . ." he replied, "but if I am not to have your ministrations at my bath, might I request a razor instead?"

"Of course. Now keep still while I bathe your head," said Miss Blakelow. "Ned, how came you not to tell me about this? I would expect a prank of this nature from Jack but not from you. I thought you were the sensible one."

Ned colored. "Marcham sent that damn popinjay and his man of business to go through all of our possessions, Georgie. How could I do nothing when we are about to be evicted from our home?"

"Well, that explains it then," agreed Lord Marcham without a moment's hesitation. "The perfect reason to kidnap a member of the peerage."

Miss Blakelow glared down at him. "Sir, will you be quiet?"

He spread his hands. "What? I am showing remarkable consideration, under the circumstances."

"You are not helping, so please be quiet. Ned, why is Lord Marcham here?" asked Miss Blakelow in a voice that froze the blood in his lordship's veins. He looked at her leisurely while she was distracted by the task at hand, thinking that while she was not an Incomparable, she could have been said to be a very attractive woman. Her eyes were green and set under dark arched brows, her skin smooth and bronzed by the sun, her nose small and straight, her chin firm, and those full lips, which he had thought quite remarkable from the beginning of their acquaintance, were parted in an unconscious invitation to be kissed. He acknowledged within himself a desire to know what those lips felt like beneath his own and found that it was not a new sensation. Why, when he could have his pick of society beauties, was he fantasizing about a slip of a girl without fashion, exceptionable beauty, fortune, or position? In short, she had nothing that should attract him. And yet attract him she certainly did.

"We did it for Thorncote," said Ned belligerently. "I could not just stand by and watch Will's inheritance—oh, dash it all, I didn't want to see you out on the street, George. Jack and I and the girls could live with some relative or other, probably not together, but we would have had a home. But you have no one. You have no money. You would have ended up in the workhouse."

"Well, I hope not," said Miss Blakelow brightly. "I might have become a governess or . . . or something."

"Or something," echoed his lordship, his eyes twinkling at the very improper image that flashed into his mind.

She glared at him, knowing what he was thinking. "Or some-thing *respectable*."

"But where would be the fun in that?" he teased.

Miss Blakelow decided there and then that Lord Marcham was every bit as depraved as his reputation had suggested. She deliber-ately slapped the wet cloth around his face and had the satisfaction of hearing him gasp at the cold. "A seamstress."

"With your eyesight? Oh, no," said his lordship.

Miss Blakelow froze.

Her eyesight. She groped for her pocket and her glasses and suddenly remembered that she was wearing nothing but her nightgown. She folded her arms self-consciously across her bosom.

"Too late to shut the stable door after the horse has bolted," he said, smiling faintly at her obvious embarrassment.

"Ned, help his lordship downstairs. I must get dressed."

"Must you?" murmured the earl.

Miss Blakelow looked around for something to throw at him.

"And I am happy to say that I was right," he continued as the lad helped him to his feet. "You are much improved without those wretched glasses. You appear to me to be able to see without them perfectly well."

"Ned, I am sure that his lordship would prefer a *cold* bath after being cooped up in this hot attic all this time," said Miss Blakelow, glaring at their noble neighbor. "Pray see to it."

CHAPTER 9

HIS LORDSHIP, MUCH RESTORED by a bath and a fresh change of linen, was making a hearty breakfast in the parlor with the Blakelow family looking on with varying degrees of trepidation.

He was making them await his decision, savoring every mouthful of the fare that had been placed upon the table for his enjoyment.

Miss Blakelow was quite astonished, watching him from the other end of the room as he steadily packed away a considerable amount of cold meat and bread and washed it all down with a tankard or two of ale. Her brother William had a healthy appetite, but nothing at all compared with this man. She stared at him, rather wondering at his athletic physique; it was amazing to her that he was not round enough to rival the Prince Regent.

The earl leaned back in his chair and popped a grape into his mouth, watching with some amusement the faces of the Blakelow family, evidently all gathered to watch him eat as if he were a freak act in a traveling show. They all looked expectantly at him, as if fearing that the Bow Street Runners would arrive at any moment and cart them off to prison.

His eyes flicked around the room. The aunt had finally put in an appearance at the breakfast table, concentrating on demolishing the huge sweet pastry on the plate in front of her. Plus Ned, Marianne, Catherine, and Elizabeth, every one of them blond-haired and pale-eyed, like peas in a pod. There was another brother, his lordship remembered, William. He recalled that he was like the others. Jack was darker in coloring, more like his eldest sister, and his eyes fell upon Miss Georgiana Blakelow, her chestnut-colored hair once more hidden under her thick white cap, her glasses perched upon the end of her nose, and her figure once more swathed in the black, featureless mourning dress that he was fast learning to despise. Another image came all too readily to mind, the image of her in a threadbare nightgown, the curve of her waist and a breast silhouetted by the candlelight, her long slender legs moving toward him with seductive grace, and her glorious hair down around her shoulders.

"I will agree to your terms," he announced at last.

The occupants of the room let out a collective breath and grins broke across their faces.

"On one condition," continued the earl.

"Which is?" demanded Ned belligerently, still clearly smarting from his lordship's tongue-lashing earlier that morning.

Lord Marcham paused. So here was the moment. Was he certain? he asked himself. Why, when he had failed to speak the words to Lady Emily Holt, was he now considering speaking those very words to a woman he hardly knew? Was it the way something inside him leapt whenever their eyes met? Was it the laughter he saw lurking in her eyes or the passion he saw when she had burst into his home and pulled a gun on him? He had rarely felt such an attraction for anyone before, even the reputed beauties with whom he'd had enjoyable affairs. Something about the way she looked at him made his heart double its speed. He found himself wondering once again what it would feel like to hold her in his arms. He knew she'd be good for him. He promised himself he'd be good for her. And ultimately, he wanted her and knew there was only one way to achieve his aim.

"I would ask your sister, Miss Georgiana Blakelow, if she will do me the honor of accepting my hand in marriage," said the Earl of Marcham, calmly raising the tankard of ale to his lips and watching the lady in question over the rim as he drank.

Miss Blakelow was obliged to grip the back of the chair to steady her as the room spun before her eyes.

"What?" demanded Ned, surging to his feet wrathfully. "You will not!"

"I need a wife. You have deprived me of the hand of Lady Emily Holt and so I need a replacement. I find that I cannot bear the thought of going through the elimination process again, and so I may as well take the nearest eligible female and have done with it."

"The elimination process?" echoed Catherine. "Is that how you choose your wife, my lord?"

"It is as good a method as any other," his lordship replied, putting down his tankard.

"What about love?" asked Elizabeth.

"What about it? You don't imagine that I am in love with your sister after two hours' acquaintance, do you?"

"I think that any of us would rather die than see her married to you!" flashed Ned, his face red with anger.

The earl pushed away his plate, his hunger apparently sated at last. "Indeed?" he said politely. "You may get your wish if I were to inform the authorities as to what has gone on here the past few days."

"You are mad," breathed Georgiana.

"Quite possibly," he conceded, turning his eyes at last upon her. "And so, my bluestocking, what do you say?"

"You cannot be serious. You cannot wish to marry me . . . Do you?" she asked.

"Not in the least," he replied with unflattering bluntness. "But I do need a wife. You seem to be the nearest unwed female of marriageable age. I can conceive of worse fates than being married to you."

She put a hand to her head. "But every proper feeling must rebel. You . . . I mean . . . I am not of your world, my lord. Your way of life is . . . is so . . . You must see that it would not answer."

"I see nothing of the kind."

"And you are engaged to Lady Emily Holt," she pointed out.

"Lady Emily married Thomas Edridge two days ago by special license."

Miss Blakelow was astonished. "Did she?"

"They had been fond of each other for some time. I . . . er . . . merely bumped their heads together and made them see sense. So you see, there is no reason for you to concern yourself with Lady Emily. But your unruly family has stopped me from informing Lord and Lady Holt that there was to be no wedding yesterday. No doubt the world thinks me a cad of the highest order."

"Indeed, we are very sorry for it."

"Are you? Well, I am not sure that I am," replied Lord Marcham.

"Oh," said Miss Blakelow.

"You and your revolting family have made me realize that if I cannot have love, I will at least have laughter with the woman I marry."

"I see," she replied, much struck by this revelation. "Then why not consider Mrs. Finch. Newly widowed and young. She's always laughing."

"She squints."

"Or Miss Kate Busby. She would make you a creditable wife. Pretty as a picture and sweet natured too."

His lordship grimaced. "And she would run a mile every time I tried to make love to her."

Miss Blakelow shot him a look, then regarded the stunned faces of her youngest brothers and sisters. "You forget yourself, my lord. There are impressionable minds present."

"My apologies. I mean only to say that I want fire, not ice."

"Please let us drop this subject," she said coldly.

"And you are most definitely fire."

"My lord—"

"Does the thought of intimacy with me terrify you?" he asked her gently.

She could not meet his eyes. "Will you stop speaking to me in that way?"

"It needn't," he continued regardless.

"How romantic!" cried Marianne, her hands against her heart.

"Oh, shut up, Marianne," recommended her brother tersely, at which juncture Marianne promptly burst into tears. "There is nothing romantic about it."

"Oh, Lord, there she goes again!" said young Jack, expressively rolling his eyes. "Women!"

His lordship's lips twitched. "Exactly so. Well, Miss Blakelow, what is your answer?"

The lady clasped her hands before her. She took a deep breath. "I should thank you for the very great honor you have done me in making your proposal, but I do not think that you meant to say it. What I mean to say is that I think it surprised you as much as it did me to hear yourself speak those words aloud."

The earl was mildly irritated that she had read him so unerringly. *Very well, Miss Blakelow, if plain speaking is what you are after, then plain speaking you shall have.* "You are not my first choice and I doubt I am yours, but we will deal tolerably well together."

"And is that what you want of wedlock?" she demanded. "To *deal tolerably well?*"

He shrugged. "I am no romantic, Miss Blakelow."

She gave a scornful laugh. "You do surprise me."

He pushed back his chair from the table. "I need a wife. I need an heir."

"I'm sure you do," she replied with heightened color, "but I am unable to give them to you. I am neither of marriageable age nor inclination. I thank you for your very flattering offer—"

"My *what?*"

"Your very *kind* offer," she corrected primly, "but I cannot accept."

"Why not?"

"Because I don't wish to be married."

"Every woman wishes to be married."

She raised her chin. "Not this one."

"I don't believe you."

"I don't care what you believe."

"You refuse me?"

"I'm sorry, my lord, but I do."

A silence fell across the room. The younger siblings of Miss Blakelow had followed this exchange as if watching a ball thrown back and forth, their eyes alternately swinging from the face of their eldest sister to his lordship and back again.

The earl stood up and bowed stiffly. "Very well then. I bid you all good day. I am not an unreasonable man, and I give you three months to resolve your affairs. But I trust you will be ready to move out of Thorncote at the end of that time."

He tossed down his napkin upon the table, sketched the merest outline of a bow, and was gone.

CHAPTER 10

IT DID NOT TAKE his lordship long to discover that news of his encounter with highwaymen on the main road to Holme Park had spread far and wide. That he had been waylaid by adolescents hell-bent on revenge was a fact he was not about to divulge when he was widely considered a formidable marksman. He was a man with a certain reputation to keep up, after all, and he was considerably embarrassed to have been caught napping.

Not a man to prevaricate, he went the next day to Lord Holt and disabused him of the notion that he was to gain the Earl of Marcham for a son-in-law. Any hopes that Lady Holt cherished that the marriage would still take place were dashed in an instant when Lord Marcham informed them that their daughter had married Mr. Thomas Edridge several days before. The reaction to this news was all that his lordship had hoped for, and the memory of the sour look upon her ladyship's face was one that would give him pleasure for some time to come.

He told them that he had made a mistake, and that he should never have raised expectations of matrimony in their daughter's breast. He was looking for a wife, and he had believed himself to be utterly indifferent to whom he chose to fill that role. It proved to be the opposite. He was in fact very particular about whom he wanted.

His lordship reimbursed them every last penny of their expenditure, going even as far as to pay for the satin shoes his bride wore while she married Mr. Edridge. He put a large wad of notes into Lord Holt's clammy fist and watched the chubby fingers close around it with indecent haste.

He rode home feeling much relieved, as if the weight of the world had been lifted from his shoulders. He wondered how Miss Blakelow had slept after his proposal. He smiled as he imagined her lying awake, wondering at his sanity and his reason. Did she think that he was mad? Did she think that he was toying with her? The image of her silhouetted body in her threadbare nightgown flashed into his mind. He smiled again and took the road to Thorncote before he knew what he was about.

He found the family entertaining two male visitors. When Lord Marcham was announced, young Jack Blakelow was being lectured very sternly by a ponderous-looking man in his early thirties with a ruddy countenance, auburn whiskers, and fleshy lips. The man seemed determined that the whole county should hear his strictures and spoke in so loud a voice as to drown out the announcement by the butler that they had a visitor. No one was aware of his lordship's arrival, and he was able to observe the scene unnoticed. The butler and the earl exchanged wry smiles, and then the butler went away and his lordship melted into an alcove, the better to enjoy the entertainment.

The fleshy man rolled back and forth upon the balls of his feet, looking down his nose at the young lad. Clearly this gentleman considered himself a father figure of sorts to the Blakelows. "I'm sure it was very amusing to you, but I can assure you that I don't find it so," the man said.

"I said I was sorry, Mr. Peabody," said Jack petulantly, scuffing his toe against the carpet.

"I hope you are, young man. In my view, a boy of your age should have been packed off to school long ago. And young Ned here. The best thing for boys is hard discipline."

Ned Blakelow, clearly fuming that a man who was not even related to them should seek to undertake the chastisement of his younger brother, snapped, "Jack already knows he was in the wrong, and he does not need you to tell him twice."

"Enough, Peabody. The boy has said he is sorry," said the other visitor, a quiet, elegant man seated on the other side of the fireplace.

"It's alright for you, Bateman. It was not your carriage that was assaulted," said Mr. Peabody, his cheeks red with anger.

"Hardly that. It was a boyish prank, nothing more," replied Mr. Bateman calmly.

"A boyish prank? Have you any idea how much that carriage cost? The paintwork alone cost well over—"

"Mr. Peabody," put in Miss Blakelow hastily, "come and sit by the fire and have some tea."

"Yes, do," exclaimed Marianne, giving him her most winning smile.

"And have a cake," chimed in Kitty, brandishing the plate at him.

"Or a biscuit," said Lizzy, thrusting another plate under his nose.

Not immune to being the focus of female attention, the gentleman was persuaded to sit down and partake of some tea.

"As much as I admire you, Miss Blakelow," continued Mr. Peabody, "and respect your opinion, I do not think that you fully understand how to handle young men. They are a rowdy bunch and much inclined to get up to mischief as soon as your back is turned. It is my belief that they should be packed off to school without delay and from there sent to Oxford. Nothing like an education for ridding a young man of his wilder tendencies. Don't you agree, Bateman? And another thing . . . I saw you wandering alone in the field above the house the other morning. You must know that it is highly improper for a delicate female to be abroad entirely unescorted."

"Oh, what nonsense," said Miss Blakelow, mildly irritated. "I am long past the age where I give a fig for that."

"But you are an innocent, impressionable female. And we all know whose estate borders Thorncote." He paused to give her a significant look. "The Earl of Marcham, ma'am. You cannot pretend to be ignorant of *his* lifestyle. His reputation is scandalous. I won't go into detail, but suffice it to say that there are stories . . . orgies, parties, and drunken assaults on the women of the village."

"Hardly," said Miss Blakelow, suppressing a peculiar desire to laugh at the outrage on Mr. Peabody's face.

"You do not take me seriously. I can tell by your face that you do not."

"What business is it of ours if the earl wishes to throw a party?" she demanded reasonably.

"Quite right," said a voice from the doorway.

"Lord Marcham!" cried Marianne. "However did you get in here?"

"Your butler showed me in some moments before," he said in his deep voice, "but you were . . . ah . . . otherwise engaged. You were saying, Peabody?"

Miss Blakelow spun around so quickly that she knocked her cup of tea flying, and it landed unerringly on Mr. Peabody's pantaloons. He shrieked, stood up, and dabbed at the offending wet patch with a napkin. He looked so much as if he had wet himself that it was all the Blakelows could do to keep from laughing.

"Oh, sir, I do *beg* your pardon!" cried the lady, seemingly genuinely mortified.

"No matter, Miss Blakelow," replied the man stiffly. "I know you would not do such a thing deliberately. Really, it is no fuss at all. To be sure these are a new acquisition and of the finest material, but it is of little matter, my dear, little matter. I went to London for them especially, and I fancy that they look very fine, very fine indeed. But rest assured, I know that you would not have done such a thing deliberately. Such good friends as you and I are. I am certain that no such thought would enter your head."

Lord Marcham, raising a silent brow of inquiry at Miss Blakelow as she came forward to greet him, saw the look of pure exasperation on her face, and he struggled to suppress a smile.

"It appears," he remarked in a low voice only she could hear, "that you must try harder to be rid of him."

She looked up at him, a guilty flush stealing into her cheeks. "I beg your pardon?"

"I meant only that he appears to be more persistent than you may have thought. Good aim, by the way. I shall be wary should we ever play billiards together. What a penchant you have for attacking a gentleman in the unmentionables!" he marveled in a low voice. "First you rendered Harry Larwood unable to perform the most basic of natural functions after you assaulted him at my house, and now Mr. Pearbody suffers the ignominy of tea spilled over his very fine pantaloons. Remind me to keep my unmentionables well away from you."

"Then don't tempt me into assaulting them," she whispered. "And it's Peabody. Not Pearbody."

His eyes met hers. "Shall I kiss you here and now in full view of everybody? I begin to think that only drastic measures will see him off."

She choked on a laugh. "No, you wretched man, don't you dare!"

"Then shall we begin again in the proper manner?" He grinned as he made her his bow and took her hand. "Miss Blakelow, how do you do?" he asked, the very picture of politeness as their gaze met again, and he squeezed her fingers for the briefest moment before releasing them.

"Don't ask."

"I see. And may I ask, what has Jack done now?"

She lowered her voice, although they were already speaking in an undertone. "He scrawled the word 'Peabrain' into the muddy paintwork of Mr. Peabody's carriage."

"Ah," said his lordship.

"And it is not funny."

"No."

"Then stop laughing."

He spread his hands. "I'm not."

"Yes, you are. I can see it in your eyes. Why are you here?" she demanded. "What do you want?"

"Well, that is not very polite, is it?" he asked, amused.

"Can you not see that I have my hands full?"

"Yes, but you always have your hands full. I am here to see you."

Her eyes narrowed. "Why?"

"Why, for the pleasure of your company, ma'am."

"Tosh," she said and then in a louder voice, "Are you here to pick up where your man of business and the odious baronet left off?"

"Ah. Yes, I heard about that. I can only apologize."

"Anything you see here that takes your fancy, my lord?" she demanded.

"Indeed there is."

"I meant the paintings."

"I can assure you, I had no idea Sir Jeremiah had any intention of paying you such a visit, and if I had, I would have put a stop to it. Sarah went behind my back."

"She wants Thorncote."

"Yes. Her husband's land is all in Ireland. She wants a home in England. And the Thorncote estate neighbors Holme Park, where she grew up. It is not really so very hard to understand."

She stared at him with narrowed eyes. "Do I have your word, as a gentleman, that you had no part in it?"

"On my life," he said and bowed.

Miss Blakelow eyed him speculatively, saw that he was in earnest, and smiled. "Then won't you allow me to introduce you to our guests?"

The earl smiled affably as she drew him forward and the introductions were made. The man with the fleshy nose was introduced as Mr. Joshua Peabody, the eldest son of a friend of the late Sir William Blakelow. He owned Goldings, a large estate on the Worcestershire border. The reserved gentleman, the earl discovered, was Mr. Samuel Bateman, from a wealthy family that lived in Loughton and as quiet in appearance as he was in character.

That both of these gentlemen were in pursuit of Marianne, his lordship soon dismissed when he saw the way they looked at the eldest Miss Blakelow. He knew a moment of surprise. Given that she was a virtual recluse, he had not considered that he would have competition for her hand.

"Are you related to my Blakelow friends, Mr. Peabody?" asked Lord Marcham as he accepted a cup of tea from Georgiana's hand.

"I consider myself some sort of cousin, I suppose," he answered, dabbing at the stain on his trousers. "Their dear father and mine were good friends. Sir William Blakelow was a very fine man. He would have done anything for his children . . . anything at all."

"I'm sure he would," replied the earl politely, looking around at the sadly dilapidated state of the furnishings and the stained bare patch on the wall where a painting had once been. *A father so fine that he gambled away their home out from under their feet,* he thought. "I am sure that you would agree that such a kind father would have left his children's future well cared for?"

"Yes, of course. Sir William was nothing if not thorough in all matters of business."

"Indeed? And so if he thought that his youngest sons would benefit from a school education, he would have no doubt arranged it?"

"Er, yes . . ."

"Or if he thought that Miss Blakelow needed the assistance of a guardian in making her arrangements for the family, he would have arranged that too?"

Miss Blakelow blushed at his lordship's inference. "I do not believe such an arrangement exists, my lord."

"Quite so," agreed his lordship smoothly.

Mr. Peabody bristled. "I only mean to counsel Miss Blakelow in areas where I think she needs it. Our families have always been close, and as William is often away, I look after them in his absence."

"Very commendable, Mr. Peabody, but that will no longer be necessary," said the earl. "As the hopeful future brother-in-law of Sir William Blakelow of Thorncote, if such decisions are needed, then I will take them—in conjunction with my wife, of course."

"Your wife?" echoed Mr. Bateman, staring from Marianne to Catherine to Elizabeth and then back at the earl.

"Yes."

"And do you imagine that Marianne, Kitty, or Lizzy would have a man like you?" demanded Mr. Peabody.

"Not for one moment," replied his lordship. "And as I have not asked them to marry me, then such a conclusion is, dare I say it, impossible."

Mr. Peabody scratched his head. "Then . . . who?"

"Miss Georgiana Blakelow."

The lady in question closed her eyes in silent pain as the room seemed to explode around them.

"What?" shrieked Mr. Peabody.

"Impossible," said Mr. Bateman, his face pale with anger. "She would not have you. I would rather marry her myself than see her shackled to you."

"I'm sure Miss Blakelow is overcome by your kindness," said his lordship dryly.

Miss Blakelow was in fact looking around her for something to hurl at their noble visitor. Everyone in the room stared at him, mouths agape.

"Please, Mr. Bateman, Mr. Peabody, pay no heed to his lordship's jokes. He is mad," Miss Blakelow said and heard the earl give his low laugh. "I am not going to marry anyone, I can assure you. Lord Marcham thinks it amusing to pretend there is an agreement between us—"

"You?" demanded Mr. Peabody, as if the lady had not spoken. "But you . . . I mean . . . you are a . . ."

"Yes?" inquired the earl softly.

The portly gentleman gulped, remembering suddenly the stories of the duel his lordship had fought as a young man. "But you hardly know her," he said, settling on the safest complaint that popped into his brain.

"I know her well enough to know that I wish to marry her. And so if any chastisement needs doing, I will do it . . . Jack?"

"Yes, my lord?"

"Consider yourself duly chastised."

"Right . . . oh . . . is that it?"

"That's it. And you are barred from fishing for a week."

"Er . . . right."

"But you don't even *like* fishing—" Kitty began. "Ow! I don't see why you should kick me, Jack Blakelow!"

"You seem to forget, sir," said Ned, ignoring all this with a cold smile, "that our sister refused you. All of us heard her turn you down."

The earl smiled. "When you come to know me better, you will realize that when I want something, I invariably get it."

"Lord Marcham?" said Miss Blakelow, smoothing the material of her gown over her knee.

"Yes, my love?"

"Not this time," she said with a sweet smile, but as their eyes met through the lenses of her spectacles, hers held the distinct gleam of a challenge.

"Georgie is the best of sisters, but she has no great opinion of men or mankind. What made you choose her as your bride?" Marianne asked the earl. "You must know that she has vowed never to marry anyone? It is common knowledge."

"Hush, Marianne," said Miss Blakelow quietly.

"You may think you know her but you don't, my lord," continued her sister regardless. "She had any number of beaux when she was young and refused them all."

"Indeed?" he replied, meeting Miss Blakelow's gaze. "A veritable little heartbreaker."

The lady blushed and looked away.

"She doesn't *want* to be married," declared Marianne.

"I see. Well, what does she want then?" asked his lordship.

"She is happy to stay here with us," said Kitty.

"Yes. And although she is not strictly related to us, she has always managed everything creditably," said Marianne.

"And is like a mother to us all," put in Lizzy.

"I see," said the earl. "And what will happen when all of you marry? And when William brings his new wife to live at Thorncote? Do you imagine the future Lady Blakelow will be happy to have her sister-in-law running the house for her?"

"She will come and live with me," said Marianne gallantly.

"And me," said Kitty.

"She will be the dear kind teacher to our children that she was to us."

Although this impassioned speech was intended to be a compliment, it hit Miss Blakelow like a slap around the face with a dead fish. She tried to smile and failed.

Lord Marcham saw the look of consternation on Georgiana's face and longed to box Marianne's ears. "What an attractive prospect to be sure," he said. "But perhaps your sister would prefer to have children of her own to love and nurture. And I own, I would like nothing more than to try to give them to her."

There was an audible gasp in the room, and Miss Blakelow blushed scarlet.

"Sir!" cried Mr. Peabody. "There are ladies present."

"So there are . . ." agreed the earl, picking up his cup and sipping from it. "Miss Blakelow has given up her youth and prospects to look after you brats. It is time she did something for herself."

Miss Blakelow protested. "What nonsense! I did not give up anything."

"That's not what I heard," he said.

She sank into brooding silence, wondering how much Aunt Blakelow had told him.

"You, my lord, are a disgrace!" said Mr. Peabody, almost as red as a holly berry.

"So I have been told."

"To speak of the . . . the marital act . . . in front of impressionable young minds is simply not to be borne!"

"If these young minds are anything like mine was at their age, then they probably already know more about it than you do," replied the earl.

A collective giggle answered this remark, and Mr. Peabody stormed from the room. Mr. Bateman sat quietly in the corner, disapproval emanating from every pore.

The earl's eyes twinkled engagingly as they rested upon his reluctant fiancée. "Well, that got rid of him, my love; I told you I would achieve it, didn't I?"

"My lord Marcham, might I have a word with you in private?" asked Miss Blakelow, a steely edge to her voice.

He set down his cup and smiled. "I thought you'd never ask."

❧

"What exactly are you up to?" Miss Blakelow demanded, watching as the party retreated to stroll in the gardens. His lordship held the door open for her, and as she brushed past him, she trod on something and tripped, only just catching herself before she ploughed face-first into his chest.

"*That* was my foot," he said with a pained expression on his face.

"Sorry," she said awkwardly.

"What did you do with that money I gave you for the new spectacles? You clearly have not made use of it. If I find you have spent it on any of the Blakelow brats, it will be very much the worse for you—"

"What are you doing?" she interrupted with some impatience. "Are you determined to shame me in front of the entire neighborhood?"

"Not at all. You wanted to be rid of Pearbrain, did you not?"

"His name is Peabody. Please try and remember it. I did . . . did wish that he might go away . . . but not like *that*. And I wish that you wouldn't say that I have given up my youth and prospects and beauty for my brothers and sisters, for it is not true, you know."

He looked down at her, a warm light in his eyes. "I didn't say that."

"You did."

"Not your beauty. I didn't say it for I don't think it."

"Then you need spectacles even more than I do," she said caustically.

He smiled. "My eyesight is fine and I suspect yours is too."

"Did I or did I not refuse your offer of marriage the other day?" she demanded.

"You did."

"I did. I am glad that we are in agreement over that. So why then, given my very clear refusal, have you just announced that we are to be married?"

"I didn't. I announced my *intention* to marry you. That, my girl, is entirely different."

"I am not going to marry you. Can you understand that?"

He gave her a twisted smile. "I will allow that you are not ready to marry me at the present moment, but I hope that once you have discovered that you cannot live without me then you will change your mind."

There was a loud groan from the lady.

"Yes, my love?"

"I will not change my mind. I won't marry. I cannot marry. There, can I be any plainer?"

"Why not?"

She rolled her eyes. "I am not having this discussion with you. Please consider this my final answer."

"Very well. I will come to an agreement with you. I will not send details of our engagement to the newspapers just yet."

"How kind."

"Yes. We will be friends first."

"*When* are you going home?" she asked, as if his presence gave her exquisite pain.

He grinned. "When you have agreed to ride with me tomorrow."

"Then you will have a long wait, my lord."

"A walk then, by the lake."

"No."

"You are being rude to me today," he marveled.

"And you are making decisions for me and I don't like it," she said tartly, trying to move past him.

He caught her elbow in his hand and held it fast. "Don't you?" he asked in a soft voice. "I venture to think that you like it a great deal."

She blushed and tried to remove her arm. "You flatter yourself. I know it amuses you, my lord, to mock me because you think I have no experience of men. But I do not find it amusing, and I wish that you would find yourself another flirt."

"Is that what this is all about? You think I am teasing you?"

"I think we both know that you are amusing yourself at my expense. Now, please let go of me, or we will be remarked upon."

He released her. "You will allow me to tell you that your Peabody fellow is a great deal too busy in your affairs, ma'am."

She glared at him. "No, *you* are a great deal too busy in my affairs. You are no more my choice of husband than I am your choice of wife."

He smiled. "Then that shows how little you know me . . . and yourself for that matter."

With this very perplexing remark he let her go and watched her disappear into the rose garden with Mr. Samuel Bateman. He left soon afterward, sure in the knowledge that Miss Georgiana Blakelow was thinking about him—perhaps not in the most flattering of terms, but she was definitely thinking about him.

❧

"My dear Miss Blakelow," began Mr. Bateman slowly, ten minutes later, "forgive my impertinence, but marriage to the Earl of Marcham?"

She gave him a speaking look as they found a seat at one end of the rose garden. "There will be no marriage, never fear. Pay no heed to his lordship, Mr. Bateman."

"Pay no heed? The man is a . . . a scoundrel."

The note of shock in his voice made Miss Blakelow want to laugh, and she bit her lower lip and sucked it under until she had controlled herself. "This is his idea of a jest only. He seems to take enjoyment from baiting me."

"Baiting you?" he repeated. "But why?"

She shrugged and adjusted the shawl around her shoulders. "He has likely never come into contact with someone like me before. As part of my work with the church, I wrote a pamphlet, you may remember, condemning his morals and behavior. No one was more surprised than I was when it was published across half the country." She smoothed the worn skirt of her gown over her knees and gave him a rueful smile. "I think he is looking for revenge."

Mr. Bateman reached under the slats of the bench and pulled out a weed from between the gravel chippings. "I would never have thought a man like him would be bothered if a hundred such pamphlets were published."

"I agree. But for some reason he seems determined to punish me by pretending to have an interest in me."

"The thrill of the chase," he said distractedly.

She smiled. "Something like that. I don't believe he has ever been turned down by a woman before. And his pride is wounded."

"And such pride too."

"Oh, I don't say that he has insulted me or accosted me in an improper manner. Merely that he has made it his mission to make a fool of me."

"How any man could make a sport of such a pure and gentle creature is beyond me," Mr. Bateman said earnestly.

Miss Blakelow, who considered herself anything but pure and gentle, pulled a face. "He is bored."

"Do you think so indeed? Bored with his wealth and position? I wish that I had the opportunity to be bored with his advantages," he remarked, and then colored as if remembering that he was supposed to be a Christian man. "My apologies, ma'am, I meant only that he has a world of opportunity spread before him. He has no reason to be bored. He may go where he likes, buy what he wishes, and marry who he wants . . . Others, younger sons especially, are not so lucky."

"I don't say that he is bored of his position, merely that he is bored of his life. Women come two-a-penny to a man like him. He is only making me the object of his attentions because I am different. A novelty." She smiled brightly. "Do not worry for me. He wishes to make me fall in love with him so that he might cast me aside. And I am in no danger of giving him what he wishes."

"Well," he replied. "If the man becomes intolerable, let me know."

"That is very kind of you, Mr. Bateman. What do you plan to do? Fight a duel on my behalf?"

He balked a little, unaware that she was teasing him. "If I must," he replied, running a forefinger between his neck and the collar of his shirt.

"Dear sir, pray don't be ridiculous. I was jesting. Now tell me, are you planning to attend the dance next week with your mother and sister?"

"Yes, at least I think so, if my sister has recovered from her cold. Will you be there too, ma'am?"

"Me?" she said, rather taken aback. "Oh, Lord no. It has been a long time since I have shown my face in Loughton. No, my aunt will accompany the girls. She enjoys it, you know, sitting and chatting with her friends."

Miss Blakelow remembered the horrible, tedious evenings, sitting amongst the dowagers and the chaperones, dressed in some featureless, dull gray gown that no one noticed, her obligatory spectacles hiding her from the world, her foot tapping longingly in time to the music. She watched with every other dowager present as the young people set about having fun and yearned to join the dancing herself. It was torture. No, let Aunt Blakelow go and leave her in peace.

"If you are worried that you will want for a partner, ma'am, I should be honored to lead you out," said Mr. Bateman.

Miss Blakelow smiled. "That is kind of you, sir, but I do not dance. My eyesight is so bad that I constantly crash into people, and my memory so lax that I forget all the steps. No, don't worry for me. I shall be happier at home with a book."

They rose then and meandered their way through the gardens to the lake, where the rest of the party were engaged in skimming flat pebbles across the surface of the water. Mr. Bateman discovered a hitherto unknown talent and was soon lost in the laughter of the moment. As his hand curled around Marianne's, instructing her how to hold the stone, Miss Blakelow smiled like the veritable matchmaking mamas whom she so deplored.

CHAPTER 11

"WHAT *CAN* YOU HAVE found at Holme to entertain you all this time?" complained Sir Julius, looking at his friend through his quizzing glass. His lordship had come down to London on business. Within the hour, news of his arrival had reached a good number of his acquaintances. He had been invited to dine by three particular friends, and a note had been brought around to his house asking him to present himself at his mother's house as a matter of urgency. Having been in London several days and having failed to abide by her wishes, the earl was bracing himself for an imminent visit from the countess. As his lordship had a very fair notion of what his mother wished to ask him about, he was much relieved to have found Sir Julius upon his doorstep instead.

The Earl of Marcham smiled. "I have been busy."

"So I hear. Planning to get yourself leg-shackled, by all accounts."

There was a short silence.

"News travels fast," observed his lordship, reaching for a slice of toast.

"Don't be a fool, March. You have proposed to two females in the space of a month. Of course news of *that* is going to travel fast."

"Pass the marmalade, would you?"

"You're not seriously contemplating marriage with this girl are you?" asked Sir Julius. "I thought I could count on you to shun matrimony to the end of your days."

"I cannot afford to, Ju. In case it has escaped your notice, I am in need of an heir. And for that I need a wife. More coffee?"

Sir Julius shook his head. "Who is she?"

"Does it matter?" countered Lord Marcham evasively.

"Oh-ho, touchy! Are you afraid that I might steal her away, Rob?"

His friend smiled. "Not in the least. But she is a gentlewoman and not likely to welcome a carte blanche from you."

"Who said anything about carte blanche?" asked Sir Julius, wounded. "I may wish to get married myself. Describe her to me."

Lord Marcham smiled and picked up his coffee cup. "She is not your sort, Ju."

"Which means that she is something out of the ordinary and you wish to put me off the scent," said his friend with a knowing look.

"Undoubtedly. I wish to have her all to myself."

"A beauty then?"

"In an unconventional way—yes. You will find out for yourself once I have . . . er . . . secured her affections."

Sir Julius thoughtfully rubbed the long scar on his cheek with the knuckle of his thumb. "You are confident of success?"

His lordship merely smiled and sliced his toast in two. He looked over at his friend. "And you? Are you serious about matrimony?"

Fawcett shrugged and took a sip from his tankard of ale. "I am in no rush. I am in no great hurry to leg-shackle myself again to any female. This time I plan to be much more exacting in my choice. Marry in haste and you wake up one morning a few years later lying next to a woman who you neither like nor desire. Were I not a widower, such would still be my lot in life. Heed my warning, March. Ask your brother if you don't believe me. None knows better than Hal."

"He always said you were a cold fish," remarked his lordship, before taking a bite of his toast.

"Hal was the best of good friends, but the biggest fool of my acquaintance. Handsome as they come and a dashing red coat to boot. Not surprising he had half the women in London on the catch for him . . . more women after him than you, March. God alone knows what possessed him to hitch himself to Mary's wagon."

The earl, who knew very well what caused his brother to hitch himself to Mary, ate his toast and remained silent. He generally considered himself to be open-minded where his brother's love affairs were concerned and would only interfere when it was strictly necessary. But when Hal had gotten a young woman of a sickly disposition with child and had been proposing to leave her to her own devices, his lordship had felt obliged to step in. Affairs with married women, widows, or opera dancers were generally tolerated by society, if the participants were discreet, but to seduce a young innocent? That was too much, even for the earl. Lord Marcham had induced his brother to do the honorable thing before knowledge of the pregnancy was out, and the couple married. The child, a girl, was born as sickly as her mother and did not live to see her first birthday. Although relations between the two brothers had since been cordial, Hal had never quite forgiven him for forcing him into an unhappy, if respectable, marriage.

"You know that Mary died, don't you?" asked Sir Julius, thoughtfully playing with an unused fork on the table.

"Yes. I received a letter from Hal last month informing me of the fact."

"Very sad business. Always ill, that girl, from the moment he married her. Between you and me, Rob, she barely let him touch her."

Lord Marcham lowered his eyes. "She was a . . . singular female."

"Frigid," said Sir Julius with an expressive look in his eyes that showed exactly what he thought of that behavior.

"I think she was rather hurt by—well . . . it's none of our business, is it?"

Sir Julius watched his friend, wondering what he had been about to say. Some subjects were forbidden, it seemed, even to a lifelong friend. The Holkham family always had closed ranks against the rest of the world—even against the people they considered their friends. It was a trait that irritated him. He always felt shut out and marginalized by the blood ties, which it seemed were stronger than even the closest of friendships.

"How is he? Is he coming home? I suppose there is nothing to hold him in Brussels now. He was only there for Mary, after all."

"And the war," said his lordship.

"Yes, but he's shot of all that now. A fresh start for him back home is what he needs."

"I had an idea on that very subject that I wished to discuss with you."

"By all means."

"A neighbor of mine has fallen on hard times. The woman's father lost his estate to me at the faro table," said Lord Marcham, leaning back in his chair. "It's in the devil of a state, of course, and will need careful supervision to bring it back up to scratch. I was planning to sell it, but then I had an idea that I might gift it to Hal, give him something to do. Something to think about besides Mary."

Sir Julius raised his quizzing glass and frowned at his friend through it. "Lord, Rob. Can you see Hal as a farmer?"

The earl smiled. "Not exactly. But they have a decent man there who would shoulder most of the responsibility."

"Where is the place? What is it called? Do I know it?"

"I doubt it. It's a pretty enough little estate with a fair-sized house. Thorncote, owned by Sir William Blakelow junior, currently to be found losing money hand over fist at the faro table. A boy so wet behind the ears he has not the sense to know when he's about to lose his inheritance."

"Lord, not that chubby blond fellow who puts me in mind of a goat?"

"The very same. His family are about to be turned out of their home, and all he cares about is cutting a dash—and, I may add, squaring up to me."

"Blakelow . . . weren't we recently speaking of someone named Blakelow?" mused Sir Julius.

Lord Marcham smiled. "Your pamphlet."

"Eh?"

"'The immoral Lords of Worcestershire and their pursuit of buxom lovelies in the bedroom'—or whatever that thing was called."

Sir Julius Fawcett gaped. "Not *her*?"

"Miss Blakelow, author and arbiter of moral excellence."

"Well, I'm blowed," breathed the other man.

"Would you believe that she came to me asking for my help?" said his lordship. "The gall of the woman quite took my breath away. She wanted me to lend her money—a lot of money—and this after she had dragged my name through the mud. I said no, of course."

"What does she look like? Is she as horse faced as we feared?"

The earl made no answer but reached for the coffee pot to refill his cup.

"You dog, March!" cried Sir Julius, laughing. "You dog!"

His lordship merely smiled.

"I knew it! I knew that you wouldn't let that pamphlet go unchallenged! You had to have your revenge somehow, and now you will take her home from her—but what will you do with the family? You cannot turn them out onto the street, Rob."

"I understand that the younger Blakelows have relatives living whom they can call upon for assistance . . . So what do you think?"

Sir Julius shrugged. "It sounds as good a place as any. And close enough that you can keep an eye on Hal."

"That was precisely my thinking. I think he's a little low in spirits as one might expect after such a loss."

"Did he love Mary then?" asked his friend, looking surprised.

"I don't think love came into it. But she was his wife, after all."

"And what, may I ask, are your plans for Miss Blakelow?" asked Sir Julius with a grin.

"Miss Blakelow . . . is to live with me."

A pale eyebrow rose. "The devil she is . . . with you? As your wife, my lord, or as your mistress?"

His lordship smiled. "Miss Blakelow does not approve of me or my ways."

"I see. Then I fail to understand how you can assume that she will live with you. You can kidnap her, of course, but I hardly think that behavior of that sort will be tolerated in this day and age."

"I will do whatever it takes—what in God's name is that racket?" said the earl as sounds of hysterical female voices emanated through the thick walls from his hallway.

"Robert?" cried an imperious voice. "Robert Louis Edward Phillip Holkham. Show yourself this minute!"

"Oh, Lord," muttered the earl, throwing down his napkin, "what on earth can she want now?"

"I imagine," answered Sir Julius, leaning back in his chair as one preparing to be hugely entertained, "that your mother has heard of your imminent engagement."

"Robbie? Are you in there?" The door was thrown open and the Countess of Marcham stood upon the threshold, a picture of outrage in purple silk, a shawl around her shoulders that grazed the floor, and a bonnet of such vast size upon her head that her son rather marveled at her being able to get through the door. She fixed him with her fulminating glare, her ample bosom heaving with indignation. "There you are. What, may I ask, is the meaning of this?"

"The meaning of what, Mama?" asked his lordship, dutifully rising to his feet.

"Your *engagement*," she said with almost violent passion. "Another one!"

"Won't you sit down, ma'am?"

"Don't you try that flummery with me! Tell me at once, is it true that you have made an offer for that . . . that *Blakelow* creature?"

"You may not choose to sit down, but I have not finished my breakfast, so you will forgive me if I continue with my toast."

"Answer me!" she said, coming farther into the room, leaning heavily upon her parasol, which looked as if it might well give up under the weight it was forced to bear.

"Yes, it is true," her son replied calmly.

"Are you not aware that she is the author of that . . . that *rag*?"

"Precisely what I said," put in Sir Julius helpfully.

"Are you not aware that you have been most viciously maligned?" demanded her ladyship.

"As the stories are for the most part true," replied Lord Marcham, "I rather think she is guilty of nothing more than dredging up my past—disagreeable though that may be."

"You defend her?"

"Not in the least."

"Who is this woman that she should dare to criticize you? A poor nobody, that's who. And you make the woman an offer? I thought you had lost your mind when you announced your intention to marry Lady Emily Holt, but at least she has breeding! A Miss Blakelow? Nobody had ever heard of her before she wrote that . . . that drivel! Who is her father, pray? Who are her family? Are you expecting to go up in the world with this alliance?"

His lordship gave up on his toast and pushed back his chair, allowing his eyes to coolly assess his enraged mother. "No, ma'am, I am expecting to be happy."

Sir Julius picked up his eyeglass and examined his friend through it. "Happy, do you say?"

"Happy . . . yes."

"With *her*?" asked her ladyship. "How can you be?"

"Because I like her."

The countess pulled out a chair and collapsed into it. "You *like* her?"

"Yes, ma'am. I like her," said the earl, looking amused.

"Define 'like,' March," said Sir Julius. "Like as in enjoy her company, or like as in wanting to take her . . . er . . . clothes off . . ." his voice trailed off as he encountered the chilly stare of her ladyship.

"Both," replied his lordship calmly.

"A woman of no fashion or beauty?" said the countess. "A woman with no connections or expectations or title? A woman, in short, who is so far beneath your company that she is not fit to shine your boots?"

"She is a gentleman's daughter and that is good enough for me. Now if you will both excuse me, I have an appointment in an hour."

"Stay precisely where you are, young man!" said her ladyship in a voice that seemed to shake the glass in the windows.

"With all due respect, Mama, I am a little old to be put over your knee. I am a grown man and will make my own decisions."

"Like you did with Lady Emily Holt, you mean?" she snapped.

His lordship smiled coldly. "That young lady was bait for a trap that I was foolish enough to fall into. She was innocent, I believe, in the schemes that her parents hatched. She was as relieved as I was that the match between us fell through."

"And how do you know that you haven't once again fallen into a trap?" demanded his mother. "How do you know that this Blakelow creature is not another money-grabbing harpy who wants you only for your purse?"

"She has a point there, Rob," put in Sir Julius. "You have to admit that it is a consideration. Especially as you told me that she was after your blunt to save her family's property."

"There!" said her ladyship triumphantly. "I knew it!"

"Miss Blakelow is not that kind of woman. She is good, kind, and decent. She is also proposing to pay me back for any monies lent to her." He walked toward the door. "You may not approve, Mama, but for the first time in my life, I have found someone who makes me smile, someone whose absence from a room makes me sad, someone whose eyes seek mine when there is a good joke to be shared. For the first time in my life I wonder what it would be like to hold that person when I am old and gray. And *that*, in my experience, is a most promising start. Now, if you will excuse me, I must go."

And with that, and stopping only to peck her upon the cheek, he went away.

"Well," fumed Lady Marcham, flinging down her parasol. "*Well!* That is how he speaks to his own mother! That is the son whom I bore into this world and nurtured and raised. Ungrateful boy!"

Sir Julius looked longingly at the door, wondering how he could get out of the room without appearing rude. "I . . . erm—"

"This is how he repays me! This is how much he thinks of his father's name . . . of his father's inheritance! Are that woman's children to run free at Holme? Is her blood to taint the Holkham name for future generations?"

"I . . . what a fetching bonnet that is, my lady."

"And I am just expected to sit back and let him throw himself away on a . . . a harpy? No and no!"

"No, my lady."

"I will not let that woman wreck my son's future. I will not stand idly by and let that odious creature take him from us. Oh, no!" said her ladyship. "She will find out exactly what I am made of!"

CHAPTER 12

Miss Blakelow was busy polishing the copper late one morning the following week when John appeared before her to inform her that his lordship had called and was waiting in the parlor to take her out in his curricle for a drive.

The lady's first inclination was to ask John to inform the earl that it was not convenient and that he should come back again another day. She had started to relay this message to her butler, but when he gave her one of his looks, the one that contained that perfect mix of skepticism and "tell him yourself," she was persuaded to give it up. She untied her apron, hastily put on the cap and spectacles, and went into the parlor.

He was standing by the fireplace, talking to Aunt Blakelow, when she came in, and Miss Blakelow did not miss the swift but thorough assessment the man gave her figure as she appeared. She lifted her chin and wrapped her arms protectively across her bosom, but on seeing the gleam of amusement that stole into his eyes, unfolded them again.

"Good morning, my lord," she said, clasping her hands before her. "Did you have a good trip to London?"

"Certainly I did, thank you," he replied. "How do you do? Your aunt has just persuaded me to take you out for a drive, and I have to say that I think it a capital idea. It is a glorious day, and I have a fancy to see the far side of the lake where there is a grotto, or so I have been told. My curricle awaits, ma'am, if you would send a maid for your shawl and bonnet?"

"I told you before that I am too busy to drive out with you."

"What nonsense. Do you never stop for luncheon? Even paragons of womanly virtue such as you have to eat, and I have brought a picnic. Now, what say you to that?"

"Of course she will be pleased to go with you, Lord Marcham," said Aunt Blakelow, ignoring the glare she received from her niece.

Miss Blakelow gritted her teeth. "I don't wish to appear rude, my lord—"

"Good, that settles it then," he replied promptly. "Go and fetch your bonnet."

"Do you ever take 'no' for an answer?" she complained.

He grinned. "Not when I want something. I'll wait for you here."

For some inexplicable reason, it took her an age to decide what to wear. It was a warm autumn day, and yet she tugged on a thick winter pelisse because it was smarter than the old cape she habitually wore. She changed her gown three times and ended up back in the one that she had been wearing earlier. She put on her glasses and a hideous bonnet that she had only bought because it completely hid her hair and cast her face into shadow, which greatly added to her straitlaced image. By the time she was dressed to her own satisfaction, it was fully forty-five minutes before she finally returned to the parlor.

"Well," he said as she entered the room. He stood by the window, impatiently slapping his gloves against his thighs. "If this is how you treat your beaux, it is not surprising that you have never married."

"I don't have any beaux," she said.

"No, and I don't wonder at it. You probably frightened them all away with that bonnet."

Miss Blakelow took a firm grip on her temper. "Are we going for a drive, my lord, or not?"

"Yes, if my horses have not expired through boredom in the last hour. I was beginning to wonder if you had become stuck in your own chamber pot."

Aunt Blakelow had a coughing fit, which sounded suspiciously like laughter.

"I have not kept you waiting above forty-five minutes," Miss Blakelow said, with a defiant toss of her head.

"Only because you did not have the nerve to keep me waiting a full hour. But I'll wager you were tempted to try it to teach me a lesson, weren't you?"

Miss Blakelow lowered her eyes as a guilty flush stole into her cheeks. "I was undecided as to whether I needed a shawl or a spencer or a pelisse."

"So instead you chose that great thick redingote, which I'm sure is just the thing for a freezing winter day . . . but in the warm sunshine outside, you will be wishing it at Jericho within the space of five minutes."

"Have you finished?" she demanded.

"And when we are married, such a hideous bonnet as that will be forbidden. As will be those spectacles," he remarked, moving to the door and holding it open for her. "In fact, I may cheerfully burn half your wardrobe and not repine. Good day, Aunt Blakelow. I shall return your niece forthwith."

It was on the tip of Miss Blakelow's tongue to retort in kind, to lash out that he was dressed like a court card, but he looked so immaculate, so elegant, and so handsome that the words died upon her lips. He led her out to his waiting curricle, and before she had time to set one booted foot upon the step, he had placed his hands on her waist and lifted her high up onto the seat as if she were nothing but a featherweight. Her stomach performed a perfect backflip as her feet left the ground, or maybe it was because his hands held her so firmly that she felt funny inside. She opened her mouth in surprise and to protest, but before she could form the words, he had set her down and removed his hands. He looked up at her, a devil lurking in his eyes, daring her to protest.

"Yes, Miss Blakelow?" he asked softly.

"Nothing, my lord."

A smile curved the corners of his mouth as he walked away to the rear of the equipage, said something to his groom, and then swung up onto the seat beside her. He took the reins in his gloved hands while the groom jumped onto the seat behind them, and in a moment they were bowling down the drive.

"And so, Miss Blakelow, show me it all."

"I beg your pardon?"

"I do not wish to see the beauty spots that your aunt was pleased to show me the other day. I wish to see the warts."

She stared at him as if she could hardly believe her ears. "Do you have a hankering to see an estate in decline, my lord? Do you have a desire to see a property ravaged of all its wealth by a man trying to pay off a gambling debt?"

"Certainly I do."

"I can show you tumbledown barns in bad state of repair, farmers' cottages with leaking roofs, and rotting crops in the fields because there is no one left to harvest them."

"Then by all means do so."

There was a silence.

"I wish that I could believe you to be in earnest," she said seriously.

"I am very much in earnest. How am I to know what is to be done at Thorncote if no one will show me where the problems are?"

She flashed him a smile. "Then turn left at the end of the drive."

❧

"Well, what do you think?" Miss Blakelow asked him a good while later as they sat on the grass in the warm October sunshine by the lake, eating from the picnic basket that his lordship had brought. She reached into the basket and took out a pastry, pulling it apart with her nimble fingers.

They had driven the length and breadth of the estate, inspecting rickety bridges, crumbling walls, and broken fences, talking to the tenants and discussing plans for improvement. Miss Blakelow was cautiously optimistic that she had persuaded him to help at last and stole a furtive glance across at his profile.

Lord Marcham shrugged and gazed over at his horses, which were grazing nearby, the groom in attendance. "I think that Thorncote is in a very bad way," he answered.

"Yes," she agreed thoughtfully, nibbling a piece of her pastry.

"I also think that it would take a very large sum of money and an army of men to bring it back into good order. And I am asking myself why I should put myself to the trouble."

Miss Blakelow stared at him, her temper bubbling under the surface. *Put yourself to the trouble,* she thought angrily. *Yes, it's much easier to turn your back, isn't it, my lord?* She gave herself a mental shake and took herself firmly in hand; getting angry with him was not likely to get her what she wanted. "Because you will make a tidy profit when the estate comes to the good again," she pointed out calmly.

"And what if it does not come to the good?"

"It will."

"What if you disappear to get married and leave the running of the estate to your brother? Who by all I hear is just as hopeless with money as your esteemed father. Who will care about my money then?"

"I won't get married," she said, staring at her lap.

"How do you know you won't? You are still young. There are still . . . opportunities for you."

She pulled a face at the thought of being in any way physically intimate with Mr. Peabody. "Thorncote is my home. I will live here for as long as I am able."

"And what if you fall in love, Georgie?" he asked quietly, watching her.

She ripped apart another piece of her pastry with a scornful laugh. "I have done with love long ago."

"And what if love has not done with you?"

"It has, I can assure you. If this is your indirect way of asking me if I mean to marry Mr. Peabody . . . ?"

He shrugged. "It might be."

"I could not accept Mr. Peabody. As I have told him on numerous occasions."

His lordship raised a brow. "Is Mr. Peachybody an overly ardent suitor, Miss Blakelow?" he guessed. "Would you like me to have a word with him?"

"There is no need."

"Has he touched you?"

She looked uncomfortable and did not entirely answer his question. "I believe William has warned him off."

"Your brother is good for something then," Lord Marcham muttered, picking up a plum and biting into one end of it.

"And what do you mean by that remark?"

"Did Peabody insult you, ma'am?" he asked again.

"He . . . he tried to kiss me . . . that's all."

"Where is your brother? Why is he not here to defend you from such men, and I may add, help you to rescue Thorncote?"

"William lives in London."

"And shows no concern that his estate is about to be taken from him," said his lordship scornfully. "I have been criticized for many things in my time, but never apathy where Holme Park is concerned. Have you written to him?"

"Yes."

"And?"

"And he has fallen in love."

"I'll bet," said his lordship caustically. "No doubt he has been fortunate enough to fall in love with a lady of means. How very timely."

"If you already knew, my lord, I wonder why you took the trouble of asking me."

"To see if you'd tell me the truth. I had the dubious pleasure of seeing your brother while in town last week. He wanted to call me out."

"Call you out?" she repeated incredulously.

"Yes. The wretched boy seems to think me responsible for the death of your father. He threw a glass of wine in my face and demanded that I meet him."

"Did you meet him? Pray tell me! Oh, sir, tell me that you did not."

She clutched at his arm and found to her dismay that she had grasped his hand instead. He looked down at her hand on his as if her touch surprised him, and she hastily withdrew it.

"Of course I didn't," he replied, somewhat distractedly. "You do have a good opinion of me, don't you? Well, whatever you may think of me, I have not yet resorted to the murder of children."

She blushed, aware that by touching him so casually and familiarly, she had overstepped the unspoken boundary of her own making. His eyes finally rose to hers, and she gulped at the message she read there.

"But he threw wine in your face . . ." she said, pressing on with the conversation in an attempt to divert his attention away from her embarrassment.

"Yes, and I took great pleasure in kicking him down the stairs for his trouble."

"Oh, you brute! You hurt him."

"I sincerely hope so. And allow me to warn you that should your revolting brother come sniffing around my youngest sister, I *will* hurt him and take great pleasure in doing so. A fortune hunter," said the earl. "What truly repulsive relatives you have, Miss Blakelow. Tell me why I should sink my blunt to rescue such a selfish object as your brother?"

"Because it is his inheritance, my lord, and I would have thought that you of all people would understand that."

"I do understand it. But what I fail to understand is why you care more for that than your brother does."

There was a silence as a flock of geese flew overhead. Miss Blakelow looked down at her hands.

"If I were to consider helping you . . ." continued the earl, "I would not wish to have Mr. Bateman living here at my expense."

Her head snapped up and she stared at him. "What do you mean?"

"You know very well what I mean."

"Mr. Bateman has not yet asked me to marry him," she said, in a small voice. "And I do not believe that he has any such thought in his head. I think him in love with Marianne but too afraid to broach the subject with her."

"He seems very concerned with your business. What would you say if he asked you?"

"That, my lord, is none of your business."

"I think that if I am to invest my money in this place, then it is very much my business. If I were to give you the money, it would be as much an investment in *you* as Thorncote. You love this place. You are the driving force. As soon as you leave, the estate will fall back into disrepair."

"And I say again, that I will not leave. I have nowhere else to go."

"Have you not, Miss Blakelow?" he asked softly. He picked up a plum and pushed the smooth skin gently against her lips until they parted under the pressure. She was so surprised by the sudden intimacy of the move that she stared up at him in confusion, her eyes searching his, her heart pounding hard in her breast. His hand was warm. The touch of his fingers against her cheek had set off a quivering in her belly that was alien yet achingly familiar. She had forgotten this. She had forgotten the thrill of a man's touch. It unfurled inside her, like a seedling growing toward the light. Desire. She had not felt it in a very long time. She wondered if he felt it too. Women were two-a-penny to a man like him. Did he feel this umbilical cord of connection between them, or was he merely toying with her, showing her the power he had over her? For all her grown-up good sense, part of her wanted nothing more than to throw caution to the wind, feel his arms around her, his lips on hers—propriety be damned. So much for keeping a safe distance, she thought. So much for that protective wall she had built around her heart. It had been breached easily, by nothing more than the casual brush of his hand.

"Bite, Miss Blakelow," he coaxed, his eyes on hers, and for once he was not teasing. The strange, intense heat in his gaze was unfamiliar to her and she questioned it. Could it truly be her who inspired such a look?

The moment was too much. It was too suggestive, too intimate. The longing in her heart had been too long ignored to be allowed free rein now. She pushed his hand away and stood up hurriedly.

"It's getting late," she said, dusting her skirts. "I should go."

⁂

"Well?" asked Aunt Blakelow on Miss Blakelow's return.

"He is considering investing in Thorncote," she replied, tugging the ribbons of her bonnet undone. "But he does not like William."

"Not like him? I cannot imagine why he would. William has hardly endeared himself to his lordship by blaming him for your father's death. Besides, his lordship moves in very different circles, you know."

"Yes . . . I'm sure he does."

Aunt Blakelow saw the consternation on her niece's face and said, "Georgie? What is it?"

Miss Blakelow sighed and flung down her bonnet on the table. "William tried to call Marcham out."

"What?" shrieked her aunt.

"I know, I know . . . the wretched boy is determined to ruin all of us."

"Call him out? But why?"

Miss Blakelow told her aunt all that Lord Marcham had told her.

"Has William been gambling again?" asked Aunt Blakelow, aghast.

"Yes, I think so. He aspires to Marcham's set but does not have anything like enough money to survive in that company. There is a very good chance that we will have another spendthrift in the family, every bit as irresponsible as Papa was."

"Have you heard from William?" asked her aunt.

Miss Blakelow took off the spectacles. "Yes, a short note only to say that he has fallen in love with the most ravishing creature, who also just happens to have a fortune of thirty thousand pounds."

"Oh," said Aunt Blakelow dejectedly.

"Was there ever anything so vexing? Just when it seems that Marcham is beginning to become interested . . ."

"What can we do?"

"I will write to William once again and request him to come home. Thank heavens that some of the money was put into trust for him when his mother was alive. She at least did not want for sense."

"No indeed," agreed Aunt Blakelow. "Dear Jane was an excellent woman. And . . . and you and his lordship . . . ?"

Miss Blakelow's eyes flew to her aunt's, and a guilty color stole into her cheeks. "I beg your pardon?"

"Are you . . . I mean . . . you seem to be—"

"No."

"I thought perhaps . . ."

"Well don't. Don't think anything."

Miss Blakelow remembered their picnic and her embarrassment as he had fed her the fruit. She shouldered the memory away, uncomfortable with that moment of tension between them, as if a thread had been drawn out to snapping point. She had been aware of his eyes, the close proximity of his body, the warmth of his hand, the soft pressure of the fruit between her lips. She reddened painfully.

"Did he kiss you?" asked Aunt Blakelow, watching her closely.

Miss Blakelow stood up. "Aunt! How could you ask such a thing? Of course he didn't!"

"Do you wish that he had?"

Miss Blakelow was momentarily robbed of speech. She put her hands on her hips and stared in disbelief at her aunt. "No, ma'am, I do not!" she managed.

"Be careful, Georgie," warned the older woman. "He is not a boy."

"Do you think that I don't know that?" demanded her niece hotly.

"He knows exactly what he's doing. He's as adept at playing a woman as he is at playing cards."

"Dear Aunt, do you think that I am foolish enough to let him seduce me?"

"I do not know what may happen when you are alone with a man like him."

"We were not alone. His groom was there," said Miss Blakelow, glaring at her. "And nothing happened."

"No? Then why are you so angry?"

"Nothing happened," she repeated. "Do you think me so weak as to be in danger now, after all these years?"

"I think you sensible enough to keep him at arm's length," said Aunt Blakelow, "but I also think you are lonely enough to fall for his charm. And let us not beat about the bush; he has plenty of charm."

"I am a grown woman, Aunt. I am no longer a silly young girl whose head is turned by a handsome man."

"Possibly not. But he is every inch the rake that the world knows him to be. And if he has decided that he wants you, then he will not give up until he has achieved his goal."

Miss Blakelow shook her head in disbelief. "I am going upstairs."

"By all means. But think on what I have said. He knows it has been a long time since your heart has been touched. And he knows your pride is vulnerable to a little male attention."

Miss Blakelow stormed out of the room, too incensed to speak. She ran up to her bedchamber, threw herself on her bed, and buried her face into her pillows. The scene at the picnic came back to haunt her. His eyes on hers, the air crackling with animal attraction that she could no more deny than the need to breathe.

That he was out merely to seduce her was a thought that had already occurred to Miss Blakelow. The thought that he was pretending to show an interest in her merely as part of some game was so lowering that she wanted to cry. She might be an old maid, but she was still a woman with feelings, and she was not stupid. She knew that he was toying with her. She buried her face deeper amongst the pillows, wishing that the bed would swallow her whole.

Lord Marcham had come too close. It was time to retreat to the keep, draw up the bridge, and wait it out until the siege was over. With any luck he would get bored and go away.

CHAPTER 13

"OH, LORD, HERE HE comes again!" groaned Jack, watching the ponderous Mr. Peabody as he made his way toward them across the front lawn. The buttons of his coat seemed to sigh under the strain. "He's always showing up here unannounced and uninvited. George, you are not seriously going to marry the fellow, are you?"

Miss Blakelow, seated on the bench under the willow tree, laughed as she set another stitch in her embroidery. "No, you ridiculous boy, I am not."

"Thank the Lord for that. I could not bear to come and visit you if you did. All that prosing and lecturing and sermonizing is enough to send a fellow mad."

"But he does seem particularly keen on you, Georgie," said Marianne, "which is flattering, to be sure."

"Is it?" asked Catherine doubtfully. "I'd rather have Lord Marcham."

"Kitty!" gasped Marianne. "Of all the improper things to say!"

"I meant given the available choices," she qualified quickly and then colored. "He has a much better figure than Peabrain."

"And he doesn't have wind like a cannon going off either," put in Ned.

This comment naturally produced a fit of the giggles, which even Miss Blakelow found hard to resist. She turned her head away to hide a smile as she was momentarily diverted by the thought of Lord Marcham doing anything so inelegant.

"How do you know he doesn't?" demanded Lizzy, her face alight with laughter.

Miss Blakelow put aside her embroidery. "If you cannot speak in a way befitting a young gentleman, Ned Blakelow, then I suggest that you do not speak at all," she said severely.

"But he thinks we're all deaf!" complained the young man.

"What did I just say?" asked Miss Blakelow.

Ned colored and looked away moodily.

"Mr. Peabody has been very kind to us, and we must show him the respect due to a friend of Father's," said Miss Blakelow, "however trying that may be at times."

"He tried to kiss you, George, have you forgotten that?" demanded Jack, throwing a ball up in the air and catching it again one-handed.

Miss Blakelow silently cursed her youngest brother as the rest of her family assimilated this new fact with horror. William and Jack had caught Mr. Peabody in the act six months ago, and Miss Blakelow had sworn them both to secrecy.

"He did *what?*" demanded Ned, sitting bolt upright on the grass.

"Thank you, Jack," murmured Miss Blakelow wryly.

Her young brother flushed and looked guilty. "Sorry, I forgot."

"Mr. Peabody?" breathed Marianne, staring at her eldest sister in wonder. "Oh, George, how horrible."

"I never thought he had it in him," said Lizzy, plucking a blade of grass beside the blanket on which she was sitting.

"He probably had to lie down for half an hour afterward," put in Kitty, giggling.

"He certainly did, because William landed him a facer," Jack confided.

"Oh, I wish that I had seen that!" said Ned, his eyes gleaming.

"It was a beautiful jab. An uppercut to the jaw, which shook the old fellow's bone box, I can tell you."

"Can we talk about something else?" asked Miss Blakelow in pained accents. "He is nearly upon us and will hear you."

"Not him. Deaf as a post. Did his whiskers tickle, Georgie?" asked Ned, grinning.

Miss Blakelow picked up a conker and threw it at him.

She stood up as Mr. Peabody approached and forced a smile. "How do you do, sir? It is such a lovely day that we thought we would come and make the best of the sunshine."

"Good day, Miss Blakelow. What a pretty picture you make to be sure. Quite enchanting, my dear," he said, taking her hand and petting it. "Of course, I should have guessed that you would be outside on such a day as this. You do love to be outdoors, do you not? I went to the house, and your servant told me that you were not at home. And then I chanced to see young Jack there sneaking out of the door, and I wondered if you had all come out to take the air."

"Yes," agreed Miss Blakelow with a smile, "we always come out here when we can."

"What my sister actually means is that we saw you coming down the drive in your gig, and we ran out here as quickly as we could to avoid you," said Ned in such a low voice that only his siblings heard him. He caught Georgiana's eye and, chastened, stood up with his cricket bat. "Come on, Jack, let's hit a few balls."

Miss Blakelow watched enviously as all her brothers and sisters hastily departed, leaving her entirely alone with Mr. Peabody. She begged him to be seated and took the other end of the bench, placing her embroidery between them.

"How is your mother, Mr. Peabody?" she asked, desperate for a topic of conversation.

"She is well, thank you, ma'am. And your aunt? I do not see her with you today?"

"No, she is visiting friends in Loughton."

There was an awkward silence, both of them watching as Jack and Ned stripped off their jackets, folded them, and cast them on the ground to use as wickets. Ned took the ball and ran in to bowl to his brother, who was poised catlike at the makeshift stumps, the bat in the air.

"Miss Blakelow," he began.

"Oh, do you see that bird? How pretty it is! I think it is a crested hornbill . . . thing."

Mr. Peabody looked dubiously at the stubby brown bird. "I think it's a thrush, ma'am."

"Oh . . . but such a pretty thrush . . . Oh, Mr. Peabody, please don't," she begged as he took her hand.

"Dearest, most beloved creature. I must be allowed to speak. You are always surrounded by your relatives—this is my only opportunity to speak to you alone. It is not such a place where I would wish to make such a declaration, but if it must be, then I am not one to cavil. You must be aware of my intentions; indeed I believe the whole of Loughton may know what they are. I have admired you from the very first moment I saw you—well, almost the first moment . . . It was the day you came to Goldings to meet Mother, and you were so kind and dutiful that I knew then that I had to have you for my wife. Adorable creature, say that you will be mine. Indeed you must, for anyone may know that Thorncote is by no means certain to stay in your family. And where will you go then? You need a home, Miss Blakelow—Georgiana, if I may?—and you and I both know that 'our little secret' makes it unlikely that you will find happiness with another man."

Miss Blakelow tried to withdraw her hand. Her father, bless his rotting soul, had seen fit to divulge some of her past to Mr. Peabody during an evening when they had played cards together, as they frequently did, and Sir William had grown more inebriated as the night drew on. That Mr. Peabody should be privy to the most intimate details of her personal life felt like a violation to Miss Blakelow, and every time he referred to "our little secret," she cringed and grew angry and wished to tell him to go to a very warm place. She wondered how Mr. Peabody would like his dirty linen washed in public and examined by the entire world.

"And I will be a most attentive husband." He took her hand to his lips and covered it in moist kisses. Miss Blakelow shuddered with revulsion.

"Please, Mr. Peabody, you are already aware of my feelings on the subject," she said, trying to pull her hand away.

Jack took a swipe with the bat, and there was a sharp cracking noise as the ball was hit down the hill toward the house. A flurry of Blakelows chased after it, and Jack ran happily between the make-shift wickets, leaving their eldest sister entirely alone with her suitor.

She tried to remove her hand. "Mr. Peabody . . . I told you on the last occasion that I—"

"My angel," he said, clasping her to his breast. His breath was warm on her cheek, and he smelled vaguely of camphor.

"Mr. Peabody, I must insist that you let me go," said Miss Blakelow firmly, turning her face away as her hand found her embroidery on the bench between them.

"I must have you," he declared, covering her faces with kisses. "We must be married immediately. I must make you my own in every way." His hand slid to her breast and squeezed it.

Miss Blakelow's hand found the needle, prized it loose of the material, and plunged the end sharply into his thigh. The result was immediate and effective. He yelped and sprang up from the bench, clutching his leg. The siblings paused in their game of cricket and turned around and stared at the sight of Mr. Peabody practically hopping on one leg.

"My dear Miss Blakelow, what have I done to deserve such treatment from you?" he asked reproachfully.

"I would have thought *that* was obvious," remarked a wry voice from behind them.

Miss Blakelow and her suitor whirled around to find Lord Marcham leaning nonchalantly against the trunk of the tree, his arms folded across his chest, a hint of a smile upon his lips.

"You!" exploded Mr. Peabody, his already red face turning purple.

"Your servant, Peapod," replied his lordship, bowing slightly. "Your servant, Miss Blakelow. What a glorious afternoon, is it not? I don't blame you for leaving the house in favor of the country-side in such unseasonably warm weather. But as your neighbor and friend, ma'am, I must counsel you against sitting entirely alone with a strange gentleman. It is really not the done thing, you know."

"Strange gentleman?" repeated Mr. Peabody, outraged. "I have been coming to this house for years!"

"Then you should know that it is highly improper for a gentle-man to be alone with such a delicate female as Miss Blakelow."

She glared at him. "Indeed? No doubt you would not object half so strongly if the gentleman in question were you?"

"Oh, no, not then, Miss Blakelow, but I am an entirely different case," agreed the earl. "And as your prospective bridegroom, you will allow me to have a vested interest in . . . er . . . keeping your charms entirely for myself."

Miss Blakelow, still holding her embroidery needle, was seriously tempted to attack a fleshy part of his lordship's anatomy with it. She continued to glare up into his dancing eyes. "You are *not* my prospective bridegroom, and who I choose to see or be alone with is entirely my own affair."

He raised an amused brow at that. "Is that so, Miss Blakelow? Would you like me to leave you alone with Mr. Peaham?"

She stared at him and the message in her eyes was clear: *don't you dare.*

He smiled affably. "I see that you understand the situation tolerably well. We will say no more about it."

"What are you doing here, my lord?" demanded Peabody, still rubbing his thigh.

"Attending to my property," replied the earl.

"Thorncote is yours then?"

His lordship smiled. "Thorncote and everything in it," he said with a glint in his eye.

Mr. Peabody flushed purple. "I see that I am wasting my time here."

"Good. I'm glad you begin to understand," said the earl.

Mr. Peabody bowed stiffly to Miss Blakelow. "It is clear to me, ma'am, that you prefer the company of this . . . this scoundrel to a man of decency. You must allow me to say that I am disappointed in you. A dalliance with a man of his sort can only lead you into the sort of situation that would be detrimental to your reputation and your character. I warn you against it most strongly. Marriage to this man would make you miserable."

"Not as miserable as if she married you," put in the earl, leisurely taking a pinch of snuff and putting it to one nostril.

Miss Blakelow shot a smoldering look at the earl before turning to her wounded suitor. "Indeed you mistake me, sir. I have no intention of marrying Lord Marcham. I assure you that he is only saying those things to provoke me. It seems to amuse him to pretend that there is an engagement between us. Why not come in with us and have some tea? Aunt Blakelow will have returned by now."

"Capital idea," said the earl, "then you, Peahead, can talk to the aunt and I may have Miss Blakelow all to myself."

Mr. Peabody ignored this interruption, raising himself onto the balls of his feet as he invariably did when he was giving a sermon. "And this is the man whom you prefer?" he demanded. "You choose this *rake* over a man of decency, of principle . . . in short, a *gentleman*?"

"Rake I may be," said the earl, putting away his snuffbox, "but I have never yet forced my attentions on a gently bred woman. And by the very familiar embrace that I have just witnessed, it seems that you, Peabrain, cannot say the same."

Mr. Peabody's eyes bulged as if they would pop from his head. "You, sir, are a disgrace!"

Lord Marcham yawned and examined his fingernails. "Has he gone yet, my love?"

"Any woman of high moral principle, as I had thought you to be, would recoil at such a union."

"Mr. Peabody, I can assure you, I have no intention of marrying anyone," said Miss Blakelow roundly. "Please believe me when I tell you that marriage to Lord Marcham is of little interest to me."

Mr. Peabody puffed out his chest as if she had not spoken. "You have been charmed by a pretty face. I had not thought it possible. I had thought, Miss Blakelow, that you were a woman of superior sense, but I see now that I was wrong. I count myself fortunate to have escaped from such an unhappy union. I therefore announce that I have withdrawn my offer. I will now take my leave of you." He bowed stiffly, straightened his cravat, and strode away.

"Hurry back, won't you?" said the earl.

Miss Blakelow whirled on her lordly neighbor. "Are you satisfied?"

A wicked glint stole into his eyes. "I could be . . . if you were to give me such an embrace as you just gave him."

She glowered at him and felt her cheeks color but was too angry to speak.

"What?" he asked, laughing as he spread his hands.

"You have upset Mr. Peabody."

"No, *you* did that. Something to do with a needle, I believe."

"How long have you been standing there?" Miss Blakelow demanded.

"Long enough," he replied coolly, admiring her figure as she bent to fold up the blanket that Lizzy had been sitting on.

"And you didn't think to make your presence known?"

"That would have been rude in the extreme. Mr. Peabody was making his declaration. It probably took the poor man a month to work up the courage."

"You feel sorry for him?" she asked incredulously.

He shrugged. "I feel sympathy for any man attempting to make you an offer—I know from experience that it is not for the fainthearted."

"You . . . oh, how I loathe you! You stood there while he was . . . while he was . . ."

"Pressing his attentions?" he suggested sweetly.

"Yes . . . and you did nothing. You did not lift a finger to intervene when you must have known that his suit is not welcome to me."

"How was I to know that it was unwelcome? You have hardly made me your confidant, have you?"

"You stood there and listened, knowing all the while that his kiss was of all things the most repugnant to me. What if he had gone further? Would you have stood there and watched?"

"Oh, I would have stepped in then, but you did not look as if you needed my help. You repelled him most efficiently. In fact, I consider myself fortunate to have learned a valuable lesson. When kissing Miss Blakelow, ensure that any sharp objects—needles, pins, nails, and such like—are out of arm's reach."

She folded up her embroidery and threw it into the basket.

"Dearest, most beloved creature," he said softly, laughter quivering in his voice.

She glared at him. "Don't."

He clutched his hands to his breast in perfect imitation of Mr. Peabody. "My angel."

She wrestled with the urge to laugh and conquered it. "Lord Marcham, you are the most detestable, odious man alive."

"Adorable creature, say that you will be mine," he begged.

She threw a cushion at him, and he dodged it neatly, grinning broadly. "I must say, he did talk a lot for a man passionately in love. He should have kissed you," recommended his lordship. "You can't berate a man when your mouth is otherwise occupied."

"No, he should not have kissed me," she flashed, blushing hotly. "I cannot think of anything more repulsive. Except, of course, kissing *you*."

He smiled, unperturbed. "Naturally."

She glanced up at him over the top of her spectacles as she bent to pick up another blanket. "Why are you here, my lord? Shouldn't you be fleecing some poor man at the card table or something equally noble?"

"That was yesterday, ma'am," he replied glibly. "I always fleece men of their property on a Wednesday. Thursdays are for flirting outrageously with one's neighbors."

"And Fridays?" she asked, shaking off the other blanket.

"Oh, drinking oneself into a stupor," he said, smiling, "but not *all* day—one does need to eat, you know."

"And Saturday you spend all day in bed," she put in before she had given herself permission to speak the words aloud. She had meant that he would spend all day in bed to recover from a day's drinking, but suddenly realizing how it could be misconstrued, she stopped and flushed to the roots of her hair. Judging by the look of unholy amusement that came into the earl's eyes, he had *definitely* misconstrued it. She cursed her unruly tongue. Why did she always manage to put her foot in her mouth when he was near?

"My dear Miss Blakelow, I'm shocked," he murmured.

"You know very well what I meant," she said in a stifled voice.

"Do I?" he replied, his eyes dancing. "I hardly dare hope that you were making me an offer."

"You," she choked, "are deliberately trying to make me blush."

"True," he agreed smoothly, watching the delicious pink tinge that colored her cheeks, "but I assure you it is utterly irresistible."

"My lord Marcham, you must allow me to tell you: aware though I am of your . . . your lifestyle and your . . . how shall I say . . . *misdemeanors*, it is highly improper of you to speak to me of such things as—" She broke off, realizing into what dangerous waters her tongue was leading her.

"What things?" he asked, his face the picture of innocence.

"That I would . . . that we would . . . oh, you know very *well* what things!"

"That you would beg me to go to bed with you?" he asked, his voice quivering with laughter.

Miss Blakelow closed her eyes in pained silence. "Did you have to say that quite so loudly?"

"Given that you were a key witness at one of my infamous parties, I would doubt you are as offended by our conversation as you pretend to be. But let me reassure you on one thing: you would not need to beg me—I'd happily spend all day in bed with you."

She turned away to hide her face, acutely embarrassed. "You—oh, go away!"

He laughed and folded his arms. "Come here."

She eyed him suspiciously. "No."

His lips twitched. "Miss Blakelow, you really should try to improve your manners, you know. They really are not at all the thing. I regret that I find it necessary to hint, but you should be aware when going about in company, it is not at all the done thing to be quite so blunt. A few words in the manner of beating around the bush would, I am persuaded, serve you better. An approved response might have been, 'No, thank you, my lord.' Now why don't you try it? These manners may seem strange to you at first but it will get easier in time."

She listened to this in long-suffering silence. "My lord, if you do not wish me to deal you the same treatment I gave to Mr. Peabody, then I suggest you desist baiting me."

"A truly terrifying prospect to be sure, but as you have now put away your stitchery, I feel tolerably safe. Well, if you won't come to me, then I will have to come to you."

She balked a little as he drew near, but she stood her ground, her heart pounding a little strangely as he came to stand directly before her, his body no more than a foot away from hers. She glanced up at him warily as he reached out his hands and, before she knew what he was about, gently pulled the spectacles from her nose. So convinced was she that he had been going to kiss her that this outcome took her completely by surprise, and she felt excessively foolish, like a green young girl, and wondered if her thoughts had played out across her face.

He watched her with a funny little smile as he took his handkerchief from his pocket and began to clean her spectacles. "Mr. Peabottom's attentions have smudged your glasses," he said.

"Oh," she said, turning her face away in confusion. She felt naked without her spectacles and hardly knew where to look as she felt his eyes on her.

"Why do you hide your face from me?" he asked.

She forced a laugh. "I . . . I don't."

"You always turn away. Do you feel so vulnerable without your glasses?"

"Please, may I have them back?"

"What did that fellow mean 'our little secret'?" inquired the earl.

She blinked at him, giving her best impression of an innocent wide-eyed look.

Lord Marcham frowned. "He said that 'our little secret' would prevent you from finding happiness with another man. What did he mean?"

She colored and looked away. "Nothing. Mr. Peabody pretends an intimacy with this family that is entirely false. He was a confidant of my father's, and as such he makes it his business to know all our business, whether we wish him to or not."

"I see . . . but you did not answer the question, Miss Blakelow," he said gently.

"May I have my glasses back now?" she asked, disturbed by the watchful expression in his eyes.

"Where do I know you from?" he mused.

"I . . . I beg your pardon, my lord?"

"The first time you came to Holme I was left with the distinct impression that we had met before."

Miss Blakelow's heart began to pound sickeningly. "Certainly we have," she managed as coolly as she was able. "We are neighbors, after all, my lord."

He shook his head. "I remember you from somewhere else . . . and I cannot quite place it."

"Perhaps I look like another lady of your acquaintance?" she suggested.

"Perhaps," he agreed.

"I am sure you have been acquainted with so many bookish females over the years that we all look the same to you; it must be all that time you spend in church praying for forgiveness."

"Perhaps you are right," he agreed, a smile in his eyes. "Because my behavior is such that I need a lot of forgiving, isn't that right?"

"Quite so."

"Here, Miss Blakelow, are your glasses."

"Thank you," she replied, lifting her hands to take the spectacles from him. Her fingers brushed against his for the briefest of moments, and she felt a tug of attraction so strong that it robbed her of the ability to think or to even breathe.

"How old are you?" he demanded suddenly, frowning, his mind still evidently puzzling over where they had met before.

She looked up at him. "That is an impertinent question, sir."

"You cannot be more than five and thirty, surely. To be sure you are not in the first bloom, but you are not yet in your dotage."

"Thank you," she muttered. Miss Blakelow, who was in fact nine and twenty, took this comment in bad part. Then, sensing his amusement, she looked at him and saw the mischievous gleam in his eyes and knew that he said it deliberately for revenge.

"Yes, Miss Blakelow, I am that outrageous, and if you come to know me any better, you will realize that trying to shame me does not work, because I don't have any scruples. Now, you may leave your shawl here. You cannot play cricket with that thing around your shoulders."

CHAPTER 14

THE EARL OF MARCHAM, dressed in a rich brocade dressing gown at nine the following morning, looked up from his newspaper as the sound of an almighty crash came from the hallway beyond the breakfast parlor, where he was seated. He winced and looked at his butler, who was clearing the table of the breakfast things. "Davenham, what was that racket?" he asked in pained accents.

"I believe it is your lordship's sisters, sir. Lady St Michael and Miss Holkham—they have come to stay," said that faithful servant in a quaking voice.

"Both of them?" he demanded.

"Yes, my lord."

"The devil they have," the earl said, pushing back his chair by its armrests and striding across the room. He yanked open the door and stepped out into the Great Hall.

A succession of trunks and valises and bandboxes littered the stone floor in every direction. Servants—*his* servants—were running to do the bidding of the tall, imperious woman standing at the foot of the staircase. "You, Brook, is it? Please see to it that my trunk is taken up straight away. I wish to change out of this traveling dress immediately. Davenham? Davenham? Where are you—? Ah, there you are! Please ask the cook to prepare us something to eat immediately. I'm famished and I'm sure Harriet is too. Where is my brother?"

Lord Marcham immediately shrank back into the shadows cast by the staircase. He heard his butler clear his throat. "He went out riding, my lady. He is not expected back for some time."

His lordship, who had in fact already been for his early morning ride, smiled. Good old Davenham. The man always did cover for him in times of need.

"Gone out riding before nine?" repeated Lady St. Michael. "Robbie? What, were there worms in his bed?"

"I believe his lordship rises much earlier these days than when you lived with us, my lady."

"I see. No doubt the influence of his fiancée. Perhaps she is not so bad after all."

Footsteps ran lightly up the front steps and then a girl, no older than eighteen, burst into the hall. "Is Robbie here?" Lady Harriet asked breathlessly, the voluminous plume on her bonnet wafting in the breeze. "I have so much to tell him!"

"He's out riding," said her ladyship bluntly. "Can we get this bandbox out of the way? Someone is going to trip over it in a minute."

Lady Harriet looked around her in wonder. "What a lot of baggage we have! I knew we should not have gone shopping in Oxford. Oh, Robbie, *there* you are! Why are you hiding in the dark? Come here where I can see you."

Lady St. Michael spun around and narrowed her eyes on her brother's rather irritated-looking face. She gave him a knowing look. "Hiding from me, Robert?" she asked sweetly.

He came forward, smiling. "Always, dear Sister. I find it preserves my sanity."

She pecked him upon the cheek. "Coward," she said softly.

"Termagant," he retorted in kind.

"Oh, Robbie," cried Harriet, hurling herself at his chest. "I'm so glad to see you."

He kissed the top of her bonnet, the only part of her available to him, and nearly had his eye taken out by her feather in the process. "Hello minx," he said affectionately.

"Is it true that you are to be married?" she demanded, her big gray eyes searching his face.

He was a little taken aback. *How the devil did she find out about Georgie so quickly? Mama has been busy,* he thought grimly. "I hope to be," he replied.

"What is she like? Is she pretty? Is she as tall as me? Does she sing and play? Does she dance?"

"If you would ask one question at a time, I might stand a chance of answering you. Yes, she is pretty. Yes, she is as tall as you . . . rather taller in fact. And I have absolutely no idea as to her accomplishments."

Lady Harriet looked perplexed. "You have no idea of her accomplishments?" she repeated. "How can you fall in love with someone and not know their interests?"

He carelessly flicked a forefinger against her cheek. "You do it all the time, love."

"Be serious, Robbie. I heard that her family are horrid fortune hunters. Are you certain that she feels for you just as she ought?"

"I think there is every chance that she feels precisely nothing at all for me," he said, guiding her into the library.

"Then why are you wishing to marry her?" asked Lady Harriet as her sister came in and closed the door.

His lordship looked from one sister to the other and sighed. "Don't you wish to change your clothes after such a long journey?"

"In a minute," replied Sarah, Lady St. Michael, folding her arms. "Answer the question."

His eyes settled on one of the paintings without really seeing it. "Because she intrigues me . . . and I haven't felt like that in a long time."

"Then, Robbie," blurted Harriet, "what I have to say will shock you exceedingly. I was at the Grants' ball last week, and I wore my celestial blue crepe with the rosebud trim—and you needn't roll your eyes at me, it is of all your habits the most annoying—and Anne Ellis said that Sir William Blakelow's pockets are to let. She said that he does not have a penny to pay his London debts let alone save Thorncote. He was planning to throw one of his sisters under your nose so that you might marry her. Miss Marianne Blakelow is a trap set for you. I had it from my friend, who had it from her brother, who is a friend of William's."

"Er . . . and why are you telling me this?" asked Lord Marcham, utterly uninterested in anything William Blakelow did or said.

"Why are we . . . ? Because you are going to marry Marianne Blakelow. Don't you see? He is on the hunt for a fortune for his sister."

He stood up and moved behind his desk. "Oh, I am well aware of that. But you seem to be misinformed—which, given that you have just spent several hours in a carriage with Sarah, is surprising. Miss Marianne Blakelow and I are not now, nor have ever been, engaged."

His youngest sister looked from him to Lady St. Michael and back at her brother again. "Not engaged? But you just said that you were!" cried Lady Harriet, much confused.

"I said that I *hoped* to be . . . but the lady I spoke of was not Miss Marianne."

His youngest sister clapped her hands together with glee. "Didn't I tell you, Sarah? Didn't I tell you that Robbie wouldn't marry such a horrid, scheming creature as Marianne Blakelow? Oh, why did you not tell me, Sarah? How infamous of you to keep me in the dark all this time! Who does Robbie wish to marry? Who is she?"

"Keep your voice down—the servants will hear you. She is a worse match for him than ever Lady Emily Holt was," said Lady St. Michael coolly, "which is why I was not going to give credence to the rumor in the carriage with our maids listening in."

"Thank you, Sarah," said the earl, "but I will marry whom I choose, I believe."

"Refreshments are served in the breakfast parlor, my lord," announced Davenham with exquisite timing.

"Davenham?"

"Yes, my lord?"

"Remind me to increase your wage," said a very grateful Lord Marcham.

❧

The earl's discomfort was markedly increased when an hour later his mother arrived, complaining about the damp, and immediately set about stoking up the temperature in the drawing room to such a degree that he could not bear to be inside it with a coat on for longer than five minutes.

"Robbie!" she said, waving him down to kiss her cheek, bestowing upon him a smile so sickly sweet that he immediately became suspicious.

"Mama," he replied, by this time dressed in a beautiful wine-colored coat and pantaloons the color of oatmeal. "To what do I owe the honor?"

"We were worried about you."

"Really?" he asked doubtfully. "Should I be flattered?"

"You know, you wretched boy, that I am worried sick about this proposed match of yours."

His lordship cast his eyes heavenward in a bid for divine assistance. "Please, Mama, let us not discuss it again. I have no wish to argue with you."

"Darling Robert, you were always my favorite, you know," she said.

Lord Marcham struggled to hide his irritation. His mother's tricks had ceased to work on any of her children many years ago once they had realized how adept she was at playing one off against the other.

"Are you warm enough?" asked his lordship rather sharply.

"Yes . . . but—"

"Good, then you won't mind me opening one of the windows, will you?"

The countess spluttered, looking for an answer that wouldn't further set her son's back up, and decided that that particular battle would be better saved for another day.

"Has Sarah told you?" the countess asked.

"Has Sarah told me what?" he asked with a feeling of distinct foreboding.

"Harriet is to have a ball."

"Jolly good. Just don't expect me to come, and she can have as many as she chooses," he returned crisply.

His mother coughed. "Harriet wishes to have a ball . . . *here.*"

"I'll wager she does. I wish to fly to the moon, but it isn't going to come true."

"Now, Robbie, don't be difficult," said his mother. "It was her home too, remember?"

"So it was. But it is my home now, and I do not wish to host a ball," he said, casting himself onto a sofa.

"Why? What objection can you have?" his mother demanded.

"Objections plural."

"Such as what? What pray do men know about organizing a ball?"

"They know about paying for them, ma'am, and that is my first objection: the expense."

"Oh, pooh and nonsense. What is there to pay for in a trifling ball?"

"Flowers. Food. Champagne. Candles. The orchestra. Not to mention the rig you will turn her out in with jewels and the like. Slippers. Stockings, et cetera, et cetera—no, Mama, let me finish. The fuss. The servants have enough work to do in this house without organizing a ball. It needs to be coordinated, and I have no inclination to waste my time in such a fashion. The noise. The night of the ball, I will not be able to sleep with all that racket going on, so I will be forced to attend or go for a prolonged stay with Uncle Angus in the Hebrides because he will be the only one of my relatives not at the ball. The crush. No doubt everyone will want to be there, and you won't be able to get to the food for wading through feathers and waistcoats and sweaty bodies. Not to mention the heat, swooning females everywhere, and matchmaking mamas all dead set on pairing me off with their hatchet-faced daughter. The hassle. Ten to one Harriet will fall in love with some unsuitable wretch, as she always does at these things, and then it will be up to me to play the tyrannical brother and sort it all out. And finally, the infernal giggling. Guaranteed that every female within a fifty-mile radius will be prating on about the wretched ball every minute of the day: what they will wear, how many feathers they will put in their hair, and who they will dance with until every gentleman, including me, is driven to distraction. No, Mama. I do not want a ball in this house."

A short silence greeted this little speech.

"Well, if those are your *only* objections, I cannot see that they are insurmountable," said the countess.

His lordship opened his mouth to say something and then closed it again.

"You may invite Lady Phoebe Halchester," she added as a sweetener. "I heard that you were fond of her . . ."

Lord Marcham nearly threw his teacup at the wall. "I have no interest in inviting Lady Phoebe. But as you bring it up, that is another objection. I would be forced to invite her, for it would look very odd if I did not."

"Has he agreed, Mama?" asked Harriet, popping her head around the door at that moment.

"Nearly, my love, nearly," replied the countess.

His lordship closed his eyes.

"Oh, Robbie, wouldn't it be famous?" cried Harriet, coming to sit on the sofa beside him. She grabbed his hand and held it tightly in her own. "I am so grateful to you for letting Holme host my ball. I think we will have a splendid time. Dearest, best of brothers, I knew that you would agree. And you may bring your mysterious lady too."

"I have not agreed to host your ball, and I realize at this juncture that you may wish to take back the part about 'best and dearest of brothers,' but so be it. I do not have the time or the inclination to host your ball, and I rather think you are much better off using the house in Grosvenor Square. I will happily hand you the keys. There you may invite whom you like, when you like, and arrange it all to your own satisfaction. I will even assist you with paying for it."

Lady Harriet's face fell. Large glistening teardrops welled in her eyes. "Oh, Robbie, you don't mean it."

"I do mean it. And you can forget the waterworks. They won't work on me. I have resisted women ten times as manipulative as you in my time."

"But—"

"No, I'm sorry."

"There you are! I have been looking for you everywhere!" cried Lady St. Michael, who came into the room at that moment. "Heavens, isn't it warm in here? Well, I have just seen the Lady's bedchamber, and I must say, Robbie, it has been very tastefully done. It used to be pink in Mama's day, but I rather like the pale green. It brings a springlike freshness to the room that is very appealing. What decided you upon changing it after all these years?"

"Er . . . it was looking a little tired."

"Well, it looks wonderful now. One would almost think it had something to do with planning for the future Lady Marcham."

Her brother stood up, gave her a tight smile, and walked out.

❧

To escape the three female relatives in his house, a day later, Lord Marcham walked the two miles over to Thorncote in the early afternoon. There he found Miss Blakelow vigorously pulling up weeds from one of the flower beds. On spying him from a distance of one hundred yards, she threw down the trowel, hastily donned her glasses and lace cap, and succeeded in smudging mud halfway across her face.

"You needn't wear them on my account," he called out as he came up to her. "It is patently obvious to me that you don't need them for gardening, so why you think you have to wear them to talk to me is beyond my comprehension."

"And a good day to you too, my lord," she retorted, bending once again to rip up a particularly fine specimen of dandelion. "Are you here to discuss the estate? Or business? Or have you merely come here to annoy me?"

He folded his arms and rested against the wrought-iron gate, leaning back to get a good view as she bent over. "You're in a good mood today," he remarked. "Get out of bed on the wrong side, did we?"

"Any side of the bed in this house is the wrong side," she muttered angrily. "It makes no difference what mood I may be in when I get into bed, but I always wake up to the same problems. Most of which are caused by knowing you."

He frowned thoughtfully. "Come to think of it, which side of the bed *do* you sleep on?"

"Why can that possibly interest you?" she fired at him over her shoulder.

He shrugged. "When we are married, we will share a bed. I thought it only polite to ask the lady which side she preferred."

"You being such a fine gentleman," she said witheringly.

He dazzled her with his smile. "Exactly. I tend to prefer the right side, but I'm prepared to compromise." His eyes drifted slowly down her trim form. "I'm sure you'll make it worth my while."

Miss Blakelow gasped and stood up in a hurry. She came toward him, waving the muddy blade of the trowel under his nose. "You are beyond anything! How dare you speak to me like that?"

He spread his hands, half laughing. "Like what?"

"Like . . . like we are already married, which you know very well that we are not!"

"Come, Georgiana, you cannot tell me that you are innocent of what occurs between a husband and wife?"

"If you do not stop talking to me in that odiously disrespectful manner, I will have you thrown off this estate. Do you understand?"

"I love it when you're angry."

Miss Blakelow thought she might explode. "I am not one of your lightskirts, my lord," she said crossly.

"No indeed, you are not," he murmured, frowning. "What has gotten into you today? You must surely know that I was teasing you? I meant no disrespect."

"You are trying to shock me, aren't you?"

"Not at all," he replied smoothly. "I was merely referring to the very great pleasure to be had when you become my wife."

She clapped her hands over her ears. "Enough! I will not discuss this subject with you, which you must realize is highly repugnant to me."

He bowed. "Then I apologize unreservedly. We will henceforth confine our conversation to the weather and books and your aunt's many health remedies and mending shirts and pruning."

"As you wish."

"And the best cut of meat to be had for a winter broth and other edifying subjects that I cannot at this moment think of."

"Very proper," she approved.

"And I may well die of boredom," he added.

"We can but hope."

"What say you to a discussion about the underlying engineering principles behind Stephenson's locomotive?"

"If we must. I am sure that it would be most instructive."

"Or whether I am corpulent enough that I should start wearing a corset?"

"Stop trying to make me laugh."

"I wish that you would."

She flung down the hand fork she was holding, and it landed vertically with its tines in the soil, spearing the earth. "Nothing amuses you more than to put me out of countenance, does it? You love to mock me and I do not like it."

"I was not *mocking* you; I was *teasing* you. There is a difference," he said patiently. "What is the matter?"

"You and that wretched ball. I have heard nothing else all day but dresses and silks and satins until I am thoroughly sick of it."

He frowned. "What ball?" he asked, although he already guessed.

"*What ball*, he says. For your sister," she said, ripping up a daisy and hurling it at the bucket.

"I am not holding a ball for my sister," he said calmly. "And I told her so in no uncertain terms when she arrived yesterday."

"Well, it is common knowledge in Loughton."

His lordship swore under his breath.

"Exactly!" fumed Miss Blakelow, clawing at a particularly stubborn buttercup root.

"And why has that put you in such a foul temper?" he demanded.

"Because my sisters are obsessed with having new dresses for the occasion and there is no money. Not a penny. And they have talked of nothing else all week."

His lordship looked down at his boots. "And, if there *were* a ball . . . and if there were money to be found for your finery . . . would you come?"

"Don't be ridiculous. What would I do at a ball? Sit and make polite chatter with the old tabbies? No, I thank you."

"You would dance and enjoy yourself like all the other young women."

"I am *not* a young woman," she said, wrestling with a clod of couch grass. "I'm not a child, my lord. I don't want a new dress, and I don't want to dance at your ball. My problems are far bigger than that. Look around you. Thorncote is on its last legs. How Marianne and Kitty and Lizzy can think about your stupid ball when they are soon to be turned out of their home is beyond me." She wiped a tear away angrily with one gloved hand.

He laid a hand on her shoulder. "Hush, love."

She shrugged him off. "Don't you *hush* me! It's alright for you! You have more money than you know what to do with. *You* are not about to be turned out of your home!"

"And neither would you be if you had accepted my offer."

She paused, staring at him. "What offer?"

"Thorncote in exchange for my hand in marriage," he said simply. "I believe I made it perfectly clear that I was willing to help you set this place back on its feet but that I want something in return."

"You are already getting a return. A very good rate of return," she pointed out hotly.

"It will be a number of years before Thorncote is paying me the interest you offered me. I want something else while I wait."

She stared at him and he smiled. "A bribe," she said caustically.

"I wouldn't quite put it that way . . ."

She bent over and tidied all the escaped weeds into the bucket.

He watched her, waiting. "Well?" he asked, inclining his head, a gentle smile on his lips. "Do we have an agreement?"

She straightened and picked up the bucket, walking toward him. She looked him straight in the eye. "I told you before that I am not one of your lightskirts. I am not for sale, my lord."

She brushed past him onto the gravel path, and he rolled his eyes in exasperation.

"What do I have to do to get through to you?" he complained.

"You have done enough already," she flung at him over her shoulder. "You have ruined my life!"

"Hardly."

"You have!" she cried, yanking on a buttercup root with all her might. "You have taken my father's estate away from us so that we are forced to split the family up and move away—no, let me finish! You have refused to help us with Thorncote so that we may keep it for ourselves and have given us three months to leave. Look at these gardens! How am I supposed to look after them on my own? And the house? And the farm? How can one woman set to rights the mismanagement of twenty years? I cannot do it alone. I can't. And I asked for your help, but you were too selfish to give it, because you never consider anyone but yourself. And so I watch as day-by-day my home rots around me. And you come here expecting me to joke with you when you have shamed me in front of my neighbors by saying that you wished to perform the marital act with me, and now you are holding a ball, which has taken such a hold over my sisters that I cannot get a sensible word out of them from morning until night!"

Where the tears of Lady Emily had left him unmoved, even irritated him, he found the angry tears of Miss Blakelow upset him to such a degree that he had come forward while her tirade was in full flow and laid his hands upon her shoulders, intending to pull her into his arms.

But she shook him off, slapped his hands away, and glared at him, leveling the fork at him as if it were a weapon. His closeness unsettled her, and she stumbled away from him until several feet of bare earth were between them.

"What are you doing?" she demanded.

He held up his hands and backed away. "I was merely trying to offer you comfort, that's all."

"I don't need comfort from you. I don't want anything from you, do you understand me? Ever!" she cried and choked on a sob.

"Perfectly," he replied stiffly.

Miss Blakelow had held her emotions in check for so long that now that they'd broken through the surface, she gave them free rein. "I never want to see you again as long as I live. You have brought nothing but misfortune to my door. I wish I had never laid eyes on you!" A part of her knew the lion's share of her anger was directed at her father and her brother, but since neither of them were there, she used the next best available target: Lord Marcham.

There was a long moment of silence while his eyes scanned her face as if looking for confirmation that she really meant the words that had just left her lips. His jaw worked; a muscle ticked angrily in his cheek. "Very well, ma'am," he said coldly, "as you wish."

Miss Blakelow put a hand to her mouth, watching his broad back as he walked away, and the sobs came. She put out a hand to call him back, to say that she did not mean it, but he had gone.

CHAPTER 15

Lord Marcham stormed into his house half an hour later and made straight for the drawing room, where his two sisters and his mother were seated by the fire.

"Robbie, there you are. Davenham said you had gone to visit our neighbors at Thorncote," said Lady St. Michael. "How do they do? Dreadful business about the father. Gambled away everything, or so I've heard. But Miss Marianne Blakelow is as pretty as a picture, so perhaps she's the reason you spend all your time over there?"

His lordship was definitely not in the mood for his sister's prying questions. "You have, all three of you, disobeyed my wishes," he said, standing before them and speaking with cold controlled anger. "You have spread the news abroad that this damned ball of yours is going ahead when I expressly forbade it. You have forced my hand. Very well. You may have your ball. But I am not parting with one single servant to organize it nor one single penny to pay for it. I do not wish to hear about any of the arrangements, and I do not wish to be consulted on anything. This is your ball. You will organize it and you will pay for it. And for God's sake open some windows. It's like a Turkish bath in here."

With that he strode out of the room, slamming the door behind him.

"Well," said Lady St. Michael. "That went well."

"At least he has agreed to it," said Harriet.

"Yes, but who's going to pay for it?" groaned their mother, holding vinaigrette to her nose.

Lady St. Michael gave a self-satisfied smile. "Robert."

"Robbie?" repeated Harriet. "But he just told you in no uncertain terms that he would have nothing to do with it."

"He did."

"Then how are you going to persuade him?" demanded her mother.

"I'm not. But the delectable Miss Blakelow is," said Lady St. Michael.

"Sarah, what are you up to?" asked the countess through narrowed eyes.

"Since Robbie is determined that none of us will sway him from marrying the wretched female, then let us use her to our advantage. He is hoping to fix his interest with this girl, is he not? All we need to do is make her think that he has arranged the ball just for her and she will do the rest. Rapturously happy females usually assist gentlemen in parting with their cash."

"Yes," said Harriet, frowning prettily. "But how do you know that Miss Blakelow wishes for a ball? According to what Mama says, she is dreadfully straitlaced."

"I think it's all a ruse. I think it's Marianne Blakelow he's interested in. Since when did you know Robbie to fall for any but the most stunning blonde? I am going to take a drive over to Thorncote this afternoon and see her for myself. The rest I will leave to human nature."

Miss Blakelow, having watched his lordship's back as he walked away until he was no longer visible, allowed herself a hearty cry in the privacy of the rose arbor, wiped her puffy eyes, and sniffed inelegantly. It had started to rain softly, the tiny droplets bouncing gently on the leaves of the climbing roses. But she remained there as the bench grew dappled with wet around her and her old black gown grew damp.

She knew that she had been unreasonable. It was not his fault that there was no money. It was not his fault that her father had gambled it all away. If it had not been Lord Marcham who had won the estate at the card table that day, then it would have been some other gentleman. And would she have turned up on his doorstep demanding reparation? Probably not. His lordship just happened to live within the neighborhood, unluckily for him. He owed her nothing at all.

She *had* been unreasonable and not only to Lord Marcham. He had turned up not ten minutes after she'd had a blazing row with the girls—that was what had put her in a foul mood, and she had taken all her frustrations out on him.

Miss Blakelow had caught her three younger sisters going through her solid walnut trunk in the spare bedroom that had once belonged to her mother. The lid of the trunk had been opened and the layers of diaphanous tissue paper cast aside. Shawls of fine lace were strewn across the floor; ribbons of every color exploded from the wrapping like fireworks; opera cloaks and glasses, fans, reticules, and slippers languished everywhere. The carpet was covered in flashes of scarlet ribbon, white lace, deep-blue velvet, and green satin. Dresses had been pulled from the armoire, dresses that Miss Blakelow had worn during her season over a decade before. Marianne was trying on a riding jacket of wine velvet that the young Miss Blakelow had worn when riding in Hyde Park. Kitty was wrapping herself in a cloak of dark-green wool, and Lizzy, unknowingly the worst offender, was holding up to herself a Grecian white gown trimmed with exquisite pink rosebuds.

On seeing the gown again, Miss Blakelow was transported back what seemed like a hundred years to the innocent girl she had been at the age of nineteen. She had worn it on the night of her first party, when she had been presented at Lady Carr's ball. That was the first time she had met him, the man who had so completely broken her heart.

"Oh, Georgie, look!" had cried Marianne. "See how the color suits me. It is terribly old-fashioned, of course, but it could be altered."

"Take them off," snapped Miss Blakelow, suddenly gripped by anger out of all proportion to the crime committed.

"This gown is *so* beautiful, Georgie," breathed Lizzy. "May I borrow it to wear to the ball?"

"No, you may not."

The words cracked through the air like a whip, and the three younger sisters looked at each other in confusion.

"We were only having a look, Georgie," said Marianne. "We meant no harm."

"Take them off this minute. They are not playthings," said Miss Blakelow, picking up a pale-pink satin slipper from the floor and flinging it angrily back into the trunk.

"Let us put them away for you, the way we found them," coaxed Kitty, sensing their eldest sister's mood.

"I don't need your help. Please just leave me alone."

Marianne laid a hand on her shoulder. "We're sorry—"

"Don't any of you ever think of anyone but yourselves?" demanded Miss Blakelow, her cheeks flushed with anger. "Do you never think of anything but your own pleasure? It hasn't even registered with you that we are going to be thrown out of Thorncote in eight weeks' time, has it? You should be worried about your future and where we all will live. Instead of that, all you can think of is dresses and balls. You have no comprehension of the problems we face. You have no comprehension of what I feel, because you never ask and you do not care. You have no respect for my property. You have no respect for my feelings. These are not your things. These are not your toys. They are mine, and you had no right to go through them without even asking my permission. You assumed control over them as if they already belonged to you. Trying them on, telling me how they can be altered to fit you. I don't *want* them altered. They were cut to fit me, and they will stay that way. If you have to go to that wretched ball in a hessian sack, I will not give you my things. Now get out, all of you, before I say something I regret."

Tears flowed, doors slammed, recriminations would follow. Ned sternly chastised the three girls for their stupidity.

Perhaps the strain of the last few months had finally taken their toll. Perhaps her anger was born out of frustration that she could not afford to buy the girls new dresses herself. Perhaps.

In that moment, when she had seen Lizzy swathed in the evening gown, she had been reminded of her own youthful folly. It was like uncovering an old wound, healed on the surface but still raw and deep underneath. The pain was still there, pain at the memory of the fool she had made of herself. The heat of the ballroom came back to her, the press of people, the perfume, flowers, and sculptures, the dresses and the dancing. Champagne flowed through her senses. His smile was dazzling and warm. She was pronounced a hit. The whole of London was at her feet.

From that moment on, she and Aunt Thorpe had been inundated with invitations to balls, routs, and parties. Vouchers were given for Almack's; a box was hired at Vauxhall Pleasure Gardens. The opera and the theater became her second home, and she dined out nearly every night of the week.

She was no heiress and had little wealth to offer a gentleman, but it was the force of her personality, coupled with her youth and beauty, that made her the talk of the ton. She had no shortage of male attention, and she was widely anticipated to make a very good match. Such a promising beginning—the envy of other girls—all to be dashed in a moment of folly.

"I thought you'd be out here," said a voice behind her.

Miss Blakelow's head snapped up. It was Aunt Blakelow. The older woman sat on the seat beside her, pulling her shawl closer about her shoulders.

"It's very damp out here, Georgie. Not at all good for my bones, you know, and not good for you either. Heavens, look at the weeds under this tree. I shall have to see what can be done. Not that I am any good at gardening, mind you, but even I know how to rip up a bit of long grass."

In a move that would have astounded their lordly neighbor, Aunt Blakelow pulled a small flask from the hidden pocket in her skirts and handed it to her niece.

"Brandy," said Aunt Blakelow. "By far the best health product you can buy, in my view."

Miss Blakelow took a hearty mouthful and gratefully swallowed the fiery liquid. It warmed her belly and seemed to put steel back into her spine.

"The girls told me what happened," said her aunt gently.

Miss Blakelow nodded lamely.

"Dear Georgie, is it still so painful after all these years?"

"Aunt, don't, please," said Miss Blakelow, struggling with her tears.

"What's done is done. There is no point repining."

"I know."

"You just have to make the best of it. You made your bed, as they say, and no one but you must lie on it."

"I know that too," croaked Miss Blakelow.

"Do you begrudge the girls their chance to be admired? They were only playing and dreaming as young girls do."

"Yes. And that's only natural. But when I saw Lizzy standing there so sweet faced and innocent, I saw myself as I was at their age. And I was so fearful in that moment that they might end up like me."

Her aunt gripped her hand. "Is life here so very bad?"

"Oh, no," cried Miss Blakelow, kissing the back of her aunt's hand. "How can you think such a thing? You have been my rock, Aunt. When all fell about me, only you stood firm. And I am as fond of you as I was of my own mother."

"Dear girl. I would not see you cry for all the world."

"I cannot help crying sometimes, Aunt. I love Thorncote, truly I do . . . but . . . but I sometimes wish . . . for more."

"Love."

"Yes," whispered Miss Blakelow.

"I thought you had vowed against men."

"Oh, I have," replied Miss Blakelow, laughing. "Frequently."

"But you still hope."

"Yes . . . I cannot seem to help myself. Do you despise me for it?"

"How could I when I still feel that way myself even at my age? You look shocked. I am still a woman, Georgie, and my heart still quickens when a handsome man enters the room. Of course you will continue to hope and that is natural. But you have a past, and there are not many men willing to live with that."

"No," Miss Blakelow agreed, taking another swig of the brandy.

"Don't expect too much, my love. That way brings disappointment."

Miss Blakelow nodded, choked by tears. "I suddenly realized today after all these years just how vulnerable I was at that age. If you had been there, Aunt, things might have been different. I would at least have had someone to advise me. Aunt Thorpe was very adept at firing me off, as the phrase goes, but not so good at guiding me through the pitfalls of girlhood. I was young and silly and arrogant and vain. I thought I had the world in my hand. But in truth, I realize now that the world had me under its heel."

Aunt Blakelow reached for the flask and took a swig herself. "Has Marcham recognized you?"

Despite herself, Miss Blakelow blushed. "He knows that we have met before, but he cannot place me."

"Good. Then let us hope that it stays that way. If he remembers, then we should all be in the suds. We should go in. The clouds are gathering. I think there's going to be a downpour. Heavens, Laura has left the washing out on the line. We shall have a pantry full of soggy washing in five minutes—"

"I was dreadfully rude to him, Aunt . . . earlier," blurted Miss Blakelow. "He came here hardly ten minutes after the argument, and I . . . and I said some things that I bitterly regret."

"Water off a duck's back, my dear. Ten to one a man with a skin as thick as his has forgotten it already—who is that? There is a carriage coming along the drive. Are we expecting visitors?"

Miss Blakelow stood up, wiped her eyes, and looked across at the approaching coach with its smart navy panels and gold crest emblazoned on the sides. She groaned and a million contrary thoughts entered her head, the main one being panic.

"Isn't that one of Marcham's carriages, Georgie?"

"I think so . . . Dear Aunt, I cannot face them. Not now. Pray don't ask me."

"You may have to—they have just seen us. Wave, my dear, wave. Let us go in, and leave the talking to me. Now, dry your eyes, put your glasses on, and wipe your face. You have mud on your nose. There. A few deep breaths. A smile. And you will be fit to be seen."

They walked briskly up the path as the coach swung around in a languorous curve before the front door. As two ladies were handed down from the carriage, Miss Blakelow and her aunt hastily entered the house through a side door. Miss Blakelow removed the apron she had been gardening in and cleaned away as much mud as was possible. She and her aunt entered the drawing room and were seated precisely ten seconds before Lady St. Michael and Lady Harriet Holkham were announced.

"My dear ma'am," said Lady St. Michael, stepping forward with a smile to greet Aunt Blakelow. "How do you do? I was so sorry to learn of your brother's death. Please allow us to offer you our condolences."

Aunt Blakelow curtsied. "Thank you, my lady. Won't you sit down?"

Tea was ordered, pleasantries made, and the ladies all sat down. Miss Blakelow chose a chair as far away from Lady St. Michael as it was possible to be, away from the direct light from the tall window. She sat upright, dreading what was to come, feeling out of place in her own drawing room. She had studiously avoided this woman for ten years, and now here she was, sitting down to drink tea with her.

"Well," said Lady St. Michael, smiling brightly. "Isn't it pleasant to see old friends again? Our brother is out this afternoon, so we thought we would come and pay you a visit, but really it was no trial because it is always pleasant to be at Thorncote." She looked about her, keeping the rather fixed smile pinned to her face. "Is Marianne not with you today?"

"She is otherwise engaged, my lady," said Aunt Blakelow. "Girls in this day and age are always visiting with friends, and they walk into Loughton to visit the shops as regular as may be—"

"Such a sweet girl. I haven't seen her for an age. Did she have her London come out? I don't remember hearing that she did."

"She was unfortunately in mourning, my lady."

"I see. Well. I'm sure she will find herself much sought after in Worcestershire. One does, you know, when one is young and pretty. And how much places change over the years when one would always hope that they stayed the same!" continued her ladyship. "It is the same at Holme Park. Robbie is forever bringing in some newfangled invention to improve this and that, when I had much rather keep it the way it was. But then I don't live there. And I suppose if I did I might feel differently." She spied a clock on the mantelpiece and went toward it. "My brothers and I were always straying onto your land when we were young. Is it very shameful of me to admit it? But you had much the best hill for sledging for miles around. What a pretty clock this is! I should think it quite an antique now."

"It is Georgiana's, my lady. She inherited it from her mother," said Aunt Blakelow.

Miss Blakelow, who still hadn't forgiven her ladyship for sending two men to value the contents of Thorncote house, was less than enthusiastic to be in the woman's company again. Georgiana was highly conscious of her own appearance and her rough worked hands and wished that the old threadbare carpet would swallow her whole. She saw the beauty of her ladyship's fine complexion, the curling blue plume that seemed to kiss her forehead, the navy spencer buttoned neatly at her wrists, and felt every inch the country bumpkin. She turned to look at the young Lady Harriet and was almost struck dumb by her likeness to her brother. Soft black curls framed an extremely pretty face with a small straight nose, the familiar gray eyes, and sweeping dark brows. The girl smiled at Georgiana, looking at her with frank curiosity, unconscious that her thoughts played out across her face.

The tea was brought in and Miss Blakelow poured for their guests, peering over her spectacles so that she shouldn't embarrass herself by spilling it.

"Have you lived at Thorncote long, Miss Georgiana?" asked Lady Harriet as she accepted her cup of tea.

"All my life," she replied, saying the lie without thinking. "Well, very nearly all of it."

"That explains it then. I knew that I recognized your face from the moment I saw you. Isn't it funny how one never forgets a face even after years and years apart? But I spent much of my childhood at Holme," said Lady St. Michael as she nibbled on a biscuit, "and we must be of a similar age, you and I, so we must have met before. We probably sledged down Thorn Hill together."

Miss Blakelow smiled uncomfortably. "Yes. Probably."

"Robbie was always the maddest of us all," her ladyship continued. "Always set off down the hill headfirst with little regard for his safety. Mama was driven to distraction by him. All those bumps and bruises. And Hal would always try to copy his big brother with disastrous results. Do you remember the time that Robbie broke his leg, and we had to drag him all the way back to Holme on the sledge?"

"Yes," said Miss Blakelow, who had no such recollection.

"And up he would be the next minute, determined to join the fray again. Those boys were inseparable," she said, becoming wistful. "They did everything together in those days. I, being only a mere girl, was more often than not considered the hanger-on. Oh, the innocent days of youth. Life was so much simpler then, was it not? What a pretty view you have from this window! And the formal gardens once the jewel of the county. The lake at Thorncote was always my favorite, you know. If you were to move that chair to the right, you may find your view improves . . . But how rude of me—you will of course have your furniture just as you wish it . . . How is your brother William? He must be quite grown-up now. I'm told that he is a very handsome fellow, but then he always was. I remember Marianne and William and little Kitty, but Lizzy was hardly even thought of then, a mere twinkle in her mother's eye." She paused, laughing. "William was too young to play with Hal and Robbie, of course. Ten years in age difference seems like a lifetime at that age, does it not? It is the strangest thing, Miss Blakelow—your face is so familiar to me and yet I cannot place you. I'm very sorry for it because it is excessively rude of me, but I cannot ever remember having seen you at Thorncote before."

There was a brief silence.

"I have lived here seven years, ma'am," replied Georgiana stiffly. "Before that I spent much time abroad."

As soon as the words had left her lips, Miss Blakelow knew that she had made a huge mistake. She'd already said she'd lived there most of her life, and now she was contradicting herself. She was distracted; the arguments of the day weighed heavily upon her mind, and she had spoken without thinking.

Lady St. Michael raised a brow. "Abroad? How fascinating. Well that would explain it then. But how came you to be separated from the rest of your family? Was not your father always living at Thorncote? Forgive me, I am a little confused."

"Do have a sip of tea, Miss Blakelow," said Lady Harriet. "You do not look at all the thing."

"Thank you, I will be better directly," she replied, casting a pleading glance at Aunt Blakelow.

"Did you say that you were staying in the district for long, Lady St. Michael?" asked the elderly Miss Blakelow, coming to her niece's rescue. "I must confess myself glad to see the family back at Holme. It was empty for so many years while Lord Marcham was in London. And such a shame to see a house like that deserted. But now he is back, perhaps we will have a family settled there."

"Perhaps," smiled Lady St. Michael politely.

"And if Robbie marries, we will have lots of nephews and nieces," said Lady Harriet.

"Drink your tea, Harriet," commanded her elder sister.

"Well, I for one would like to be an aunt," said Harriet. "It will be years before I have children of my own. And Robbie won't be one of those stuffy fathers who are afraid of their children acquiring a little dirt. He is most likely to get down and play on the floor with them, earl or no earl."

"Harriet," said Lady St. Michael sharply. "Please pass the biscuits."

"So," said Harriet excitedly, almost shoving the plate of biscuits in her sister's face. "Are you all going to come to my ball? You shall all be invited."

"My nieces have talked of nothing else, my lady," said Aunt Blakelow.

"Is it not exciting?" cried Lady Harriet, clapping her hands.

Lady St. Michael gave a chilly smile. "Forgive my youngest sister; she is very excitable. My brother was not keen on the idea at first, but he has finally been persuaded. I am determined that you all should come—you too, Miss Georgiana, should you wish it, although I believe that you don't often go out as a general rule."

Miss Blakelow smiled wanly but made no answer.

"Well, if you should wish to come, I am sure we can find room for you. One more is no trouble."

"Thank you," murmured Miss Blakelow.

"Oh, you *must* come," said Lady Harriet imploringly. "You will be missed if you do not."

Miss Blakelow opened her mouth to make a reply, but her aunt rescued her once again.

"His lordship was keen to hear my recipe for chicken broth, which I told him about when he was good enough to call upon us the other day. It is of all things the best cure for an upset stomach. Or for a cold. I swear by it and so, I can assure you, does my maid. All my dear late brother's children were brought up on chicken soup. There is a secret, you know, in the recipe. A certain extra something."

Lady St. Michael's smile became fixed. "Indeed?"

"I always say that one cannot do better than an old family recipe, my lady. All these new ideas come and go, but what is best in my book is good old-fashioned chicken soup. Good fresh ingredients straight from the farm and made fresh in the pot. My grandmama wouldn't have it any other way. If you ever have a need of it, do not hesitate to ask. I am always happy to give up a family secret for the Holkhams."

Miss Blakelow choked on her tea.

"Well," said Lady St. Michael hastily. "We must be going. Thank you for a most entertaining afternoon. I hope that you will visit us at Holme very soon."

"We will, my lady, thank you," said Aunt Blakelow.

"No, don't get up, Miss Blakelow; you look quite fagged to death. Good day to you."

Lady Harriet followed her sister out of the room but then ran back and produced a letter from her reticule and pressed it into Miss Blakelow's hand. "This is from my brother, ma'am. He said I was to give it to you personally. Good-bye. I hope we may meet again."

The carriage rattled away, and Miss Blakelow collapsed with relief into her chair, shoving his lordship's letter between the cushions out of sight.

"Oh, Georgie!" said Aunt Blakelow, when she had seen the ladies to their carriage. "How came you to say you had lived abroad?"

Miss Blakelow groaned and put her head in her hands. "I know, I know. I just didn't think."

"She smells a rat. Always was a busybody that one and always will be. She knows we are hiding something . . . and it took a double dose of chicken soup to get rid of her."

Her niece smiled wanly. "She never did like me."

"Oh, nonsense. She doesn't like anyone. Do you know, you can tell a lot about a person by how they react to chicken soup? I find it most instructive."

"And how many chicken soups did it take to get rid of Lord Marcham the other day?"

"He wouldn't go. Three chicken soups, and I threw in the mustard plaster as well just to be sure, but drat the man, he seemed determined on seeing you."

CHAPTER 16

Miss Blakelow opened Lord Marcham's letter in the privacy of her bedchamber. As she broke the seal and unfolded the wafer, several pieces of torn paper fluttered to the floor. Frowning, she picked them up and turned them over; they seemed to be bills for tailors and chandlers and wine merchants. Then she saw a thicker docket with her brother's strong handwriting, declaring his intention to hand over Thorncote to Lord Marcham in lieu of gambling debts. The docket had been ripped in half.

> *Dear Miss Blakelow,*
> *These are the bills for all your family's debts, which I acquired as a means to have Thorncote. They belong to you. Your debt to me is from this moment dissolved. I hope this will relieve you of the necessity of having to leave your home and of ever having to see me again, which was the fervent wish you expressed this morning.*
> *Your ever obedient servant,*
> *Robert Holkham*

Miss Blakelow slowly lowered her hand to her lap, his lordship's letter still between her fingers. She could hardly believe her eyes. Why would he do this? The money he was owed ran into thousands. Why would he give up his advantage and Thorncote? She went to her writing desk and seized her pen.

Dear Lord Marcham,

I return these bills to you along with my sincere apology for the hateful words I said to you this morning. I hope you know that you will always be welcome at Thorncote.

I am grateful for the sentiment but I cannot accept your gift. It is too much. You must allow me to repay my debt to you in full. I will arrange payment for sixty-two pounds, which I believe takes care of my father's hat-makers' bill. The rest I will pay you as soon as I am able.

Yours affectionately,

Georgiana Blakelow

The letter was given to her maid, and it was dark when that lady returned to Thorncote in his lordship's gig, driven by his lordship's head groom. Betsy's excitement at having a ride in such a "bang up" equipage was such that it was many moments before Miss Blakelow ascertained that she had another letter for her from Lord Marcham. She almost snatched the note from the maid's hand.

My dear Miss Blakelow,

While I cherish your note, you must allow that sending torn pieces of paper to each other is rather futile. So instead, I have placed all the bills onto the fire.

As to payment—you know what I want,

R

❧

"Well, *I* liked her," announced Lady Harriet, reaching for a pastry at breakfast the following morning.

"She was a plain little nobody who thought she was the Queen of Sheba," said Lady St. Michael tartly.

"She was shy," insisted Lady Harriet. "You can be so judgmental sometimes, Sarah."

"I don't recall any girls named Georgiana Blakelow living at Thorncote," put in the countess. "Marianne, Catherine, and Elizabeth are all I remember. And an elderly aunt—funny creature, always talking about her ailments. Then there was Sir William's first wife, Sophia, and his second, who was Jane or Judith or some such thing—or was it the other way around? Not that I ever paid particular attention. One doesn't, you know, when one lives a life of continual pain. Your father was always more familiar with Sir William than I was. Frightful man—Sir William that is. Very unruly eyebrows."

"I am relieved to hear you say that you do not recall her, Mama," said Lady St. Michael as she picked up her knife, "because I don't recall her either. Robbie and Hal and I were always at Thorncote growing up, and I don't remember ever seeing her there as a child. I had never heard of the name until yesterday."

"Whose name?" asked Lord Marcham, coming into the room at that moment. He was dressed for driving in buckskins and a close-fitting navy coat. He sat down at the head of the table and, at a nod of the head to Davenham to bring him some coffee, absently picked up the newspaper.

"Georgiana Blakelow," said Lady St. Michael.

"What about her?" asked her brother, his eyes on the front page of his newspaper.

"She claimed to have lived at Thorncote all her life, and yet I do not recall ever hearing her name before. Then she changes her tune and admits that she had in actual fact only been there for seven years and had lived abroad before that."

"Yes. So?" said the earl, as the butler placed his breakfast before him.

Lady St. Michael rolled her eyes. "Why would a daughter be sent abroad on her own when the rest of the family stayed at Thorncote?"

"Any number of reasons," his lordship replied, picking up his knife and fork.

"See, I told you!" cried Lady Harriet. "She might have had schooling abroad or gone to visit relatives or anything."

This thought had occurred to Lady St. Michael, but she was on the brink of discovering a secret and not to be put off her course. "She's hiding something," she announced.

"Oh, what tosh, Sarah," said Lady Harriet. "You are just miffed because she didn't bow and scrape enough for your liking."

Lady St. Michael bristled. "I tell you she's hiding something. Did you see her face when I asked her why she lived abroad?"

"Leave the woman be," said Lord Marcham.

"You may choose to ignore it if you wish, but something about her story stinks to high heaven. And I know her from somewhere—I know I do. I recognized her face the moment I saw her."

"Yes," cried Lady Harriet, "probably because you have seen her at Thorncote."

Her sister shook her head and spread her pastry with marmalade and sliced it in two. "Not here . . . I have seen her somewhere else. Perhaps when I stayed with Grandmama in Cheltenham. I cannot quite place her."

"Sarah," said her exasperated brother. "I asked you to leave the woman alone. She has enough on her plate without being subjected to one of your witch hunts."

Lady St. Michael stared at him. "And who is she to you that you defend her so?"

"A friend."

"A friend? How close a friend?"

"That is none of your damn business."

Lady St. Michael and her mother exchanged glances.

"If I didn't know you better, I would almost think you in love with her," said his sister, toying with a fold in the tablecloth.

He gave her an acid smile. "Sarah, you are nothing if not typical of your sex. I only have to call a woman my friend and you have me in love with her."

"I know you to be on the hunt for a wife. But I must say, Robbie, I thought your taste ran to curvy blondes, not slender brunettes. The woman looked as if she could do with a decent meal inside her."

"Can I please eat my breakfast in peace?" he demanded, carving himself off a wedge of beef.

"So it really is not the blonde piece. Well, well, perhaps you have grown up at last."

Lord Marcham sighed heavily. His home had been invaded. Even the quiet of his library was no longer sacred; his eldest sister had no qualms about tracking him down, whichever corner of the house he chose to hide himself in. He needed to escape for a few hours to regain his sanity. "Davenham?"

"Yes, my lord."

"Please have my curricle brought round at once."

"Yes, my lord."

His lordship visited a small shop in the town of Loughton. He ducked under the door and made his way to the counter, the hem of his greatcoat fanning out behind him as he slowly drew off his gloves. He looked critically at the bolts of fabric behind the counter as a small woman appeared. He told the lady that he wanted to buy five ball gowns: three for young ladies just about to enter society, one for a matron, and one for a woman who was perhaps aged nine and twenty.

The woman beamed at the thought of so much new business and brought down several bolts of white, pink, and cream material for his inspection. Lord Marcham approved these but also requested a pale blue, which he rather thought would suit Miss Marianne Blakelow. For Aunt Blakelow he chose a bronze satin with matching headdress and for Georgiana, a deep-red silk. He instructed the woman to visit Thorncote with the material and her pattern book and to send the bill to him. He then reached into his pocketbook and left a deposit before tipping his hat and leaving the shop.

When the modiste arrived at Thorncote a couple of days later, Miss Blakelow was out on the estate speaking to Mr. Healey regarding repairs to an outbuilding; thus she had no knowledge of Lord Marcham's gift. On entering the house, she heard much giggling and excitement coming from the parlor and was perplexed as to the cause. She walked into the room and halted dead on the threshold. Amongst swaths of material and patterns, measuring tape, and pins were her sisters, clustered around a tiny woman who was holding a swatch of cream-colored lace up to Lizzy's face.

"Oh, there you are, Georgie!" cried Kitty. "Only try to guess what has happened! Lord Marcham has arranged for us to have new dresses for the ball!"

Miss Blakelow blinked at her. "New dresses?"

"Yes, come and look," said Marianne eagerly. "I am to have this blue, which I have to say is *just* what I would have chosen myself, Kitty is to have the pink, and Lizzy the cream."

"And Aunt Blakelow is to have this bronze satin with the most delightful feather headdress to match. Isn't it gorgeous?" demanded Lizzy.

Miss Blakelow looked at her aunt, who would not entirely meet her gaze. "I see," she said.

"And you are to have this one," said Kitty.

"*Me?*" said Miss Blakelow incredulously.

"Yes, miss," said the modiste, bobbing a curtsy. "His lordship chose it for you himself."

"Did he indeed?"

"I think it will be beautiful. It's the color of crushed raspberries," said Marianne wistfully.

Miss Blakelow wondered dismally how many of his lordship's mistresses had been clothed in the same color. "We cannot accept this."

"Oh, I knew she'd say something like that!" wailed Lizzy.

"We cannot. It is kind of him but it is too much. Girls, help the lady pack her things up, and we'll have John bring the carriage around to take her home."

"Oh, George, no . . . please," said Kitty. "You don't have to accept his lordship's gift if you don't wish to—but Marianne, Lizzy, and I do. And Aunt Blakelow too. It has been years since we had new dresses. Please, George. Please don't take this away from us."

Miss Blakelow could say no more.

She had a great deal of difficulty tracking his lordship down. A ride to Holme Park proved fruitless. Davenham informed her that he had gone to visit a friend and wasn't expected home until late.

As she had spent the best part of the ride over there rehearsing a speech, she was disappointed not to have the opportunity to say it aloud. She started home as a sunset was staining the clouds with pink, and the black leafless branches of the elms scratched at the October sky.

She hadn't long left Holme before it proved too dark to see her way back through the fields, so she decided to join the main road as soon as she could. A clump of trees screened her from the view of any oncoming traffic, and as she nudged her horse to jump the shallow ditch, a rider appeared, flying around the bend in the road with coattails streaming out behind him. The mash of hooves whipped up mud as he went, and it was all that Miss Blakelow could do to keep her seat. Her horse whinnied and reared just as the gentleman managed to bring his sweating steed to a plunging halt. His dog, a hunting hound of some description, set to barking, and before Miss Blakelow had a chance to grasp the reins, she was thrown clear of her horse.

"Hell and damnation," cursed the man, controlling his own horse with difficulty. "Damn fool woman. Don't you know that is a blind corner? What possessed you to stand there?"

Miss Blakelow moved gingerly, touching her hand to her forehead. "My apologies, sir. I was taking a shortcut."

"Are you alright?" he asked sharply, coming toward her.

She nodded lamely and tried to get up, but the world was spinning around her head. Two iron hands gripped her under the arms and lifted her bodily onto her feet.

"There," he said, picking up her fallen whip and handing it to her. "Are you able to ride home?"

"Yes, sir. I'm sorry to be so much trouble."

"Never mind. Come over here and I will lift you onto your horse. Are these your spectacles? I fear my horse has trodden on them."

"No . . . no matter. I have a spare . . . I mean . . . oh . . ."

And for the first time in her life, Miss Georgiana Blakelow fainted dead away.

❧

It was no mean feat to convey an unconscious woman and two horses back to Holme Park, but he managed it, and so he told Davenham when he reached the house. A footman rushed forward to take Miss Blakelow from his arms and the gentleman, relieved at last of his burden, was able to relinquish his hat, gloves, and greatcoat. He was trying to restore a semblance of order to his hair in the hall mirror, when a voice shrieked, "Hal!" at full volume, and a moment later, Lady Harriet cast herself into his arms.

"Well, well," he said, clumsily patting her back. "I said I should be here for your ball, didn't I?"

"Oh, I am so happy to see you. When did you get here? Where is your luggage? You are staying this time, aren't you? Pray say that you are!" She perched on tiptoe and kissed his cheek. "Now my ball will be perfect, for everyone I love is here—well, except Caroline, but she'd never come anyway."

"Now let go of my sleeve, Harry, do. Twenty shillings a yard this material cost me," he said.

"Then more fool you," said the cool voice of Lady St. Michael as she came down the main stairway. "Hal . . . is it you indeed?"

"Sarah, how do you do?" he replied, setting aside his youngest sister and going to greet her ladyship. "When you put on that sour face, you put me in mind of a bulldog."

"Thank you," she replied. "Are you here alone? Yes, I feel sure that you are. The handsome widower comes to try his luck with the hay-chewing populace of Loughton."

The Honorable Henry Holkham smiled, but the expression did not reach his eyes. "You really are the most frightful snob, Sarah; I don't know how Edward puts up with you. Congratulations, by the way. I hear you are expecting a happy event."

Lady St. Michael smiled. "Shall we go in to Mama? She will be wondering what all the noise is about."

"By all means. Where's Rob anyway?" he asked as Harriet looped her arm through his and led him through to the drawing room.

"I have absolutely no idea. Out courting his lady love, belike," Lady St. Michael said over her shoulder. "Have you dined?"

"Yes, thank you . . . His lady love, you say? Never tell me he's fallen in love at last?" he said incredulously.

"She is nice," said Lady Harriet impulsively. "Well, *I* like her. But Sarah doesn't."

"And I can probably guess why," said Hal.

"Have you brought a change of clothes with you or are you going to smell of the stables all night long?" asked Lady St. Michael.

"My valet follows with my luggage so you will have to wait. Hello, Mama. Lord, isn't it hot in here?"

He bent down to kiss his mother where she was reclining on a sofa. She swathed him in an embrace of sickly scent.

"Hal! Is it you indeed? I knew that you would come, for your sister's sake. Sarah thought you would not, but I knew you'd do anything for Harriet. How are you, dear boy? You have lost weight, haven't you? And you look pale."

"Yes, yes. I'm fine. What's this I hear about Robbie falling for the ball and chain?"

The countess began to fan herself vigorously. "Pray do not mention it. I do not wish to discuss it. The boy has taken leave of his senses. She's lured him. With arts and witchcraft. She's lured my poor Robert." She plied a tissue to her eyes. "My poor boy is taken in. Taken in by a . . . a harpy!"

"Oh, hardly that, Mama," said Lady Harriet, rolling her eyes.

"Good for him!" grinned Hal, accepting a glass of sherry from the butler. "Is she a prime article?"

"No, that's the thing. She's perfectly ordinary, and none of us can understand his fascination with the woman," said Lady St. Michael.

"Sticking your nose in my affairs again, Sarah?" asked a cool voice from the door.

The company jumped collectively and Lady St. Michael reddened slightly. She turned serenely in her chair toward him. "I have said nothing that I would not say to your face."

"Hello, Rob," said Hal, setting down his glass. "Have you stolen the best-looking girl in the neighborhood for yourself?"

His lordship, who had not until that moment noticed his brother, halted at the sound of his voice. "Hal, what the devil are you doing here?" he asked in pleasant surprise, coming forward to shake his hand.

His brother grinned and stood up to clasp his hand and clap him on the back. "I heard some ball or other was taking place."

"Oh, not you as well. I have heard enough about the wretched ball from the women of this house to last me a lifetime. When did you arrive?"

"Less than fifteen minutes ago. How do you do? I swear this place gets farther and farther away from the main road every time I come here. Nearly got run over."

"Run over?"

"Yes, you know where that sharp bend is by the drooping tree? A woman flew around the other side, and it was all I could do not to run her down."

"How exciting!" said Lady Harriet.

"My horse reared and her horse reared and Brisket—my new puppy, you know—was yapping for all he was worth, and I rather think the poor girl hit her head."

"And no doubt you offered her your manly breast to lean upon," remarked Lady St. Michael dryly.

"She passed out in my arms and I brought her here. Come to think of it, where is she? A footman took her from me. But I suppose someone ought to check on her."

"I'll go," said Lady St. Michael, standing and snapping shut her fan.

"And I think I owe the poor girl a new pair of spectacles because Firestar trampled all over them with his great hooves."

Lord Marcham had been staring down into the fire, but at that his head shot up. "Spectacles, did you say?"

"Yes, great thick ugly ones—what did I say?" complained Hal as his brother strode from the room.

Lady St. Michael gave a grim smile. "It seems, Hal, that you have run over his paramour."

❧

Lord Marcham took the stairs two at a time. He found his housekeeper coming out of one of the spare bedrooms.

"Mrs. Haskell, the lady who was brought here, where is she?" he demanded.

"She's in the end bedchamber, my lord, and resting now. She took quite a tumble, and there's a nasty gash on her head."

"Has the doctor been sent for?"

"He's on his way, my lord . . . but you cannot go in there; she's in bed and it's not decent—"

"Decency be damned," he muttered, flinging open the door.

In the center of the room in the large canopied bed, Miss Blakelow lay supported by white pillows, her skin almost as pale as the bandage around her head, and her hair for once free of the white lace cap. Her dark locks fanned out across the pillow like liquid mahogany. Her eyes were closed, her eyelashes a perfect delicate fan against her cheeks, her right eye bruised and blackened, as good a disguise as ever her spectacles had been.

The earl approached the bed and sat on the edge of it, taking her hand in his. Her eyelids fluttered open and she looked at him for a moment, uncomprehending. Her green eyes, unencumbered by her spectacles, were clear and beautiful. She blinked and recognition came.

She smiled. "Oh, it's you."

He squeezed her hand. "My—" He broke off and cleared his throat. He looked down ruefully at her black eye. "You did take a tumble, didn't you? How do you feel?"

"I have a headache," she said.

He gave her a slow smile. "Well, if you will go gallivanting around in the dark . . ."

"I was looking for you," she said softly.

"Were you? Ought I to be flattered?"

"I don't think so. I was going to tell you that we were very touched by your gift but we couldn't accept it," she replied, wondering vaguely when he was going to let go of her hand.

"I might have guessed, I suppose. And does this decree come from all the Blakelow women or just my little bluestocking?" he asked.

She gave a wry smile. "Well, I must confess that if I were to force my sisters to give up their chance of a new dress, I'd have a riot on my hands."

"So then. Accept my gift with a good grace."

"It was very kind of you, but I could not wear such a dress."

"You don't like the color? I thought it would suit . . ."

"I think the color is beautiful, and I'm sure your last mistress did too," she said.

His lips twitched appreciatively. "My last mistress did *not* have a dress that color, and if she had I would have liked it exceedingly."

"I'm sure you would. It is a color that commands attention."

"Which is why I would very much like to see you in it."

"If you would not be offended, my lord, I would like to exchange it for something more . . ."

"Dull?" he suggested.

She pretended to glare severely at him. "Yes."

"Well, I *would* be offended. Mortally offended. I have seen you in enough gray and black and purple to last me for a lifetime."

"My lord, please, you do not understand. If you wish to pay for a dress for me, then let me change it to one that I may wear. I will not wear a ball gown. I don't go to parties. I may choose a fabric half the price of the red silk and probably make myself two day dresses for less money than it costs to make one ball gown."

"And what will you wear to Harriet's ball?" he demanded.

"I am not going to Lady Harriet's ball," she said, trying gently to disengage her hand from his grasp.

"You damned well are," he replied, holding her hand rather tighter.

"I am not. I cannot," she said in a quiet voice.

"I want you there. If I am forced to attend the wretched event, then I will at least have someone there I choose to talk to. And, I may add, someone to dance with who does not bore me rigid."

"Please, my lord," she said, trying not to smile. "Don't be angry with me."

"You are going, even if I have to ride over to Thorncote myself and dress you with my own hands . . . which, now I come to think of it, does have a certain appeal . . ."

A footstep sounded outside the door and Lady St. Michael took in the scene. Miss Blakelow tore her hand from the earl's but not quickly enough.

"Robbie, get out of here before you ruin this girl's reputation for good," complained his sister wearily, coming toward the bed.

His lordship stood up hastily. "I was checking that Miss Blakelow was comfortable."

"I will see to her. Ask Mrs. Haskell to bring one of my night-gowns, would you? It is not at all the done thing for her to be wearing one of your nightshirts."

"Well . . . I'll . . . I'll bid you good night then, Miss Blakelow."

She turned her head on the pillow. "Good night, my lord."

"Out, Robbie! Out!" Lady St. Michael said, pushing him through the door and closing it behind him. "Men are impossible, are they not, Miss Blakelow? Always under one's feet. You will forgive my brother's intrusion, I am sure. It was kindly meant."

"Lord Marcham was not intruding," Miss Blakelow replied softly.

"Well, and are you comfortable? Mrs. Haskell seems to have done a reasonable job bandaging you up, at least. Can I do anything for you?"

Miss Blakelow licked her dry lips. "If your ladyship could arrange to send word to Thorncote. I fear they may be worried. I should have been home hours ago."

"Of course, my dear. I will ask my brother to send the carriage for your aunt. I am sure you would wish to have her staying with you."

Miss Blakelow tried to raise herself up on her elbows. "There is no need. I shall be well again tomorrow and hope to return home in the morning."

"That's as may be," said Lady St. Michael, pushing the patient back down onto the pillows, "but my brother won't let you leave until you are quite well again, Miss Blakelow. I shall send up some soup for you. Try to get some sleep."

CHAPTER 17

"And how is the patient today?" asked his lordship the following morning, hovering outside the guest bedroom where Miss Blakelow was sleeping.

"A little groggy, my lord," replied Aunt Blakelow, as she closed the door, "but on the mend."

"Can I see her?"

"She's sleeping at the moment. Best to leave her."

He nodded stiffly and smiled. "Very well. Perhaps later."

He turned to go and Aunt Blakelow bit her lip. "Oh, go on then! But don't tire her out."

The earl flashed a boyish grin and placed his hand upon the doorknob. "I won't, ma'am, thank you."

Miss Blakelow was sitting up in bed when he entered the room, staring out of the window, apparently deep in thought. She turned her head when the door opened and self-consciously pulled the covers up to her chin.

"Someone's feeling better," he observed as he closed the door.

"Good morning, my lord."

He took a few steps farther into the room. "Did you sleep well?"

"Yes, thank you. You have been very kind."

He pulled up a chair beside the bed and sat down.

"Sir, I have been thinking," she began.

"Oh, Lord," he murmured.

She glared at him but the look was spoiled by the smile tugging at her mouth. "You needn't look like that."

"I always look afraid when women get that look in their eye," he commented, bracing one booted foot across the opposite knee. "It means I am either just about to be put to a great deal of expense or a great deal of trouble. Come on then, out with it."

"Thorncote."

"Ah . . . I was wondering when we would get to that."

"The debts. I cannot let you write them off. Indeed it is most kind of you but—"

"Nonsense."

"But you must let me at least *try* to pay them back. It may take me some time, but I will do it. I swear I will."

"Please put them out of your mind. I did it for purely selfish reasons. You can have no notion how enjoyable it was to tear them up."

Miss Blakelow looked down at her hands. "I want to do something for you in return."

Several rather powerful images flashed through his lordship's mind at that moment, and he was hard-pressed not to smile. But he had no desire to be in her black books again, so he quashed the suggestion that sprang to his lips in favor of something less contentious.

"There is no need, Miss Blakelow. To see you restored to full health is all the thanks I need."

She reached for the glass of water on the table by the bed and sipped from it delicately. "I would like to return home this morning," she said, "if I might impose upon you to borrow your carriage?"

"My carriage is at your disposal, ma'am, but I believe the doctor advised that you stay here for a couple of days."

"There is no need. I am very much better already."

"Are you going to argue with me about everything?" he asked, amused.

"No, my lord."

"Well," he said, standing and pushing the chair back against the wall. "I promised your aunt that I would not stay too long. Please let me know if there is anything you need."

"A book?" she replied, her eyes flicking over him as he walked to the door.

"Something instructional and morally improving? Fordyce's *Sermons* perhaps?" he asked with a smile.

"I do not believe such a work exists amongst your collection, my lord."

"Then you'd be wrong," he replied with a hand on the door-knob. "And no, it is *not* used as a paperweight; I have actually read it."

"And enjoyed it?"

"I'm a rake, Miss Blakelow. I'm afraid there you are pushing the realms of possibility too far."

She smiled and snuggled down under the covers. "Choose me a novel, if you please."

He bowed. "Something frivolous coming up."

Miss Blakelow watched him until he had closed the door. She looked around her at the tasteful decor of the room, the rich embroidery on the bed curtains, the thick carpet on the floor, and remembered her own threadbare room at Thorncote. She had not known such luxury since she had stayed with her Uncle Thorpe in London for her season all those years ago. She wondered, had she not been so reckless with her own reputation as a young girl, whether she might now be mistress of a home such as this, with fine clothes and furnishings, jewels and carriages, servants at her beck and call, and a husband to have and to hold at night. Many a woman would jump at the chance to have all these worldly goods; women sacrificed much for a secure financial existence, but Miss Blakelow wanted more. She wanted love. If the earl was unable or unwilling to give her his heart, then she'd sooner die an old maid than marry a man who was not truly hers. These reflections inevitably transported her mind back to the day of the picnic, and in the quiet of his home with the scent of his cologne still in the air, she closed her eyes and allowed herself the fantasy of being his.

❧

Miss Blakelow was persuaded to stay at Holme for two days. She read two very frivolous books, one of which was a gothic romance that was so preposterous that she pronounced herself surprised that his lordship would countenance its presence upon his hallowed bookshelves. They fell into a routine of sorts; he came to see her once briefly in the morning and again for a longer visit in the afternoon, when they played chess while Aunt Blakelow changed the dressing on her head. The only blot on her landscape was Lady St. Michael, who seemed to delight in bursting into the room uninvited at any hour, once catching Miss Blakelow about to use the chamber pot.

Miss Blakelow was angry at the woman's intrusion and was at a loss to explain it. Nothing would have pleased her more than to have told the woman to get out. But it was not her room and not her house. She was a guest. And a guest deeply beholden to the Holkham family, at that.

It was during his lordship's afternoon visit on the second day that things came to a head.

Aunt Blakelow had gone for her afternoon nap, leaving her niece alone with their host. He was seated on the edge of the bed, as he usually was, and the chessboard sat on Miss Blakelow's lap. She was pondering her move when she slanted a deeply wicked look at him from under her brows and asked, "Is it true that you fought a duel when you were only sixteen?"

He looked up from contemplation of the pieces. "Where on earth did you hear that?"

"My brother. He said you nearly killed your man, cool as you please, and went out drinking afterward."

Lord Marcham shifted uncomfortably. "There are lots of stories about me. Not all of them are true."

"Is that one?" she asked.

He sighed. "It is true that I fought a duel when I was sixteen. But I was *not* 'cool as you please.' I was little more than a boy and frankly terrified."

"Oh."

"Yes. Now concentrate, Miss Blakelow. I am about to take your queen."

"But is it true that you gambled Holme Park away on the turn of a card and lost? And then won it back the very next moment?"

He leaned back, frowning. "What's brought all this on?"

"Nothing . . . I'm just trying to gauge exactly how debauched you are."

"I see," he said stiffly.

She gave a gurgle of laughter. "Dear sir, please don't be angry. I'm just curious. One hears so many stories . . ."

"I am glad that you find my past so entertaining."

"I have upset you."

"My dear girl, it would take more than that to upset me. But I am not altogether proud of all my . . . er . . . youthful achievements."

"So is it true?" she asked quietly.

He folded his arms. "It's partly true. It was not Holme that I nearly lost but my house in London. It was the height of folly and I'm not proud of my behavior, but it's true."

Miss Blakelow kept her eyes lowered. "But you regret it now you are older and wiser?"

"Of course. I was lucky no serious harm was done but it could have been a disaster. I was young and naive. What other excuse is there? I'm sure not even the irreproachable Miss Blakelow could claim she never put a foot wrong in her youth."

She was genuinely taken aback. "Me? I can assure you, I am the very last person who would ever claim that."

"Then why, if you admit to fault yourself, did you write that pamphlet about me? That smacks a little of hypocrisy, do you not think?"

"I know you must question my motives, but I genuinely care for the fallen women of society, those who have no choice but to submit to the will of men. I . . . I know a little of their circumstances, and I find it intolerable that many of them are blamed and punished by the world we live in for giving in to their desires or just trying to provide for their families, when men are equally as responsible." She paused and felt heat climbing her face. "I wrote it as a warning to all young women to be wary. Besides, what better way to divert attention than to point the finger at someone else? And your shoulders are broad enough to take the weight."

"Why me? There are a hundred or more such men."

"Because I grew up living within the sphere of your influence, at Thorncote and in London. I felt I knew you better as a subject than any other man." She paused and looked down at the chessboard and gave a wry smile. "And I suppose part of me wanted to punish you for daring to beat my father at cards and take Thorncote from us."

"Will anyone ever replace Thorncote in your affections, I wonder?" he mused.

She shook her head, smiling. "Never. It is the place I love best in the world. It gave me a home when every other door was bolted against me."

"Why would anyone bolt their door against you?" he asked, frowning. "I cannot imagine you can ever have done anything to earn anyone's displeasure."

Her eyes fell away from his. "A lady's reputation is a fragile thing, my lord. It seems that I did not show mine enough care."

"You were ruined then?" he asked curiously, in as gentle a voice as he could manage. "What could such a sweet-natured creature as you possibly have done to offend?"

She shook her head as tears sprang into her eyes, unable to answer him for the sudden choking sensation in her throat. She found she could not speak the words. She looked away as a tear slid down her cheek.

Lord Marcham reached across a hand and tucked a curl of her hair behind her ear. He would not press her for more if it upset her so. "And if I told you that my door was open for you now and always—could you ever consider this house as your home?"

Her heart leapt at the sudden touch of his hand. "I think it would be presumptuous for me to do so," she said.

"Not if you were my wife."

A silence fell. Miss Blakelow kept her eyes lowered. "If I am to be your wife—"

"If you are to be his wife, you had best have a very forgiving nature," said Lady St. Michael suddenly from behind them. "He has a mistress in town and probably another in Loughton."

Miss Blakelow jumped and overset the chessboard. All the pieces rolled and fell onto the counterpane and the carpet.

His lordship turned and glowered at his sister. "Thank you, Sarah, thank you very much indeed."

She smiled her bittersweet smile. "Anything to help, dear Robbie. You seemed to be unable to tell dear Miss Blakelow that which she most needed to know. You are wanted downstairs, by the way. You may leave Miss Blakelow in my care."

"Your care, Sarah? Why does that thought send a shiver down my spine?" he muttered.

She smiled. "You needn't look so worried. Your secrets are safe with me."

He hesitated, a chess piece in his hand, reluctant to leave his sister alone with Miss Blakelow. What stories would Sarah tell her? How much further would he sink in the eyes of Miss Georgiana Blakelow?

"Go, Robbie," commanded his sister. "Miss Blakelow is to have a wash and you will be very much in the way."

Lady St. Michael closed the door on her brother and stared down at Miss Blakelow. She set down a pitcher of water. "My brother is very entertaining, is he not? You should know precisely the sort of man he is if you intend to marry him. He is rather a selfish creature, who takes little interest in anything but the pursuit of pleasure. Did you think that he had reformed his character just for you? Do you think you will be able to convince him to give up his mistress after you are wed? You poor little innocent. You'd best not let your heart become involved, my dear. It is much the best thing to look upon it as a business deal, for ten to one he will return to his old ways within a year. You said you wanted to know how debauched he is? Be under no illusions, he is not called a rake for nothing."

"He is not debauched," said Miss Blakelow firmly, "merely bored."

Lady St. Michael raised a brow politely. "Indeed? You know him so well on only a month's acquaintance?"

"I know that he has been a good and kind friend to me."

"Friend," scoffed Lady St. Michael. "Is that what you call it? Trust me, when a man's primary motive is to bed you, it is not friendship that he's offering."

Miss Blakelow threw back the bedcovers and swung her legs over the side. "I'm not listening to this."

"How long do you think he is going to be happy living here in the middle of the country with you and nothing for entertainment but sheep and fresh air? He is an inveterate gambler, my dear. He spends days of his life in one gaming hall or another. He drinks to excess. He frequents the homes of opera dancers. Rural Worcestershire will not hold him for long and neither, to be blunt, will you. Be warned, this is no green boy you trifle with."

"Why are you doing this?" Miss Blakelow demanded as she disappeared behind a screen and whipped the nightdress over her head.

"Because I don't want to see my brother unhappy . . . or you, for that matter. Whatever I may think of you, I would not wish to see you trapped in an unhappy marriage for the rest of your life."

"I'm touched by your concern," said Miss Blakelow coldly as she pulled on her shift, "but you are suffering under a delusion. I have no intention of marrying your brother or anyone else."

"I am relieved to hear it, Miss Blakelow."

"I have not given Lord Marcham any reason to believe that we are anything other than friends," she said, throwing on her gown.

"Then you had better reassert that intention. My brother is looking for a wife and he seems to have chosen you."

"Only because he has not found a replacement for Lady Emily Holt," said Miss Blakelow. "To be frank with your ladyship, he wants a brood mare to give him a son. And that is . . . not what I want. He had best look in another direction for his wife and so I have already told him."

"You are not then in love with him?" asked Lady St. Michael.

Miss Blakelow struggled with the fastenings on her dress. "I . . . I am not."

Her ladyship seemed to relax. "And you have no intention of accepting him were he to make you an offer?"

"I have already refused him," said Miss Blakelow quietly.

"You relieve me, Miss Blakelow. I have to own that you relieve me a great deal."

"But he will marry one day, my lady, and you had best get used to the fact. He needs an heir and that is something that even *you* cannot give him."

There was a chilly silence.

"And what do you mean by that remark?" demanded Lady St. Michael.

"Merely that you will not always be the first woman in your brother's life," said Miss Blakelow, as she pulled on her boots. "I suspect that you are rather used to having him all to yourself . . ."

Lady St. Michael gave a scornful laugh. "If you say so."

". . . and you don't like the thought that one day he might choose his wife over you."

Lady St. Michael simmered with anger. "I want him to be happy."

"With a lady of your own choosing, no doubt," said Miss Blakelow, wrapping her cloak around her half-fastened dress. "A lady who won't answer back. A lady who you may order around as you choose."

"How dare you?"

"Does your brother continually flout your choices for him?" mocked Miss Blakelow, pulling her hair into a bun and thrusting it under the hood of the cloak. "Poor Lady St. Michael. You try so hard to choose him someone you think he should be happy with and, drat the man, he'd rather choose his bride himself."

Miss Blakelow came out from behind the screen, dressed in haphazard style but decent nonetheless. Her appearance would not pass public scrutiny, but her cloak hid the unfastened buttons of her gown from view. "I won't stay in this house with you for another second, Lady St. Michael. I am going home. I will let you explain to your brother the reason why I have gone. Good day."

Miss Blakelow found an entrance to the servants' staircase and yanked open the door. She flew down the rough stone stairs, her hand gliding along the cold metal banister rail, her boots echoing on the steps as she ran. She did not want to be caught by his lordship or anyone else; she was so close to tears that any further confrontation would completely overset her composure.

She followed the stairs down and down until she emerged in a small lobby. The servants' hall was to her left, the great long table empty, a huge clock on the wall above it, no doubt to remind them that even their leisure time belonged to the master. She sped out of the door in front of her and found herself in the stable yard.

A stable hand was looking at her curiously from one of the stalls.

"Can I help you, miss?" he asked, wiping his fingers on his trousers.

"My horse was brought here two days ago, a black mare with a white flash—"

"Down its nose. I know, miss. Were you the lady that had the accident?"

She smiled. "Yes. But I am recovered now and should like to go home. Would you be able to saddle her for me?"

"Right away, miss."

Miss Blakelow was in an agony that his lordship would find her at any second and ask the reason for her departure. And she could not face him. She could not let him know that his sister had chased her away by reminding her of the thing she already knew: Lord Marcham was not the man for her.

Lord Marcham stood behind his desk in the library, bracing his fists on its surface so that he leaned over it and could look into his sister's face. "What the devil was all that about?"

Lady St. Michael bristled. "Nothing."

"Nothing? You decide to tell an innocent female that I have a mistress in town and another in Loughton, and you tell me it was nothing?"

"May I remind you, Robbie, that *she* broached the subject? She wanted to know how debauched you were."

"She was asking me about the duel, not my mistresses," he said furiously. "But you took great delight in telling her, didn't you? I could see it all over your face. No matter that I haven't had a mistress for some considerable time."

"Oh, poor foolish Robbie. Do you expect anyone to believe that?" she mocked.

He paused, a muscle pulsing with anger in his cheek. "What else did you tell her?" he asked, controlling his temper with an effort.

Her ladyship adjusted the shawl around her shoulders. "I told her nothing that she could not have heard from anyone else."

"What else did you tell her?" he demanded again, more insistently.

"That you gamble and drink and see opera dancers. She needs to know what you are, Robbie. She has some nonsensical notion that you have reformed yourself for her, just as every other female did who ever set up a flirtation with you. They all think they can change you. And they are all wrong."

He folded his arms and sat on the edge of his desk, staring coldly down at her. "You think that you know me so well, don't you?"

"I know you better than she does."

"I don't think you do. You have no idea what I want. You have no conception what my thoughts are on anything. The man you have described so exhaustively to her was the man I was ten years ago. You are intimately familiar with my reputation, but you do not appear to know *me* anymore."

"She has addled your brain. Your lust for her has clouded your judgment. You cannot tell me that you are serious about this woman?" said her ladyship, rounding on him. "Who is she? Who are her family? A second-rate baron with a gambling habit? Don't make me laugh."

"Why are you determined to ruin this for me?" he demanded.

"Because she's lying. She's hiding something and I don't trust her."

He rolled his eyes and flung himself away from the desk. "Just because you don't remember sledging with her? For God's sake, Sarah, grow up."

"I was telling the story about how you broke your leg sledging on Thorn Hill."

"It was Hal who broke his leg, not me," replied his lordship.

"Exactly!" she cried triumphantly. "Exactly right. And yet she said that she remembered it was you."

"It's hardly a crime, Sarah."

"Do you remember her from when we were children?" Lady St. Michael demanded suddenly.

"I have to confess that I don't."

"No, and neither do I. The point is that she lied. She said she lived here all her life and then changed her tune. Why would she do that unless she has something to hide?"

"I have no idea," he said, throwing up his hands. "Maybe she's forgetful. I don't know and I don't care."

Lady St. Michael stood up and came toward him and laid her hand upon his shoulder. "I'm only doing this because I don't want to see you hurt."

He shrugged her hand away and moved toward the door. "Leave Miss Blakelow alone and keep your nose out of my affairs. I won't warn you again."

"You can't keep away from her, can you?" said her ladyship, her voice rising with hurt and anger. "Look at yourself, running up to see her like a lapdog. Well, she's gone, so you are wasting your time."

"Gone?" he thundered, pausing with a hand on the doorknob.

"She went home the best part of an hour ago."

There was a silence.

"Why you little—" He broke off, controlling himself with an effort. "I mean it, Sarah, leave her alone."

"She's not in love with you, Robbie," said Lady St. Michael as she watched him wrench open the door. "You're deluding yourself. She doesn't want you. She told me so herself—"

But his lordship had gone.

CHAPTER 18

MISS BLAKELOW SPENT THE next few days in a kind of torpor.

She told herself and her Aunt Blakelow that she was resting; the bruise to her eye made her an unsightly companion, and she spent much of the time in her room, reading and pondering her future. She stared listlessly out of her bedroom window, looking at the unkempt gardens with frustration, almost as if she could hear the weeds growing in the October rain as she languished in her room, wondering what she should do.

His lordship did not visit the day after she had returned to Thorncote, or the day after that, or any time during the week that followed. He seemed to have decided to keep his distance; perhaps his sister had managed to persuade him to drop their acquaintance. Perhaps he had realized for himself that she was unremarkable and was quite prepared to forget her. In any event, she missed him and could not quite fathom why his absence affected her so.

It was two weeks after her riding accident when a traveling chaise appeared at the front door and her aunt, Mrs. Thorpe, stepped down onto the gravel drive. Miss Blakelow had always been fond of Mr. Thorpe, her mother's elder brother, but she had failed to understand what he had seen in his wife, a cold, selfish woman with a hard, bony core where her heart should be. When Mr. Thorpe, her kind, gentle uncle, had died, Miss Blakelow had been left in the care of his wife, who had made it her mission to marry the young Georgiana off at the first opportunity.

Miss Blakelow and her aunt had never been close; it was this aunt who had been pushed into bringing her out all those years ago and who was intimately acquainted with everything that had befallen her since. That Mrs. Thorpe disliked her, she knew; that she had only agreed to champion her because she had married the brother of Miss Blakelow's mother, she also knew. So it was with trepidation that Miss Blakelow reluctantly went down to the parlor, where the woman was examining the thickness of dust on the mantelpiece.

The woman had her back to her as Miss Blakelow entered the room and gave a cold smile to no one in particular. Mrs. Thorpe was a thin woman—all bones and sharp edges—with pronounced cheekbones, a beak of a nose, small dark eyes buried deep in their sockets, and an oily curl of iron-gray hair resting immovably against her forehead as if it had been dipped in melted butter and had set hard. She wore a pewter-colored pelisse of satin and a small mean bonnet with a wilted, semivertical feather.

"So this is where you've been hiding yourself," remarked Mrs. Thorpe, turning at last to examine her niece. Then she froze. She gaped. She stared. She looked her over from head to toe and could do nothing but blink at her.

"Hello, Aunt," said Miss Blakelow in her calm, quiet voice, smiling vaguely at the reaction.

"Good God . . ."

"Won't you please sit down? Can I offer you some refreshment?"

Mrs. Thorpe opened her mouth to say something and then closed it again. Her mind drifted back the decade since she had last seen her niece—a young, vivacious, and beautiful girl—and tried to reconcile that picture with the staid, drab woman who stood calmly before her.

"Well," said Miss Blakelow with a kind smile, "I have already arranged for some tea, and then you may decide when it arrives."

"But you . . . you look so . . . I would not have recognized you for all the world."

"I am a little older, ma'am."

"Yes, to be sure . . . so are we all . . . but Good Lord. I would never have imagined . . ."

"No," replied Miss Blakelow, "and I hope that others do not 'imagine' either."

"But this . . . I mean, I came here after news reached my ears concerning you, Sophie—"

Miss Blakelow winced at the use of the name from her past; it reminded her of her youthful folly. She was Georgiana now. "My name is Georgiana Blakelow. I would be grateful if you would commit it to memory."

"Yes . . . of course." Mrs. Thorpe sat down heavily. "Good Lord, if your uncle could see you now."

Miss Blakelow smiled. "He would be a good deal surprised."

"He would indeed . . ."

"And so, Aunt? What is your reason for coming all this way?"

Mrs. Thorpe gave herself a mental shake. "I have come to speak to you on a delicate matter . . . concerning my daughter."

"And how is my cousin?" asked Miss Blakelow. "She must be seventeen by now."

"Eighteen."

"And . . . and has she had her come out, ma'am?" Miss Blakelow blushed faintly as she asked the question; the memories of her own disastrous come out were still fresh in the minds of both women and pervaded the air like a stench.

"This season gone was her first," replied Mrs. Thorpe somewhat awkwardly. "And you may imagine that she was a great success. I hope she may achieve a very good match indeed."

There was a silence. Miss Blakelow could not help but feel that her aunt was making the comparison. There was no doubt that the young Miss Thorpe would obey her mother's wishes, even if her cousin had not.

"I wish Charlotte every happiness," said Miss Blakelow.

John then appeared with the tea tray and several moments passed in silence while Miss Blakelow saw to the refreshments.

"It is her happiness that concerns me. It has come to my attention that your brother is on the lookout for a wife," said her aunt.

Miss Blakelow blinked. "William is four and twenty, ma'am. He is old enough to decide for himself when he wishes to marry."

"That he may be, but all of London knows that he does not have two shillings to rub together," said Mrs. Thorpe, twitching the skirts of her gown over her knee.

"He has an allowance, which I believe his mother put in trust for him."

"Yes, expressly to keep it from the grasping hands of his father," returned Mrs. Thorpe somewhat acidly.

"Well, whatever the reason," replied Miss Blakelow in her calm way, "he has a little money for the future."

"He is on the hunt for a fortune. Surely you must know that? From all I hear, he is well on the way to establishing himself in debtors' prison unless he finds himself a wife with means."

"I know nothing of that. I think that William will marry for love when the time comes."

"Love? You still prate of love? And where, pray, did all that talk of love get you?"

"We are not discussing me, Aunt—we are discussing William, although why he is any of your concern, I cannot imagine."

"When he is chasing after my daughter, then it is very much my concern," retorted Aunt Thorpe.

There was a silence.

"I see," said Miss Blakelow gravely.

"He has been seeing her behind my back. Secret assignations. Meetings in the park, and Charlotte without even a maid to lend her respectability."

Miss Blakelow was silent. She had heard from Lord Marcham that William was hanging out after a fortune, but never had she supposed the object of his desire to be Miss Charlotte Thorpe.

"I need not tell you the seriousness of the situation. You may imagine how concerned I am as a mother. And William without anyone to guide him, in short, as much a loose cannon as ever his father was. Charlotte is to come into a considerable fortune. I will make no secret of the fact that Sir William Blakelow is not the man I wish to see her married to."

"If money is his true object, then very likely someone richer will come along and your Charlotte will be safe."

Mrs. Thorpe gaped at her in an expression that always reminded her niece of a trout. "And is that all you have to say?"

"What do you expect me to say?" asked Miss Blakelow, sipping her tea.

"That you intend to do something."

"And what do you imagine that I may do? I am not William's guardian. He is a grown man and may marry where he wishes."

"He may not marry where he wishes," said Mrs. Thorpe, her small pearl earrings bobbing violently under her earlobes.

"Ten to one it is an infatuation that will be over before Christmas."

"You are very calm about it. But then, it would be in your interest to see him married off to a fortune, would it not? Your beloved Thorncote would be saved."

Miss Blakelow was amused. "My dear Aunt, with all due respect, if William's object is to save Thorncote, he will need to look for a much richer heiress than your daughter."

Mrs. Thorpe bristled. "You will do nothing?"

"I can *do* nothing. I have written to him and requested that he come home so that we may discuss what is to be done about the future of the house and that of the girls. When he comes I will speak to him."

"And when will that be? After he has spent all my daughter's money, no doubt?"

Miss Blakelow smiled and set down her cup. "That will depend upon whether Charlotte is willing to give it to him," she said quietly.

Mrs. Thorpe turned purple with anger. "Well, I begin to think I have come on a fool's errand."

"I begin to think that you might be right," agreed Miss Blakelow.

"Oh, you are a cool fish, aren't you? Sitting there with that smug smile upon your lips. Well, you will no longer be amused when you hear what I have to tell you. I could not believe it when I heard the story, and having seen you, I believe it even less."

Miss Blakelow raised a brow in silent inquiry.

"It has been brought to my attention that you have been encouraging the attentions of the Earl of Marcham," said Mrs. Thorpe.

Miss Blakelow, despite her best efforts, blushed faintly. "Indeed, ma'am?"

"It is being said that you have set your cap at him," said Mrs. Thorpe, "and that he has set you up as his latest flirt. Now, miss, what do you have to say to that?"

"That it is untrue."

"Do you deny that you have encouraged his society?"

"I deny that I have done it through any other reason than to secure the future of Thorncote," said Miss Blakelow promptly.

"Has he offered to make you his mistress?" demanded her aunt.

Miss Blakelow was beginning to lose her temper. "He would not insult me by such a suggestion, ma'am."

"No?" sneered Mrs. Thorpe very, very softly.

Miss Blakelow struggled for calm. "His lordship has behaved toward me in a manner every inch the gentleman. He may have a reputation, but he has not laid a finger on me."

"He will," replied Mrs. Thorpe assuredly.

"You know the earl? You are in his confidence?" demanded Miss Blakelow.

"Anyone may know what he wants. I know his type. And so, my girl, do you. None better."

Miss Blakelow paled. "You pain me, Aunt, by your language—"

"Do you not remember? Are you so fixated with him that you forget everything you learned? God knows that it is abhorrent to me to speak of that time in your past—"

"Then don't speak of it," flashed Miss Blakelow, her eyes blazing.

"Your mother entrusted you to my care—"

"My mother did no such thing," replied Miss Blakelow coldly.

"And in that capacity, I must counsel you against the folly of courting a man like Marcham."

"I am not courting him. We are friends."

"Friends? You cannot be friends with a man like him. Sanity precludes it. Honesty, decency, and delicacy preclude it. You must know that a woman who links her name to his, even in friendship, is finished in the eyes of society?"

Miss Blakelow smiled coldly. "Lord Marcham has been a good friend to me."

"Do you have no care as to your reputation?"

"I did. As you can see, I have taken great care of my reputation. I have crafted a new one to fool society." Miss Blakelow paused and with a wan smile indicated the clothes she wore. "And now my pristine reputation has replaced the tarnished one I made in my youth. My reputation defines me as Lord Marcham's defines him—even though we both loathe our public faces. In that respect we are very similar, he and I."

"Surely you are not foolish enough to believe he means marriage?" exclaimed Mrs. Thorpe, her pinched eyes as wide as they could be.

"I believe that his lordship intends to marry someone," replied her niece calmly.

"Oh, I'm sure he does—he must, at any rate—but *you*?"

"I have a headache, Aunt. I hope you will excuse me, but I must go and lie down for a while. I will ask John to bring your carriage to the door."

"Take a good long look at yourself, my girl," said Mrs. Thorpe, who stayed seated in her chair, continuing as if her niece had not spoken.

Miss Blakelow stood and went to the fireplace, where she pulled the bell cord. "I have no desire to do so, however, and I must ask you to leave."

"You have lost your youth and your looks and much more besides—heaven knows who will take you now. Your course is run, Sophie. You had your chance and you threw it away, and now you live upon the charity of a family who are not yours—"

"John, please be good enough to bring Mrs. Thorpe's carriage to the door."

"Yes, miss."

Her aunt stood but made no move to leave. "I did my best by you. I made you the hit of the season, didn't I? I promised Mr. Thorpe that I would. I did it for his sake, because he loved his sister so, and when she died he wanted nothing more than to see her daughter creditably established. You had gowns and bonnets and lace. You had suitors vying for your hand. You had all of London at your feet. You might have had anyone—anyone you wanted! And how did you thank me? You threw it all back in my face! I tried to see you suitably established with a man of means but you rejected him—"

"He was nearly fifty," put in Miss Blakelow hotly, "and I was barely nineteen."

"And you might now have had a home of your own instead of living upon someone else's charity," flashed Mrs. Thorpe. "Do your so-called brothers and sisters know what you are? Does Lord Marcham?"

"Your carriage is nearly ready, Aunt. I must beg you to leave."

"Does he know? Do you think he will want you after that? And what do you think your friends in Worcestershire will think of you once I tell them who you are?"

"I care not for your threats. You may have fired me off very creditably, but the thing that I wanted from you most, you were unwilling to give: affection. The only person in your house who gave tuppence about me was my uncle. But he was ill and dying. And once he had gone, you and Charlotte and my other cousins treated me like the village leper. One of the reasons I did what I did was to escape from you, ma'am."

The butler appeared and fixedly stared at the floor, awaiting further instruction.

Mrs. Thorpe drew on her gloves. "You see to it that your brother stays away from my daughter, or I will make it impossible for you to live in this county or any other."

The woman stalked from the room, leaving a wake of sickly perfume behind her.

Miss Blakelow sat down heavily in a chair and put her forehead into her hand.

"Here, miss," said a gentle voice. She looked up to find John offering her a glass of wine. She smiled her thanks and took it.

"John?"

"Yes, miss?"

"I think it's time that we moved on again."

"Yes, miss. Begging your pardon, miss, but where will we go?"

The young woman sighed. "I don't know, John. I honestly don't know."

CHAPTER 19

"And so, Miss Blakelow, have you missed me?" Lord Marcham asked, casting a swift smiling look at her profile. He had stayed away purposely, hoping that his absence might make her heart grow fonder.

He was taking her out for a drive in his curricle. It was a beautiful but cold November day, the sky a cloudless swath of blue, the sunlight golden upon the autumn leaves. They had reached the boundary of her father's estate and had taken the road up into the thickly wooded hills. Lord Marcham had left his groom to kick his heels at Thorncote until his master returned. If Miss Blakelow noticed this improper behavior, she did not mention it. It might be improper, but the moment of privacy was the perfect opportunity to tell his lordship that the neighborhood was gossiping about them and that it would be best if they didn't see each other for a while.

"Given that I only saw your lordship a couple of days ago, I rather think that unlikely, don't you?" she replied, looking away from him and out at the fields that rolled away to the hills. Her spectacles impeded her sight, and she peered over the top of them when she thought that her companion was distracted enough with his driving not to notice.

"Oh, too cruel. It has been at least a week. And when I think how I have lain awake thinking of you."

"Pooh. What nonsense."

"Lain awake, I tell you. In an agony to know if I have featured in your dreams."

"In my nightmares, quite possibly," she muttered.

His lips twitched appreciatively. "Now that is not very charitable of you, Miss Blakelow, is it? When I have dreamed of holding you close in my arms—"

"And my knee in your unmentionables?" she put in sweetly.

"I see that I will have to purchase a pair of iron breeches."

She turned her head aside to hide a smile. "They would be in very great danger of rusting from disuse, my lord. I'm quite sure you spend a considerable portion of your life—" She broke off hastily, suddenly realizing that she was once again engaging in a highly improper conversation with this man.

"You were saying, ma'am?" he prompted.

"Nothing."

"You were about to say that I spend a considerable portion of my life without any clothes at all?" he suggested, a teasing smile around his mouth.

She stared at the distant trees, a swath of red mounting up her neck. "No, my lord, I was not."

"Well, I should hope not, indeed. To hear a woman of your unimpeachable character talk in such a shocking manner—"

"Don't," she said quickly, a little more harshly than she had intended, her recent encounter with her Aunt Thorpe still very much on her mind. To be accused of encouraging a man like Lord Marcham, to be thought fast, to have the neighborhood into which she had been welcomed, criticizing her for a flirtation with a rake was intolerable. How had Mrs. Thorpe known about her friendship with the earl? Someone must have told her.

"And to think you wrote a pamphlet condemning my morals," he added, a gleam of unholy amusement in his eyes.

"I said don't!" she cried.

He frowned at the very real distress in her voice. The laughter in his eyes vanished as he brought the horses to a sudden halt and turned on the seat so that he could see her face. "Now what's amiss?" he asked.

"Nothing, my lord," she replied, averting her face and trying valiantly to compose herself once again. She knew he was only jesting, but the manner of her conversation with her aunt was so fresh in her mind that any reference to it was like a finger jabbed into a gaping wound. That he should mock her for her past indiscretions when she had already suffered that and worse from others was simply too painful. She could endure anyone else's ribbing on the subject of her folly, but not his. "Please drive on."

"Not until you tell me what's wrong. You must know that I was teasing you," he demanded, utterly perplexed by her consternation. Where was the Georgie of old? Where the woman who gave quite as good as she got? Something was wrong, and his lordship would not rest until he found out what it was.

"I wish that you wouldn't," she replied in a small voice.

He tried to look into her face, but it was cast into shadow by the deep brim of her bonnet. "Miss Blakelow," he said quietly. "You must know that I would not willingly give you pain for all the world."

She swallowed hard on a curious lump that seemed to have formed in her throat. The gentleness in his voice was nearly her undoing. "Please drive on," she said again. "We are blocking the road."

He watched her for a long moment, looked as if he might say something further, and then appeared to let it go. He flicked the reins and the horses moved forward. "Well, we shall confine our discourse to safer waters then. What say you to crop rotation?"

She was relieved and grateful to him for changing the subject. "Must we?" she asked, dutifully looking mortified at the proposed topic of conversation.

His face took on a look of mock horror. "Crop rotation and the espalier training of soft fruit trees."

"Oh, Lord."

"I am relieved to hear you say so, Miss Blakelow. You may tell me instead the history of your life."

She pulled a face. "I do not consider that subject any improvement on crop rotation."

"How is it that you have lived at Thorncote all these years, and yet I have never before met you there?" he asked, guiding the horses with an expert hand over a narrow humpbacked bridge.

"There is no mystery, my lord. You were not often at Holme Park before this summer, and I am not often away from Thorncote. We did meet once, in Loughton, I believe, at an assembly-room dance a number of years ago."

"Did we? I do not remember. Did we dance together?"

"I believe you only danced with the prettiest girls, my lord," she murmured.

"Then I feel sure we must have danced together."

She smiled but the expression did not reach her eyes. She was all too familiar with the cheap flattery of men and had become immune to it. "Do you think so indeed? For everyone knows me to be a great beauty, do they not?" she mocked gently.

He looked at her sharply. "*Now* what have I said? I gave you a compliment, ma'am."

"So you did," she agreed and clasped her hands in her lap. "I think you should stop the carriage, Lord Marcham."

"And why would I do that?"

"Because we are about to have an argument, and I do not wish to upset you."

"Too late for that," he replied, his mouth set hard. "You have already accused me of being the sort of man who bandies false flattery about to suit my own ends. I will take leave to inform *you*, ma'am, that I may be a man of a certain reputation, but I am not a sycophant."

"I apologize if I offended you, my lord."

"And what would be the point of an apology that you do not mean?" he demanded, giving rein to his anger. "You think me vain and idle and selfish, do you not?"

"No, my lord," she said softly, and her heart broke a little at his tone.

"You think that I spend all my time drinking and gambling or seducing women. You don't think me capable of a sensible thought on books or politics or art, do you?"

She shook her head, hating herself for making him think that way about himself. "That is not true."

"You think my sole aim in life is fleecing men like your father of their property for the amusement it affords me. It has not occurred to you that the reason that your father was so determined to sit down at the faro table with me was to fleece me of *my* property. I had already told the man to go home twice, but he would not listen. He was on a winning streak and was convinced he would add a great deal of my fortune to his winnings. Well, my naive Miss Blakelow, he was wrong. I have lost a great deal of money to men a lot cleverer than your father."

"Put me down. I wish to walk home," she said coldly.

"Does it upset you to confront what he was? I told you before and I will tell you again, Sir William Blakelow was a fool. He was a moderately well-off man who lived life as if he were as rich as a king, and you and your family have paid for his folly."

"Please stop the carriage," she insisted, her voice dripping with icy disdain.

"But *you*, ma'am," he said, turning to look at her, his eyes on her face. "*You* baffle me exceedingly. Why do you never wish to talk about your past?"

"Stop this carriage at once, my lord!"

"For reasons I have yet to fathom, you are hiding behind those spectacles and hideous clothes of yours to stop anyone getting too close. Heaven forbid that a man should be able to see beyond the mask and admire the woman underneath. Heaven forbid that a man should desire you. What now, Miss Blakelow? I have seen past your disguise. What else will you throw at me to push me away?"

She made no answer to this and looked stonily at the road ahead. What could she say? She could no more deny the truth of his words than the need to breathe in and out. He was right, after all.

"Do you suppose that thick spectacles will stop me from kissing you if I want to?" he demanded.

She spun around to face him with a gasp. "If *you* want to?" she repeated incredulously. "What about me and what *I* want? For your information, I don't want to be kissed by you or anyone else."

"No?" he asked softly, his eyes on hers. "Would you like to put that theory to the test?"

She stared back until she lost the battle and looked away. "Let me down at once."

He brought his horses to a standstill under the shade of an apple tree and looped the reins over his knee. "You do not answer me because you know it is not true. Look at me, Georgiana . . ."

She kept her face averted, her hands clinging to the side of the curricle, as if it were a raft in a storm. "Please, my lord," she whispered. "Don't."

He pulled off his driving glove and reached a hand across to gently cup her chin. "Look at me."

She turned reluctantly to gaze into his eyes.

"What have I ever done to make you fear me?" he whispered.

"N-nothing, my lord," she stammered, struggling to keep her emotions in check.

"Have I ever given you cause to mistrust me?"

She shook her head.

"Then what is the matter?" he asked. "Why do you pick an argument with me?"

"Because I cannot do this," she said.

"You cannot do what?" he asked.

"Please, my lord. This . . . *acquaintance* of ours . . . must be at an end."

He shook his head in bafflement as if to clear it of cobwebs. "Why? I don't understand."

"People are talking. They are saying things about me. Things that I cannot defend for as long as we are friends."

"What things?"

That I have set my cap at you. That you are going to make me your mistress. That you will cast me aside when you grow tired of me. And my Aunt Thorpe is threatening to tell you everything about me and I could not bear it. I could not bear to see the condemnation and disgust in your eyes.

"You know what things," she whispered.

There was another silence.

"And so you would cast me aside to save a little gossip?"

"Hardly anything so paltry, my lord. A little gossip, as you call it, can ruin a woman's life."

"And you care for that more than you do for my friendship?"

She choked as her sadness lodged like a ball in her throat. "No . . . yes . . . I have to."

There was a sharp, painful silence. "I see." His fingers traced the outline of her cheek, his thumb tracing the sensitive curve of her lower lip. "To hell with the gossips," he said, "to hell with them all. You are a passionate creature. You were made for love. And I was made for you. Let me love you, Georgie."

So he had said it. Her Aunt Thorpe had said he would, but Miss Blakelow had refused to believe he was just like all the other men of her acquaintance. He wanted her to be his mistress. Well, at least now it was out in the open. No more games; they had found the truth at last. She felt the bitter sting of disappointment in the back of her throat. She was going to cry. And soon, but she'd be damned if she would cry in front of him.

"Oh . . . you—you cad!" she cried.

He blinked at her. "I beg your pardon?" he replied.

"You would like that, wouldn't you?" she continued, her voice shaking with anger. "I believe that's all you have ever wanted from me."

"What are you talking about—?"

Miss Blakelow stared at him, heavy tears brimming in her eyes, slowly shaking her head in disbelief. "Would you like to do it right here on the seat of your curricle, my lord? Or would all that heaving and groaning frighten the horses? But I'm sure for a man of your considerable talent and expertise that would present no trouble at all. You are, after all, a master of seduction. Shall I hitch up my skirts right here, my lord, or shall we find a barn?"

His lordship had the distinct sensation that he had just stepped into horse manure up to his neck. He saw the blaze of anger and hurt in her eyes and held out his hand in a placating gesture. "I think that you have misunderstood me."

"Oh, I understood you perfectly, my lord. I can readily believe that a woman whom you haven't bedded must be a serious fascination to you. No doubt that was what the marriage proposal was all about to begin with. Just a way to get me bedded sooner—preferably before the vows were spoken so you would never have to actually say them."

"Georgiana—"

"I must be a rare specimen indeed, one who must be studied. There must clearly be something wrong with me if I have not succumbed to your charm, is that not right?"

"That is not what I meant."

"How is it that you have not already had me?" she demanded. "That is what you are asking yourself. You have walked with me, ridden with me, taken me for picnics, flirted with, and flattered me. You even paid for that ridiculous ball gown. And women have fallen into your bed for less, have they not?"

"You know very well I meant nothing of the sort—"

"I believe you set out to seduce me from the first moment you found out that I wrote that pamphlet. You swore for revenge, did you not? And what better way to punish a bluestocking than to rob her of her virtue?"

He grasped her wrist. "You have deliberately misunderstood me. You know that I meant no insult, but you have been determined to pick a fight with me from the first moment you laid eyes on me this morning. Why? What has happened?"

"Nothing."

"Someone has said something to upset you, haven't they? Is it my sister? Has Sarah upset you?"

"It is not your sister. I am just sick and tired of men and their assumption that every woman is fair game. I came to this part of the world to escape from men like you—" She broke off, her voice choking on a sob.

He pulled her around to face him again. "Men like me . . . what the devil does that mean? I'm a gentleman. I do not make indecent offers to gentlewomen no matter how attractive I may find them," he said angrily.

"No? Why do I find that hard to believe?"

"Because you have lost all faith in my sex, that's why. You think all men are like him."

"Him? Who are you talking about?" asked Miss Blakelow as she felt the color drain from her face. She knew precisely whom he was referring to.

"You tell me," he said, glaring down into her eyes. "The man who broke your heart. And he did break your heart, didn't he, Georgie? He stamped all over it."

She struggled to release her wrist from his grasp. "Let me go."

"Do you still love him?" he demanded. "Is that why you push every other man away?"

"Let me go!"

"Or is it that you are afraid to love again in case you get hurt?"

"And why is it that you immediately assume that I am lovelorn because I am not falling into your arms? It never occurs to you that I simply don't want you, does it? You have no interest in me, but you pretend that you do because you have made a bet that you can make me love you. It is all a game to you. You mock me by pretending to be attracted to me. But look at me. What do I have that you could possibly desire? Why would you prefer me to Marianne or any other beautiful girl in the neighborhood? It is laughable. And I would be grateful if you would credit me with a little intelligence. The only reason you come here is for revenge, pure and simple."

Lord Marcham clenched his teeth with frustration. "If I set out with any such intention, it has been many weeks now that I have forgotten it in the pleasure of your company."

She laughed scornfully, shaking her head in disbelief. "I am *not* going to marry you. I do not even like you. Your lifestyle is abhorrent to me as is your pursuit of the most vulnerable in our society at the card table or in the bedroom."

There was a chilly silence.

"Indeed?" he inquired at last, his voice like ice. "How very kind of you to enlighten me as to my faults. I realize that to such a paragon of perfection as you, I must be a sad disappointment indeed."

She flushed. "You force me to be blunt, my lord."

He struggled for a long moment to retain his composure, a muscle flexing in his jaw. "As you wish, ma'am," he said coldly, taking the reins into his hands, "as you wish. You win. I officially give up. Go and be happy playing schoolmistress to your sisters' children. I care not. I wish you joy of this solitary existence you have chosen, and I sincerely hope that you may not live to regret it."

"I won't."

"We will see, won't we? Live your life alone if you wish, but don't expect me to do the same. I'm tired of loneliness. I need someone to hold at night even if you don't."

She stared at a distant clump of trees, unable to say another word. The thought of him living with another woman as his wife, holding her close in his arms at night, made her so unhappy that her previous resolve not to cry in front of him was broken, and the tears fell unheeded from her eyes.

"Well, let us turn around and go back. I will not trouble you with my acquaintance any longer," he said coldly.

He swung the curricle about, and they drove in silence the entire way back to the house, where his lordship's groom helped Miss Blakelow down and took her place on the seat next to his master. She had hardly set foot upon the gravel when his lordship set the vehicle in motion once again, and she watched it in misery until it had disappeared through the lodge gates.

Now that their friendship was over, Miss Blakelow mourned the loss of it like a severed limb. She had driven their friendship over the edge, willingly, determinedly, because there had been no other choice. She simply could not risk her reputation again—there was too much to lose. If William married Charlotte Thorpe, her aunt would carry out her threat to tell his lordship the whole history of her past, and she could not bear to see it in his eyes when he found out that the woman he thought he knew was a lie.

CHAPTER 20

A WEEK LATER, TWO men galloped over the rise, their coattails flapping out behind them, their faces chilled by a cold November breeze. They reined in as they crested the hill and looked down on Thorncote, the house nestled prettily amongst the trees.

"Well, and are you going to let me have a look at your beauty?" asked Hal, grinning across at his brother.

Lord Marcham's horse pranced restlessly, and it took him a moment to calm his steed. "If we must. But I am not altogether sure who you may mean."

"Oh, this gets better and better! So there is more than one beauty at Thorncote? I *thought* you were keeping your cards close to your chest. Don't trust me with her, do you?"

"My dear Hal, precisely what are you talking about?" asked the earl, looking pained.

"The chit Sarah tells me you are hanging after. The one you spirited out of the house before I even managed to get a look," complained his brother. "Not fair, big brother, not fair at all. To keep all the best sport for yourself when you must know that Holme is as dull as dull can be."

Lord Marcham shrugged. "The doors are unlocked. No one is forcing you to stay if you find it tedious."

"Now, Robbie, don't get in a miff. I like Holme well enough, but you must allow that compared to London, the country is a little slow."

"My dear Hal, there are three young and extremely pretty Blakelow sisters and one spinster aunt for you to try your charms on. Not even you can find fault with that."

"And Georgiana?" asked his brother, a smile on his lips.

The earl looked away to the hills behind the house on the other side of the valley, where a lone figure, no more than a pale blur at this distance, was slowly moving toward a farm gate. "By all means," he replied. "I wish you luck with your endeavor. You'll need it."

"Speaking from experience, Rob?"

His lordship made no reply but patted the neck of his horse.

"Oh-ho!" cried Hal, grinning. "Here's a to-do! Lovers' tiff, eh?"

Lord Marcham threw him a scornful look. "To have a lovers' tiff, as you term it, one would actually have to be in love. And I don't think Georgiana Blakelow is capable of any such emotion."

His brother's grin broadened. "She *has* upset you, hasn't she? Is that why you have been in the foulest temper all week?"

The gray eyes swung around sharply in his direction. "Can we go?"

"Go home? Not a bit of it," replied Hal cheerfully. "I want to see the delightful Marianne. She is quite something out of the common way, or so I'm told."

"She is," his lordship agreed. "If you like meek and mild."

"And you don't like her?"

"Me? God no. Not in the way you mean, at any rate."

"Sarah thinks that you secretly wish to make a match of it," mused Hal airily.

"Does she indeed? Then Sarah is sadly mistaken."

"Come on then," cried Hal, urging his horse into a canter. "You may introduce me!"

❧

Hal Holkham could hardly believe his eyes.

This was Georgiana Blakelow? This oddity was his brother's beauty? This strange-looking woman who was wearing a very large, ugly, and outmoded cap upon her head was the woman with whom he was infatuated? He must be queer in his attic!

Why, when his lordship could have the company of the most stunning women society had to offer, had he fallen for this nervous creature who stared at the floor through thick glass spectacles and covered any curves she may have had under a greatly oversized mourning gown? Apart from the fact that she was clumsy and spilled half the contents of the teapot across the tray, she also spoke no more than a handful words from the moment they arrived until the moment they took their leave.

That she and Marcham had fallen out was obvious; they barely spoke two words to each other for the entire duration of the visit. Hal watched his brother and noted with amusement how often his eyes strayed across the room, not seeking the angelic countenance of Marianne Blakelow, but seeking instead the stony features of the eldest sister.

And the strangest thing of all was that the woman seemed to show no interest in the earl. In fact she seemed far more interested in watching *him*. Hal would look up and find her staring at him, hastily turning away when she was caught in the act. What the devil was the woman staring at? Did he have a pimple on the end of his nose or something?

He decided to ignore her, trying to stave off the nagging sense that he knew her from somewhere, and instead focused his eyes on the perfect youthful bloom on Marianne's downy cheeks. She really was the most delectable little piece. Too bad if his brother had cast his net into other waters. This girl was all eager attention and blushes, and he'd be damned if he wouldn't have a little dalliance while he was in the neighborhood.

⁂

Miss Blakelow was never more relieved than when the two gentlemen stood up to leave.

To endure the icy, resentful stare of Lord Marcham was bad enough, but to sit opposite Hal Holkham for the first time in ten years, to be forced to watch him flirting with Marianne, was more than her nerves could bear.

She exchanged a long meaningful look with John as he showed the visitors to the door, and she soon pleaded a headache and went to her room.

Hal Holkham was here. She paced the floor, her fingers trembling.

Hal Holkham. She put a shaking hand to her head and swore in a most unladylike manner.

What did this mean? Had he recognized her? How long would it be before others found her too? How long before her past threatened to rip her from her family? She couldn't bear the thought of being separated from Marianne, Kitty, Lizzy, Ned, and especially young Jack.

Mr. Holkham had sat opposite her, a cup of tea in his hands, looking every bit as handsome as she had remembered. He had paid her no attention, of course—why should he? He did not recognize her. She had gone to great lengths to ensure that no one should know her. But the way he looked at her, as if trying to place her, was disquieting to be sure.

She had peered at him over the rim of her cup, taking in his figure, his face, his smile. She couldn't help it. Her eyes were drawn to his face as if he were magnetic. He seemed to sense her stare and looked in her direction and then uncomfortably looked away. He smiled uncertainly, as if feeling out whether she was friend or foe, but she could not return the gesture. Her mind drifted back to the last time she had seen him, to that sordid inn, miles from anywhere. His arms, warm and safe . . . comforting. He looked thinner, older, slightly world-weary, but he was still her Hal.

And then she had sensed other eyes upon her and knew that his lordship was watching her. She could feel his scrutiny, the critical, resentful stare burning into her face. His expression when they parted was not one she would easily forget.

She stalked to the armoire in the corner of the room and pulled down the cloak bag that was always kept packed and ready for an emergency flight.

Had he guessed? How much did Marcham know? And did he blame her for it as every man she had ever come to care for had?

"I thought that's what you'd be thinking," said a low voice behind her.

Miss Blakelow whirled around as the door closed. "Oh, John, what choice do I have?"

"He didn't recognize you."

"He was looking at me," she cried, flinging the bag onto the bed. "I could tell he sensed something."

"He did *not* recognize you, miss," he said again, coming toward her.

"I have to go. Now. This minute," she said, unfastening the bag and opening it.

"We can't, miss. We're not ready."

She picked up her book and flung it into the bag. "Then I'll go on ahead. I'll send word where I am."

"And bring *him* direct to your door in the process," said John with gentle admonishment. "I won't let you do it. I swore to your papa that I would look after you, and I'm not letting you wander alone without even me for company."

"But, John, don't you see? If Hal has found me, it's only a matter of time before *he* finds me too. And I can't allow that."

John put his hands on her shoulders and turned her to face him. "You have become as dear to me as a daughter. Do you honestly think I would let anything happen to you?"

She looked into his well-worn and rugged face. "I'm tired of running, John."

"I know you are, miss."

"And I'm frightened."

He clumsily patted her shoulder. "There now, don't you cry. Old John Maynard still has a trick or two up his sleeve."

"No," she said, wiping angrily at her tears. "I mean . . . I'm truly grateful to you . . . for everything . . . but no more. Not this time. You've followed me from pillar to post since my mother died. You gave up your own chance of a family and happiness to look after me."

He blushed. "Nah, miss. It's not so bad. And I'd do it again if the decision was mine to take."

"Dear John, you have been such a good friend to me. But enough. You love Thorncote. You are married. You have Janet now, and I won't let you give her up for me. The time has come for me to shift for myself."

"And what do you plan to do, miss? Where will you go?"

"I don't know," she replied.

Her faithful servant cleared his throat. "As the wife of the Earl of Marcham, you'd have his protection . . ."

Her eyes lit with fire. She remembered the way he had looked at her, and she was determined that she would never ask him for anything ever again. "No!"

"No man would dare go up against his lordship—"

"I do not need his help."

"Begging your pardon, miss, but I think you do."

"I'd rather marry Mr. Peabody than marry a man who has less idea of marital fidelity than . . . than the Prince of Wales!" she flashed.

"I know you and he have fallen out . . ."

She glared at him. "Do you?" she asked dangerously.

"My Janet is friendly with the housekeeper up at the big house, miss. The word was that you sent him to the roundabout, and that he was not best pleased about it."

Miss Blakelow fumed. So now her private conversation with his lordship was all over Loughton? "Indeed?"

John swallowed. "Janet told me that he—um, well, perhaps I'd best not say."

"She told you that he what, John?" she pursued with narrowed eyes.

He shuffled his feet. "I'm not sure as I should say, miss."

"John, you had better tell me."

Her servant colored and looked at the floor. "Janet told me that he fell asleep in the bed where you stayed when you were knocked off your horse, miss."

Miss Blakelow opened her mouth to say something, thought better of it, and closed it again.

"He's taken your refusal awful bad, miss."

"Good," she said, swiping a miniature portrait of her mother from her bedside table and throwing it in the bag.

"They say he's hardly eaten a thing all week."

"I don't care," she declared.

John reached into the bag, took out the tiny painting, and set it back upon the table again.

She glared at him. "What are you doing?"

"I could have a word with Janet, who could drop a word to her friend up at the house that you were of a mind to have him."

"And have all the servants knowing my business?"

"Begging your pardon, miss, but they know it anyway."

She put her hands on her hips. "I will *not* marry Robert Holkham. Can I be any plainer?"

"It would solve a good many problems."

"And create a good many more," she muttered, pulling a bundle of letters from a drawer and flinging them into the bag. Marrying Lord Marcham would mean telling him the truth about her past—all of it. The thought of looking into his eyes as she told him, knowing he would in all probability despise her, was simply unthinkable.

He bit his lip. "Lord Marcham is . . . is a man of the world. Chances are that he'll understand your predicament better than most."

She shook her head. "He won't."

"You don't know that."

"I do know it. Men—present company excepted—are hypocrites. He once told me that men of his sort did not fall in love with women like me."

John, recognizing the signs of a stubborn female digging in her heels, said no more. But once his mistress had calmed down enough to stop trembling, he managed to elicit from her a promise that she would not run away that night and went even so far as to encourage her to put the bag back on top of the armoire.

The next morning brought a brief letter addressed to Miss Blakelow from her brother William who was still in London. She opened it with some impatience and was little satisfied with its contents.

On the subject of her Aunt Thorpe's demands that he cease his dalliance with her daughter, Charlotte, he merely wrote that Mrs. Thorpe had a mouth that put him in mind of a horse he once had sight of at Tattersall's. He was hoping to come to Thorncote for the earl's ball but could not be certain, as he had been invited to stay with a friend, Mr. Boyd, who was a capital fellow.

Miss Blakelow screwed up his note and hurled it into the fire. Foolish, silly boy! Did he not know what he endangered by playing with the affections of Charlotte Thorpe? Did he not know how close to ruin they all were?

She hastily seized a pen and paper and wrote to him again, demanding that he come home immediately. So distracted by her thoughts was Miss Blakelow that she had forgotten to pick up her glasses and cap before she left the room, and thus, when Hal Holkham entered the drawing room in the middle of the afternoon in pursuit of Marianne, he was rather shocked to find a familiar face looking back at him.

So entirely was Miss Blakelow thrown by the encounter that she knocked her sewing basket over, and silks of every color tumbled onto the floor. It gave her an excuse to avert her gaze, however, and for several minutes she was employed in retrieving her belongings while keeping up a stream of utterly pointless conversation about the weather as if nothing in the world were wrong.

Oh, where was her aunt? Where was Marianne? She was desperate for rescue, for this man was staring at her as if she were a ghost. She swallowed, blushed, and stammered something about needing to go upstairs.

"Sophie?" he whispered.

"Who?" she asked, in a valiant attempt to continue with her ruse.

He stared at her, his mind clearly trying to make sense of what he saw before him. "Who the devil . . . ? Who are you?"

"We met the other day, I believe," she said brightly, in an attempt to bluff her way through the situation. "I am Georgiana Blakelow."

His boots gleamed in the sunlight as he walked toward her, and he bowed. His eyes were dark and held hers, and she felt as if she could swim in their depths.

"Sophie? Is it you?" he asked softly.

She moved away. "I think you are mistaken, sir. I know of no one by that name—"

He turned toward the fireplace, took a stride toward it, and then spun around to face her once again. "I—I don't believe it. I thought you were dead."

She swallowed hard. "I say again, my name is Georgiana—"

He narrowed his eyes in triumph. "I *thought* I recognized you the other day! I was racking my brains all the way home, but I couldn't quite place you . . ."

Miss Blakelow felt a rising sense of panic as the situation seemed to be slipping beyond her control. "If you will excuse me, sir, I have an appointment. If you are looking for Marianne, she has walked into Loughton. She will be back within the hour, I daresay. Good day to you."

He laid a hand on her arm to detain her. "No, don't run away . . . Sophie. It is you, isn't it?"

Miss Blakelow's eyes slid from his. What was the point of continuing to deny it? He had recognized her.

He laughed and shook his head. "Oh, this is famous! To think of how we all looked for you but you vanished into thin air! And this is where you have been hiding all this time?"

She did not answer him.

"Oh, what a good joke it is! Two miles from Marcham's door! Just wait until I tell Caroline! How she will roar with laughter!"

Her eyes shot to his face, and she grasped his arm imploringly. "Oh, no, you must not. Please promise me that you won't tell anyone who I am."

He looked slightly taken aback. "Not tell anyone? Not tell Caro, your dearest friend?"

Miss Blakelow shook her head. "I cannot risk it. If he should find me . . ."

"He?" Mr. Holkham grew quiet. "Is he still after you then?"

She gave a laugh that was utterly bereft of humor. "Oh, yes. He'll never give up."

"I did not know that it was you the other day . . ." he said. "I mean . . . when I knocked you from your horse."

"I took care that you should not know me. I took great care that no one should know me."

He nodded slowly. "Georgiana Blakelow. The perfect ruse."

She shrugged. "She has served me well enough."

"Does my brother know about us?"

She shook her head and dropped her eyes to the floor. "No. And it must stay that way. No one can know who I am, Hal. No one. You must promise me."

"But why?"

She looked up at him. "Because I am still in hiding. Because I cannot allow my reputation to catch up with me. Because I would not inflict my past upon my brothers and sisters, that's why."

"Who knows what happened but you and I?" he asked.

His voice was deep and intoxicating, and listening to him, she was transported back to when he had persuaded her to run away with him ten years ago. He was handsome. His voice was like silk. She had known men like him before and they were dangerous.

"Do you forget that I was ruined in the eyes of the world?" she asked in a low, calm voice.

"The world is a great deal too ready to listen to gossip."

"I think that we gave the world enough to gossip about, Mr. Holkham," she said acidly. "We were away for three days."

"And who knew?" he asked again. "Your Aunt Thorpe. Julius. You and me."

"Yes, and your mother and your sister and all the servants. Not to mention your *wife*, who you conveniently forgot to mention, then as now," she added scathingly.

He colored faintly beneath his tan. "It was not intended to be that way."

"No?" she asked. "How was it intended then? You left me alone in the middle of nowhere without a penny to my name. Was that an indication of how much you cared for me, Hal?"

"I was young and foolish," he said. "I know that you hate me. God knows you have good reason."

"I don't hate you."

"I hope that's true. I truly regret what happened," he said. "You must believe me. I know what I did was wrong. But my feelings for you were real—I swear it. I loved you."

"Don't." The word rang out in the room, and she immediately held out her hand as if to ward him off. It was too much. It was too painful. The memories still cut deep.

"My little Sophie," he said softly. "I used to call you that . . . remember?"

"Don't, Hal . . . please."

"It is so good to see you again after all these years," he whispered, coming toward her. "And you are still so beautiful. You have hardly changed in ten years."

Miss Blakelow laughed unsteadily. "You're such a poor liar, Hal. You always were, you know."

He smiled, relieved that he had broken down some tiny corner of her defenses. "We were inseparable for a time, weren't we?" he asked, his voice warm with nostalgia. "I always remember that summer with such fondness. We used to talk about everything. So free and easy in each other's company. So different from Mary and me . . . But you were a secret and no one could know, not even our families, so we had to pretend in public that we were nothing to each other. And we danced at balls as if we were strangers, when we had just been out on the terrace kissing only moments before . . . and we stole glances across the dining room at each other when no one else was looking. And there were all those meetings after dark, when your aunt had gone to bed. Those kisses in the moonlight. I remember those kisses, Sophie. They kept me warm on all those lonely nights in Brussels. Mary and I—we were never intimate and I was so desperately lonely. Then along came my little Sophie, a beautiful slip of a girl, who stole my heart and told me that she'd keep it safe for me forever. Do you still have it, Sophie? Do you still have my heart?"

She closed her eyes, finding some inner resolve from somewhere. For years she had fantasized about this meeting, about seeing him again and what she would say to him. She had practiced speeches that were meant to tell him how little he had meant to her, how utterly forgettable his kisses were, how she had long ago forgotten his touch . . .

But all these well-rehearsed monologues were forgotten in his presence. His voice was seductive, as smooth as chocolate, slowly pulling her under, sucking at her resolve until it melted away. "I don't know," she answered.

"Am I nothing to you then?" he demanded in a low voice. "Have you forgotten me so easily?"

"Easily?" she repeated. "Hardly that."

"I have not forgotten you. I still have the lock of your hair that you gave me. Do you remember?"

"Oh, stop! Can't you see?" she asked passionately. "It is over. It was over before it ever began."

"I tried to find you. You ran away and I searched everywhere, but you vanished into thin air."

"I don't believe you," she whispered.

He seized her shoulders. "It's true. Look at me."

She slowly raised her eyes to his.

"Had I known that you were hiding from me in plain sight for all these years . . . not three miles from Holme Park . . ." He gave a rueful laugh. "What I wouldn't have done to make you mine. How long I have waited to see you again," he said. "I have dreamed of this moment."

And so have I, she thought. *You will never know how much.*

"It feels like coming home to have you near me."

The door opened and Miss Blakelow sprang away from him, but not before Marianne had seen her almost in Mr. Holkham's arms. She stood on the threshold and stared at them, wide-eyed with shock.

※

Miss Blakelow knocked upon her sister's door. "Marianne? Can I come in?"

"No!"

"I must speak with you."

"Go away!"

"It was not what you think."

"Go *away!*"

Miss Blakelow ignored this imperative instruction, pushed open the door, and then closed it softly behind her.

"Do none of the locks work in this wretched house?" complained Marianne, burying her face into her pillow.

"I know. Most inconvenient when one wishes to be on one's high ropes, is it not?" returned Miss Blakelow.

"I am not on my high ropes."

"No, dear," soothed her sister, sitting down upon the bed beside her.

"You have stolen him from me," Marianne sobbed.

"Nothing of the sort. He was not yours to steal and he certainly is not mine."

"You are the meanest creature. You wish to keep me here as an old maid, don't you? You wish me to remain as your companion so that you may not live out the rest of your days alone!"

Miss Blakelow, a little hurt by this speech, laid a gentle hand on her sister's shoulder. "I wish to see you married to a man who loves you, Marianne."

"You frighten off every gentleman who has ever shown any interest in me," cried Marianne into her pillow.

"Not a decent man."

"Mr. Holkham *is* a decent man."

Miss Blakelow shook her head. "I am trying to protect you."

"I don't need protecting."

Miss Blakelow sighed and looked at her hands for a moment. "I made a mistake when I was your age, younger than you even, and all I want is that you should not make the same mistake and end up like me."

"But they are my mistakes to make. How am I to find out if a gentleman really loves me if you frighten them away?" cried Marianne, surfacing from under her pillow.

"Mr. Henry Holkham is a man known to me by . . . by reputation. Take it from an old hand that he is not marriage material."

"He's not?"

"No, love."

"Who is then?"

"That nice young man who worships you."

"Which young man?"

"Samuel."

"Mr. Bateman?" repeated Marianne, wrinkling her nose. "But I have known him for an age."

"He is a good man."

"But he is hanging out after you, Georgie."

"Yes, and spends a good deal of time staring at you," said Miss Blakelow warmly.

"But he is more like a brother to me."

Miss Blakelow smiled and smoothed the golden curls on her sister's head. "He does not think of you as a sister. Trust me, I know that look."

Marianne blushed. "But he ignores me most of the time. He thinks that I am immature."

"He is hiding his feelings because he doesn't believe that you return his affections."

"Oh, Georgie, I want so much to be in love!" Marianne cried wistfully.

Miss Blakelow smiled. "Be patient and it will happen in its own good time. Sometimes it creeps up behind you when you are least expecting it. You are young. Your time will come."

"And has yours?"

Miss Blakelow smoothed the counterpane on the bed with her hand. "Love is for the young. I am far too old and too cynical and too practical in nature to fall prey to such an emotion. I had rather be content than in love."

Marianne wrinkled her nose. "But that sounds so dull."

"It is safe. Your heart cannot be broken if you choose not to give it away." Miss Blakelow stood and kissed her sister's forehead. "Give yours wisely, Marianne; that is the best advice I can give you."

CHAPTER 21

As it were, Miss Blakelow did not receive an invitation to attend Lady Harriet's ball.

Her sisters and her aunt received their beautifully finished white cards, and they exclaimed over Georgiana being omitted, wondering if her invitation had become lost, and she endured it all with a stoicism that she did not feel. She forced a smile and shrugged and said it was of little matter to her.

She was hardly surprised; Lady St. Michael had been less than warm in her dealings with her, after all. But the knowledge that her society was not valued by anyone at Holme, not even Lady Harriet, was mortifying indeed. She would not have gone to the ball anyway; she dared not, given that half the guests may have recognized her, and especially given her recent argument with the earl. But the fact that he had made no move to see that she received an invitation, even for the sake of appearances, so utterly depressed her that she could not bear the sight of the ball gown he'd arranged to have made for her, and she buried it deep at the back of the armoire.

It was little more than a fortnight to the event, and Miss Blakelow had still not heard from William as to when he would return to Thorncote. That he was deliberately ignoring her request to avoid having to pay his debts in Worcestershire seemed likely. It also occurred to Miss Blakelow that he might be so far in debt as to make a return journey home by post chaise a prohibitively expensive undertaking, and the only alternative was to travel by stage, which he probably found unpalatable. She thought him a little cowardly as a consequence and was disappointed that he had not the courage to face up to his responsibilities.

Miss Blakelow attempted to put the events of the past fortnight behind her. She had heard that Lord Marcham had gone to stay with friends and was expected to be away for some days. Why this depressed her when she had resolved to break all acquaintance with the man was a question she could not answer.

Outwardly, she threw herself into bringing Thorncote about. She spent most of her time in the garden, particularly the kitchen garden, attempting to restore some vestige of order. But privately she was planning to leave Worcestershire, the surrogate family that she had adopted, and the man whose smile had started to haunt her dreams.

It was time to move on again, to push the past even further away, especially now that Hal Holkham was back. It was so strange to see him again after everything that had befallen her. She had imagined that she would be angry with him for lying to her, or at least failing to volunteer the information that he was married. He had treated her shabbily, but they had both been so very young, both needing someone to understand and love them. Perhaps that was why she could no longer feel angry with him? Perhaps she recognized at long last that he had needed their brief affair as much as she had.

He was still handsome. He was still dashing and charming, and she had no doubt that half the young women in the neighborhood would be in love with him before the week was out. She remembered how persuasive he'd been, but she knew that she wouldn't have acceded to his wishes had she not wanted to do it herself. He'd merely been a release for her unhappiness and made her feel that anything was possible if they were together. Would he tell Marcham of their history together? Would he disclose the innermost secrets of her heart? Miss Blakelow could not take the chance.

She needed to leave Thorncote, and soon. If Mrs. Thorpe had found her, after all these years, then very likely the man who was hunting her would too. He was not stupid, and although she had managed to evade him for many years now, he was nothing if not persistent. He had promised he would find her, wherever she went, and that he would never let her go until he had what he wanted— the whereabouts of his son. She and John were the only two people in the world who knew where the boy was; after all, they had rescued the lad from his father and brought him back to England all those years ago. But Miss Blakelow knew he would never give up until he had the boy back. She knew she could not wait for him to find her again. And now, with Hal's return, it was only a matter of time.

Another new identity was forming in her head. A widow, perhaps . . .

⁂

Miss Blakelow's three sisters wished to attend the dance at the assembly rooms in Loughton to practice their dance steps before the ball at Holme Park. Aunt Blakelow was concerned that Georgie was a little depressed and persuaded her to go, with the promise that it would cheer her up. In a moment of weakness, she reluctantly agreed.

Once at the event, she regretted her decision, as she spent a rather miserable evening sitting with her back against the wall amongst some of the older ladies, watching the dancers with haunted eyes. Her misery was compounded when, halfway through the evening, Lord Marcham unexpectedly arrived with another gentleman whom she did not recognize, Lady St. Michael, and Lady Harriet. Miss Blakelow wanted to sink through the floor.

His arrival caused much speculation; he had rarely attended such gatherings before, and within moments every matchmaking mama present had him firmly in her sights. That he was on the hunt for a wife became the chief topic of conversation amongst the ladies surrounding Miss Blakelow, and she could hardly keep her countenance as they teased her that her sister Marianne was by far the prettiest girl in the neighborhood and had no doubt caught his lordship's eye.

Miss Blakelow hardly dared raise her eyes from the floor as he moved in front of where she was sitting, the memory of their argument still fresh in her mind. He asked a lady in a dark-red gown to dance, and Miss Blakelow could not help stealing a glance at him as he swept the woman onto the floor. He was exquisitely dressed in a black coat that hugged his shoulders and satin evening breeches. He danced well, his smile was as devastating to Miss Blakelow's senses as ever it had been before, and he looked so handsome that she found herself jealous of every woman, beautiful or not, who came within a five-yard radius of him.

It was when the dance had finished and he was returning the lady to her chaperone that he caught sight of Miss Blakelow, who had at that moment gone to fetch refreshments for herself and her aunt. She froze in the doorway, nearly causing an elderly gentleman to smash into the back of her, and she slopped a little of the lemonade from one of the glasses onto the floor.

Their eyes met. In a fleeting glance, she saw his eyes flick downward to take in her ugly headdress, the glasses, the shawl, and the drab dove-gray gown and then move back to her face. He looked vaguely amused, as if he had expected her to be dressed in such a fashion and was not at all surprised at the less-than-stunning result. He opened his mouth to say something but then seemed to recollect their last meeting and the smile vanished from his eyes. He bowed with cold civility and immediately moved away.

Miss Blakelow was thrown into such a state of turmoil by this encounter that she did not listen to Aunt Blakelow's conversation for a full five minutes afterward. The look in his eyes when he took in her appearance wounded her pride. The smirk on his lips told her that he knew she had deliberately chosen the most hideous dress in her meager collection to quell any rumors that she was encouraging his advances. She could not help but feel the gathered company would compare her attire to the exquisite garnet-colored gown of the blonde girl who was currently on his arm and find it wanting. She began to feel sick. The room was hot and airless and she was wearing a shawl that she did not need. She put a hand to her head as the room spun around her, the lights dazzling like a kaleidoscope.

"Georgie? Are you alright? You don't look at all the thing," said Aunt Blakelow, her voice coming to her as if down a long tunnel.

"Excuse me, Aunt. I need some fresh air."

She moved swiftly toward the stairs, barging between two gentlemen and murmuring words of apology as she fled. The staircase was swarming with people, mostly moving upward toward the dancing, like a tsunami of feathers, satins, and jewels. Over the headdress of a middle-aged woman in a purple turban, she spied a familiar-looking face at the foot of the stairs. She gasped as recognition came thick and fast, like a tidal surge, pushing the events of the last thirteen years aside like driftwood, and she was momentarily paralyzed with shock.

He was here!

He'd found her. Oh, God, he'd found her at last. She felt fear prickle down her spine.

She had to get out of there, now.

The first step swam before her eyes, and the carpet loomed up to meet her. At the last moment, when she was sure she must fall, a strong arm grasped her waist, and she was clamped to the chest of an unseen gentleman following her down the stairs.

※

Miss Blakelow came to and found herself lying full stretch upon a sofa. She opened her eyes and memory flooded back. She focused on her aunt's face, looking down at her with a concerned expression in her eyes as she chafed her hand.

"He's here," croaked Miss Blakelow.

"Yes, my love, don't get up. You rest there for a moment."

Miss Blakelow seized her arm. "No, Aunt, you don't understand. The man who . . . *He's* here."

"Here?"

"Yes. I must get up. I must leave here. Tonight." She swung her feet to the floor and gingerly sat up.

"My dear, you cannot leave in the middle of the night. Where would you go?"

"I don't know," whispered Miss Blakelow.

"He's not here, Georgie. It's your imagination."

"He's here, I tell you."

"What would he be doing at Loughton on a Thursday evening? Since when did he ever leave London?"

Miss Blakelow winced, remembering the one time she knew he had left London—because she had been with him. She thrust the memory aside.

Aunt Blakelow picked up a glass of wine and put it to her niece's lips. "Drink this. You have had a fright, that's all. It's just brought on one of your nightmares."

"It was *not* a nightmare. I saw him."

"Georgie, calm yourself. He is not here. My dearest girl, you have nothing to fear."

"But, he was there . . . on the stairs," said Miss Blakelow, confused. "He was coming up the stairs as I was going down. Someone caught me as I fell."

"Lord Marcham caught you," said Aunt Blakelow soothingly.

Miss Blakelow gaped at her. "Lord Marcham? How? I mean . . . really? Are you sure?"

"He carried you in here and laid you on that sofa himself."

"Are you sure it was Lord Marcham?" asked Miss Blakelow, unconsciously looking at the glass in her aunt's hand.

"I may be an old fool but I am not in my dotage yet. Now, you drink that wine like a good girl, and I will arrange for the carriage to take us home."

❧

Miss Blakelow had determined that she and John would leave Thorncote while the rest of the family were attending the ball at Holme Park. They had slowly and discreetly been packing away their things and moving them one trunk at a time to a disused outbuilding, where they were stacked neatly against the wall, awaiting the time when they would be loaded onto a carriage and borne away along with Miss Blakelow and John.

Over the years living at Thorncote, she had accumulated many things, some of which she would take with her, many of which she would leave behind. She would take her mother's portrait, her father's fob watch, and her meager collection of jewelry, but the wooden trunk that contained Miss Blakelow's fine clothes that she had worn at her come out, she would leave behind. The dresses that her sisters had coveted, she bequeathed to them, giving them permission to alter them how they chose.

She had written several letters—to her Aunt Blakelow, to her brothers and sisters at Thorncote, and to William—but one letter in particular she found impossible to write. A week after the dance in Loughton, she tried yet again, writing to Lord Marcham, that she was sorry, that she had to go away, and that she would always consider him to be—she screwed it up and hurled it into the fire.

To add to her misery, Mr. Peabody arrived midway through the afternoon, resplendent in a strawberry- and white-striped waistcoat that assaulted the eye in such a manner as to test the limits of even Miss Blakelow's self-control. Aunt Blakelow made an excuse and retired to her bedroom, leaving her niece in high temper that she would abandon her to this man's relentless ardor. That Aunt Blakelow thought that she should marry him was becoming increasingly clear. Thorncote's future was by no means certain, and if she became Mrs. Joshua Peabody, both of the elder Blakelow spinsters would have a roof over their heads.

"My dear Miss Blakelow," he said, coming into the room as the door closed behind him. "Your aunt is feeling indisposed and has gone for a lie-down. I hope that nothing serious is amiss?"

"Nothing at all," she replied blandly, her eye kindling with irritation as she remembered the way her aunt had hastily vacated the room. "Won't you sit down, sir?"

"Thank you," he said, taking the chair she had indicated, which was half the room's length away from hers.

"Are you alone this afternoon?"

"Yes, the girls have walked into Loughton to purchase some ribbon, and the boys are gone fishing. Since his lordship bought Ned and Jack fishing rods, they seem to have found a love for it. And they go to escape from talk of the ball," she added, smiling.

"Ah yes, the Holme Park ball. Well, I have received my invite. Do you go, ma'am?"

She shook her head. "No. I do not go to parties."

"I am sorry that you shall not be there, but knowing your peculiar circumstances as I do, I cannot wonder at it."

Miss Blakelow felt her temper rising. "Indeed? Do my circumstances mean that it is unseemly for me to dance?"

"Oh, no, no. I merely meant that you would not want to draw attention to yourself, giving rise to the sort of gossip that one must deplore. For although I condemn the nature of 'our little secret' and its having come about, I would wish to protect you from the harsh lash of public opinion. And it is on this subject that I come to you today . . . No, no, my dear, do not look so vexed . . . Your aunt wrote to me and asked me to come."

"My aunt?" repeated Miss Blakelow.

"Yes. She is worried for you. Apparently you had a mishap at the assembly rooms last week."

"I was a little hot and felt faint, that is all," she replied, becoming a little annoyed at her aunt's interference.

"She said you were hallucinating."

"Mr. Peabody, I was hot and I fainted," said Miss Blakelow. "That is the sum total of the events."

"And I understand that Lord Marcham used the occasion to foist his attentions onto you," said Mr. Peabody haughtily, looking down his considerable nose at her.

"Hardly," she retorted, "he stopped me from falling down the stairs."

"And had his arms about you. Your aunt is concerned that his attentions are becoming very marked and that you return his affections. Is that so, Georgiana?"

Miss Blakelow severely doubted that her aunt thought any such thing, or, even if she had, she would not have said as much to Mr. Peabody. Her aunt had made it perfectly clear that she thought Georgiana should encourage his lordship's attentions to save Thorncote, but that was where her admiration of the earl ended. It was one thing to use her feminine powers of persuasion to obtain his participation in a business investment, but quite another to be foolish enough to fall in love with the man.

Miss Blakelow struggled to keep her anger in check at Mr. Peabody's continued interference in her affairs. Was this man to know everything about her? Was there no part of her life that was sacred? Had someone told him about everything she did? Who she saw? When she used her chamber pot? She remembered that painful scene when he had first discovered her past; he seemed to revel in every detail of the affair, as if he somehow derived pleasure from imagining her so vulnerable and entirely alone with a man.

"Mr. Peabody, you have been good to us since Father died. Indeed, you have been very good to me too, but that does not give you the right to question my private life."

"Oh, but I think it does. Your father bade me look after you."

"Yes, and you have done so. But I am a grown woman, and I am quite capable of making my own decisions."

"Forgive me, Miss Blakelow, but I must disagree. Given your past transgressions, I hardly think you can know what is best for you. Your decisions have been anything but successful thus far."

"I was *nineteen*, sir," she said indignantly.

"Yes, nineteen and innocent as to the ways of men."

"Indeed," retorted Miss Blakelow. "But I am fully alive to them now, I can assure you." *You and your groping hands have educated me to that, Mr. Peapod,* her mind added furiously.

"But I am willing to put your past behind us. I am willing to put your youthful follies down to inexperience, and although many a man could not forgive such an outrageous slip from delicacy, I am prepared to put my reservations aside and offer you the protection of my name. I am convinced that your passionate tendencies have been cured and that you are now a reserved young woman who I would be pleased to call my wife. I am aware that there will always be this awkwardness between us arising from the knowledge of your past indiscretions, but I promise you that I will do everything in my power to evict them from my mind."

"You are too good," she answered with barely disguised sarcasm.

"I have been brought up to see the good in people where others believe all hope is lost. I understand that your brother is to be married and intends to bring his bride to live at Thorncote. Your aunt has asked me if I will take your brothers and sisters into Goldings. And I replied that I would. And your aunt too, if you wish it. My mother is concerned that your brothers and sisters will plague her, but I have assured her that they are well-behaved and pleasant young people—although Ned is a little belligerent and Jack needs schooling to whip him into shape and Marianne is a little too vivacious for a young woman of her age—" He stopped and smiled. "But we may discuss all this once we are married. You will wish to order bridal clothes, and to that end I will leave you some money—"

"Mr. Peabody," she interrupted hastily, "you hardly allow me to answer. Indeed, I am grateful for the very great honor that you have done me by asking me to be your wife, but I must tell you again that it is impossible."

"You have no choice, my dear," he replied. "Where will you go? You have run from one relative to the other until they are all used up. You are penniless. You are friendless. You have no one."

A steely light entered her eyes. "I have a little money and my own wits, and I can assure you that they will serve me well."

"Perhaps they might. But what of your family? Do you have enough money to feed and clothe and house a family of seven? Never mind about the debts that young William is piling up in London."

"Mr. Peabody, I don't wish to pain you, but I don't love you."

He looked at her blankly. "Love? My dear Miss Blakelow, of course you don't. I wasn't expecting that you did."

"You do not love me?" she asked.

He chuckled. "Yes, yes, women like to hear things like that, don't they? Certainly I do, my dear, I'm very fond of you."

Miss Blakelow turned away. "I must be allowed to think."

"Naturally, I will leave you to make your preparations."

"Mr. Peabody, I have not accepted you, nor have I agreed to my family living with you. I must have time to consider. You do understand?"

He rose to his feet. "Of course, of course. I understand that it must be a difficult decision for a woman who has been single for so many years. So now I will leave you, my dear, and return tomorrow."

❧

"You can't do it!" cried Marianne. "I won't let you!"

Miss Blakelow sighed. "I have not yet decided that I *am* going to do it."

"But you'd have to kiss him and . . . and submit to . . . other things," said Marianne, a comical look of disgust on her face.

Miss Blakelow, who had been considering that very unappealing fact herself, tried to be sensible, even though in her heart of hearts she knew she could never consent to such a marriage. Assuming she could stomach being intimate with Mr. Peabody, marriage to him would only be a temporary solution. Sooner or later, the man hunting her would find out where she had gone, and Miss Blakelow was certain her new husband would be no match for the man.

But in the short term, if the world thought her engaged to Mr. Peabody, would it silence the rumors concerning her and

Lord Marcham? Would Lord Marcham himself stop pursuing her once he found out she had accepted another man? It was a consideration. She had promised Mr. Peabody that she would think about his offer and that was exactly what she planned to do—even if she knew her own heart well enough to know that she could not lead the poor man on by accepting him. However irritating he could be, he did not deserve that. "I am not romantic, Marianne . . . at least, I cannot afford to be. Mr. Peabody is offering to give us a home at Goldings . . . *all* of us."

"I cannot live with that man," said Ned, tossing a ball of wool at the wall and catching it as it rebounded into his hand. "I *will* not live with him."

"We do not have many options," said Miss Blakelow simply. "Mr. Peabody is one such option."

"And so is Lord Marcham," Kitty pointed out.

Miss Blakelow colored despite herself. "Lord Marcham is not willing to loan us the money to set Thorncote to rights. I had hoped he would see it as an investment, but it seems that he is not interested in helping us."

"He will if you marry him. He said so," returned her sister.

"I'd rather live at Holme Park than Goldings any day," said Ned. "Lord Marcham may be a rakehell but he's not a bore."

"No, and he's handsome," put in Lizzy, arranging a shawl around her shoulders. "And he has a very good figure."

"And he has bought us new dresses for the ball," added Kitty.

"Why won't you marry him, George?" asked Marianne.

Miss Blakelow felt uncomfortable as five pairs of eyes swiveled in her direction and stayed pinned to her face. "Because I can't."

"Why?" asked Lizzy.

"Does it have something to do with when you lived in London?" asked Jack, lounging in one of the window seats.

"Yes," said Miss Blakelow, "it has something to do with that."

"What happened, George?"

Miss Blakelow looked down at her hands. Perhaps her brothers and sisters were old enough to know the truth now—perhaps they had even guessed it. Besides, after ten years, she was sick of carrying her burden of lies. "I was extremely foolish, that's what happened."

"You fell in love," guessed Marianne.

Miss Blakelow was silent.

"Yes," said Kitty, " . . . with a man who was . . . unsuitable."

"Why unsuitable?" asked Lizzy.

Miss Blakelow sighed. "Because he was married already and he did not tell me."

"Oh."

"His wife was an invalid and lived in the country. Because I was supposed to marry another man, a wealthy man who was considerably older than I was. I kept my love for this married man a secret . . . and thus, no one was able to warn me that he was . . . a rake."

"What happened?"

"I was ruined," said Miss Blakelow shortly, bringing that particular subject to an abrupt close, "which is why I cannot marry Lord Marcham. Mr. Peabody knows what happened because Father told him, against my wishes, I might add, but he told him nonetheless. Mr. Peabody is kindly prepared to disregard the past."

"Magnanimous of him. No doubt he will remind you of the fact every moment of the day," muttered Ned with astonishing insight for one so utterly inexperienced in the ways of the world.

"He is a kind man . . . and he has been good to us."

"He is a pompous, conceited bore," said Ned.

"Why do you not tell Lord Marcham your story?" asked Lizzy.

Miss Blakelow shook her head, imagining the scene, imagining the look of disgust that would come into his eyes, the same look that had come into another man's eyes when she had told him. "I can't."

"But he is a man who does not care for public opinion. If anyone is likely to understand, it is him," said Ned.

"Yes, and he'd probably congratulate you for doing something half so daring," Marianne said, laughing.

Given that the man who contributed to her ruination was Lord Marcham's brother, Miss Blakelow highly doubted that. She stood up. "I cannot. You are young . . . You do not fully understand."

"We do understand," said Ned. "You fell in love and you made a mistake. Women do it every day."

Miss Blakelow's bottom lip trembled at this young man who was growing up before her eyes. "In my experience, men are not so forgiving. Mr. Peabody is an unusual case. I must go and think."

"What is there to think about? Go and find the earl and tell him that yes, please, we would like to come and live at Holme Park," said Ned.

"And that we would like to learn to box like he does . . . well, Ned and me anyway . . . please," put in Jack.

"And that we won't spend *all* his money on dresses," said Kitty with a giggle.

"And that you will marry him just as soon as it can be arranged," said Lizzy.

"And that you love him," added Marianne simply.

CHAPTER 22

"Isn't that Peabody?" asked Hal Holkham of his brother as he rode up to him.

"I do believe it is. What a coat to be sure," marveled his lordship, riding a magnificent gray horse into Loughton high street, "a pea-green coat for a Peabody."

Hal chuckled. "You are too cruel, Robbie."

"I would be a lot less cruel if he weren't so damned worthy," he replied. "He always looks at me as if I were recently excreted from the back end of his horse."

Hal laughed. "And so you were."

"Thank you," he responded lightly. "Good morning, Peaham." He tipped his hat, intending to pass on.

"Indeed it is," replied Mr. Peabody from atop his gig as he gathered the reins into his hands. "A very good morning indeed."

"You are jolly today, Mr. Peabody," observed Hal with a friendly smile.

"I am the happiest of men. Miss Georgiana Blakelow has agreed to be my wife."

The earl's gray horse skittered at the sudden tug his master performed upon the reins, and it took his lordship a moment to calm his startled mount. He glared at Peabody from under a thunderous brow. "What did you say?"

Mr. Peabody smiled smugly. "I have already sent an announcement to the papers. I am the happiest of men. Not even you can kill my mood today, my lord. Well, I must be off. I have arrangements to make. Two hundred guests and very likely more. A grand affair and the lady dressed in the finest clothes Loughton can buy. I will send you an invitation, never fear."

"Don't bother," recommended the earl savagely.

"You have lost, Marcham. The game is up. The lady is mine, and I intend to give her a babe to swell her belly just as soon as I can."

It was fortunate that Hal placed his hand on his brother's arm at that moment, for his lordship had started to move toward the portly gentleman with such a grip on his riding whip and such a vicious look on his face that Hal feared for the other man's safety. "Not here, Rob," he said.

His lordship wrestled with the urge to drag the man from his carriage and throttle the life from him with his bare hands. "You had better watch your tongue, Peabody, or I swear . . ."

Mr. Peabody smiled into the furious face of his lordship. "I see that you can remember my name when you wish to, my lord. Well, good day to you both. I must get along. The wedding will be at Goldings in January. I am off to buy the lady a gift. What say you to pearls? Or are they too young for a lady of Miss Blakelow's advanced years?"

Hal gave him a chilly smile as his brother whirled his mount around in the direction they had just come. He heard the sound of rapidly retreating hooves as his lordship urged his horse into a gallop. "I believe pearls are the established gift, sir. Good day to you."

He turned his own horse around, following his brother, who was by now practically out of sight. It was no very difficult task to guess where he was going. He urged his horse toward Holme Park and mentally sent Miss Blakelow his sympathies.

※

His lordship threw the reins to a groom and ran lightly up the front steps at Thorncote house to knock imperatively upon the front door. On being told that Miss Blakelow was not receiving visitors, he barged past the startled butler and strode into the hall, calling out her name.

John took one look at the earl's face and instantly abandoned any vague plan he may have had of throwing his lordship out of the house; if he was not much mistaken, Lord Marcham was in a rare old taking. He quietly closed the front door and watched with a wry smile as their lordly neighbor took the stairs two at a time. There would be fireworks before the day was through or his name was not John Maynard.

The earl found Miss Blakelow in her bedchamber, seated by the window with a book. He entered the room and virtually slammed the door behind him. She started and the book fell from her hands, her eyes wide and her mouth open in surprise.

"How dare you barge in here?" she demanded, standing up swiftly and reaching for her glasses from the dressing table.

"Don't you *dare* put those damned things on!" he fumed, her spectacles becoming the irrational focus of his anger.

Miss Blakelow glared at him and pointedly disobeyed him, pushing them over her ears. "I need them to see with and I do not take orders from you—"

"You see perfectly well without them," he said, as he flung down his gloves upon the corner of the bed and strode toward her. He took her spectacles from her face, dropped them to the floor, and very deliberately crushed them with his heel, mashing the twisted metal and broken glass into the carpet.

She gasped. "How dare you destroy my property?" she demanded.

"And this!" he said, yanking the ribbons of her cap from her hand and flinging it onto the fire. The low flames swamped it in a riotous dance of golden heat. "There is only one thing your ugly caps are good for, and that is kindling."

She was speechless with anger. It took her several moments to summon the words to convey her feelings. She moved toward the door and opened it, her hand upon the doorknob. "You are insufferable. Get out of my room and get out of this house."

He stared at her for a moment from across the room, tight-lipped, rigid with anger. "Well, madam, I hear that congratulations are in order," he said in no gentle voice.

Miss Blakelow blinked at him. "Congratulations?" she repeated frostily. "For what?"

"Your engagement. Do you pretend to be ignorant of it?"

"I do not know what you mean."

"Don't you, by God?" He flung away to the window and stared out for a moment before coming back to face her. "And am I to receive an explanation as to why you have accepted that pompous idiot Peabody, when you have so roundly rejected me?"

Miss Blakelow stared at him in confusion for a moment, and then she closed her eyes as the realization dawned on her that Mr. Peabody had taken her vow to think about his offer as an acceptance of it. As angry as she was with Mr. Peabody for forcing her hand, she was fast becoming even angrier at Lord Marcham's assumption that she needed to ask his permission before accepting another gentleman. And just because she had seen fit to turn down his offer, that did not mean that she needed to justify to him or anyone else why she wished to accept another man, however pompous he might be. She calmly folded her hands before her, forming a desire to teach his lordship a much-needed lesson.

"You are being overly dramatic, my lord. I have never given you cause to believe that there was any agreement between us. I made it perfectly clear at the outset that I was not interested in matrimony."

"No," he agreed, "although it seems that matrimony with Peabody suits you just fine."

"Whom I choose to marry is none of your business," she said frigidly. "Now I must ask you to leave. It is highly improper for you to be in here—"

"I thought you had sworn not to marry any man," interrupted his lordship rudely. "If that is the case, then why is Peabody accepted when the rest of mankind is kicked aside?"

She lifted her chin mutinously. The words were on the tip of her tongue to deny the rumor, to shout from the hilltops that she'd rather die an old maid than marry a man as loathsome as Joshua Peabody, but she kept quiet. Perhaps if Lord Marcham thought her engaged to another man, he would finally stop pursuing her, and she need never tell him about her relationship with his brother. He would go back to London and find amusement with another woman. She could leave without fear of him coming after her. It would give her enough breathing space to get far away. "Mr. Peabody is . . . familiar with my circumstances," she said guardedly.

He frowned at her. "What circumstances?"

"I am unable to . . . I must ask you to leave. Immediately."

"What circumstances?" he repeated. "Tell me."

She shook her head. "I cannot tell you . . . It is . . . I cannot."

"Is it so very bad then?"

She made no answer and stared at the floor in silence.

"Oh, I see," he said, making an impatient gesture with his hands. "I am not good enough for your confidence, is that it? I am not to be trusted with it. And yet you choose to confide in Mr. Peabody."

"He has been a friend of the family for years," she said coldly. "And who I choose to confide in, my lord, is—"

"And have I shown myself to be unworthy of your confidence?" the earl demanded.

"You don't understand."

"Damn right I don't," he replied, balling his fists against the mantelpiece.

She flinched at the anger in his voice. "Shouting at me is hardly likely to induce me to confide in you, my lord."

He suddenly came toward her and so caught her by surprise that she did not have time to move. She was trapped against the wall. He reached out a finger and lifted her chin so that he could look into her face.

"Am I so very bad, Georgie?" he asked in quite another tone, a tone that tugged at Miss Blakelow's heartstrings. She could not look at him. She stared at the folds of his cravat, judging her gaze to be safe there.

"No, my lord," she whispered.

"Am I not handsome enough for you? Is that it? Too old, perhaps? Or are my manners completely beyond the pale?" he asked softly.

She shook her head, confused by his sudden change of tack. His anger she could cope with, but these gentle reproaches against himself slipped under her guard and tore at her resolve.

"Perhaps you would rather see me in that hideous cherry-striped waistcoat he wears? Or lavender-colored pantaloons? I am obviously far too dull a creature for a woman like you."

"Oh, don't . . . You don't understand . . ." she cried, her voice choked by emotion. "I need to provide for my family."

"Then let *me* provide for them," he said. "If you think that Joshua Peabody is going to become a father figure for those young brothers of yours, then think again, my girl. The man is far too self-ish to be bothered with any of them."

"He is a good man . . . who . . . who I am grateful to."

"Grateful?"

"Yes."

"Well, I can remedy *that*," he said promptly. "Take Thorncote. Take the whole damn lot and be grateful to me instead, and we'll be married just as soon as I can arrange it."

She shook her head, smiling faintly.

"Georgie . . . am I so repulsive to you? Can you not stomach me as your husband?" he whispered.

"It's not that," she said in a tremulous voice, looking down at her hands as if they held the answer. "But I . . . I cannot bear to have my heart broken again. It . . . it took me many years to find some sort of peace . . . here, at Thorncote. And I know that I am not enough for a man like you. You think you want me now, but that is because a woman who refuses you amuses and fascinates you—for a while anyway. But the novelty will wear off soon enough, and I don't want to be cast aside when you tire of me."

"What nonsense is this?"

"It is true, my lord. You are used to . . . to taking your pleasures wherever you find them. But I am a selfish creature, and if you were my husband, I would not want to share you with anyone else." She turned away and walked to the fireplace. "And now I think you should leave."

There was a silence.

"So that is it?" he asked, staring at her. "You have already made up your mind about me. You have already found me guilty of adultery when I have not even placed my ring upon your finger."

She returned no answer. In truth, she could not.

300

"I am not leaving this room until you convince me that you don't love me," he said, squaring his shoulders.

She gasped. "You are unbelievable!"

"Well?" he demanded.

"No, my lord, shocking as I know it must be to you, but I am not in love with you."

"Really."

She glared at him. "I don't mean to give you pain, much though you deserve it, but although I esteem you—"

"You what?"

"If you will allow me to finish, my lord, I was about to say that I esteem you and have a little affection for you, it is true, and we have become friends—good friends—but that does not mean that I—"

"Friends be damned," he muttered, coming across the room with several long strides, and before she knew what he was about, he had jerked her into his arms. He took her chin in one hand and turned her face up to his. "Do you mean to tell me that you have not imagined us like this?" he whispered.

"Let me go," she said, her eyes searching his face, her breathing fast and shallow.

He did not heed her request but instead pulled her rather tighter against him. "Do you mean to convince me that you have not lain awake wondering what it would be like to let me make love to you?"

She braced a hand against his chest, her heart beating wildly as she stared up into his eyes. "You should not speak to me of such things, my lord. It is highly improper."

"What nonsense. You are no milk-and-water miss to be shocked by a little plain speaking. I want you and I think that you want me too."

"You flatter yourself," she said, hearing the lack of conviction in her own voice. She was trembling from head to foot with fear and excitement and a heady longing that she thought had been exorcised from her heart years ago. Now, here with this man, his strong arms around her, protecting her, cherishing her, she yearned to throw all caution to the wind, lay her head upon his chest, and unburden herself to the one person she had grown to trust above all others. She could not deny her attraction to him. Oh, yes, he was handsome, but mere physical appeal was not likely to touch an experienced heart such as hers. It was a connection between them, this strange invisible thing that coursed from one body to another, binding them together, until they both knew what the other was thinking as if they were one mind.

A voice inside her head reminded her that he was a rake and of the attendant dangers of such a situation. His affairs with the opposite sex had been as notorious as they were numerous. How many other women had fallen for him in such a way? How many society beauties had he held like this, making each of them feel that she was the only woman in the world who mattered? What if he did not truly love her back? What if his feelings for her were nothing more than an infatuation because she was different? She'd had some knowledge of what an infatuation felt like at the hands of Hal Holkham. It had not been a pleasant experience. What if she gave in to the dearest wish of her heart and told him everything, laid herself bare before him—and what if he then could not forgive her?

"If I do not speak the truth, then why are you trembling?" he asked.

"I'm not."

"You are. Georgie . . ." he whispered with the ghost of a laugh. "I think you have imagined yourself in my arms as I have imagined myself in yours. Deny it if you dare."

His mouth swooped down to lock with hers in a kiss that shook her almost to her knees. His arm was an iron bar around her waist, holding her tightly to him as if he would never let her go. His other hand lay tenderly against the angle of her jaw, caressing the skin of her throat and the hollow above her collarbone. She felt as if she ought to breathe, but it was beyond her; he had robbed her of the ability to function in a normal manner. Her arms were trapped between them, her hands laid flat against the lapels of his coat, and of their own volition crept up around his neck. He showed no sign of relinquishing his hold upon her, nor of breaking the kiss; rather he took it deeper, tilting his head so that he could have greater access to all of her mouth.

As he felt her arms return his embrace, his tongue found and entwined with hers. He groaned at the pure pleasure of it. God, this was wonderful! She was kissing him back with a passion and intensity that staggered him. The rake in him wanted to carry her over to the bed and make her his. But he wouldn't. She deserved better than that. She deserved the best of him, and he would not dishonor her in such a way.

He kissed her and went on kissing her even as someone entered the room behind them and gasped at the sight of Miss Blakelow locked in his lordship's arms.

It was Miss Blakelow who came back to reality first and started to pull away.

"You cannot deny it, Georgie," his lordship said, staring down at her with eyes the color of a stormy sky, his breathing slightly labored. "Marry your Joshua Peabody if you wish, but don't expect me to watch you do it."

He turned without another word, pausing only to retrieve his gloves from the bed.

Aunt Blakelow stared in shock from her niece to the earl and back again as he strode from the room. Their eyes met. Miss Blakelow saw the condemnation in her aunt's face and turned away.

"Oh, Georgie . . ." said her aunt.

Miss Blakelow held out a hand as if to keep the disapproving words at bay, tears starting in her eyes. "Don't," she whispered.

"My dear girl, what can you have been thinking of?" she demanded.

Her niece shook her head, momentarily unable to speak for the choking sensation in her throat.

"He was in your bedchamber . . . I cannot . . . You *must* see the impropriety of such behavior. My dear Georgie, you of all people should understand the very great danger of—"

"Please, Aunt. Don't," begged Miss Blakelow, steadying herself with her hands upon the dressing table. She touched her fingers to her lips. Her mouth still tingled from his lordship's kiss; her body yearned for the comforting warmth and strength of his embrace. Georgiana Blakelow hadn't been kissed like that in a very, *very* long time.

Tears swam before her eyes. He was right. How could she deny it? She had responded to his caresses willingly enough; indeed she had returned them most ardently. She was in very great danger of losing her heart to him, if she hadn't already. All her determination not to succumb to his charm had failed. She was as vulnerable now as she ever had been in the past, to the joy of having a love and keeping it for her very own. She had learned nothing. The brutal, painful lessons of her youth had not rid her character of its passionate will. And she had realized it in the earl's arms. He had awoken feelings in her that she had convinced herself no longer existed. She had put them out to pasture, buried them deep. But one kiss was enough to rouse her longings. She looked around her, seeing the familiar drapes, the wall hangings, the portraits on the wall, as if for the first time.

"You were *kissing* him," said Aunt Blakelow in a low voice, coming farther into the room. "Tell me at once what has happened in this room."

Miss Blakelow made no answer. She closed her eyes in pain.

"Georgie?"

"Nothing!" cried Miss Blakelow. "Nothing save a kiss."

"You are certain?"

"Yes, I am certain!"

"I am relieved to hear it. I wish to know to what extent you have been encouraging his advances."

Miss Blakelow swung around. "*Encouraging* him?" she repeated blankly. "How can you talk so? Have you not heard me refuse him repeatedly? Have I not told you on several occasions that I have no interest in wedding him?"

"You have," Aunt Blakelow agreed, folding her hands primly before her, "most emphatically. But I am not a fool. I have seen the way that you look at him. And so it seems has his lordship. I feared how it would be. He seemed determined to set you up as his latest flirt from the start of your acquaintance. And doe-eyed looks to a man of his kidney—"

"I did not give him *doe*-eyed looks," flashed Miss Blakelow, annoyed and embarrassed.

"Georgie, have you learned nothing?" asked her aunt, coming toward her. "Are you still so easily lured by a handsome face?"

"You pain me, Aunt, by speaking so."

"I thought you had more sense."

"*You* encouraged me to go out driving with him! You seemed *very* keen on his company," retorted Miss Blakelow.

"Yes," said her aunt, "but only because it was a means to an end. I thought our primary motive was saving Thorncote. Had I any inkling of your feelings . . . Had I known you were foolish enough to fall in love with the man, like the very greenest school-room miss—"

Miss Blakelow could stand no more. She swiped her cloak from the chair and ran from the room.

CHAPTER 23

"CAROLINE, WHEN WILL YOU let me take you out of this house," asked Lord Marcham. It was two days later, and he had come to London to visit his sister. He paced impatiently over to the window of her drawing room and looked out across the narrow street.

"I like this house," Caroline replied as she set a stitch in a shirt she was mending. She looked fondly at the garment in her hands, her son's shirt, her lad who was fast growing up before her eyes.

"It's small," said his lordship crushingly. "And wouldn't James like to live at Holme with all the animals and miles of parkland to call his own?"

"I am sure he would. But I have my pride, Robbie. We are happy here and it's perfect for my needs. We don't all need a palatial mansion, you know."

"You are living like a pauper when you don't need to."

"Hardly," she said, smiling and setting aside her stitchery.

Lord Marcham nodded at the pile of young James's books on the table. "Does Julius give you anything to help with the upkeep?"

She turned her eyes upon him. "Julius? What, pray, has he to say to this?"

"He is the father, isn't he?"

Mrs. Weir colored faintly. "*Stephen* is the father."

"Stephen had been dead six months when you conceived James. Either yours was the longest pregnancy in history or your arithmetic is sadly awry."

"Why are you here, Robbie?" she demanded.

He held up his hands. "Alright, alright, I've said my piece. I just think you could do with a little financial help now and again, that's all. You won't take anything from me."

"Stephen left me amply provided for."

"He left you with a small competence," the earl corrected gently.

"Robbie, are you here for any other reason than to criticize my housekeeping arrangements?"

"Do I need a reason?" he asked, turning and leaning his hips against the windowsill.

"No," she said, folding her hands in her lap. "But you have one all the same, and I don't imagine that you were just, well . . . passing. So? What brings you here?"

"Damned if I know," he muttered, running a hand over his jaw.

Mrs. Weir looked at him thoughtfully, her head to one side like a watchful bird, observing the tired look about his eyes and the pensive look on his face.

"Are you in trouble?" she asked, watching him.

He looked surprised, and for a moment the frown on his brow lifted. "Me? God no . . . well, not the sort of trouble you mean."

"I see."

He fell once more into brooding silence.

Mrs. Weir folded her stitchery and placed it in the workbasket at her feet. She smiled. "Who is she?"

He moved away from the window and came to sit beside her. "Is it that obvious?"

"A little," she replied, patting his knee. "Tell me all."

"You said you wanted to see me make a fool of myself over a woman?" he said bitterly. "Well, now you have your wish."

"I don't wish to see you unhappy, Robbie. Never that."

He put his head in his hands. "She won't have me."

Mrs. Weir blinked in surprise. "Oh."

"I've never felt like this . . . I mean . . . oh damn it all, she's different. This time it's different."

"I see. And is she beautiful?"

He shrugged. "She is beautiful . . . to me anyway. She is not what you'd call . . . obvious. But her figure is good."

"I'm sure it is."

He glared at her. "I have not laid a finger on her."

"Do I know her?" asked Mrs. Weir, wisely changing tack at that moment. "What is her name?"

"Georgiana Blakelow. Daughter of Sir William Blakelow of Thorncote."

His sister raised a brow in surprise. "Blakelow? That's one of your neighbors, isn't it?" At his nod, she frowned. "Georgiana . . . I cannot place the name."

"No," he said gloomily, "and neither can anyone else."

"A mystery, Robbie?"

"A mystery indeed."

"Describe her to me. Is she blonde like the other Blakelows?"

"Not in the least," he said, getting up again to pace around the room. "She has brown hair and green eyes."

Mrs. Weir blinked at this very un-lover-like appraisal of the woman's attributes. "Is she tall? Short? Round? Elegant? Really, Robbie, you are hardly painting a portrait for my imagination. How do you expect me to remember her on such a description as 'she has brown hair and green eyes'? You have just described a good percentage of the women of Worcestershire."

He sighed and rubbed his fingers across his brow. "She is tall and very slim . . . perhaps too slim if you listen to Sarah. She is intelligent and pretends that she is bookish for reasons that I have yet to discover. In fact, she plays the bluestocking very well, and most of society is fooled by her little act. She would have the world paint her as a recluse, a moralizing bore, and she wears those infernal spectacles to keep the world at a distance—and, I might add, to aggravate me . . ." he said, pausing as his eye kindled with annoyance. "But I have seen the laughter in her eyes, and I know that she is not as straitlaced as she would have us all believe. It's an act, a ruse. She dresses continually as if she is in deep mourning, wears a hideous cap upon her head so that no one can catch a glimpse of her hair, and plays the part of the governess and guardian to her younger brothers and sisters, when I suspect that she would like nothing better than to waltz the night away in a man's arms. She is hiding something from me . . . from the world . . . and I do not know what it is. She won't tell me what troubles her even though she knows that she might confide in me and that I will do my best to help her if I can. I have asked her to marry me countless times, and she has refused me on every occasion. I suspect that she would like children of her own, and I want nothing better than to give them to her, but she pushes me away. She has built a thirty-foot-thick wall around her heart and as fast as I tear it down, she rebuilds it again."

He flung away to the window and leaned his shoulder against the wall, looking out. "We are good friends . . . or at least we were until last Wednesday . . . and I hoped that perhaps she was beginning to feel something for me . . . but she doesn't. She manages very well to keep me always at arm's length. She teases me—actively flirts with me sometimes—and then retreats behind her shell again. She frustrates the hell out of me. She doesn't believe that I am in earnest, and she won't believe that my intentions are honorable. She's damnably infuriating—and . . . and I can't stop thinking about her."

Mrs. Weir stared at her brother in amazement. "Well," she said at last. "That has given me a picture now, to be sure."

"So? What's the verdict?" he asked grimly.

"You certainly seem . . . taken . . . with her."

He gave a short laugh as he picked up a small vase and examined it. "Taken . . . yes, I think you could safely say that I am taken with her."

"But, Robbie, are you certain? I would hate for you to make a mistake. Do you desire her?"

"Undoubtedly. I spend far too much time thinking about our wedding night."

"But is that all you feel?"

He went very still, thinking, and then he said quietly, "I want to protect her. I want to take her troubles off her shoulders. I want to sleep next to her every night for the rest of my life." He came back to the middle of the room and sat down beside her once more. "What am I to do, Caro?"

She took his hand in hers and squeezed it. "Have you kissed her?"

He looked so uncomfortable that his sister was hard put to it to repress a smile. "I'm not really sure that that is relevant—"

"Of course it is relevant!" she cried. "If you want me to help you, then I need to know what has happened . . . Have you kissed her?"

"Yes," he admitted reluctantly.

"And?"

"And what?"

She rolled her eyes. "How did she react? Did she like it?"

He shrugged. "I don't know . . . We had argued and I . . . I forced the kiss upon her to prove a point. I was angry, jealous too, I suppose, and I let my temper get the better of me."

"I see. And did she slap your face?"

"No."

"Ah. So then, did she kiss you back?"

He cleared his throat.

She patted his knee. "So, this is good. She is not adverse to you."

"Then why has she accepted Peabody?" he demanded.

Caroline blinked at him. "Mr. Peabody? She's going to marry that dreadful man of the lavender pantaloons?"

"The very same," said his lordship gloomily.

"Oh, dear."

"Quite," he muttered.

She thought for a moment, then took a deep breath as if coming to an astounding conclusion. "She doesn't believe that you mean marriage."

It was the earl's turn to roll his eyes. "I know that! I told you only a minute ago that she won't believe me to be in earnest. Honestly, I don't know why I bother—"

"Have you told her?" she asked.

He stared at her, somewhat taken aback. "Told her what?"

She laughed. "Heavens, Robbie, of all the numbskulls . . . that you're in love with her."

He glanced at her, then at his hands, and then at the floor but said nothing, lost in his thoughts.

She squeezed his arm affectionately. "While you debate and hesitate, she is no doubt forming the opinion that you are amusing yourself with a little flirtation while you are in the neighborhood. She needs to know how you feel."

"Will you come to this wretched ball and meet her?" the earl asked.

"Do you wish me to?"

"Yes. You may convince Sarah that Miss Blakelow is not a she-devil who has come to emasculate me. Do come, Caro, if only to prevent me from drowning Mr. Peabody in the white soup."

His lordship left his sister and went immediately to his club, where he was hailed by several of his friends, who wished to know where the deuce he had been hiding himself for all these weeks. He smiled faintly and refused their invitations to dine, but requested from them the address of the lodgings where one Sir William Blakelow currently resided. On finding one of his particular friends, Sir Julius Fawcett, seated by the bay window reading a paper, he greeted him but declined to sit, on account of his needing to speak to Sir William. Sir Julius, citing boredom, folded the newspaper and declared that he would come with him.

It took the earl some time to track his quarry to earth as Sir William had spent all the previous night at the card table and was no doubt much afraid to return to his rooms for fear that creditors would find him there. His losses had been heavy, his consumption of alcohol even heavier, and the earl eventually found him sleeping off his excesses under the table at his friend Mr. Boyd's lodgings.

His lordship walked into the room, assessed the situation with one swift look, and, stripping off his gloves, kicked the boots of the sleeping man to wake him. The man groaned but did not open his eyes.

"He's not very awake, Rob," commented Sir Julius, following his friend into the room and observing the young man on the floor through his quizzing glass. "Gad, what a waistcoat."

Lord Marcham went to the stand, picked up the pitcher of water, and emptied it into the face of Sir William Blakelow. Then he calmly laid his gloves upon the table, sat down, crossed his booted ankles, and waited.

The young man surged to his feet in a storm of bluster and foul language. He looked about him as if trying to find his assailant, and on spying his lordship stormed forward. "You!" he cried. "What are you—? How dare you come in here?"

His lordship nonchalantly reached across for a towel, picked it off the washstand, and flung it in the face of the young man. "Dry yourself off, Blakelow. You are dripping water all over Mr. Boyd's floor."

"He's rather pale, March," drawled Sir Julius, observing the young man at length through his quizzing glass. "He's not going to part company with his breakfast is he?"

"I would be very much surprised if he hasn't already parted company with it," replied the earl. "Do sit down, Julius, you are frightening our friend here."

Sir Julius did as he was told, stretching his extremely long legs out before him.

"You—what do you mean by coming in here and accosting me in such a manner?" demanded Sir William, absently plying the towel to his red and dripping face.

"I wished to speak to you. You were . . . ah . . . indisposed. And that method seemed to be the most effective."

"You will meet me for this," said Sir William, lifting his fists menacingly.

Sir Julius put up his brows. "Good God, is he actually threatening you, Rob?" he asked, astounded.

His lordship smiled faintly. "He seems to have a penchant for violence—against me anyway."

"How very peculiar," observed his friend.

"I will have satisfaction," declared Sir William furiously.

"He wants satisfaction, Rob. Very bad business. And him hardly out of short coats. Not the done thing at all, but if he will force it upon you . . ."

"Hush, Julius, you interrupt Sir William," said Lord Marcham.

"Hardly out of short coats?" repeated the young baronet, practically exploding with rage.

"For God's sake, puppy, calm down," recommended his lordship. "Do you think I want to fight with you? Take a damper."

Sir William Blakelow was a bullish-looking young man with a short, thick neck and a rather stocky physique. He was a shade over medium height with a ruddy countenance, and he put his lordship in mind of young Ned Blakelow. His hair was more copper than gold and his eyes a pale blue, but he was unmistakably a Blakelow. He plied the towel to his wet shirt, glaring angrily at his lordly visitor.

"What do you want?" Sir William demanded belligerently.

The earl pulled his snuffbox from his pocket and flicked open the lid. "Sit down, Blakelow."

"I'd rather stand. I don't take orders from no murderer."

"Sit down," said his lordship quietly, taking a pinch of snuff and putting it to his nostril.

Sir William balked a little. "You cannot tell me what to do."

"On the contrary, while I hold the purse strings, I can tell you precisely what to do. Now, are you going to sit down or do I have to resort to more immediate methods?"

The young man reluctantly drew out a chair and sat down.

"Thank you," said his lordship. "I wish to speak to you on a delicate matter. Your sister came to me about two months ago with a preposterous idea. She wanted me to loan her the money to make Thorncote profitable enough again to pay the debts your father owed me."

"Eh?" put in Sir Julius, putting up his quizzing glass again.

"Exactly. That is almost to the letter what I said at the time. Now, while I admire her courage and enterprise, I am, as you may imagine, rather reluctant to invest my blunt in a sinking ship without some . . . *contingencies* . . . put in place." The earl paused and looked over at the florid young man before him. "You play deep, do you not, Blakelow?"

Sir William Blakelow flushed. "No deeper than you, my lord."

"Ah, but I can afford to pay off any debts I may incur . . . You, on the other hand, are a little . . . er . . . compromised."

"I pay my debts, sir," said the young man through his teeth.

"That's not what I heard," drawled Sir Julius.

"I do, I tell you!"

"Of course you do," said the earl soothingly, "and I would not imply otherwise. But you must see that from my point of view, I do not wish to be—how do I phrase it?—forever filling up a leaking bucket."

Sir William flushed. "I have an allowance. My debts will be paid come the beginning of the next quarter."

"Naturally." Lord Marcham smiled. "But by then, you will have another handful of debts to pay off. And a few more the next month and a few more the month after that. You will, I am persuaded, understand my concern."

"You wish me to retrench?"

"No, Blakelow, I wish you to go home."

There was a short silence.

"Go home?"

"If you wish me to help you set Thorncote back upon the road to recovery, then I need to see evidence that you are willing to put in the work to make it happen. Your sister cannot manage it all on her own." The earl paused, smoothing the fabric of his pantaloons across one knee. "And besides, she may not always be at Thorncote. She loves the place and wishes to see it restored for your sake. And I want to see you taking responsibility for your own property. I don't want to see you burdening her any longer with problems that are yours. Is that clear?"

"What has this got to do with you?"

His lordship smiled. "Here we get to the delicate aspect that I mentioned. I wish to have the honor of your sister's hand in marriage."

"What?" cried William.

"As you are head of the family, I feel I should . . . er . . . inform you that I intend to pay my addresses."

"She's barely half your age! I will not have it. It's disgusting."

"I beg your pardon?" said the earl softly but with a steely glint in his eye.

Sir William Blakelow gulped. "She is an innocent and you . . . you . . ."

His lordship raised a brow in silent inquiry.

"Are . . . not," the young man finished lamely.

Lord Marcham picked up a clock on the table, examined it briefly, and then set it down again. "Miss Blakelow is an exceptional woman. Not only does she look after your brothers and sisters and the running of Thorncote and the house, but she is also the most selfless person I have ever met."

"Marianne?" demanded William. "She does not know one end of a scythe from the other!"

"Ah . . . I think we are talking at cross-purposes," the earl said with a smile. "I wish to marry your eldest sister . . . Georgiana."

William stared at him. "I don't have a sister called Georgiana."

There was a moment's silence.

"I'm sorry?" said his lordship.

"I don't have an older sister called Georgiana."

"He don't have an older sister, March," added Sir Julius, helpfully.

His lordship suddenly felt that the carpet appeared to have moved of its own volition under his feet. He sat up in his chair, looking at the younger man intently. "I beg your pardon?"

"I have an aunt called Georgiana. She lives at Thorncote. But I doubt you wish to marry her, my lord. You can give her twenty years."

There was another silence.

Lord Marcham regarded William fixedly. "Georgiana Blakelow is nine and twenty, tall, with dark hair and green eyes. She is bookish and wears thick spectacles. *Now* tell me you don't know her."

William blinked at him. "I have three sisters: Marianne, Kitty, and Lizzy."

The earl got up and began to pace about the room. "What the devil—?" he began and then broke off suddenly, whirling around to face his prospective brother-in-law. "When was the last time you were at Thorncote?"

"I was there for Christmas, my lord."

"The Christmas just gone?"

"Yes, my lord."

"And you have never seen such a young woman as I have described?"

"Georgiana Blakelow is, as you say, a rather bookish and damnably prudish lady, who loves moralizing at the dissolute young men in the neighborhood and writing pamphlets . . . and making my life miserable. She is in her sixtieth year and spends a great deal of time dispensing health remedies to those unfortunate enough to get stuck with her."

Lord Marcham ran a hand over his jaw. "When did your mother die? Forgive the question, but I must know."

William shrugged. "Lord, years ago. Why?"

"And what was her maiden name?"

"Oh, Lord, I don't know. Bray or Gray or something."

The earl thought for a moment. The name rang no bells. He looked at Sir Julius, who shrugged; he did not recognize the name either. "And she had six children?"

"Yes. She died giving birth to Jack. Look, what is this? Why are you asking me all these questions?"

"Was your father married before?"

"No, my lord."

The earl swore under his breath.

Sir William stood up. "Will that be all, my lord? I have an appointment to view a horse at one and I need to get home to change. I say, that is a natty waistcoat you are wearing, who made it for you?"

Lord Marcham was not listening. He was staring out of the window, a frown like a furrow between his brows. "Your father . . . forgive the question . . . had no illegitimate children?"

"How should I know?"

"No wards or other dependents?"

William picked up his coat and began to put it on, shrugging it over his shoulders. "He had a stepdaughter."

The earl turned around. "What was her name?"

"Lord, I don't remember. She lives abroad. Haven't seen her for years."

"Your father married again?"

"Yes, after my mother died, although briefly. But the lady was not in the best of health, and she died not three years from their wedding. Can I go now?"

"And you don't remember the lady's maiden name?"

William rolled his eyes. "How should I? I was hardly eleven years old at the time of the marriage."

His lordship sighed impatiently, sensing that the young Sir William Blakelow, Baronet, was lying through his teeth. He wished now he had paid more attention to the machinations of his neighbor's marital affairs, but he'd been fighting abroad in Spain for much of the time in question, and for as long as he could remember, his mother had considered the Blakelow family beneath their notice. The two families moved in decidedly different circles. The natural children of the baronet and his first wife were at least ten years his lordship's junior and so were unlikely to have developed a close friendship with the Holkham children, even had the countess allowed it. By the time the late Sir William had married again, the earl was abroad with Wellington's army. "Do you have other relatives in London?"

"Only my Uncle Charles, but he had no daughters," said the young man quickly, impatient to be gone. "Can I go now, my lord?"

Lord Marcham nodded absently and picked up his gloves from the table. "Let us go, Julius," he said.

"With the greatest pleasure on earth," responded his friend and stood up. He went to the door and held it open for Sir William and watched as the young man took himself off without as much as a thank you to his host. Sir Julius smiled at his friend and followed Sir William out.

A footstep sounded in the hall, and the earl looked up to see a man loitering in the doorway in such a way as to make his lordship suspect that he had been listening at the door to at least the latter part of their conversation. His name was Mr. Boyd, and he had flinty eyes and a watchful look that the earl mistrusted. He was supposedly the friend of Sir William, but Lord Marcham had met enough unsavory characters in his time to suspect that this gentleman was befriending the young gentleman for his own ends. What could he possibly want from Blakelow? Did he too wish to solve the mystery of who Georgiana really was?

"Apologies for the intrusion, Mr. Boyd," said his lordship, pulling on one of his gloves. "And apologies for that young man's less than beautiful manners."

Mr. Boyd smiled. "Not at all, my lord. Did you find out what you wanted to know?"

"In the usual way of things, my inquiries have raised more questions than they have answered. Is Blakelow a good friend of yours?"

"An acquaintance. He has the ability to land himself in a scrape in the time it would take you to tie that neckcloth."

Lord Marcham smiled faintly as he drew on his other glove. "Taken him under your wing, have you?"

"All young men need a little guidance."

"To be sure."

Mr. Boyd clasped his hands behind his back. "I think we both want the same thing, my lord."

"Indeed?" inquired the earl. "And what is that?"

Mr. Boyd smiled again and his cold eyes gleamed. "To find Miss Sophie Ashton."

His lordship felt a distant chord of recognition, a chime against his memory. The name was familiar somehow but he could not place it. A friend of Sarah's perhaps? Or an old flame of his? No, he felt sure he'd remember her face if it had been that. His lordship decided to humor Mr. Boyd a little and see where it got him. "I see that we begin to understand one another," he said.

"I work for a gentleman who has entrusted me with the task of finding that young woman. A woman who vanished off the face of the earth. A woman who has been invisible for ten years. And I believe we are very close now, my lord, very close indeed."

Lord Marcham picked up his hat and cane. "I hope you may be right. Your client must have deep pockets to keep you employed for ten years."

"He most particularly wishes to find her. She made rather a fool of him, and he does not like to be made a fool of, your lordship, not one tiny bit. And he won't let anyone get in his way."

His lordship smiled slightly. "Good day, Mr. Boyd."

Lord Marcham threw open the door to his sister's bedroom half an hour later, and his eyes scanned the room until they found her, seated before her dressing table in her robe.

"Good Lord. Robbie, you're back. I thought you'd be halfway to Holme by now. What is the matter? Is anything amiss—?"

He shook his head impatiently and came into the room. "Sophie Ashton. She was a friend of yours, wasn't she? Tell me about her."

Mrs. Weir put down her hairbrush and turned to face him. "Sophie Ashton?" she repeated. "Why? What's the matter? What has happened?"

"Nothing. But who was she? Tell me."

Caroline looked at him for a long moment. "You don't know?"

He shook his head. "I remember the name but I cannot put a face to it."

"But surely Hal must have told you?"

"Hal? Told me what? What has he to do with it?" he asked, although he already had that familiar sinking feeling in his stomach as he began to sense another disaster of his brother's making.

"You really *don't* know what happened, do you?" she said.

"No. But I think I'm able to hazard a guess," he replied. "An affair, perhaps?"

"Yes, I'm afraid so."

The earl went over to the window and looked out, slapping his driving gloves against his thigh. There was a silence while he struggled for mastery over his feelings.

"Are you so very angry with me?" Caroline asked him at length.

He gave a long sigh and shrugged. "I can see why my family kept me in the dark for all these years—especially after the Diana Ingham affair. I warned the boy after I extracted him from that entanglement that I would not tolerate any more scandals. But he defied me and got Mary with child—she a gently bred female whose father was a respected local magistrate. I was furious. I practically had to force Hal to the altar with a gun to his head. I told him that I was done with him from that moment on."

There was another short silence.

Caroline folded her hands in her lap. "I didn't tell you because I knew you wouldn't be able to forgive him," she said quietly. "You were so angry with him over Mary. Mama begged us, Sarah and me, not to tell you about Sophie. She said you and Hal were at loggerheads already and that you would cut him from your notice if you found out that he had toyed with the affections of yet another young innocent."

"So you kept it from me," he said.

She nodded. "I'm sorry, Robbie. I should have told you."

"Yes, you should. I might have been able to help her then, even if I can do nothing about it now. I might have been able to spare her some pain at least," he muttered to himself. He walked over to the window and stared down at the road with his back to her. He was quiet for a long time, thinking. Finally he turned around. "Just to be clear, it was Sophie Ashton he ruined?"

"Yes."

He nodded, a muscle tensing in his jaw. "Are you still in touch with her?"

Caroline sighed. "Good Lord, no. I haven't seen Sophie in years. She disappeared after it all happened."

"She was the same age as you?" asked the earl.

Caroline shook her head. "She was younger than me, and I had already become a widow by then, but we became good friends," she said, looking wistfully at the wall. "She had great success. She was a hit."

"Describe her to me."

Caroline shrugged and puffed out her cheeks. "Lord, I don't know . . . beautiful, I suppose, in a rather unconventional way. She had an unusual way of arranging her hair that became her signature and all the crack . . . tall, elegant figure, but she had a vivaciousness about her that men could not resist. They were attracted to her like bees to a honey pot. It was quite a thing to behold. She'd have had *you* wrapped around her little finger, Robbie, no doubt of it. She was the daughter of a navy man, a ship's captain I believe, but he died in the West Indies some years before."

Lord Marcham moved to the fireplace. "And her mother?"

"She was dead too. Poor Sophie had nobody by the time I knew her."

"She must have lived with someone in London. A chaperone of some sort?"

"Her aunt—Mrs. Thorpe. Frightful woman. She made it abundantly clear that Sophie was a burden to her. The aunt's sole aim was to marry her off to the first rich man who came along. A candidate was chosen, the only trouble being that he was considerably older than her—old enough to be her father, in fact. But Sophie was rebellious and refused to do her aunt's bidding. Then there was the scandal, of course."

"My esteemed brother strikes again," he commented with a sneer to his lips.

"While you were busy chasing Boney, Sophie was busy falling in love . . ."

The earl laid his arm along the mantelpiece and clenched his fist. "And?"

"And she eloped with him."

"But he was already married," his lordship pointed out.

"Yes. But Sophie didn't know that. She went with him willingly, thinking they would be married at Gretna Green. Hal had only enough money to get them as far as Stevenage, and I think that was all he ever intended. She was ruined."

CHAPTER 24

MISS BLAKELOW WAS LEAVING that evening.

She had hidden from John her intentions to leave without him. She would take nothing but the money she had earned from her writing and the bag she kept packed with a few precious belongings. She had sewn her money into the hem of her petticoat and mused wryly that it would be as safe under the skirts of an aging spinster as if it were in a locked vault. The ball was that evening, and she planned to take Goodspeed from the stables and head out onto the back roads while her sisters were all dancing the night away. Ned and Jack had gone to a cockfight that evening, and however much she disapproved of such sports, it was the way of the gentlemanly set to which they aspired. By the time they all returned she would be long gone.

So occupied was Miss Blakelow by her preparations to leave Thorncote that she did not notice a parcel to her from Holme until late in the day. When she opened it, a very fine knitted stole in a beautiful silver gray shone in the candlelight as it spilled out into her hands. Frowning, she unfolded the accompanying letter.

My dear Miss Blakelow,

You must forgive me, but I have only today realized that your name has been omitted from the guest list for my sister's ball. I therefore enclose an invitation along with the fondest hope that you will come this evening. I have my brother's assurance that he will not bother you throughout the course of the evening, and so you may be comfortable on that score.

I enclose a stole that was given to me as a present. I find that it is a little old in style for me, and I think will suit you better. I hope you like it, and it is my wish that you will keep it and think of it as a peace offering. I trust you may make use of it this evening, as I think it will perfectly compliment your dress.

Yours, etc.,

Lady St. Michael

Miss Blakelow's mouth fell open. *Too old for her?* Too *old?* How dare she? She screwed up her ladyship's note and hurled it at the floor, pacing back and forth across the carpet.

"Why, Georgie," cried Marianne, who was being dressed in her new blue ball gown and watched her in the mirror, "whatever is the matter?"

Too old? How old did she imagine she was, for heaven's sake? Ninety? Why the sanctimonious, scheming—! *Oh!*

"Nothing!" declared Miss Blakelow vehemently.

"Nothing? But you look as if you might explode."

"And so I might! That hateful, odious . . . !"

Too old? Too old? Miss Blakelow paced back and forth in front of the fireplace. Of all the insulting, ill-mannered, devious women!

"What has he done now?" asked Marianne wearily as she screwed one earring into her earlobe.

Arrested by this unexpected question, Miss Blakelow halted her prowling across the carpet. "Who?"

"Lord Marcham."

"*Lord Marcham?* What has he to say to it, pray?" demanded Miss Blakelow irritably.

"I don't know, but you look terribly put out, and it is usually he who is the cause of it."

Miss Blakelow stopped dead in her tracks and stared at her sister. Lord Marcham. She hadn't allowed herself to think about him all day. If her plan to leave that night was successful, she wouldn't ever see him again. She would sneak away while he was at the ball, and he wouldn't know that she'd gone until it was too late. This was what she wanted, what she'd planned for, but now the thought sent a stab of misery through her. Could she find a way to get one more glimpse of him before she left? She imagined herself dressed in a dark cape and sturdy boots, her horse grazing behind her as she gazed longingly through the windows at the party in full swing. He would not know she was there. He would have little idea that she was hiding in the bushes for a glimpse of him while he was playing host to his guests. She would gaze upon her sisters, knowing that in all probability it would be the last time she would see them.

But part of her wanted to dance alongside her sisters as their equal, to be noticed instead of being confined to the shadows. She wanted to feel Lord Marcham's arms around her, to know that he had seen her as she really was—once, without the spectacles and her widow's weeds. Her secret was almost out anyway. What had she to lose? She would leave by midnight. What harm could an hour or two in a pretty dress do?

❧

Her desire to have one night as herself before she disappeared sustained her long enough to see her ensconced in the carriage with her sisters and her aunt, the steps taken up, and the vehicle in motion.

But when she saw the lights of Holme Park house glinting at her through the trees, her nerves returned to such an alarming degree that she asked for the carriage to be halted so that she might walk home.

"Walk home? In all this dirt?" cried Aunt Blakelow. "You will not."

"But, Aunt, I have made a dreadful mistake. I cannot go. I was foolish to even think of it. I allowed my vanity to get the better of me. Please let me go home."

"Nonsense. Enjoy yourself for once."

"Oh, yes, do come, George," breathed Marianne, radiant with excitement. "You do look so beautiful."

"I feel a fool."

"Georgie. Calm yourself," said her aunt, patting her hand.

Miss Blakelow said no more. She would try to steal away once the carriage had pulled up before the house. The girls would be too distracted to notice her slipping away into the darkness.

But the carriage halted before the house, and Miss Blakelow stood before a thousand windows ablaze with light. Every chandelier appeared to be glowing, the light refracting and bouncing off a million crystal teardrops. As she followed her sisters and the crush of guests up the front stairs and into the hallway, she saw flowers in yellow and gold and white on every available surface. Champagne flowed, the guests milled around in their finery, and she could hear the orchestra striking up for the dancing.

She turned to flee, but the press of people was too thick, like an incoming tide, sweeping all before it. She was borne inexorably toward the receiving line where Lady Harriet, Lady St. Michael, and their mother stood waiting to greet their guests. Miss Blakelow noticed with relief that Lord Marcham was absent. Perhaps he was still in London with his sister. Perhaps he had not been behind that note from his sister after all. She saw Lady St. Michael look over her appearance with a cold smile and itched to slap that lady's rouged cheek. The countess was no less warm in her greeting, and it was with relief that Miss Blakelow felt her hand warmly clasped by Lady Harriet, who expressed herself very happy to see her.

Miss Blakelow was at first amused at the reaction to her appearance. People plainly did not know who she was. She found herself being stared at openly and surreptitiously, from behind fans and through quizzing glasses. Hal Holkham, after his initial shock, openly ogled and grinned at her from across the room with gleeful appreciation. Some of the ladies from the parish who had recognized her and had only ever seen her in dull gray or black stared at her with strong disapproval, giving her the cold shoulder as she approached them. But she did not care. In a few hours' time, she would be gone.

❧

Lord Marcham saw her across the room just as he was reaching for a glass of champagne. He froze, hand poised midair, suddenly unable to perform even this most simple of tasks. The footman had to place the glass in his lordship's gloved hand himself because the man was transfixed by the sight of the woman who had just entered the room.

She was dressed in a gown of midnight-blue silk, which fell over the top of an azure-blue satin underskirt. The puffed sleeves were also made of midnight silk and were trimmed with blue silk rosebuds. The neckline slashed low across her bosom and a single sapphire on a gold chain nestled against the perfect swell of her breasts. Her beautiful mahogany tresses were arranged in a style so markedly different from the other women—who wore bunches of tight curls clustered together like grapes on either side of their temples—that several stares were directed at the simple twist of hair elegantly pinned to her head, allowing her natural waves to curl onto her shoulder. Her womanly curves were very much on show, and the spark of smiling defiance in her eyes dared anyone to object. The glasses, the shawl, the hated cap were all gone, and Lord Marcham thought he'd never seen anything quite so beautiful or so downright alluring.

"Do close your mouth, Robbie," drawled Lady St. Michael as she passed by him on the arm of her husband.

His lordship flushed, dragged his eyes away from Miss Blakelow, and sipped his champagne, trying to gather his disordered wits.

"Is that her?" asked a soft voice at his side.

He turned to look at his sister Caroline. "I don't know what you said to get her here, but you must be a genius."

"Don't thank me. Thank Sarah. She sent her a note and whatever she said, it worked."

"I'll say it did," he murmured, his eyes unconsciously straying to Miss Blakelow once again.

Caroline smiled and looped her arm through his. "Are you going to introduce me then? Or are you going to stand here all night working up the courage to go and ask her to dance?"

"I don't want to ask her to dance."

"So don't then. And when Mr. Peabody calls her wife, you may complain to someone else about it," she replied sweetly.

⁂

Miss Blakelow saw him coming and willed herself to keep the smile pinned to her face despite the memory of the last time she had seen him being still painfully fresh in her mind. He came to stand before her with his sister on his arm. He was exquisitely dressed, as always, his black coat hugging his powerful shoulders, with satin evening breeches and a simple yet elegant cravat at his throat. He looked pensive and there was a frown on his brow, and she wondered if he too were thinking of the last time they had met and that kiss . . .

He bowed stiffly. "Miss Blakelow, may I present my sister to you, Mrs. Caroline Weir?"

Caroline smiled and squeezed her brother's arm, a prearranged signal that the woman she was looking at was one Sophie Ashton. "How do you do, Miss Blakelow? Georgiana, is it not?"

Miss Blakelow could barely meet her eyes. She knew that she had been recognized. "Mrs. Weir, I—"

"Call me Caroline, if you please. We are to be friends, are we not? Well, what a sad crush it is. I knew it would be, of course, because Mama and Sarah *would* invite everybody. Robbie, is that Mrs. Grant over there? Lord, what a gown! She looks like a joint of ham. And that woman in the frightful turban who I have never before seen in my life. Who are all these people?"

Her brother shrugged. "Ask Sarah. I do not know one in ten of them."

"No, and depend upon it, Miss Blakelow, my brother here only wanted one person to attend anyway, and that person is you. He's desperate to ask you to dance, by the way."

Miss Blakelow blushed and looked down at her gloved hands.

"I am quite capable of asking Miss Blakelow myself, if I *wish* to ask her," said his lordship acidly, looking somewhat annoyed.

"Well, get on with it then," recommended his sister. "The evening will be halfway over by the time you take to the floor."

Miss Blakelow, receiving the message loud and clear that he did not want to dance with her, looked away. "I should find my aunt—" she began.

"Miss Blakelow," interrupted the earl in his deep voice. "May I have the honor of the next set?"

"I—I don't wish to force you into dancing with me if you do not wish to," she stammered, heartily wishing herself back at Thorncote and him at Jericho.

He bowed with cold civility and was about to move away, but his sister was having none of it and grabbed his arm to halt his escape.

"My dear Georgiana," she said with her most winning smile, "you *must* dance with him. Indeed, he will be insufferable if you do not. He has been like a bear with a sore head all week as it is. For the sake of the future of his line and any progeny, you must dance and put him out of his misery, because if you do not, then I may well murder him, and what then for the earldom?"

Miss Blakelow could not help smiling faintly at that.

Mrs. Weir placed a hand on her old friend's arm. "Besides, he is by far the best-looking man here, wouldn't you agree? You will make all the other women envious." She ignored the derisive snort from her brother and added, "And if you do not, Mr. Peabody is bearing down upon you and will claim your hand for this dance instead."

Lord Marcham pulled a face filled with disgust. "I do not think it is very flattering to a gentleman to be told that the only reason a girl wishes to dance with him is because his company is slightly preferable to that of Mr. Peapod."

"Very well, my lord," replied Miss Blakelow. She spoke to his cravat, unable to meet his eyes. "But I am a wretched dancer, woefully out of practice, and will step on your toes."

"My toes are at your disposal," he said, bowing again, and unsmilingly held out his arm as the set was forming, stopping only to say into his sister's ear, "Caroline, you go too far."

"So I do, but I get results, do I not?" she retorted with a smile up at him.

They took their positions on the floor, and Miss Blakelow hardly dared look at him as the music began and he clasped her hand. They performed the moves of the dance in silence, each too preoccupied to think of anything to say. It was a full five minutes in this manner before his lordship could stand it no more and said, as lightly as he could, "Miss Blakelow, you are here without your spectacles. Do you not fear to trip over a chair leg and land headfirst in the rum punch?"

His tone was light, teasing. But there was a reserve in his voice, which made her suspect that his mind was elsewhere. That kiss. That wretched kiss. She should have pushed him away. She should have done anything but submit to him. And she definitely should not have leaned into him or curled her arms around his neck or answered the insistent pressure of his lips with her own. Was he thinking of it too? Did the memory give him pleasure? Or did he regret their entire acquaintance and her ever coming to Holme Park at all?

"Indeed I am, my lord. Some clumsy oaf trod on them. I hope you will make yourself useful and point out to me such obstructions as I am likely to fall over," she replied as her eyes fleetingly met his.

"Mr. Peabody's tongue for one," he muttered, staring down the ballroom at the portly gentleman in a bad coat. "He's been staring at you all evening."

"As have you, my lord," she murmured, taking his hand as was required by the dance.

He stared at her for a moment. "It is a great deal too immodest of you to boast of your own beauty, ma'am."

"Oh, I did not mean *that*," she replied airily, "only that you are so astounded at my appearance that you cannot believe your eyes."

"I will not pander to your vanity by answering that."

It was fortunate that the dance required them to separate because Miss Blakelow was flustered by the look in his eyes. She moved through the dance, aware that he still watched her, and as they came together again, their hands clasped firmly together and she looked up into his face.

"Did you have a pleasant trip to London, my lord?" she asked.

"Subtle change of subject," he observed wryly. "Yes, thank you, I did. I went to reacquaint myself with your brother."

"How—how tiresome for you," she replied, her poise slipping a notch.

"I found his company most instructive."

"Indeed?"

"He informed me that he has no sister called Georgiana. In fact, he does not have an elder sister at all."

"He is a brother by marriage only," she said uncomfortably.

"He denies knowing you. Why is that?" he asked, looking down at her.

She shrugged as lightly as she was able. "He and I do not see eye to eye."

"Perhaps. Or perhaps he just wants to protect you from prying questions. And why would that be, Miss Blakelow?" he asked.

"I have no idea."

"You have no idea," he repeated. "Then why do I have the distinct impression that you are hiding something from me?"

She lifted her chin. "I have no idea what you are talking about. Was William able to set your mind at rest concerning Thorncote?"

"Not in the least. I think Thorncote may be damned as far as he's concerned. I think that the only person who cares for it is you. And possibly your aunt."

"And may I ask what you have decided?"

"I may make Hal a gift of it." His lordship smiled, but no warmth reached his eyes as he observed the effect of that name upon his dance partner. "Yes, my brother. I believe you are acquainted with him?"

She colored. "A little."

"A little?" he repeated. "I should say more than a little, from all I have heard, Miss Blakelow . . . or should I say, Miss Ashton?"

She stopped. A lady behind her nearly walked into the back of her, and Miss Blakelow apologized profusely. He knew. She looked up at him, steeling herself against the blaze of anger in his eyes. He *knew*. "Are you attempting to punish me, my lord, for refusing you the other day?" she asked, and was obliged to resume dancing for appearance's sake or else have the whole room staring at them.

"You flatter yourself, ma'am."

"Then why do you bring up a subject that you must know is painful for me?"

"Is it painful for you? Still?" he demanded, watching her intently.

There was a silence.

"The memory of my own folly is painful," she answered at last, her voice barely audible above the sound of the music and laughter and conversation in the room.

"You do know that he's here, don't you?" said his lordship.

Her eyes darted to his face. "If you think to discomfort me, my lord, by mentioning his name, you are sadly mistaken."

"Indeed? You would like me to think so, at any rate. His wife died, you know," he said conversationally. "Give me your other hand and turn toward me. You really are out of practice, aren't you?"

"I am sorry that his wife died."

"I'll wager you are," drawled the earl in such a tone as to imply the opposite.

She glared up at him. "I *am* sorry that Mary died. And you are a great deal too cruel to accuse me of wishing for her death and too unfair to think that Mr. Holkham's marital status should anymore be of interest to me."

He raised a brow in a supercilious look that made her long to stamp on his foot. "I am amazed that you did not recognize him before, Miss Blakelow," remarked the earl. "After all, it was he who ran you down on your horse that night on the road to Loughton. A man and a woman who had been as inseparable as you and he appear to have been, and yet he carried you to his horse and held you all the way back here, and neither of you recognized one another. It is vastly amusing, I'm sure you'll agree," said his lordship, sounding as if nothing amused him less.

"It was dark and I swooned. There is nothing very remarkable about it."

"And he has visited Thorncote on several occasions to visit Marianne, although she has apparently kept that fact from you."

"It is a friendship, nothing more."

"Friendship? Is that what you call it? And we all know what sort of *friendships* my brother makes, do we not?"

"So speaks the rake," she replied with heavy sarcasm.

He smiled. "Ironic, is it not? A man of my reputation is discovered to be an arbiter of moral excellence after all. Whatever you may think of me, Miss Blakelow, I have never seduced an innocent, unlike my saintly brother. The reason he married Mary was because she was carrying his child."

Miss Blakelow began to feel faint. The room was hot and airless; the champagne she had drunk swam in her head.

"Does the sight of him still upset you, my love?" mocked his lordship. "Well, now his wife is dead, so you are free to pick up where you left off. How convenient. Does Mr. Peabody know that his fiancée has designs on another man?" His hand tightened uncomfortably on hers as she started to pull away to run from the dance floor. "Don't," he said in a warning voice.

Miss Blakelow began to feel sick. "Why are you doing this?" she whispered.

"Is that why you refused me?" hissed the Earl under his breath. "Are you still in love with my brother?"

"No."

"He makes a very handsome widower, does he not? All the ladies of the neighborhood have been in a flutter since he arrived."

"You are cruel," she cried.

"Oh, no, my love, it is you who are cruel. To play one brother off against another. To punish me for my brother's mistakes. And I have had it from the horse's mouth. Yes, Miss Blakelow, Caroline told me everything that happened. You eloped and you were ruined. My brother was already married and failed to make you aware of the fact," he said, lowering his voice. "How can you have been so foolish? Are you so free with your reputation?"

Her eyes fell away from the angry resentment in his, the disappointment in her and the disgust. He knew everything and had already condemned her. She had feared his reaction with good reason, but nothing she could possibly have imagined would have prepared her for the look in his eyes at that moment. Well, it was not to be wondered at. Any man her stepfather had ever told had also turned away in disgust. She'd have given anything for the blissful ignorance of a couple of weeks ago, when it had seemed that nothing could taint his opinion of her. The respect and admiration that she was so used to seeing in his eyes had utterly vanished, as had the smile that she had learned to love. Only now that she'd lost it did she realize how much his good opinion had meant to her.

"I don't expect you to understand. I fell in love," she said hotly, "an emotion that *you* know nothing about."

"Don't I? How well you think you know me," he observed with a hard smile. "Clever Miss Blakelow, you think you know everything, do you not? You think that you know men so well. You think that you know me so well, and yet you have failed to spot that which is obvious to half the people in this room."

"Let me go," she hissed, trying to free her hand from his tight grip.

"When the dance has ended."

"Dancing with you is agony, my lord," she muttered.

"And I have been living in agony since our last meeting," he responded bitterly. "You have made a fool out of me."

She could not answer him; her throat was choked with tears and emotion.

"And now I find that you were in love with my brother all along. I never stood a chance, did I? Why didn't you just tell me? Or was it more entertaining to lead me on and watch me tie myself in knots over you?"

She shook her head.

"Did you set out to punish me?" he demanded. "Did you set out to bewitch me so that you might have your revenge? A Holkham broke your heart so you chose to avenge yourself on his brother. That has a certain completeness to it, doesn't it? After all, I am just a rake and I have no feelings, do I? Men like me are not worth a damn."

"You are angry, my lord, because I chose not to reveal my past to you. But you need not insult me. It is my secret, and who I choose to tell is my own affair."

"Are you honestly going to marry Hal or Peabody or anyone else after what happened between us the other day?" he asked hoarsely. "Do you kiss all your admirers the way you kissed me?"

She flushed and lowered her eyes. "What happened between us was a mistake."

"Indeed it was, Miss Blakelow. The worst mistake I ever made," he agreed, "because I haven't been able to stop thinking about it ever since."

They moved for a moment in a circle, interweaving with the other partners in the dance.

"Go to him then," said the earl, his voice like ice. "I won't marry a woman who has given her love to someone else."

The dance ended five minutes later, five minutes of icy silence that seemed like an eternity. When he finally released her, she barely stayed long enough to receive his bow before she fled.

CHAPTER 25

Miss Blakelow fastened her wrap around her shoulders in the cool hallway. It was quieter here, and she was alone but for the servants.

"I won't marry a woman who has given her love to someone else."

Those had been his words.

He knew. He knew everything. She looked longingly at the ballroom, hoping for one last glimpse of him before she left. She knew that she had to go. She knew that she would never see him again.

"Where are you going?"

Miss Blakelow jumped at the sound of the voice and turned, her heart beating loudly. She had thought that she was entirely alone. She had thought she had made her escape from the ballroom unseen, but Hal Holkham stood before her, smiling.

She adjusted her wrap. "I am going home. I have a headache."

"Stay. The night is young, and I have yet had the pleasure of dancing with you."

She shook her head. "No. I am tired and I shouldn't have come."

"Why did you?" he asked curiously. "And without your disguise?"

She shrugged. "Someone made me angry."

"Sarah," he guessed.

She colored and looked away.

"I thought so," he said. "You two never could stand each other."

She pulled the hood of her cape over her hair. "Good night, Hal."

His hand caught her arm, halting her flight. "Come into the library with me."

She choked on a half laugh. "No."

He spread his hands. "You needn't look like that. We may be more comfortable in there."

She eyed him in amusement. "So we might, but I am no longer a green girl, Mr. Holkham."

He looked amused. "I didn't mean *that*."

"Didn't you?" she asked, her tone doubtful.

"You look beautiful tonight," he said.

She playfully rolled her eyes. "Don't you ever give up?"

A grin tugged at the corner of his mouth. "I could hardly keep my eyes off you."

"When you weren't staring at Marianne, that is," she answered with a knowing look.

He gave a reluctant smile and held up his hand to acknowledge a hit. "Alright, I admit it. But she is hard to ignore."

"Indeed she is . . . for a man like you."

"Or Robert," he added.

Miss Blakelow stiffened. "Lord Marcham is not short of beautiful women for company."

"He is a man like any other. Why shouldn't he enjoy a beautiful woman when he finds one?"

"Because there are rules."

"Rules are made to be broken," he murmured, coming closer.

"For men, perhaps."

"You broke rules once before," he said softly.

"Yes, but I was nineteen and very foolish."

"You were adorable."

She laughed scornfully. "Hal, stop."

He spread his hands, the picture of innocence. "What?"

"The chance of some sport is not to be passed by, is it? You are worse than your brother."

He leaned his shoulders against the balustrade with folded arms. "Not worse, Sophie. The same. We are not so very different, he and I."

"Neither of you can think past the gratification of your own pleasure, whether it comes from a bottle or a bedroom—but at least *he* respects a virtuous female."

"Perhaps. But unlike me, Robert is a dreamer. He believes in love."

"And what do you believe in?" she asked.

He smiled. "I believe in making it."

She was unimpressed by this speech. "A predictable response, Hal. Did you not think of growing up in Brussels?"

He looked amused. "Where would be the fun in that?"

"You might actually pass one calendar year without an outraged father, husband, or fiancée on your heels and a horsewhip in their hands. Try it. You might like it."

He tilted his head on one side, examining her like a bird. "You have changed, Miss Ashton."

"I have had to."

He took a few steps toward her, smiling. "But I wonder if this cool aloofness is a ruse and that the passionate creature I remember so well is still lurking underneath?"

She tried not to gulp as he came to stand before her. She willed herself not to flinch or balk and raised her eyes defiantly to his.

He gave a soft laugh as he saw the fight in her stare. "Yes . . . most *definitely* you have changed," he said.

"Go home, Hal. Marianne is not the fool that I was. She will not give up her kisses so easily and you cannot—"

He silenced her with his mouth. For a moment she resisted him, struggling against his embrace, but then something in her gave way and she leaned into him, savoring his closeness, smelling his cologne, feeling his arms around her after all these years apart. So many times had she dreamed that she would one day be back in his arms, that she would once again feel his desire, if not his love.

But this was wrong. Somewhere along the line they had become the wrong arms, the wrong lips, and his kiss aroused nothing more in her than the desire to be kissed properly by the man whom she craved to hold close.

"Hal . . ." she whispered, closing her eyes, searching . . . trying to find something. A feeling. A thrill. Anything. Trying to recapture those feelings that had been hers so long ago . . .

He bent his head and kissed her again, this time very gently, almost reverently. She opened her mouth beneath his, offering herself up to him, waiting for him to come and take her, waiting for the passion, waiting for that old familiar feeling to tremble in her belly. But it didn't.

She drew her mouth away and simply stared at him.

"Hal," she whispered.

She put her arms around his neck and looked up at him as their eyes met. And in that long moment, Miss Blakelow felt the years fall away. All the hurt and anger and resentment were unimportant now. It was over.

He had not been deliberately cruel and heartless all those years ago. He had not intended to use her for his own ends or ruin her life. He had been weak, that's all. He was a weak man trapped in a loveless marriage. He had given in to his youthful passions at the expense of his honor, and she realized now that he had been every bit as naive as she. He had not intended to cheat her or break her heart. They had both been young and foolish and unable to reconcile their feelings for each other to the world in which they lived.

In that moment, she forgave him much. The ten years of hurt slid away, and she saw him as he really was: not a hero from one of the novels she read as a young woman, but a real man who made very real mistakes.

"Hal, it's over," she said softly.

He sighed. "I know."

"You're kissing me as if I were your sister—or at least it feels as if you are."

"Sister?" he repeated, horrified. "Well, dash it, Sophie, that's not exactly flattering."

"I'm sorry."

"It's too late then," he said sadly.

"It would never have worked, you know . . . you and I."

"Wouldn't it?"

"I realize it now even if I didn't before."

"Perhaps you've met someone who suits you better?" he suggested.

She lowered her eyes from his. "I don't think I'm suited to anyone, Hal. I am the poisoned chalice. Everything I touch turns sour. No matter where I go or what I do, my past continues to haunt my future."

"Then change it."

She gave a scornful laugh. "Oh, how easy you make it sound. I wish that I could."

"You can."

"How?"

"Stop running away. Face it head on."

She shook her head.

"Robert needs to know what happened," Hal said gently.

"I can't," she whispered, emotion closing her throat.

"You have to tell him." His hands slid down her arms and took her hands in his. "Tell him, Georgie."

She looked up at him, surprised to hear that name on his lips. She had always been Sophie to him.

"You are Georgiana now," he said. "Your life is here now. These people are your friends. This is your home. No more running."

She reached up on tiptoe and kissed his cheek. "Good-bye, Hal."

She stepped away from him, but not before she had seen the man hovering over his shoulder. Lord Marcham stood in the doorway, watching.

Their eyes met for a long moment before he turned back to his guests.

✾

Lord Marcham stood in the entrance to the ballroom, half watching the dancing but with one eye to the hallway, waiting for his brother to come back . . . or Georgiana . . . or both of them together.

A woman passed by and nodded a greeting to him but he did not notice. His attention was caught by the scene taking place in the hallway, which would decide his future happiness. He saw a movement out of the corner of his eye and watched as his brother came back in through the front door. Davenham closed it, and Hal said something to the butler and smiled.

Hal was smiling, damn him. He looked happy. His lordship felt his stomach clench into knots. He was happy for him. Or at least he *should* be. He was his brother, after all.

Hal had spent years in an unhappy marriage—why shouldn't he now marry the woman he had fallen in love with all those years ago? All the best to him. He wanted nothing but Hal's happiness, he told himself. It was all he ever wanted. Now Hal had a second chance at matrimony, a chance for love, and children, and a future. He should take it with both hands.

And Georgie? Well. There had been women before her and there would no doubt be women after her. He was a rake, wasn't he? It was expected of him. He would take a mistress. A mistress with green eyes and chestnut hair. And in the moments after intimacy, he would be grateful to wake up still a single man, without responsibilities. He would still be free.

He had lived thirty-six years without love, and he had no doubt that he could survive another the same. Sarah was probably right. He was not the right man for matrimony. He was too jaded, too selfish, too used to taking his pleasure where and when he chose. And he found Georgiana intriguing, but she was not beautiful enough to hold his interest for long. There would be other women. There were bound to be. Since when had he stayed with any woman for more than a year?

He was as immoral as he was dissipated. He had been warming Lady Burford's bed at the age of eighteen, when Georgiana was still taking lessons from her governess. It would have been laughable if it wasn't so tragic. How could he change a lifetime of bad behavior? How could he let her marry a man who had never had any kind of meaningful relationship with a woman in his life? A man who had never had an interest in a woman beyond her seduction? How did he know that it wasn't merely lust that he felt for Miss Blakelow? And once he'd had her, how soon would the novelty of married life wear thin? And how long before he would look to other quarters for excitement? The chances were that he would be unfaithful within a year.

And yet . . .

"Robbie, you're not dancing," Hal said, coming to a halt before him.

Lord Marcham gathered his gloomy thoughts together and threw them from his mind. "I'm ready for my bed."

"Already? What kind of rake goes to bed before midnight?"

"The bored kind," responded his lordship.

His brother chuckled. "Oh, dear, that bad, is it? Not enough scantily clad females here to hold your interest? Or is the play at the card table a little tame for such a hardened gamester such as you?"

"Exactly so."

"Well, it can't be that bad. Find yourself a pretty girl and make yourself agreeable."

"I'm not in the mood."

"You? Not in the mood to chase pretty girls? Impossible."

Lord Marcham forced a smile. Given the thoughts that had so recently been revolving in his head, this wasn't exactly what he wanted to hear. "Even a rake needs a night off now and again. My age, you know."

"Hardly. You'd probably drink me under the table without any trouble at all. Us married men, you know, dull dogs I'm afraid."

"How was the happy reunion? Am I to wish you joy?" asked Lord Marcham in a desperate bid to change the subject. He sipped his champagne, keeping his eyes on the dancers on the floor before them as they interwove in a country dance, their flushed and happy faces in stark contrast to the wretchedness he felt inside.

He'd sworn he would not ask. He'd told himself that he was uninterested in whatever arrangement his brother and Georgiana had come to. But he had seen that kiss. He had witnessed her slipping her arms around his brother's neck, and the sense of gnawing jealousy made him want to place his fist with some force into the center of Hal's handsome face.

Hal turned and saw his brother's look and smiled faintly. "So you *are* interested after all," he commented.

His lordship raised a brow. "Of course I'm interested. You're my brother."

Hal gave him a knowing smile. "Doing it much too brown, big brother, much too brown indeed."

"If she is to become my sister-in-law, then I wish to know," said Lord Marcham coldly.

Hal looked amused. "Why?"

"Why? Because I was planning to give Thorncote to you, that's why," he said stiffly. He paused and cleared his throat. "I was thinking of it as a wedding gift."

"Keep little brother busy so that he cannot get into more trouble?" murmured Hal.

"Something like that."

"And are you going to come over and check my progress with the farm thirty times a day, just so that you may have the excuse to ogle my wife?"

The earl clenched his fist. His wife. Christ. His wife. He felt as if he might be sick. Never had two words made him so blazingly angry. "Not at all," he replied with all the appearance of calm. "I have no intention of interfering. I will move back to London. I find Holme a little dull, I must confess."

His brother gave him another knowing look. "And would you find it half so dull if Georgiana were living here with you as *your* wife?"

Their eyes met.

"Are you deliberately trying to goad me into losing my temper?" demanded his lordship.

"It appears as if I don't have to try very hard to achieve that effect."

"Hal, I swear, by all that is holy—just watch your damned tongue."

"I am grateful for your offer—to buy Thorncote for us, I mean—but that won't be necessary."

His lordship's eyes fixed upon his brother's face. "Why not?"

"Because I intend to return to Brussels."

"Brussels?" the earl repeated. He felt the blood drain from his face. He was taking her to Brussels. He would never see her again . . .

Good, he told himself. Then she would not flaunt her new-found happiness in his face. She was going to Brussels, and that would spare him the pain of seeing her happy with another man, of watching her belly swell with his babe. It would never stop him imagining. It would never stop him dreaming. But at least she would be out of sight if not out of mind.

"Yes. I rather like it there. I have made friends, and Mary's family has been very good to me. You should come and visit us there now that the war is over."

Lord Marcham could take no more. He nodded lamely. "We'll see."

"No, I mean it. It will be a pleasure to have you visit. I'm sure Georgiana would like to see you."

His lordship made no answer.

"She thinks of you as a very good friend," Hal said, watching the tortured look on his brother's face with some amusement. "I will have the bedchamber next to ours redecorated for when you come."

The room next to yours? So I can hear you making love to her? No and no and dammit—no!

His lordship drained his champagne glass. "I need some air," he said, putting down the glass on the mantelpiece with such force that he nearly broke it.

"Good idea. I'll come with you."

Marcham held up his hand. "No. I want to be alone."

"Yes, that's the ticket. Go and mope on your own in that gloomy library of yours. That will help."

His lordship stared at him. "You are *goading* me? Do you know how close I am to rearranging your damnably handsome face?"

His brother laughed quietly. "You have it all wrong, you know."

His lordship thought that he might well explode. He clenched his fists, his belly sour with pain and anger and jealousy. "Hal . . . don't . . . just don't."

"Rob, you fool, stop glaring at me. You're not going to hit me."

"I wouldn't count on it."

"It's over, can't you see that? There is no attachment between Georgiana and me anymore."

The earl's eyes shot to his face. "What do you mean?"

"We are different people now. Sophie has long gone and Georgie has taken her place. And I have other interests . . ." His eyes flicked toward the ballroom, where Marianne Blakelow was talking with a friend.

"I don't understand. I thought that you and Georgie . . ." His voice trailed off. He couldn't put it into words.

Hal shrugged. "It was so long ago. I will always be fond of her, of course."

His lordship stared at his brother, hope soaring in his breast. "Hal, don't tease me on this subject—are you certain?"

"As certain of anything in my life! Why don't you go to her?"

"Because it's useless. She won't have me."

"And why won't she have you?"

"I don't know." Lord Marcham ran a hand through his hair. "Well, that's not strictly true. I think she doesn't believe that I wish to marry her. She thinks that I'm shopping for a wife and any available woman will do."

"I see. And who gave her that impression?"

The earl swallowed. "I did."

"You did," Hal repeated.

"Yes. I asked her the first time because she was convenient and, oh, it's a long story, but she seemed to be the answer to my prayers. But as time went on, I began to think that we might suit, more than suit." He paused, scuffing one beautifully shod foot against the floor. "Sadly I was the only one of us who thought so. She thinks that I will be unfaithful to her."

"And will you?"

"No."

The word surprised him. Or not the word but the way he said it. He said it without hesitation, without having to think it through. He knew that if he was given the chance of love after all these years, he'd be damned if he'd throw it away.

"And have you asked her to marry you since?" Hal asked.

"Of course I have."

"And what does she say? What *precisely* does she say?"

"That she cannot marry me."

"Ah," said Hal, as if everything had suddenly become clear.

"Ah, what?" demanded the earl.

"Not that she doesn't *want* to marry you, but that she *can't*. She's scared to tell you what happened. She's frightened that you will despise her for it."

"Despise her for what? Do you know what happened?"

Hal smiled faintly. "Yes. But I think that she should be the one to tell you."

"She won't tell me," replied his lordship bitterly. "She'd tell everyone else *but* me."

"You idiot, Robbie. That's because she's head over heels in love with you, can't you see that? Your opinion of her matters to her a great deal. She doesn't want you to think badly of her."

Lord Marcham stared at him. "Are you sure?"

"As sure of anything in my life. Go to her. Ask her what happened at the White Swan. And do it now Rob; she's planning to leave."

"Leave?" his lordship barked.

Hal smiled. "If I know my little Sophie, she is right now packing her trunk."

Lord Marcham looked at him for a moment and then started toward the stairs to change out of his evening attire.

"Oh, and Robbie?"

His lordship turned, one hand upon the banister. "Yes?"

"Do not think too badly of her—or me, for that matter. If it counts for anything with you, I know what I did was wrong."

Their eyes met for a long moment.

"Will you be here when I get back?" the earl asked.

"I don't think so."

His lordship nodded and was gone.

CHAPTER 26

Lord Marcham arrived at Thorncote to find the house utterly deserted.

The front door had been left open, and it bounced against its hinges in the breeze—a fact he observed with a sense of deep foreboding. No groom or stable hand came to see to his horse; no butler came to take his hat and riding whip. He dismounted and led his horse to a stone balustrade and looped the reins around it. He ran lightly up the front steps and entered the house. It was as quiet as a tomb.

Out of the corner of his eye he saw a slip of white paper on the floor. He stooped to pick it up and turned it over in his hands. It was a letter, and he tilted it to the moonlight and swiftly read the contents. The note was short and to the point. It was from Mrs. Susan Thorpe. William Blakelow had eloped with her daughter, Charlotte, a week ago. Mrs. Thorpe blamed Sophie for putting thoughts of love into her daughter's head. The aunt was writing to inform her niece that Miss Ashton's whereabouts had been known to Mr. Boyd and his master for several days, and she hoped that justice would be served.

Lord Marcham swore under his breath and strode from room to room, the sounds of his footsteps echoing on the stone floor as he called out Miss Blakelow's name. Every room was silent and dark. There was no one: no John, no servants, and no Georgiana.

He took the stairs two at a time and hurried along the hallway to her bedchamber. The door stood ajar. He pushed it open and was relieved to find it occupied by its owner. A single candle burned on the dressing table in front of Miss Blakelow, who stood with her back to him. She started and whirled around, her eyes wide with alarm.

"Oh, it's you . . . You startled me."

"I apologize, Miss Blakelow," he said stiffly as he came into the room. "I didn't mean to alarm you. Is everything alright?"

"Of course," she answered with a nervous laugh. "Why wouldn't it be?"

"Then why is the front door wide open? And this letter? Who is Mr. Boyd's master?"

She looked at him for a moment and then picked up a small painting from the table by her bed and dropped it into a bag.

"Where is John?" he asked when she made no answer.

"I—I gave all the servants the evening off."

"Then it is a good thing that I have come. A deserted house with no one to attend you and this man hell-bent on revenge—"

"Oh, what tosh," she replied with some impatience. "I am big enough and old enough to look after myself. Why are you here? Shouldn't you be attending to your guests?"

The earl shrugged and quietly closed the door. "No one will miss me."

"No one will miss the great Earl of Marcham?" she repeated, casting him a skeptical look over her shoulder. "I find that hard to believe. What do you want?"

He turned toward the fireplace and kicked the smoldering log to life. Orange flames erupted around it.

"I wanted to see you," he said. He leaned his fist against the mantelpiece, his eyes taking in the cloak bag on the bed. "You're leaving?"

"You know I am," she replied, as she lifted her hands and unpinned the tiny flowers that adorned her hair.

"Where are you going?" he asked.

She shrugged. "Who knows? Everywhere. Nowhere. No one cares at any rate."

"I care," he said.

"Do you?" She smirked and sent him a pitying look. She pulled another pin from her hair and cast it into a china bowl on the dressing table.

"I spoke to Hal," he said conversationally, the toe of his boot scuffing against the edge of the threadbare rug. "He told me to ask you what happened at the White Swan."

Her eyes flew to his. She was silent for a moment but then shrugged and said, "Nothing. Everything."

"My brother told me that you were there together."

"Yes. We eloped—did you know that?" she replied with a brittle smile. "And your mother sent Sir Julius Fawcett after us to bring us back. She was not best pleased at the thought of her precious son being corrupted by a harpy, so Julius found me there . . . but I ran away."

"Hal broke your heart."

"Yes." She paused and rallied her spirits. "And now I must go. My brother William has eloped with Charlotte Thorpe and my past is about to catch up with me. I can no longer remain in this neighborhood. I cannot risk Marianne and the girls being ruined by association with me."

"You can't leave. I won't let you."

355

She raised a brow at him. "And how do you plan to stop me? Tie me to the chair?"

"If I have to."

"You won't do that. Because you know that you'd have to keep me prisoner all the days of my life. One day I would run from you."

He stood watching as she pulled her hair free of the pins and teased each glossy skein so that it fell around her shoulders. He stared at her, his head full of her voice, her perfume, her intoxicating nearness, and he longed to touch her. She filled his senses like a drug, and all he could think about was the proximity of the bed.

"Don't go."

She looked at him and smiled. "You'll have forgotten me within a week."

He silently shook his head.

"I tried to warn you away, did I not?" she said as she sat down on the stool before the dressing table and began to brush her hair. "But you were stubborn and you would not listen. In typical male fashion, you had to have that which you were told you could not have. And the more I told you that I was not interested in matrimony, the more you wanted me. The great challenge was to seduce the bluestocking, was it not, my lord? But little did you think that you were the one being duped."

She pulled the sapphire drops from her ears and unfastened the necklace at her throat. Then she placed the jewels carefully in a blue velvet roll and tied the ribbon. They were all she had left of her mother's jewelry—the rest had been sold by her stepfather.

"Duped? What do you mean duped?"

She smiled into the mirror and briefly met his eyes. "You once called me a heartbreaker. You meant it flippantly, but little did you know how accurate you were." She paused and kicked off her satin slippers. "Poor Robbie. Never been in love before, have you? And the first time you fall, you fall for a woman with no heart."

"What's happened? Why are you being like this?"

"Like this, my lord? I am being like this because this is who I am."

"No," he said. "This is not my Georgie."

"This *is* me," she insisted, twisting around on the seat so that she faced him. "I am not Georgiana Blakelow. I'm nobody—can't you see that? After I was ruined, I had to run. I was shunned by the world for my affair with your brother and fearful of being found by the man I had traveled across an ocean to escape. I changed my name repeatedly. I have been a widow, a governess, and a paid companion. I have lived amongst thieves as well as the most respectable people in society. I have been every woman and no one. I have acted so many parts that I do not know who I am anymore." She broke off, a sob catching in her throat. "And I have left a trail of broken hearts behind me. And now I add the best to my portfolio—the Earl of Marcham, no less," she cried, flinging up her hands. "How many women would love to claim that?"

He came toward her and seized her shoulders and pulled her off the stool. "Stop it."

"I set out to break you from the moment I saw you. I have avenged myself on men up and down the country, didn't you know?" she jeered, staring up into his eyes, her own moist with unshed tears. "I warned you to stay away from me. I am broken."

He shook his head. "You are pushing me away again. I don't know why but—what is this all about? What game is this now?" he demanded, his fingers biting into her shoulders. He jerked her roughly into his arms, her hands trapped against his chest. His hand came up to cup her chin, turning her face up to meet his. "Tell me, is this a lie?" he demanded hoarsely a moment before his lips came down on hers.

He kissed her long and hard, his lips almost bruising in their intensity, his arms so tightly around her that she could scarcely breathe. He kissed her until she was fairly drunk with it, intoxicated with his nearness and the pressure of his mouth on hers. He kissed her until only the need for air forced them apart.

She threw him a mocking smile as she forced her eyes to meet his and said archly, "La, as I said, my lord, men like you are easily duped. For all your famed experience with women, it seems that *you* cannot tell an actress from the real thing."

He stared at her, his eyes ablaze. "You were *not* acting," he said savagely.

"I'm sorry, but I was," she replied.

He released her suddenly and almost flung himself away from her.

"How clever you thought you were. How superior. You thought I would just fall at your feet, did you not, my lord? The great rake seducer merely clicks his fingers and the plain little spinster is expected to jump into his arms."

He laughed, a harsh, abrasive sound. "Plain, innocent spinster? Hardly! You are the same as all the rest, beauty and avarice and treachery in equal measure. And I thought you were different. I came here to convince you to stay, although why I put myself to the trouble, I know not."

"Did you indeed? With rough kisses and promises of fidelity? Do you think that your suit is in any way attractive to me, my lord?"

A muscle pulsed angrily in his jaw.

"You have me all worked out, do you not?" he asked bitterly.

"I know you," she countered.

"No," he answered. "It seems that you don't know me at all."

There was a silence.

"Well then," she said at last. "Perhaps our parting is for the best."

"I begin to think that it is," he agreed moodily.

"We wouldn't suit, you know."

"So it seems. I count myself fortunate to have escaped from an alliance that can only have made both of us profoundly unhappy."

She flinched as if he had slapped her. "You had much better leave. It is late and your absence will be remarked upon."

"Where has my Georgie gone?" he whispered, almost to himself. "I want her back."

"She never existed, my lord," she answered. "She was a fabrication."

"She did exist," he insisted. "I held her in my arms and I kissed her."

She tossed her head. "The woman you speak of was a creature of my imagining. All I did was play a part." She moved toward the bed, flinging a book into her bag. "Will you unfasten my gown, my lord?" she asked, turning her back to him and lifting her hair aside. "My maid has the evening off. And as you are here, you may as well do the one thing you do so well."

Mechanically he lifted his fingers to do her bidding, but he struggled to do one of the very things he had anticipated doing with great pleasure on their wedding night. His fingers were clumsy, and the buttons seemed to develop a mind of their own.

"You'd make a terrible lady's maid," she commented with a mocking smile as she moved away from him and shrugged the gown forward off her shoulders. "It is a wonder to me that you managed to seduce any women at all if it took you that long to disrobe them."

"Will you *stop*?" he thundered.

She swallowed hard, flinching at the tone in his voice and the expression on his face, but she had come too far to give up now. "Are you going to watch me disrobe?" she asked with a shaky smile, her act slipping a notch. "Stay long enough and you will witness my use of the chamber pot too. Only imagine how that would contribute to your edification."

His lordship could take no more. He strode out of the room, slamming the door behind him.

And with him departed Miss Blakelow's act.

Her resolve crumbled, and she sank onto the bed in her undergarments and stared at the floor.

※

From the shadows of the room a movement flickered in the darkness. Candlelight gleamed along the barrel of a pistol.

"You have done well," said a low male voice.

"I've done what you asked," Miss Blakelow said coldly to the shadowy figure.

"So you have," agreed the man.

"And you'll let him go, unhurt?" she asked, raising her fearful eyes to his.

The man smiled, and Miss Blakelow felt a shudder ricochet along her spine. "If he does not interfere."

"He knows nothing," she said.

"I only have your word for that."

"He knows nothing, I swear it."

"Very well, my dear. Then I suggest that you make haste changing your clothes. Mr. Boyd, would you please ensure that she does not take too long? And if she tries to escape, hit her over the head. After last time, I am taking no chances."

Miss Blakelow was allowed ten minutes grace to change her clothes and was then escorted downstairs to the library, where she saw her nemesis seated behind her father's desk. She stiffened as the man came out of his chair.

He walked forward, a lazy, self-satisfied smile upon his face. She felt her knees threaten to give way beneath her; her hands were cold and clammy, her heart thudding hard. She stared at him, disbelieving what her eyes told her even though she had known for the last ten years that this time would come. He'd found her. And she knew now that the face that she'd seen at the assembly rooms but a week before was his. It was not a face from a nightmare, but a real living and breathing man.

"You have what you want," she said. "Let John and the servants go."

The man smiled. "Ah, but I don't have what I want, do I?" he replied softly.

She swallowed hard and lowered her gaze. "I don't know what you mean."

"Don't take me for a fool, Sophie."

Sophie. She had been so many different names, living off her wits since her ruin at the hands of Hal Holkham, that she could not remember who Sophie Clayton was anymore.

"What are you doing here?" she demanded, looking about her for a weapon.

He gave a soundless laugh. "I think you know the answer to that. Forgive me, my dear, but remembering our last encounter, I have taken the liberty of moving the paper knife and the fire poker out of reach. You may sit down."

She lifted her chin defiantly. "I will stand, thank you."

"Still so haughty," he marveled, coming forward to stand before her.

"Let me see to John. Where is he?" she demanded.

He smiled. "He is . . . er . . . sleeping and will do well enough without your ministrations. I hope you pay him well, my dear. The poor man has had a good deal of trouble on your behalf over the years."

"Leave him out of this. He did nothing but follow my orders. It is me you want. Let him and the others go."

"Do you know that I nearly caught you once?" he asked, ignoring her request with a smile.

She raised a brow in silent inquiry.

"You were going under the name of Mrs. Cork and living on the last of the funds that your uncle had given you. John was posing as your husband, and it was barely a year after your fall from grace. But you did not have your story straight, did you? You slipped up. And I broke down the front door barely five minutes after you had left; your sheets were still warm. I nearly had you then, but the trail went cold. You vanished into thin air. Now I realize that you had already begun to transform yourself into your aunt, or something very much akin to her. I applaud you for that, my dear."

She had to look up a long way into his face. He towered over her, and as her eyes met his, she tried to repress the shudder that went through her. He reached out a hand and cupped her chin, tilting her head from one side to the other. "Well, well," he said, "still a beauty, aren't we?"

She stood her ground, staring doggedly up at him. "And you are still a snake."

He smiled. "Have you any idea how long I have spent looking for you?" he whispered, his breath on her face.

"As long as I have spent avoiding you," she retorted.

"Your Aunt Thorpe sent word to me of where you were. She really doesn't like you very much, does she? She informed me that you had been here all the time, when I had begun to think you'd gone back to the West Indies. After all, that was the rumor."

"I considered it. America too."

"I congratulate you, my dear. Georgiana Blakelow was the perfect disguise. The deliberate use of your aunt's name caused us much confusion, I must confess. Two ladies named Georgiana, living together and yet each denying the existence of the other. Your family closed ranks around you. William did admirably well. He denied all knowledge of you as a sister or even living in this house—and I would know, for I was there. You should be proud of him. But I am not a man who gives up easily, my dear. And this scar that you gave me at that inn on a hot summer's night long ago aches to be with you." He took her hand and forced it to cup his face, forced her fingers to splay across the smoothness of the scar. "Does it repulse you, my love? Do you know what it is like to be stared at by children? Do you know how many women have turned away from me in disgust because of this mark that you gave me?"

"If women turn away from you in disgust, it is because they see what kind of man you are," she said, yanking her hand out of his.

He nodded slowly. "You will pay for that remark, my dear. Boyd?"

"Yes, master," said the man, who had returned to the room. "The carriage is ready."

Miss Blakelow looked with deep foreboding from Mr. Boyd to the face of her tormentor. "What are you going to do?"

"Firstly, I want to see if you are as pretty under that gown as I imagined," he said.

The skin on her neck began to crawl. "No."

He grabbed her hand and pulled her across the room to the door.

"No," she said again, more firmly.

He halted them and pulled a blade from his pocket and laid the cold steel against her cheek. "If you scream, I will mark you the way you have marked me. Do you understand?"

She nodded, her eyes wide with fear.

"And then, my dear, you will tell me where he is."

CHAPTER 27

SOMETHING, A NAGGING FEELING that all was not well, assailed Lord Marcham. Thorncote had been utterly quiet: no servants, no fires lit, no John.

And Miss Blakelow never went anywhere without John.

His lordship swore under his breath as he swung himself back off his horse and looped the reins once more around the balustrade. He strode to the rear of the house and across the stable yard. The gravel crunched underfoot as he walked over to a horse that had been hitched to an old gig. For lack of anyone to guide her, the horse had wandered toward a green verge of grass where she was happily munching away, towing the gig with her. The horse eyed him warily as he approached, her eyes wide and bulging like cue balls on a billiard table. He murmured soothing words to the animal and called softly, "John?"

A path led under a brick archway. He followed it and found that it gave onto a small kitchen garden from where he could make his way into the back of the house. The kitchen, pantry, and other rooms were all quiet and still. Now very worried, he picked up a knife from the wooden table in the kitchen and gripped it in his hand as he moved into the servants' dining hall. It was empty. There was no sign of life. He turned—

A sound. A muffled moan came to his ears. He whirled around in the direction of the noise and moved cautiously toward the stairs, his heart pounding hard. Another moan led him through the doors and into a room where the silver was once kept and polished. The shelves were empty now, the silver sold long ago to pay off Sir William's debts.

He called John's name again. There was a pause and then a muffled but frantic attempt to answer him. Lord Marcham ran to the back of the room. There, trussed up like Christmas geese and covered in strands of straw, were John Maynard and four frightened servants all bound and gagged and looking up at him with pleading eyes. His lordship crouched down beside John and untied the gag around his mouth. The butler's head was bleeding, and the side of his face was sticky and warm with blood.

John gratefully sucked in great lungfuls of air. "He's got her," he gasped.

"Who's got her?"

"We stayed here too long and now he's found us. It's my fault, my lord. I should have listened to her when she said that it was time for us to move on. But we were so happy here and neither of us wanted to leave and now it is too late—"

His lordship held up his hand to stem the flow of garbled speech as he tried to make sense of it. "Whoa, gently, my friend. You mean Georgiana?"

"Aye, my lord. He's taken her, and the Lord only knows what he'll do now he's found her again—I have to go after them. Untie me, quickly, if you please. I have a fair notion of where he's headed."

"I will come with you," replied the earl, using the knife to attack the rope, which bound the man's hands and feet together.

"No, my lord."

"Who is this man?"

John looked at him with something akin to pity in his eyes. "Her brother-in-law. She hoodwinked him, and he has never forgiven her for it."

"There, you are free. Can you stand?"

"With your lordship's help."

The earl helped him to his feet and then set about untying the other servants.

"You need a doctor," said Lord Marcham, frowning at the fall of blood on John's face.

"No time for that. I must go after them."

"You are in no fit state to go anywhere. Tell me where they have gone."

"He's obsessed with her, my lord."

"John," the earl demanded. "*Tell* me."

❧

Miss Blakelow stood by the curtains, shivering in the draft from an ill-fitting window. She folded her arms across her chest, wondering if she would survive the jump to the ground below without breaking a limb. She drew back from the window, deciding that it ought not to be attempted. She looked about her for a weapon but found the room to be utterly devoid of clutter. It possessed a bed, a dressing table, a mirror, and a table, and there wasn't so much as a hairbrush on any of the surfaces, nor a candle by which to see her way around.

Her head throbbed. They had forced some vile substance down her throat, which had knocked her semiconscious. Then, as she struggled, someone had hit her over the head. She reached up a hand and felt the bump of a bruise and a rough patch of congealed blood at her temple. She had been unconscious for several hours, long enough for her to be secreted away and locked in this room.

She heard footsteps in the hallway. A key rattled in the door and it opened. The tall figure of a man stood silhouetted against the light from the hallway.

"Come," he said, beckoning with one hand.

Warily she followed him. He led her along the hallway and down a flight of stairs that curved in a beautiful arc to the grand hall below. Light shone from a doorway, and she was pushed toward the room.

It was a dining room, and at one end of the long table sat her nemesis, watching her over the rim of his wineglass as he drank. He smiled a cold smile of triumph and indicated that she should be seated at the other end of the table.

"Eat," he invited. "You must be hungry."

"What time is it?" she asked, her voice dry and croaky.

"Seven or thereabouts."

"Where am I?"

He smiled again. "Sit, Sophie. Eat."

She pulled out a chair and sat down. A pewter plate was on the table before her; no knife, no fork, not so much as a spoon was given for her convenience. He clearly didn't trust her not to use even the simplest object as a weapon.

"Am I expected to eat using my fingers?" she demanded.

"You've done a lot worse. Try the bread. It's good."

"What are you going to do with me?" she asked, cautiously putting a wedge of bread in her mouth.

"Well, that depends."

"On what?"

"On how reasonable you are willing to be."

The bread was indeed good. She pulled off another piece and ate it greedily.

"Where is he, Sophie?" he asked in a voice as quiet as death.

Miss Blakelow felt a shudder echo along her spine. "Who?" she replied, stalling for time to think.

"I advise you to think carefully before you decide to play me for a fool."

She swallowed her mouthful and washed it down with a gulp of wine. "I told you before. He died at sea. As did my mother. There was a storm and the ship sank. A lot of people died that day."

"How then did *you* survive?"

"I nearly didn't," she replied calmly. "The water was cold; I was practically unconscious when they picked me up."

He brought his open hand down upon the table, and the pewter plates jumped as if frightened of the sound. "Don't lie to me!"

"I am not lying."

"Then how do you explain the fact that the ship you departed on was a day ahead of the storm? I have it here. See this?" he demanded, pulling a creased sheet of paper from his pocket and waving it at her. "This is a list of the ship's passengers on the day you left. A woman, a baby, and a girl with the surname Crane. The ship, the *King's Glory*, arrived safely in Liverpool, precisely when it was due and with no loss of life."

"Then it is incorrect. I have told you before, and I will tell you again, he died at sea. And it doesn't matter what you do to me, it won't alter the truth."

"The truth!" he repeated angrily, flinging the piece of paper to the floor. "You wouldn't know the truth if it landed on you. I know he's alive. I know it."

"Then you will spend the rest of your life searching for someone who does not exist."

"He's my son!"

"A fact that only seems to concern you now that he's dead," she retorted with spirit. "You were too busy chasing women to notice that your wife was dying and that your newborn son was set to follow her to the grave."

"You had no right to take him away from me. You stole him."

"Yes," she agreed, her eyes blazing. "That I did. You made my sister's life a misery from the moment she married you. I don't think there was a maid in the house who you hadn't tried to seduce. You are repulsive. And Mother and I knew that if we left for England, the child would have a better chance of a future without your polluting influence."

He was up and out of his chair in a trice and strode toward her. She steeled herself as he reached her, and the blow he dealt her across her jaw sent her reeling off the chair and onto the floor. He crouched down, leaning over her, grabbed her hair, and twisted the dark gleaming mass around his fist. Something heavy in his pocket banged against her head.

"*You* are the polluting influence, my love," he hissed. "Does he realize that his aunt is nothing but a cheap whore?"

She brought her hand up to slap him hard across the face, but he easily swatted it away with one arm.

He laughed harshly. "Touched a nerve, did we?"

"Go to the devil," she recommended, struggling against his grip.

"You thought I was dead, didn't you? You thought that I would not come after you because I had been killed in that fire. Did you set light to my bed, Sophie? Do you add attempted murder to your list of crimes?"

"I wish that I'd had the forethought to do it," she retorted, shoving her hands against his chest, "and I wish that it had succeeded."

"I was hard on your heels from the moment I arrived back in England. And what did I find? A mysterious Miss Sophie Ashton whom no one had ever heard of before had taken the ton by storm." He broke off with a laugh, tugging her hair to bring her face up to his. "I will never forget the first time you saw me. You stood there in your ball gown, with your new name and your cleverly concocted new life, staring at me as if you had seen a ghost. It was perfect. And that very evening you eloped. And whom did Lady Marcham engage to bring back her wayward son? Why, the loyal family friend. Could there ever have been a moment of greater triumph? Finding you in that sordid inn, three miles from Stevenage. I could have crushed you then had I chosen to. You were still warm from Hal's arms when I arrived, just after he had deserted you. And oh what a sight you were."

Miss Blakelow struggled to keep control of her emotions as she slowly worked her hand toward his pocket. "I had run away with the man I loved best in the world only to discover that he had deceived and abandoned me, without money or transport or even a servant to lend me respectability. I was utterly lost. Ruined. But even that degradation was not enough for you, was it? You would not be happy until you had broken me."

"All I wished for was to know the whereabouts of my son. That's all I ever wanted."

"No," she hissed. "You wanted revenge. And were I not able to cut you with that knife and run, you might well have had it."

He leaned forward until his face was no more than an inch away from hers. The scar on his cheek was deeply rutted by the firelight.

"I will ask you for the last time," he snarled. "Where *is* he?"

She spat in his face. "I will never tell you. Do you hear me? Never!"

As she spoke these words, she grasped the butt of the pistol still inside his pocket, wrapped her finger around the trigger, and pulled.

❦

Lord Marcham heard the sound of a pistol shot as he dismounted his horse. He and John exchanged a swift glance. They had ridden long and hard, and their horses were sweating profusely.

His lordship threw his reins to John and ran to the front door of the hunting lodge, pounding his fist loudly against the wood. There was no answer. He tried the door but it was bolted against him. He ran to a ground-floor window, picked up a large stone from the rockery, and threw it against the glass. The window smashed in a pool of glittering shards as the sun threw its first pink rays into the sky. Using another stone, he chipped at the remaining stalactites of glass until there was a hole big enough and safe enough for him to pass through. He laid his hands upon the sill and hoisted himself up off the ground and through the window.

He knew the house well. He had been there on numerous occasions as a guest. Hunting parties, lavish dinners, female entertainment to follow.

Cautiously he pulled the pistol from his pocket and made his way through the house, his body tensed, listening for sounds of life. A distant clock chimed the hour. He heard John scrambling through the window behind him.

Suddenly a rustle of skirts caught his eye. A pale shape was moving along the wall toward the front door.

"Halt right where you are," said his lordship, aiming the pistol at the shape.

"You need not fear me, my lord," said a soft voice.

"Georgie," he whispered, relief surging through him at the sound of her voice. He thrust the pistol back in his pocket and was at her side in several quick strides. He saw the welt on her temple and the cut on her lip, and he lifted his hand to touch her face, but she jerked her head away. A stray curl fell forward across her forehead.

"Did he do this to you?" he demanded.

"There . . . there was a struggle," she replied quietly.

"Damn him to hell."

"Have I killed him?" she asked, her eyes full of fear and glistening with tears in the gray dawn.

"I don't know."

"I think I've killed him," she said, her hands trembling. He took them into his own and chafed them.

"You're cold," he said.

She gave a nervous laugh, disturbed by the warmth of his fingers on hers. "Yes," she agreed sadly. "Always. Cold of body and cold of heart."

"Don't say that," he whispered. "You know that it isn't true."

"It is true. You don't want me, my lord. Trust me. Disaster follows me wherever I go," she said. Her bottom lip trembled and a tear rolled down her cheek.

He reached out a hand and gently wiped the tear away with his fingers. "I *do* want you," he replied. "You will never know how much."

She wanted to lay her head against his chest, feel his arms around her. Warm. Safe. Comforting. Home. She looked up into his eyes, knowing it would be for the last time. If she had indeed killed Julius, she would need to leave the country that night. John would help her escape—she knew he would. But she knew she could never come back to England again, to see her family or the man standing before her, looking at her now with pleading eyes, willing her not to leave him. The sadness in her heart was almost overwhelming.

She caught a movement over his shoulder, a shadow against the wall, black on black. The familiar shape moved catlike in the darkness.

It was John.

Miss Blakelow self-consciously pulled her hands from the earl's hold. "John—your head, it's cut."

He ruefully rubbed the back of his head. "A headache, miss, but I feel much better now that I have seen you," he answered.

"And I, you. John . . . my good friend. Look after my family for me and look after yourself. You have been a true friend to me all these years. My father could not have chosen a better one." She turned back to Lord Marcham and stared up into his eyes. "Good-bye, my lord, my dear friend. I must go now before it is too late." She paused and gave a twisted smile. "You will despise me, I know, but I find I do not have the courage to face the gallows, after all."

"Georgie, wait," Lord Marcham begged, his hand on her arm. "You do not know the extent of the damage. He may yet live."

"I shot him," she said baldly, "at close range."

His hands slid to her shoulders. "Give me the opportunity to speak with him," he whispered. "I may yet be able to turn this situation to good account."

She looked up at him, her eyes searching his. "How?"

"By telling him the truth." Fear leapt into her eyes, but he tightened his grip as if to hold her. "No, Georgie, listen. I know you're frightened, but it's for the best. All he wants to know is the whereabouts of his son. If I can elicit a promise from him to leave the boy alone, we may finally lay the past to rest. Isn't that what we all want?"

"I don't trust him."

"I know you don't and nor do I, but I do trust a sworn statement on paper. Do you trust me?"

She nodded.

"Then let John take you home to Thorncote. If the situation is such that your life is in danger, then I will come immediately to you. I will take you and the boy to Bristol or Liverpool or wherever you plan to go. We can then book our passage to America."

Tears clouded her eyes. "We? You'd come with me?" she asked, her voice breaking, hardly able to believe her ears.

He stroked her cheek with the back of one hand. "I'll go anywhere with you if you wish it. So, will you do as I ask? Will you leave now and go home with John?"

She nodded, hope shining through her tears.

"Promise me you'll stay at Thorncote until I arrive? If you still wish to leave after I have spoken with you, then I won't stand in your way, but there are things I have to say to you first," he said. "Promise me you'll wait for me."

"I promise."

"Then go with John now, and I will follow as soon as I can."

She stared up at him for a moment as John opened the front door. Then she followed John out into the dawn light.

Lord Marcham watched her until she could no longer be seen through the doorway. He turned back toward the center of the house and followed the hallway until he heard voices. He moved toward them, pushing open the dining room door to find a scene of carnage. Sir Julius Fawcett lay on the floor, bleeding from a shoulder wound, his face as pale as the face of the moon. Blood seeped across the expensive carpet beneath him like a spill of Bordeaux.

"Boyd, don't mind me, go after her!" hissed the wounded man, gripping the other man's shoulder. "Bring her back!"

"I cannot leave you, sir," replied Mr. Boyd, crouching at his master's side with a pile of towels.

"If we lose her again, I will personally rip you limb from limb," said Sir Julius, grimacing with pain.

"You will do no such thing, Julius," said Lord Marcham icily from the doorway.

Sir Julius Fawcett looked up as the earl entered. "March," he muttered as Mr. Boyd plied towels to the wound. "The bitch shot me."

"Perhaps you deserved it."

"She can't have gone far. Boyd, go and bring her back."

"But, sir, you're bleeding—"

"Go after her or you'll be looking for new employment."

Lord Marcham raised his hand and leveled his pistol at the chest of the manservant. "Mr. Boyd, might I suggest that you remain where you are?"

Mr. Boyd looked warily at the pistol, then at the pale face of his master, and finally back at his lordship.

"Quite so," agreed the earl, reading the man's mind to a nicety. "You'll be much better off following my orders rather than your master's. What price loyalty, eh, Ju? You once warned me not to trust my servants."

"What the devil do you mean by brandishing that pistol in my house?" demanded Sir Julius, his forehead shiny with sweat. "We are friends. You owe me, March. You owe me this!"

"I owe you nothing."

"Boyd! Get me up! I'll go after her if you lack the courage."

"By all means," replied the earl. "And we'll watch you bleed to death all over this expensive carpet."

"You don't know what she's done to me! You don't know what she is."

A muscle pulsed in his lordship's jaw. "On the contrary, I know precisely what she is."

"She's done for me, March. The bitch has done for me."

"You'll live," drawled the earl.

"You don't understand. She took my boy from me, Rob. She stole him. He's my only son."

"So I understand. And I know where your boy is."

There was a silence.

"I beg your pardon?" Sir Julius coughed and blood welled up in his wound.

"I know where and who he is. And I will tell you."

Sir Julius stared at him as if he could not believe his ears. "Why would you do that?"

"Because I want something in return," said Lord Marcham, calmly pulling out a chair and straddling it. He laid the pistol down on the table.

"What? How would you know? You're bluffing."

The earl folded his arms along the back of the chair. "Not in the least. I've seen him. He's a fine lad."

"How do I know you're telling the truth?"

His lordship smiled. "You don't. You'll just have to trust me."

His friend raised himself painfully onto his elbows. "Go on."

"Captain Clayton was a naval man who moved his young family out to the West Indies to make his fortune. He bought a fine house and was happy and prosperous there until the fever claimed him a few years later. He had two daughters, the eldest of which he married off to the son of a plantation owner—you. Unfortunately your wife died shortly after giving birth to your first child. The bereaved family, without the captain's protection, returned to England and changed their name. Imagine a young girl of sixteen, arriving in England with her baby nephew and her sickly mother. They have little money and little knowledge of England. Where would they go? But to relatives, of course. The mother had a brother, a Mr. Thorpe, who lived in London. But Mrs. Thorpe was not keen on her sister-in-law, and soon the lady was obliged to leave. She found herself a new husband—Sir William Blakelow. Blakelow, although a man of many failings, was father to a brood of young children and was looking for a mother for them. He was willing to take the boy into his house and the daughter, Sophie. There they lived until the mother's death a few years later. Sir William, by this time in dire financial straits, had no choice but to ask Sophie to leave, hoping she would make a good match in London, but the boy stayed with his stepbrothers and sisters. Blakelow told everyone that the boy was his. His name is Jack."

"Are you certain?" Sir Julius asked, frowning. "I mean, I had considered the possibility, and I made inquiries, but I was told that Sir William was his father."

"As far as Jack is concerned, he was. After all, the boy was only an infant when he arrived in England. He has no memory of his real mother, or you for that matter. Georgie—Sophie, as you know her, is in fact his aunt, not his sister."

"And so Sophie left him there?"

"Yes, with the family he had been brought up to believe was his. Sophie reluctantly returned to the Thorpes in the hopes of securing a husband for herself. Her uncle agreed to give her a season, to launch her into the ton and achieve a good match. She took her own Christian name and her grandmother's maiden name, and Sophie Ashton was born into being. She formed a friendship. A friendship with a young widow whose husband had died in battle and who had a young son. Your son."

"My son?" Sir Julius repeated. "A second son? Who?"

"You paid court to her for a time shortly after her husband died."

"*Caro?* I don't believe it . . . I mean, how do I know he's mine?"

"Only look at him, Ju," replied the earl caustically. "He's got your damned hideous nose for one."

Sir Julius laughed and coughed and blood gurgled. "I have two sons," he said.

"They are both fine boys," said his lordship. "Don't make me regret telling you."

Sir Julius closed his eyes, nodding faintly.

"Boyd?"

"Yes, my lord?" the man said over his shoulder.

"Have you sent for a doctor?"

"Sir Julius wouldn't let me."

"Might I suggest you see to it and with all possible haste?"

"Yes, my lord," he replied, running from the room.

Lord Marcham knelt by his old friend and made a fresh swab from a clean towel and pressed it against the wound.

"All I ever wanted was to do right by him, March . . . young Jack, did you say his name was?"

"So you hounded his young aunt halfway across the globe?" demanded the earl.

"I was obsessed with finding him. I was a little obsessed with her too. I admit it," he croaked. "I wanted to possess her, make her mine. Well, *you* know."

"No, I don't."

Sir Julius grimaced. "I loved her, in my own way. But then love grew to hate. Does Caro know that you've told me?"

"Not exactly."

"So it is to be our secret."

"Yes. But I want your promise. I want you to promise me that you will give up your pursuit of Miss Blakelow, Miss Ashton, Miss Clayton, and whoever else she may have been in the intervening years. I won't stand idly by and watch you make her life a misery any longer. Do you understand?"

"You take her side against me? Such old friends as we are?"

"Were, Julius. Past tense. Any man who can treat a woman as you have done is no friend of mine. I want your promise that this is the end."

There was a silence.

"Julius?"

"Alright," said the man, wearily laying his head back against the carpet.

"In writing," insisted his lordship. "And you won't do anything to take Jack away? Or Caro's boy?"

"No. But I would like to see them."

"Well, that would be a start."

CHAPTER 28

Lord Marcham left Mr. Boyd to oversee the removal of Sir Julius up to his bedchamber while his lordship dealt with the doctor. By the time he had spoken to the housekeeper and bid her clean up the mess on the carpet, the sun had risen high into a crisp blue December sky.

There was a sharp frost on the ground as he walked to his horse, and the fallen leaves were pale and curled and fringed with silver. He breathed in the air, wondering what the coming day would hold for him as he swung himself up into the saddle. Would Georgie finally confide in him? Could she put her past firmly behind her and give herself to him, completely and without question? She had kept him at arm's length for so long and had been so determined to keep him from knowing her innermost secrets that he wondered if she could ever trust him with her heart.

John had driven Miss Blakelow back home some hours before. He wondered what she was doing. He wondered what she was thinking. He hoped she had kept her promise to stay. He didn't want to contemplate the idea that she had run from him again.

His horse was tired, and he was obliged to stop at a coaching inn where he was able to hire a fresh horse and gig to take him the rest of the way. The new horse was slow, however, and it was late in the day when he arrived at Holme Park. There he bathed and changed out of his bloodstained clothes before setting out again for Thorncote. As he rode up to the house, the sky was darkening rapidly with the approach of evening, and heavy rain clouds were moving in. He handed his reins to the stable lad and ran lightly up the front steps to the door, pulling off his gloves as he did so. He took a deep breath and knocked.

❦

Miss Blakelow picked up the looking glass from her dressing table. She examined the welt on her forehead and the ugly cut on her lip with a wry smile. She touched her fingers gingerly to it. Her skin was pale, and she pinched her cheeks to bring some color back into them. She was dressed in a dark-blue morning gown with a lace tucker made up to the throat. Her mahogany hair was uncovered and twisted into a simple chignon at the back of her head, one unruly curl dropping to her shoulder. Her green eyes were clear and unhindered by the presence of her ugly spectacles. From the outside she looked confident, elegant, and assured. Inside, she was quaking with nerves.

There was a knock at the door behind her and she bid them enter.

It was John. He stood sheepishly upon the threshold.

"Is he here, John?" she asked.

"Yes, miss. He's in the parlor."

She nodded, set down the looking glass, and rose to her feet, smoothing out the folds in her dress with her hands. "And Julius?" she said, hardly daring to ask the question.

"He's still breathing, more's the pity."

Miss Blakelow closed her eyes with relief. "I didn't kill him."

"No, miss."

She walked over to the door and put a hand on his arm. "I plan to tell his lordship everything, John. There is a chance . . . a fair chance that he won't be able to forgive me. If that is the case, then—then life here will be intolerable for me. I could not live on his doorstep and watch him marry someone else. I had rather leave than endure that."

"I understand, miss. You and his lordship need to talk. After that, if you still want to leave, then you can. But not beforehand."

"But you won't be coming with me?"

"No, miss. My Janet is with child. I reckon I'm done with running."

Miss Blakelow nodded and walked out of the room, feeling more alone than ever before. She moved along the hall to the top of the stairs, letting her hand graze the banister rail. The scene of her meeting in her bedchamber with Lord Marcham haunted her. And what of his love for her? Had she killed it the previous night when she had pretended that she felt nothing for him? Had his love withered and died under her mockery? Even if it hadn't, would he be able to forgive her for the truth she knew she must tell him now? The knowledge that she would hurt him tormented her. She longed for his arms to hold her close and for his reassuring smile.

Miss Blakelow stood for a moment on the threshold of the parlor, one hand upon the doorknob, before she opened the door. Lord Marcham was standing by the fireplace and turned around at the sound of her entry. Their eyes met.

He bowed. "Miss Blakelow."

"You wished to see me, my lord?" she asked and curtsied.

How different he was from earlier! How serious. And how she missed his warm smile. She looked at him and knew that he was still worried she would leave him. He was waiting patiently for her to tell him everything. She saw the determined look in his eyes and the rigid set of his jaw. He was not going to be fobbed off with half-truths this time. She knew she had to tell him, to risk that he possibly would not be able to forgive her, and that knowledge broke what was left of her heart.

"John said that Sir Julius is . . . alive?" she asked, hardly daring to raise her eyes to his face.

He nodded. "Recovering. He'll have a scar to match the one on his face, but the doctor thinks he'll live."

She nodded and fell silent as tears of relief slid down her cheeks. It was over at last. She sank onto the sofa and struggled to find her handkerchief.

Lord Marcham came away from the fireplace and took a seat on the sofa next to her. He yearned to pull her into his arms and comfort her but was afraid to frighten her away. So he sat there, fist clenched against his thigh. "Are you quite well, Miss Blakelow?"

She nodded, trying to smile as tears overcame her. "Quite well, I thank you," she managed through a voice choked with emotion.

"Can I fetch you a glass of wine perhaps?"

She shook her head as the tears welled up in her eyes. "No, thank you," she whispered.

"Shall I fetch your sisters? Or your aunt?"

Again she shook her head, angrily wiping at her eyes with her fingers.

"You're tired and the stress of the situation has made you emotional."

She nodded. "That's it, yes."

"Julius is on the mend now and won't be bothering you anymore. There is no need to cry."

The gentleness in his voice just made it worse. She nodded through her tears, and through her watery haze saw him take her hand.

"Please, Georgie, don't cry. You must know that your tears are a worse punishment to me than anything in the world."

She dropped her gaze to their hands clasped together. "I think we both said things that we ought not have."

"Yes," he agreed.

"I'm sorry, my lord," she whispered.

"So am I."

"Can you ever forgive me?" she asked, turning watery eyes up to him.

He reached out a hand and cupped her face, his thumb brushing away her tears. "Hush now."

She smiled tremulously. "I said such horrible things to you last night."

"And I, you," he said softly.

"Julius was in the room listening. He promised that he would not hurt you if I drove you away. I put on an act to make you leave."

"An act?"

"Julius made me say the things I did. He had a gun pointed at your head. He told me that if I drove you away, he would not harm you. So I played a part," she said, smiling sadly. "And I played it very well. I let you think that I was a . . . a grasping female. I know you must think me sunk beneath contempt. You must think that I only ever courted your acquaintance for your money, because I told you that it was so. You came to me last night to beg me to stay and I threw it back in your face."

He squeezed her hand reassuringly. "Hush now. I knew the woman you pretended to be last night was not the girl I have come to adore. I just didn't know why you seemed to have changed so completely."

"Oh," she replied quietly, the warmth and kindness in his voice unsettling her. His anger she knew how to deal with, but this sympathy toward her made her heart lurch with longing. "You told Julius the truth?" she stammered.

"Yes. I thought it was for the best," said his lordship.

"And how did he react?"

"He wishes to see Jack. He has given me his word that he will do nothing to remove the lad from his home. And I think he means it. You needn't run anymore, Georgie. It's over."

She nodded, trying to regain her composure. She took her hand from his and rose to stand before the fireplace, turning her back upon him so that she might dash her sleeve against her wet cheeks unseen. "It is late and you must be wishing for your dinner. I can offer you stew. It's not as fine as your French chef would make but—"

He moved suddenly behind her, bracing his hand against the mantelpiece so that his arm halted her retreat. "Georgie, wait," he said hoarsely, as if the words were torn from him.

She blinked, staring up at him in surprise, fearful of what he might say. She couldn't bear to argue with him again, to feel his condemnation; it just hurt too much. "My lord?"

He closed his eyes for the briefest of moments as if finding strength from somewhere and then said, "Oh, damn it all—Georgie, is there no hope for me?" He took a step toward her and then seemed to check himself, as if the leash that restrained him had jerked taut. "Is there no hope?" he asked again more softly. "Tell me that you feel something for me. Tell me that I didn't imagine it all."

She hung her head. "You didn't," she replied in a small voice.

"Then won't you tell me what it is that still torments you?"

"I find it hard to speak of."

"I know you do," he replied, "but you can trust me, I promise you. I need to know, Georgie. My happiness, nay, my sanity, requires it. If you think I'm going to let you walk out of my life again, you are very much mistaken."

Miss Blakelow sent her eyes heavenward, fighting the urge to cry still more. "I can't do it. I can't. You'll hate me."

"I won't."

"You say that now, but that is because you do not know," she replied with an angry sweeping gesture.

"Georgie . . ."

"I *can't*!" she sobbed. "Oh, why can't you just let me go? Why do you put us both through this . . . this torture?"

"Because I'm in love with you."

"Will you *stop*?" she cried, as a tear slid down her cheek. Miss Blakelow's hand shook as she rummaged without success in her pocket for her handkerchief.

Lord Marcham pulled out his own handkerchief and gave it to her. "Yes. Yes, I tell you. And when a man loves a woman, he wishes to do things to her that requires them to be married first—well, in polite circles anyway."

She shook her head. "It's too late," she whispered.

"Dammit woman, when will you ever stop running away from me?" he demanded. "Marry me. I swear to you my love, my fidelity, and my devotion until the day I die. Marry me, Georgie . . . I beg you. Put me out of my misery."

"I *eloped* with your brother," she cried.

"I know."

She wrung the handkerchief in her hands. "I let him convince me to run away with him. I thought we were to be married."

He nodded. "I know."

"Don't you despise me?"

"Despise you? No. How could I?" he replied.

"I make no excuses for myself. I wanted to do it," she said, her eyes searching his face. "It was only later that I began to regret my decision. When I found someone I wanted for my husband . . . oh, not you my lord, at least not then. No, this was years before I met you . . . a military man who told me that he loved me. So I confided my secret to him. And I saw the condemnation in his face and the disgust. He said some very unpleasant things to me. And I never saw him again. You asked me once who broke my heart. It wasn't only your brother. It was the man who followed him, who could not live with what I had done. He hurt me more deeply than ever Hal did."

"Then more fool him."

"Can you live with it, my lord?"

"Willingly. That and a good deal more."

"But everyone knows what I did. Everyone would know that your wife dishonored herself with your brother. I could not bear for you to hear everyone gossiping behind our backs for the rest of our lives."

"I don't care. Georgie, darling, I swear I don't."

"You will, when your every acquaintance remembers who I am."

"They wouldn't dare challenge the wife of the Earl of Marcham."

"And are you going to fight everyone who takes my name in vain for the rest of our lives?"

"If I have to."

"And what of your family? Lady St. Michael and your mother loathe me."

"They will learn to treat you with the respect owing to the Countess of Marcham, or I will cut them out of my life."

She shook her head. "You cannot. I won't let you shun your family and friends for me."

"I have a feeling I won't need to once they realize what a darling you are."

She dashed away another big fat tear. "I was ruined, don't you understand? I spent three days and nights away with your brother. We were intimate."

"I know," he said and half smiled. "Well, I guessed. A long time ago, actually."

"Let me be perfectly clear so that there is no misunderstanding. I am not a virtuous female. You will not be my first."

He took her face between his hands once more. "And you will not be mine."

She gaped at him. "And you do not hate me?"

"My darling, beautiful, stubborn idiot. It will be our first time together. And it will be perfect. Isn't that enough?"

Her eyes searched his face. "Truly?"

He kissed the tip of her nose. "Truly. All I care is that you love me. Do you love me, Georgie?"

She stared up at him in wonder as if waiting for the import of his words to penetrate his own brain and for him to change his mind. She searched his eyes and saw that they were full of tenderness and longing, and she knew finally that he meant it.

Shyly, she reached up a hand and touched his face; he caught her hand in his, turned his head, and dropped a kiss into her palm. She blushed and tears of joy sprang into her eyes.

"Do you love me, Georgie?" he repeated.

She threw her arms around his neck and buried her face against his chest. "Oh, Robbie! I have been so unhappy because I thought you had stopped loving me when I had just started loving you!"

His arms pulled her to him. "My love," he whispered, burying his face against her hair, inhaling the scent of her as if she were his oxygen and he could finally breathe again.

❧

In the semidarkness of the hallway outside the parlor, her hand found his, and of one accord they moved along the carpeted corridor and up the stairs, quietly so that they would not be discovered.

He followed her in silence, unquestioning, his eyes dark in the dim half-light, his hand cradling hers. The house echoed with the distant movements of family and servants, and they both understood the need for quiet and discretion. She pushed at the door to her bedchamber and pulled him inside. The dark wood door closed softly and she slipped the bolt across. She turned toward him, smiling, no words needed, knowing beyond doubt that she would not, could not, send him away. Not now. Not ever.

The room was barely lit by the remnants of the fire burning in the grate, and in the soft orange light he stepped toward her and reached out a hand. She came to him and he touched her hair, unpinning and unraveling the dark mass of it until it lay upon her shoulders, soft and gleaming in the firelight. He took a curl and entwined it through his fingers, letting the silky skein caress his skin like molten copper.

They stared at each other for an age, two halves of the same being reunited at last, happy and complete now that they had found each other. She looked up at him, complete trust shining in her eyes.

And in a trice he closed the short distance between them until they were breast to breast and his lips were on hers. He kissed her softly, tenderly, as if afraid to frighten her with too much passion. She slipped her arms around his neck, opening her mouth under his, desperate for him to hold her, desperate for him to make her his. As rain from an evening storm beat against the leaden windows, he pulled her tighter against him, deepening the kiss as he sensed her need for more. He reached for the fastenings of her gown as she reached for the buttons of his coat, and by the dying embers of the fire they freed each other from the confines of their clothing.

She met his eyes unflinchingly as her shift fell to her feet, and she was revealed to him as naked as the day she was born. Somehow she was not shy to show herself to him. She knew that he loved her and would love her still, whatever the physical imperfections of her naked form might be.

"You're beautiful," he whispered.

She laid a finger over his lips. "Don't."

She didn't want the words that he had said to others. She did not want to be reminded of the fact that he'd had many women before her. She didn't want to hear the seduction routine of a rake. This was her night, and she wanted nothing but truth.

"You are," he insisted, slipping a hand around her waist and drawing her against him once more. "You're perfect."

She reached up on tiptoe to press her lips against his, to silence him, unconsciously pressing her soft womanly curves against the hard planes of his body. He groaned as she came against him; he couldn't help it. She felt so good. He had dreamed of this moment for what seemed like an eternity.

She pulled away slightly and took his hand again.

"Are you sure?" he whispered as she tugged his hand, pulling him toward the bed.

She nodded, smiling.

"We can wait. I can go to London for a special license tomorrow morning. We can be married—"

She silenced him with her mouth, kissing him long and hard. "Love me," she whispered against his lips.

"Georgie. I want to, God knows I do, but not if you're unsure."

She took his hand and brought it to cup her breast. "I'm sure. Love me. Please, Robbie."

He kissed her then, passionately, his tongue claiming every inch of her mouth. He lifted her high in his arms and carried her to the bed, laid her down upon the counterpane, and covered her body with his own.

And as the rain lashed against the windows, they began to touch, entwining arms and legs and warm skin against warm skin in a desperate bid to get closer. The world receded, the past and previous loves and heartaches were all forgotten, and all that mattered were two new lovers reveling in the joy of a love refound. And as they explored the contours of each other's bodies, as he sank himself deep inside her in the way of lovers time immemorial, as they rode to ecstasy in each other's arms, she cried out his name, and he felt his heart burst with joy as his own climax claimed him with shuddering, uncontrollable pleasure. This was it. Love at last.

ॐ

It was early. Very early.

The room was still dark save for the tiniest sliver of gray light threading its way into Miss Blakelow's room.

Lord Marcham awoke to find her sleeping with her head resting on his shoulder. He gently moved from beneath her, then swung his legs off the bed and sat there for a moment, thinking.

She stirred, opening her eyes, and reached out a hand to touch the muscles of his back.

He turned his head. "I woke you," he said, his voice barely above a whisper.

"No matter."

"I should go."

She propped herself up on her elbow, clutching the sheet to her bosom, somehow shy now as she had not been the night before. She nodded. "Yes."

He twisted around to face her, still seated upon the edge of the bed. "The servants will be up soon. I can't be found in here," he said quietly.

She smiled. "I know."

"I don't want you to think that I'm leaving because I'm running away—"

"I don't," she assured him.

"Last night was . . . last night was everything I dreamed of, but it changed nothing for me. I still want you as my wife. I still want you to live with me."

She sat up in bed and put her finger against his lips. "Robbie, I *know*," she said softly. "You're not Hal."

There was a silence.

"So serious, my lord?" she said, smiling. "That's unlike you."

He looked troubled and stood up, pale and naked in the morning half-light, looking for his breeches. Miss Blakelow looked away, as yet unused to seeing him unclothed, but not before noting the strength of the muscles in his chest and shoulders, the patch of dark hair between his legs, and the perfect rounds of his buttocks. He was a fine figure of a man, with or without his elegant clothes.

"I shouldn't have stayed here last night," he said, pulling on his breeches. "I swore to myself that I'd wait."

"I wanted you to stay."

He ran a hand through his hair. "I'm no better than he was, am I? Last night was a test. And I failed it."

"Last night was not a test."

"You think that I came here only to seduce you."

"No."

"All I have done is confirm what you have always thought about me," he said bitterly, "that all I ever wanted from you was a night between the sheets."

"My lord, you're *not* Hal."

"I took advantage of you."

She shook her head. "I wanted it. I wanted you. I don't regret it for a single second. Last night was perfect—for me, at least. Don't spoil it."

"I'll go to London tomorrow."

"Very well."

"I want to marry you just as soon as I can arrange it."

"Very well," she said again, smiling as tears shone in her eyes.

"You will still marry me, won't you, Georgie?" he asked, an anxious frown between his brows. "You won't change your mind?"

She was touched by his uncertainty. She smiled tremulously up at him. "I won't change my mind," she assured him.

He nodded, relieved but apparently still anxious. "And you won't run away from me again? You won't leave me?"

"I won't."

"Because I couldn't bear it," he said, and his voice wavered. "I couldn't bear it if I returned from London to find you gone. Not now, not after what passed between us last night."

"My lord, come here."

"I love you so damned much, Georgie. I don't know what I would do if I lost you—"

"Robert, *come* here," she said.

He walked back toward her and sat on the edge of the bed, staring at the floor, a muscle pulsing in his cheek.

"Look at me," she whispered.

He raised his eyes to hers and she saw the torment within him. She raised her hands and cupped his face.

"I didn't run away from you, I ran away from myself," she said. "I ran because I believed that no man would ever want me once he knew my past. I ran because I couldn't believe that you could love me enough to overlook my indiscretions. But I did you a disservice. You are loyal and noble and true. You are a good, decent man and I love you desperately. I will marry you wherever, whenever you choose."

He stared at her for a moment, his eyes searching her face, and then he pulled her to him and pressed his lips against her soft cheek.

"Darling," he murmured, his eyes curiously misty. "When? How soon can we be married? I can't wait to tell the world that you're mine."

"And what about my bridal clothes? And my trousseau?" she teased, trying to lighten the mood. "Would you deprive a girl of her childhood dream?"

"Do you care for all that?" he demanded, flicking a careless finger against her cheek.

She smiled. "Of course. Doesn't every woman?"

"How long do you need?" he asked.

She shot him a sly look from under her brows, a smile tugging at her mouth. "Well, there's my gown to think of, and slippers and flowers. Plus clothes to go away in as I am in no doubt my current wardrobe would not meet your exacting standards. Three months would seem to be reasonable."

He gaped at her. "*Three* months? No, that sounds devilish unreasonable to me. I can't . . . I just can't wait that long."

Her lip trembled with laughter. "One month?"

He groaned. "I can't wait a month to make love to you again."

She smiled. "A fortnight then?"

"One week," he said firmly.

She gasped, laughing. "How can I possibly arrange everything in that time?"

"One week. And it will be hard enough keeping my hands off you as it is."

She shrieked as he lunged for her, rolling them both over on the bed, laughing as he rained her with kisses. Then the mood changed and she made a different sound altogether as he sucked one rosy nipple deep into his mouth.

EPILOGUE

THE NEWLY WED COUNTESS of Marcham had had a busy morning at Holme Park, her residence of six weeks. It was a gray day in March, and daffodils littered the grass around the house, their cheerful golden heads nodding in the breeze—a welcome hint that spring was well and truly on the way.

They had married on the first day of February. The wedding had taken a little longer to arrange than the week he had insisted upon, and it was all Georgie could do to stop him from carrying her off to Gretna Green in his impatience to call her wife. Georgie had made him promise that they would behave with the utmost propriety for the sake of their families and did not let him touch her again until the ring was on her finger. Their honeymoon had more than made up for the period of abstinence.

She checked in on Jack and found him much restored from a bout of the influenza and sitting up in bed with a breakfast tray before him. He greeted her with a cheerful hello and brought a tear of happiness to her eye when he told her that he was glad that she had married the earl. And as he demolished a plate of bacon and coddled eggs, he demanded to know when Lord Marcham would come and visit him to finish their game of cards. The earl had gone to visit the Dowager Countess and Lady St. Michael to try to heal the rift that their wedding had caused within the family. The two ladies had boycotted the ceremony, and it had been Georgie who had urged him to try to make peace. He'd been gone several days but had raced back the previous night to creep into her bed in the early hours of the morning. She wasn't even sure his valet knew that his master was back.

The countess, blushing slightly, told Jack that his lordship had been very tired after a trip to London and would visit him as soon as may be. What she didn't say was that the reason his lordship was so tired was because he had been making love to her until the small hours of the morning.

With this secret knowledge burning inside her, she went downstairs and found the whole family in the breakfast parlor, arguing over something in that familiar way that brought a loving smile to her face. Nothing had changed; they were still exactly the same here at Holme Park as they were at Thorncote. And then her eyes spotted a young man seated at the head of the table, and she almost didn't recognize him in his new attire.

"Look at you, all grown up," she said softly, noting the shadow of stubble about his jaw.

He blushed with pleasure and a little embarrassment. "And how do you like my new coat, Georgie?"

She looked at his young shoulders, filling out his coat without the need of wadding, and smiled. "You look very fine. I think Maria Callard will be quite swept off her feet."

Ned Blakelow flushed as red as a berry.

"I hear Maria Callard has very poor eyesight," said Marianne.

"Very funny," retorted her brother. "And I hear that Mr. Bateman has taken leave of his senses. He must have to have fallen in love with you, Marianne."

"How Maria Callard can prefer you to Mr. Bateman is beyond me," she replied as she bit into a pastry.

"Children, enough," said Aunt Blakelow from the end of the table. "How are you this morning, Georgie? Did you sleep well? I noticed that you retired very early."

Lady Marcham could not stop the blush that infused her cheeks. "Yes, thank you, Aunt."

The older lady stared curiously at her for a moment. "Are you quite well? You haven't caught Jack's fever, have you? You seem to be positively glowing this morning."

"I am happy that Jack is on the mend, that is all," she said, taking a seat at the table and helping herself to coffee.

"Yes indeed. Such a relief to us all. Not that I ever thought that he wouldn't recover, mind, but for a moment there it looked as if it might take a turn for the worse. But your marriage to his lordship could not have come at a better time." Her aunt picked up a letter and waved it in the air. "We have had a letter from that dreadful Thorpe woman. She says her daughter, Charlotte, wishes to take up residence at Thorncote and that we, as William's family, are not welcome. I ask you, not welcome in our own home! But as William now owns it and is unable to stand up to his new wife, it appears we have no choice but to remain at Holme Park."

"She can't do that, can she, Georgie?" said Lizzy, turning her big blue eyes on her elder sister. "Not that I wish to live with horrid Charlotte Thorpe, but it was our home before it was hers."

"I'm afraid she can. She is William's wife now and as such is mistress of his house," replied her ladyship.

"She has never even set foot across the front door, and already she has instructions on how the servants are to run the place," put in her aunt.

"Well, there is little to be done about the situation so I wish them the very best of luck," said Ned, sitting down in his chair.

"Lord Marcham has agreed to help William with the estate, but he wants to see Will applying himself in some useful manner."

"Charlotte may have a surprise in store for her if she thinks Thorncote is dripping with valuables," said Kitty, smiling.

"Oh, yes," said Marianne, "I would give my arm to see her face when she sees the state of the carpet in the drawing room."

"Or the fake Roman antiquity in the hallway," said a deep voice from the doorway.

"Lord Marcham!" cried Marianne as she stood up to greet him. "You are back. Did you have a good trip to town?"

"I did, thank you. I have been to see my mother and my eldest sister, and they have agreed to come to us at Easter."

The room hushed in astonishment. "However did you manage it?" asked Marianne. "I thought they had both sworn they would never set foot in this house again?"

"I told them that Caroline and Harriet were coming, so if they wished to see them, they would have to come to us."

"My lord," said the countess with an amused glint in her eye, "do Caroline and Harriet *know* they are coming to us for Easter?"

"They will after you write to them, my love," he replied, moving into the room as his eyes sought those of his wife. Lady Marcham's heart was beating hard and fast. He had bathed and changed and he looked immaculate as a new pin. Their eyes met, and in that instant all that they had shared and promised as they lay in each other's arms was there to read in their expressions; every touch, every kiss was relived, and Georgiana glowed with happiness.

"Good morning, my love," his lordship said, bending to kiss her.

"Good morning, my lord."

"And how is Jack?"

"Much better."

"I am glad to hear it," he replied. "And I trust that you slept well?"

She struggled to hide a smile as color flooded her cheeks. "Very well, my lord. Indeed, I am much refreshed."

His lips twitched, observing her blush and wanting to find and kiss the extent of it from the roots of her hair to the swell of her bosom. "Indeed? I am most happy to hear it. Sometimes, I find, all that one needs is one's bed when one is feeling thoroughly spent."

Lady Marcham choked on her tea, remembering how spent they both were when they left her bedchamber earlier that morning. "Certainly," she said, clearing her throat.

Aunt Blakelow stared with narrowed eyes from the earl to her niece and back again. "What has happened?"

"Shall we tell them, my love?" asked the earl of his wife with a gentle smile.

"Tell us what?" demanded Ned.

"Your sister and I are expecting a happy event."

"Oh, Georgie!" cried Marianne clapping her hands.

Lady Marcham blushed as she was hugged and embraced from all sides.

"That is such *very* happy news," said Kitty.

"Indeed, *very* happy," echoed Lizzy.

"Sir, might I be able to drive your curricle?" Ned asked, already tired of the subject.

"I realize that driving my curricle trounces my future offspring any day, but can you at least try to look happy for your sister?"

Ned grinned. "John says I have come on famously in the last month."

"If John deems you handy enough with the ribbons, then you may indeed drive my curricle," replied his lordship.

"*Thank* you, sir!" cried the young man.

Lord Marcham's eyes met those of his wife, and he managed to keep his face grave as he stepped forward to take the seat by her side.

"Let us go and tell Jack!" said Marianne, pushing back her chair.

A shout of agreement and a stampede for the door ensued. Aunt Blakelow came toward her niece. She took Lady Marcham's face into her hands and stared into her eyes.

"Are you happy, my love?" she asked.

Her ladyship nodded. "Yes, Aunt, I'm happy."

She kissed her. "Then I am happy."

She turned and held her hand to Lord Marcham, who kissed it, and then she followed her young brood of nephews and nieces out of the door.

The countess stood and put down her napkin, preparing to follow the others, but the door closed before she could reach it. An arm snaked around her waist, and she was snapped to the breast of the Earl of Marcham.

"And where do you think you're off to?" he demanded.

She looked up into his face. "To see Jack."

"Jack can wait," he said, lowering his mouth to hers.

But she evaded him. "What are you doing here? I thought you were engaged to discuss crops for the top field at Thorncote with William this morning?"

"Crops are not half as interesting as my wife; besides, I missed you," he breathed, kissing her ear, which was all that was available to him.

"Missed me?" she repeated, laughing. "You saw me only a couple of hours ago."

"I don't want to let you out of my sight," he murmured, nuzzling her neck.

"My lord," she said as his hand slid toward the hem of her gown and pulled it upward. "Stop it."

"I want you."

"Again?" she complained, giggling.

"Again and again and again," he said against her lips.

"But the servants will be in to clear the table."

"Then we'll lock the door."

"But we can't . . ."

"We damn well can. I can't get enough of you."

"I thought you were thoroughly retired, my lord?" she teased as he lifted her off her feet. "You told everyone that you had rid yourself of your rakish ways."

Lord Marcham grinned as he slid his hand under her skirts. "This rake is well and truly out of retirement, but only for you, my darling."

ACKNOWLEDGMENTS

THANK YOU TO ALL my fans and supporters and everyone who voted for me in the Amazon Breakthrough Novel Award 2014 competition. Winning the Romance category was a complete surprise and a dream come true! Thank you for making this possible.

Thank you to the team at Amazon who helped me transform my original manuscript into a living, breathing book that I can be immensely proud of. It's been a pleasure working with you.

Thank you to Christie Giraud who helped me with the original version of the manuscript and who believed in me from the moment she read the first few chapters of my very first story. Thank you, Christie!

Thank you to my wider family and friends for all your support: Andrew and Muriel, Michaela, Amanda, Philip, Sean, Stefan and Jana, David and Jean, Richard, Alex and Helen, Clive and Maggie, Marc and Bryony. Mr. T. Ruffle—you know who you are.

Special thanks also to Tony and Chris, my father and brother, who have lived every second of this with me and have shown nothing but unwavering love and encouragement. To my great friend Judy, who is always telling me off for not believing in myself—I love you, sweet-pea. And to my gorgeous husband, Tim, without whom I would not have the time to write. You have supported me every inch of the way, picked me up when my confidence was low, and encouraged me to keep writing. You know when I get that vacant look in my eye that I am off plotting in my fantasy world! Thank you for everything.

And finally to my mother, who sadly passed away before she read a single word I have written. You inspired me to write. You made me believe that anything I wanted to do was possible. I miss you every moment of every day.

ABOUT THE AUTHOR

 NORMA DARCY WAS BORN in London, but her family moved to Whitstable, Kent, when she was two, and Norma grew up living by the sea with her parents and her younger brother. She started writing when she was sixteen, but it wasn't until many years later that she began to write seriously. A graphic designer by trade, she has always dreamed of giving up design and earning a living from writing. She now lives in Kent with her husband.